Other Books by This Author

The Sea Stone Collection

Oct 2022

CALLED BACK

A Tale of Two Worlds

To Grace,

Feel the Spirit!

Kathleen Martin

KATHLEEN MARTIN

BALBOA.PRESS

A DIVISION OF HAY HOUSE

Balboa Press books may be ordered through booksellers or by contacting:

Balboa Press
A Division of Hay House
1663 Liberty Drive
Bloomington, IN 47403
www.balboapress.com
844-682-1282

Because of the dynamic nature of the Internet, any web addresses or links contained in this book may have changed since publication and may no longer be valid. The views expressed in this work are solely those of the author and do not necessarily reflect the views of the publisher, and the publisher hereby disclaims any responsibility for them.

The author of this book does not dispense medical advice or prescribe the use of any technique as a form of treatment for physical, emotional, or medical problems without the advice of a physician, either directly or indirectly. The intent of the author is only to offer information of a general nature to help you in your quest for emotional and spiritual well-being. In the event you use any of the information in this book for yourself, which is your constitutional right, the author and the publisher assume no responsibility for your actions.

Any people depicted in stock imagery provided by Getty Images are models, and such images are being used for illustrative purposes only.
Certain stock imagery © Getty Images.

Print information available on the last page.

ISBN: 978-1-9822-6953-1 (sc)
ISBN: 978-1-9822-6954-8 (hc)
ISBN: 978-1-9822-6952-4 (e)

Library of Congress Control Number: 2021910641

Balboa Press rev. date: 06/09/2021

I dedicate this book to my son, Michael, who is and always will be the center of my universe.

"This book is my legacy to you, Mike, because I am the writer. My hope is that it will touch your heart in the same magical way you have touched mine since the day you were born. I love you!"

CONTENTS

Chapter 1 1
Chapter 2 16
Chapter 3 25
Chapter 4 35
Chapter 5 42
Chapter 6 48
Chapter 7 58
Chapter 8 69
Chapter 9 80
Chapter 10 89
Chapter 11 99
Chapter 12 115
Chapter 13 125
Chapter 14 132
Chapter 15 148
Chapter 16 158
Chapter 17 166
Chapter 18 175
Chapter 19 192
Chapter 20 204
Chapter 21 219
Chapter 22 236
Chapter 23 244
Chapter 24 253
Chapter 25 264

CHAPTER 1

Pueblo Art Gallery
Phoenix, Arizona—July 15, 2016

Mike stepped from the cool interior of the Phoenix Gallery of Native Art and into the intense Arizona heat. When the glass front door closed behind him, he stood under the streetlight and lit a cigarette. With the arrival of evening, traffic was beginning to pick up. Drawing on his cigarette, he held the smoke in his lungs for only a moment before releasing it upward to mingle with the haze hanging over the street. Yes, July in Arizona was hot. But he was not about to pass up the opportunity to sell his Native American spiritual paintings in this well-known gallery. The owner, Howard Goodheart, had contacted him after seeing his paintings on Instagram. Before hanging up, Mike booked a two-week exhibit with the gallery. After gathering up twenty-two of his best canvases, he'd made the drive from Michigan to Arizona in under forty hours. When he arrived at the gallery, Howard surprised him by offering him his own display room. The smaller gallery, known as the Mesa Verde Room, was perfect for what he needed.

As he smoked, Mike winced at his reflection in the building's glass display window. His lean appearance made it painfully clear he was back to painting more than he was eating. At six foot six, he ran the danger of appearing lanky if he neglected himself for too long. Retreating into the shadow of the building, he leaned against its red brick facade and flicked the ashes from the end of his cigarette. Although this was his first visit to Phoenix, it was not his first trip to the American Southwest. After attending a Native American art exhibit in New Mexico two years earlier, it seemed that some unknown force now drew him back to this hot, arid part of the country. He just couldn't put his finger on it.

He usually traveled alone. This time, however, he'd brought his buddy Jake Moore. He wanted to show his longtime friend what it was that appealed to him in this desert country. So far, though, it was all for naught. Unimpressed with the heat, Jake refused to leave the hotel and its A/C.

Mike glanced up at the time and temperature sign in front of the Savings and Loan bank across the street—8:27 p.m. *Shouldn't it be cooling off by now?* he thought, crushing his cigarette beneath the toe of his boot. When the temperature displayed as 109 degrees, he moaned and quickly stepped back into the building's cool interior. Stopping off at the men's room, Mike took a moment to splash cool water on his face. Glancing at his reflection in the lavatory's small mirror, he realized that although he was clean-shaven, his thick dark hair now touched his collar. This, he knew, would drive his mom crazy. She would, however, approve of his crisp white dress shirt. He hated the stuffy businessman-look, but the owner suggested he cover his heavily tattooed arms. And since it was Howard's generosity that made this exhibit possible, he felt it best to oblige him.

He was counting out his loose change in front of the break-room pop machine when Nate Prescott, the gallery's twenty-two-year-old man Friday, slipped his head in the door.

"Hey, Mike, you have customers in the Mesa Verde Room," he said. "There's an old man and his granddaughter asking about one of your paintings. I offered to help them, but they insisted on talking to the artist."

"Thanks, Nate," said Mike. Dropping the handful of change back into the pocket of his faded jeans, he made his way through the main gallery. The old building was in surprisingly good condition for its age. The ceiling displayed several low, dark oaken beams, and the old flooring creaked as he walked across it. To the creative eye of an artist, these features only added to the Old West ambiance of the artwork on display. Although the first two days of his exhibit produced plenty of lookers, he had yet to have a buyer. *This could be my lucky Wednesday*, he thought, as he hurried in to meet with what he hoped would be his first sale. As he stepped into the Mesa Verde Room, his appreciation of the smaller gallery and its charm made him smile. Walls painted a soft off-white beautifully accentuated the vivid colors in his paintings. A small spotlight above each brought them to life. As an added touch, the soft tones of a Native American flute filled the room.

He spotted his potential customers in the far-right corner. The grandfather sat staring up at a particular painting. Mike pegged him as a member of one of the local indigenous tribes, as his gray hair fell well past his shoulders. Accompanying him, was a strikingly beautiful young woman with copper skin and a long braid of raven-colored hair. To accommodate the heat, she wore a pair of faded blue jeans and a white tank top that clung to her slim figure. Spotting Mike, the girl smiled in his direction, then leaned down and whispered into her grandfather's left ear.

As Mike crossed the room, the old man turned his wheelchair to face him. His wrinkled skin was proof he had spent his life in the hot Arizona sun. He wore a blue plaid western-style shirt, faded blue jeans, and scuffed snakeskin cowboy boots. Mike found his appearance typical of the region.

"Good evening, folks," he said, extending his hand to the old man. "I'm Mike Aul, the artist."

"Thank you for seeing us," said the young woman, her voice feminine but strong. Her delicate features made Mike want to grab his sketch pad. "I'm Penny White Horse, and this is my grandfather, Arthur White Horse."

"I'm pleased to meet you," said Mike. "Are you interested in a painting?"

"My grandfather is curious about this particular painting," she replied, pointing to the canvas hanging on the wall behind her. "He finds it … unique."

"Well, it's for sale," said Mike, reaching over to straighten the frame. "And yes, it is unique." *That's putting it lightly*, he thought. The painting in question had cost him in more ways than one. For months it hung in his mind like a specter. Over the course of weeks, it floated in and out of his dreams, until it slowly reached clarity. The result of those dreams now hung on the wall in front of him. The twelve-by-eighteen-inch canvas painting was of an elderly Native American man. He sat cross-legged, his body magically hovering a foot above the surface of his black-and-red Indian blanket. Bare-chested, he wore only tanned leather pants, a decorated leather breechclout, and soft-soled moccasins. Encircling his neck was a black, white, and red bone choker and a string of badger teeth. As if in a trance, his hands rested on his knees, and he stared out from the canvas through dark brown eyes. Tethered to his long graying hair was a single black eagle's feather that stood out against the large yellow sun behind him. In the background, several huge grayish sandstone buttes shimmered in the afternoon heat. This painting had cost him two sleepless nights before he had finally put down his brush. And just when he thought it was finished, he'd felt compelled to paint a large white bird in flight just to the man's left. A day later he added the symbol of the white Hopi hand to the boulder on the man's right. Only then did his mind tell him it was finally complete. It was uncanny. He had painted as if some unseen hand was guiding his brush. "Yes, this one is unique," he repeated, softly to himself.

"You've captured the heart of my people, Mr. Aul," said Penny White Horse, glancing at the other paintings displayed around her. "You've done well for a *Bilagaana*—a white man." Her friendly smile assured him that her words held no malice.

"I'll take that as a compliment, Miss White Horse," said Mike. "That is my goal. All my paintings are for sale, so please feel free to look around."

"Thank you, my son," said Arthur, turning his wheelchair to face the painting of the Native American and the white bird. "But I came here to see only this one. It speaks to me of a time long ago. You have captured its voice well."

"Tell me, where did you get the inspiration for this painting?" asked Penny, stepping over to examine it more closely.

"Well, I sort of see each painting in my head," replied Mike. "Almost like a waking dream. What I see, I paint."

"That is truly remarkable, Miguel," stated Arthur, using the Spanish version of the name Michael. "The ancestors do speak to us through dreams and visions."

"Well, these ancestors are talking my ear off," mused Mike. "I've painted at least a hundred paintings in the last five years."

"Once you begin to hear their voices, you will hear them for the rest of your life," stated Arthur. "Where were you when they spoke to you concerning this particular painting?"

"In the desert, just west of here," replied Mike. "I was on my way home to Michigan after visiting friends in San Diego. I stopped to watch the sunset from a stone bench in Monument Valley, and this image just popped into my head."

Glancing down at his watch, Mike noted the time—8:50 p.m. Knowing the gallery closed in ten minutes, he felt it was time to move things along. He was hungry, and he and Jake had dinner reservations for ten at a local steak house.

"I find your talent for detail quite exceptional," said Arthur, pulling Mike's attention away from his stomach.

"Thank you," said Mike. "Are you interested in purchasing the painting, Mr. White Horse?"

"Yes, he is," Penny replied for her grandfather. "But I see your asking price is $800. My grandfather is on assistance; therefore, he was wondering if you would be willing to take less."

Here we go, thought Mike, running his hand back through his thick dark hair. He had always bristled when people devalued his work by thinking it was not worth his asking price. His artwork was his livelihood. The talent for layering the different colors and textures onto the canvas was no different than building a house, one board at a time. Each painting cost him emotionally, as it was like baring a piece of his very soul.

"Very well, Mr. Aul," said Penny, after a moment. "I'll accept your silence as your answer. We will pay your price, as my grandfather has a great desire to own *this* painting. We've traveled many miles to purchase it."

"Like you, Miguel, I've seen this painting in my dreams," said Arthur. "Then, this very morning, the man in your painting called to me on the wind as I sat watching the sunrise. It was he who brought me here tonight."

"I'm not sure I understand," said Mike. "I've only displayed the painting this week, and I haven't seen you here in the gallery before tonight."

"Give me your hand, Miguel," requested Arthur. Taking Mike's hand, Arthur grasped it firmly and slowly eased him down to where the two men were face-to-face. Mike was astonished to find that Arthur had blue eyes. He was just about to lean away when Arthur's face suddenly changed. Though the new face was still that of an elderly Native American man, it was now strangely thinner, with a slightly wider nose. Strands of black shot through his gray hair, and just behind his left ear a single black eagle's feather dangled from a leather braid. Mike willed himself to pull away but found he was momentarily paralyzed. Then his ears caught the low rhythmic beating of a drum.

"Can you hear the *nahasdzaan assa*, the Navajo earth drum, my son?" the stranger asked him. "It calls out to your spirit."

A moment later, a white mist clouded Mike's vision, swallowing up the face in front of him. When the old man finally released his hand, Mike stood up. Shaking his head, he waited for his vision to clear. When the mist vanished, he looked around. Arthur sat quietly in his wheelchair, staring up at the painting as if the strange vision from a moment earlier never happened. Penny, her arms crossed in front of her, also stood looking at the painting. Turning, she addressed him.

"Mr. Aul, we can pay you half of the money tonight," she stated. "Will that be enough to hold the painting? I can pay you the remainder in the morning."

She, too, acted as if the vision never happened. Did it happen? Suddenly he wasn't so sure.

"Yes, of course," he said. Stepping over to the wall, he carefully took down the canvas. Glancing at the painting, he stopped. Hold on! Was he seeing things? The eyes of the old man in his painting had changed from brown to blue! And, he noted, it was *this* face that Arthur White Horse wore only moments earlier! *How can this be?* he thought. Confused, he looked to Arthur for the answer.

"Your painting is not just the result of a dream, Miguel," said Arthur, his blue eyes holding Mike's in a steady gaze. "The man in your painting is an old friend of yours from a past life."

"You're kidding me, right?" asked Mike, looking skeptical. "How is this possible?"

"The *how* is not important at this time," replied Arthur. "What *is* important is that your painting brought me here, to this gallery, to connect with you. It is destiny. Do you now see why I must possess this painting?"

"I do," said Mike. Stepping forward, he placed the painting into the old man's hands. "And, because of this desire, it shall be yours."

Mike expected no show of emotion from Arthur. He knew, instead, that the simple nod of the old man's head was thanks enough.

"Will you accept cash?" asked Penny, pulling out her wallet. "I'm afraid that's all I have."

"No," replied Mike, transfixed by the look on Arthur's face as he sat gazing at the painting in his lap. The old man's lips moved ever so slightly, as if he was speaking to the canvas.

"I'm afraid we don't have any other form of payment, Mr. Aul," said Penny, with a look of bewilderment. "My grandfather doesn't trust banks."

"I'm sorry, Miss White Horse," said Mike, turning to face her. "What I mean is, I want no payment. The painting is my gift to your grandfather. It's strange, but I suddenly feel as though I painted it just for him."

"Thank you for your generosity, Mr. Aul," said Penny, offering him her hand. "You've made my grandfather incredibly happy. For days he's talked of nothing else but this painting."

"You're most welcome," Mike replied. "I've often felt that some of my paintings were worth more than money."

"Miguel, may I shake your hand?" asked Arthur, again offering up his frail hand. Taking it, Mike half expected another vision. But Arthur remained himself. "I wish to invite you up to the Navajo reservation this weekend. Penny will give you directions to our home in Dilcon."

"Thank you," said Mike. "But I don't think I—"

"Arrive early to avoid the heat of the day," said Arthur, ignoring his protest. "Come prepared to stay a couple of days, Miguel, as it is many miles to the reservation."

"I'll have to check my schedule," said Mike, trying to recall if this was the weekend, he and Jake had planned to visit the Grand Canyon. "I may have a previous engagement."

"Very well," said Arthur, releasing Mike's hand. "I'll be waiting for you on the porch of my hogan. We've much to discuss. Come, Penny, it's time we headed for home."

"Thank you again, Mr. Aul," said Penny, handing him a small slip of paper. "Here are the directions to our home on the reservation."

For a moment, their eyes met, and he found himself looking into alluring hazel eyes flecked with gold. *Someday I'm going to paint this extraordinary face*, he thought.

"Oh yes, thank you," he stammered, slipping her directions into the front pocket of his jeans.

After seeing Arthur and his granddaughter to their small car, Mike again glanced up at the time and temperature sign at the bank across the street—9:04 p.m. A moment later the temperature displayed as 108 degrees. *Hey, it's cooling off,* he thought, stepping back into the gallery. Jake was still *not* going to be happy. Glancing into the Mesa Verde Room, his eyes settled on the vacant space where his painting had hung only minutes earlier. Still fresh in his mind was the vision he'd experienced with Arthur White Horse. And what of Arthur's words about the man in the painting "calling to him on the wind"? All this Indian mumbo-jumbo confused him. Nonetheless, he wondered what Arthur meant by his words. At the moment, however, he didn't care. He was hungry and in need of a shower. After one last glance around the room, he switched off the CD player, silencing the native flute.

Making his way back through the main gallery, he allowed his eyes to sweep over the many pieces of artwork on display. The large canvases were awash with the colorful tints and images of the desert. Several sculptures dominated a display table in the center of the room, and he stepped over to look at an impressive sculpture of an eagle in flight. Thinking it would look great on his coffee table back home, he leaned in to read the small white price tag dangling from its wing tip. The price listed made him carefully step back. The numbers only reassured him that he was *not* out of line asking $800 for one of his paintings.

Leaving the main gallery, he halted in the doorway of the small break room. Nate Prescott was lounging at the long wooden table, with his back to the door. Oblivious to his surroundings, he leafed through a copy of *Skater World* magazine.

"Nate, I'm leaving for the night," said Mike. Getting no response, he stepped into the room. It was then he noticed the pair of white earbuds protruding from Nate's ears. Guessing that the boy had his music on extra loud, he reached out and tapped him on the shoulder. Nate nearly jumped out of his skin.

"What the!" the younger man exclaimed, jumping to his feet in surprise. "Oh, it's you, Mike. Dude, you scared me!"

"I could've been an intruder, Nate," said Mike, not masking his disgust. "What would you have done if I'd come in here to rob the place? You really should pay closer attention to your surroundings. Only a fool sits with his back to the door."

"Who would want to steal from an art gallery?" asked Nate, removing his earbuds. "All they'd get are overpriced cardboard pictures that look like they were painted by a three-year-old."

"These paintings represent thousands of hours of painstaking work," exclaimed Mike, pointing to the open gallery beyond. "They're the lifeblood of at least a dozen artists, myself included! That eagle sculpture alone is … well, beyond the limits of my budget, I can assure you."

"Sorry," said Nate, throwing up his arms. "My bad."

"And please don't let Howard Goodheart hear you refer to his gallery's bread and butter as cardboard pictures. You'll be looking for another job."

"Dude, I said I was sorry," exclaimed Nate, his apology appearing anything but genuine. "I didn't mean to step on any toes. Besides, I'm only working for Uncle Howard until I can launch my new career."

"*Uncle* Howard?" groaned Mike.

"Yep!" replied Nate, grinning. "He's my mother's favorite brother, and he's helping me to achieve my dream of becoming a professional skateboarder."

"Well, good luck in that venture," said Mike. Shaking his head, he decided to let it go. He couldn't blame the kid for harboring such big ideas, as he, too, had dreamed of that very same career when he was fourteen.

"If you're ready to leave, I'll lock up," offered Nate. "I have a date."

"A what?" asked Mike.

"A date," repeated Nate. Opening a large electrical panel, he began flipping off breakers, extinguishing the overhead lights in the gallery. "You know, when a guy and a girl go somewhere for a meal. My girl, Jax, builds awesome skateboards. Someday we're going to be famous. We might even open our own skate shop."

Mike stepped out the back door of the gallery, shaking his head. It boggled his mind to think that Howard Goodheart was placing thousands of dollars' worth of artwork into the hands of this Tony Hawk wannabe.

Driving his forest-green Jeep Grand Cherokee through the streets of Phoenix, Mike let his mind revisit the encounter with the old man. This was indeed the strangest day in all his thirty-five years. The idea that the man in his painting was an old friend of his from a past life was totally bizarre. What did it mean? Perhaps he should have read the book on reincarnation his mom had given him on her last visit. It was her belief that, as eternal souls, we are each called to live many lifetimes on our journey to enlightenment. At the time, he'd smiled up at her and shoved the book into the drawer of his painting table. As far as he knew, it was still there.

Arriving back at his hotel, Mike went in search of Jake. He was not at all surprised to find him floating on his back in the hotel's indoor swimming pool. Because of the late hour, he floated alone.

"Hey, Jake," Mike called out, waving his hand to get his friend's attention. Returning the wave, Jake rolled over and swam in his direction. Mike made his way to the lounge area and sat down at one the metal tables. His chair was wet, and he immediately felt the dampness seep through the seat of his jeans. He was never one to take advantage of the great American public swimming pool. To him, it was like swimming in a freshly flushed toilet. The indoor pools were even worse, as the rooms were uncomfortably humid and smelled strongly of chlorine.

"We're eating in," Jake announced, pulling himself from the water. Running his hands over his face and hair, he stood dripping onto the blue ceramic tile. "I just learned that the Pizza Barn offers free delivery to the hotels. According to my cell phone, it's still over a hundred degrees outside. Do you remember our deal, amigo? If I came out here with you, I wouldn't have to go out into the heat."

"Pizza is fine with me," said Mike, shrugging. "Are we supposed to go to the Grand Canyon this weekend?"

"Ah, about the Grand Canyon," said Jake, dropping into the metal chair across the table from him. "There might be a slight change of plans."

"I thought you wanted to see the Grand Canyon," stated Mike. "You said it was on your bucket list."

"It is. But I sort of met this girl," replied Jake, sheepishly. "She's been using the pool the last couple of days. Dude, she's invited me to her house in Casa Grande for the weekend. Man, I am in love. Now, I know what you're thinking, Mike, but you're wrong. The house belongs to her father, which renders my intentions strictly honorable. The fact is, her father owns a successful gaming store, and he's agreed to let me test run the latest version of *Galactic Warriors III* before it goes on the market. Chloe is just icing on the interstellar cake."

"Wait. You're dumping me for some girl with a rich daddy?" asked Mike, shaking his head.

"No, I'm dumping you for the chance to battle aliens," replied Jake. "Chloe will be there to inspire me and keep me supplied with tacos and soft drinks."

"Jake, why are you wasting your time on such a childish game?" asked Mike. "Battling aliens? Really? You're thirty-six years old. That's too old to still believe in beings from another planet. They do *not* exist, dude. Aliens are right up there with Santa Claus. And everyone knows Santa Claus isn't real."

"There's no Santa Claus?" asked Jake, feigning a look of horror. "What's next? Are you going to tell me there is no Easter Bunny? I'm going to need therapy if I hang around you much longer."

"My point is, Jake, that aliens are not real," stated Mike. "You're living in a fantasy world."

"Dude, your own mother believes in aliens," said Jake, matter-of-factly. "Are you saying *she's* living in a fantasy world?"

"No, of course not," said Mike. "She's a writer. We all know writers have very vivid imaginations."

"Are you now saying your mom imagines things?" said Jake, raising an eyebrow.

"No," said Mike, sighing. "I'm just saying she has certain ideas about how the world works. For instance, she still imagines I'm going to get married, have two kids, and go to work in some boring factory job *just* for the benefits. There, I will toil for thirty-plus years, living on the edge of poverty, so I'm able to stuff all my money into a 401-K that I won't live to spend. Now *that* is using her imagination. No thanks! I'd rather be an artist."

"Well, I'd rather be a realist," stated Jake. "My mother harbors that same fantasy for me. And, if I don't find a girl soon, she's going to marry me off to the daughter of one of the ladies in her bridge club. You, my friend, are facing that same fate."

"That's where you're wrong," stated Mike. "My mom doesn't play bridge."

"Make your jokes, pal," said Jake. Plucking the white towel off the back of his chair, he ran it over his face and hair. "Seriously, Mike, you can't paint forever. One of these days you're going to have to settle down with that wife, have your two kids, and buy a dog named … Brutus."

"Perhaps," said Mike, sighing. "But right now, I need to be an artist. And everyone knows artists are loners. I am not completely dead inside, you know. I *can* appreciate a pretty face. They look good on canvas."

"I really pity you, Mike," said Jake, getting to his feet. "When I meet a beautiful girl, like Chloe, I see a really cool lady who I'd like to hang out with. Who knows? Maybe later we'll hold hands and stare into each other's eyes. You? You meet a beautiful girl, and the only thing on your mind is painting her face on a piece of cardboard. You'll die a lonely man, Mr. van Gogh."

"Perhaps," said Mike. "But unlike van Gogh, I'll die with two ears."

"Funny," said Jake. "But from what I'm hearing from my married buddies, having *no* ears is the key to married bliss."

When Mike failed to laugh at his joke, Jake grew concerned. "Okay, I made a funny, and you're not laughing," he said, taking his seat again. "What's bothering you tonight, Mike? Are you that upset I'm ditching you for someone prettier?"

"No," replied Mike. "In your case, you have to take love where you can find it."

"Point taken," said Jake. "Seriously, dude, what happened tonight? Did you blow a big sale at the gallery?"

"Negative," replied Mike. "I actually unloaded one of my best paintings."

"That's wonderful!" said Jake, rubbing his hands together. "Forget the pizza, we're ordering in prime rib from the hotel's restaurant. I'll take mine well-done, thank you. I do not consume undercooked meat. My mom claims it gives you parasites."

"Well, don't start dialing the front desk just yet," said Mike. "There's something I left out."

"Such as?" asked Jake, raising an eyebrow.

"Such as, I sort of *gave* the painting away," replied Mike.

"Like for free?" asked Jake, his mouth dropping open.

"Yes," replied Mike.

"Dude, you're totally missing the whole point of bringing your work out here to this showing," remarked Jake. "Or should I say to this 'selling'— selling being the key word here. Allow me to remind you of how capitalism works. When someone desires to own one of your paintings, you smile and hand that person the canvas. In return, they give you money. Why would you just give away your work?"

"Jake, I'm about to tell you a strange tale," said Mike. "Prepare yourself."

"Wait," said Jake, holding up his hand. "Is this about how the stinkbugs are taking over the world? It's all in your head, man. I'm telling you, it's all that health food you eat. It's not good for you."

"This is not about stink bugs," said Mike. "And that's a real threat. I read about it in *Earth Science* magazine. No, I'm talking about a real-life encounter with the strange and bizarre. This story will keep you up tonight."

"Dude, you forget that back home in Ohio I work for a rental-car business," said Jake. "You wouldn't believe the stories I get when people try to explain why there's a dent in their rental car. I've heard everything from a UFO running a man off the road, to a woman who claims she hit a drive-thru window because she had an out-of-body experience while waiting on her chicken nuggets."

"Well, this one will top even those strange tales," said Mike. "Tonight, I met an elderly Native American man and his granddaughter—"

"Wow, that is strange!" said Jake, trying to conceal his smile. "After hearing this, I'll need a night-light. I'm hungry. When are we going to eat?"

"I'll tell you all about it over a cold beer and hot food," said Mike, rising. "I'm buying. You always did listen better on a full stomach. Forget pizza. After what I have been through tonight, I need some man food. We still have reservations at the steak house at ten. It's air-conditioned. Meet me in the lobby in twenty minutes."

A half an hour later, the two friends walked into the local steak house. As they stood in front of the pedestal sign demanding they "wait to be seated", Mike took in the noisy crowd occupying the booths and tables. He was not surprised to see several of the restaurant's patrons were Native American.

"How many?" asked the pretty young hostess, pulling Mike's attention back to his appetite.

"Two," replied Mike. "We have reservations for Aul."

"Follow me," she said, leading them to a table near the back. Her long, straight blond hair held a streak of pink that perfectly matched the pink in the miniskirt she wore. Once they were seated, they studied their menus.

"I'm advising you to skip the health food, Mike," remarked Jake. "As we find ourselves in the land of cowboys and Indians, tonight we will consume the seared flesh of the domesticated bovine."

After giving their menu choices to a tall, leggy, brunette server, they sat enjoying their cold beer while they waited on their steaks to arrive. As Jake listened, Mike filled him in on his strange encounter at the gallery. When he finished, Jake motioned to the server to bring him another beer.

"Let me get this straight," he said. "When you looked into the grandfather's face, you didn't see *his* face. Instead, you saw another wrinkled face. Am I correct?"

"Yes," replied Mike, taking a sip of his beer. "I saw another face replace that of Arthur White Horse."

"Well, that's not all that strange," said Jake, shrugging. "Do you remember crazy Karla, the girl I dated when I lived in Toledo? Once, when we were fighting over a *Pearl Jam* CD, I looked into her face and saw Satan growling back at me. I let her have the CD! Besides, I'm more of a *Hootie and the Blowfish* kind of guy."

"Dude, you're not listening to me," said Mike, sitting forward. "I'm totally serious. His face changed. And that's not all."

"There's more?" asked Jake, pausing a moment to smile sweetly up at the server as she delivered his fresh beer. After she walked off, he sat back. "Go on, I'm listening."

"I started hearing the sound of a beating drum," said Mike. "And then it really got spooky. I realized the face I saw materialize over the grandfather's was the *same* face as the man in my painting. And the eyes in the painting had changed from brown to blue!"

"The brown-eyed man in your painting suddenly had blue eyes?" asked Jake, with skepticism.

"Right," replied Mike. "Oh, did I mention Arthur White Horse also has blue eyes?"

"Okay, now you've gone too far," said Jake, shaking his head. "There's no such creature as a blue-eyed Indian. I learned this fact in a documentary I watched on YouTube.I think it was called, *"There Are Only Brown-eyed*

Indians", or something. Look, Mike, I think the heat is getting to you. I know it makes me want to stay in the pool until I resemble a large prune."

"Wait. I haven't yet told you the best part of my story," said Mike.

"The granddaughter?" asked Jake, grinning.

"No," replied Mike. "I'm still talking about the grandfather, Jake. Stay with me. Arthur then told me the man in my painting is an old friend of mine from a *past* life."

"Do you believe him?" asked Jake.

"I don't know," replied Mike. "I never really bought into all that new age stuff. Well, what do you think?"

"I think this Arthur fellow is smoking his herb garden," replied Jake, shaking his head. "Did you at least get the granddaughter's phone number?"

"I didn't think to ask her," replied Mike, shrugging.

"Mike, you're hopeless!" said Jake, throwing up his hands. "You have a beautiful girl right in front of you, and you let her slip away. Why? Because you are more concerned with an old man and his hoodoo magic. And, need I remind you, they talked you into giving them an $800 painting for free. You won't be seeing them again, I assure you."

"As a matter of fact, they've invited me to come up to their home on the Navajo reservation this weekend," stated Mike.

"Is the granddaughter going to be there?" asked Jake, raising his eyebrows.

"Jake, I'm not interested in the granddaughter!" exclaimed Mike. "Pay attention. Women to me are like butterflies. I like them. If I find them intriguing enough, I'll date them. But when they start wanting to spin a cocoon around my heart, I set them free."

"Call your mom, Mike," said Jake, as the server delivered their steaks. "She'll remind you of why God created girls."

Later, as Mike lay awake in his darkened hotel room, he thought about the old man and his strange transformation. Jake obviously didn't believe him. Glancing over at the bedside clock, he noted the time—12:33 a.m. Was it too late to call his mom? Knowing he would not be able to sleep until he had this whole paranormal thing sorted out, he reached for his iPhone.

CHAPTER 2

After a couple of rings, Mike heard his mom pick up.

"Hello, Momma," he said.

"Hi, sweetie!" said his mom, obviously still awake. "I'm so glad you called. I was just thinking about you."

Of all the people on the planet, his mom was the only person who was genuinely glad to hear from him no matter how late the hour.

"How is it that you're still awake?" he asked her. "It's after midnight."

"I'm working on my new book," she replied. "It's called *The Sea Stone Collection*. It's a love story about a sixty-year-old woman who falls in love for the first time because she finds a magic stone on the beach. Poor Darrell finally gave up waiting on me and went to bed. Besides, now that I am retired, I can write whenever I choose. How are you?"

"I'm okay," he replied, wondering how best to approach the subject of his encounter.

"Just, okay? What's wrong, sweetie?" Her "mom-sense" was uncanny. "Did you and Jake have a fight?"

"What? No," he said, smiling at her innocence. "Jake and I don't fight. We respect each other's right to disagree. Mom, I have a supernatural story to tell you."

"Okay, I'm listening," she replied.

His mother listened intently as he told her about the strange encounter with Arthur White Horse.

"Is that it?" she asked.

"Yes. What do you think?"

"Well, Mike, I believe the world is filled with many things that simply cannot be explained away by science," she replied. "Obviously, something in the realm of the supernatural happened this evening. Of course, you

16

haven't given me a story like this since you were three. Back then, you were blaming everything on an imaginary friend you named Moe. You also claimed you were being stalked by a monster you called the Hoop."

"Moe and the Hoop were real, Mom," he said. "And so is this. It's hard to explain if you weren't there. I am not crazy. I saw what I saw."

"Of course, you did, sweetheart," said his mom. "Listen, Mike. The Native Americans are a very ancient people who have never wholly surrendered their traditional ways. In fact, they are beginning to reawaken from an exceptionally long sleep and are now teaching their children to live as their ancestors did. When the Europeans first came to the new world, they refused to conform to the ways of the indigenous people already occupying this land. Instead, they forced the natives to adopt their European beliefs and abandon all they had known for thousands of years. The native elders are now desperate to teach the old ways to their youth before their wisdom is lost forever."

"Do you think Arthur White Horse is some sort of a medicine man?" asked Mike.

"He could very well be just that," replied his mom. "Of course, that's a broad term. Now they prefer to be called shamans. The fact that Mr. White Horse has blue eyes sets him apart. And I have no practical explanation for why your painting changed. I guess you'll just have to call it unexplained magic."

"I don't believe in magic," said Mike.

"Well, I still do," his mom stated. "Some things just defy explanation. Anyway, the shaman was said to possess supernatural powers. They were also the keepers of the ancient wisdom. I've read tales of the tribal elders putting themselves into a trance and traveling back in time to acquire this wisdom. Hobnobbing with their dead ancestors, so to speak."

"Time travel is impossible, Mom," said Mike. "Well, maybe not if you work in Hollywood."

"You must keep an open mind, son," said his mom. "Whether you believe in time travel or not, science doesn't know everything. The old stories, I believe, hold a ring of truth. I just finished reading a book on how the Hopi believe they were brought to earth thousands of years ago by the star people."

"Wait. Are you talking about aliens?" asked Mike. "I'm sorry to scoff, Mom, but you know I don't believe in aliens."

"I prefer to call them extraterrestrials, son," said his mom. "The term "alien" makes it sound as if they arrived on earth without a passport. As you well know, I believe visitors from the stars have been coming to this planet for thousands of years. Many credible people have admitted to seeing UFOs, including several of our astronauts."

"That's in outer space, Mom," said Mike, wondering how much he should believe. "I'm in the desert. It's too hot out here for UFOs."

"That's where you're wrong," declared his mom. "The southwestern United States is considered *the* best hot spot for UFO sightings. So, keep looking up. You may just see one."

"Well, if I do, I'll take a blurry, out-of-focus photo and send it to you," he mused. "Mom, Mr. White Horse told me that he'd seen my painting in a dream and that the man in the painting is a friend of mine from a past life."

"You sound skeptical," his mom remarked.

"It's a painting of an Indian in the desert, Mom!" exclaimed Mike. "No more than an expensive cartoon. The man is not real. I saw him in my head, and I painted him. I believe Arthur's explanation is nothing more than Indian mumbo-jumbo."

"Did you read the book I gave you on reincarnation?" she asked.

"Not yet," he admitted. "I've been busy at the tattoo shop. The owners, Leo and Diane, are thinking of semi-retiring. So, I'm tattooing more as well as taking on more responsibilities."

"Well, the book will explain everything about the concept of past lives," his mom stated. "Reincarnation *is* real, even though science can't prove it. As I have told you before, we live many lives on our journey to enlightenment. What about Arthur's invitation to visit him this weekend?"

"I'm not sure I can spare the time to go to the high desert right now," replied Mike, stifling a yawn. "I'm right in the middle of a gallery exhibition, remember? But if I do go, I'll try to bring you back a story about UFOs and aliens, *if* anyone's brave enough to tell me one."

"Oh yes, please do," said his mom. "I'd love to try my hand at writing science fiction. No story is too bizarre. Got that? Will Jake be going with you?"

"No," replied Mike. "He's found a pretty face and a new computer game called *Galactic Warriors III*. I was going to take him to see the Grand Canyon, but he chooses instead to chase aliens. I find that a total waste of a good weekend. So, I guess I'll just do my laundry."

"Well, should you decide to go to the reservation, be careful," warned his mom. "Just remember you'll be among those who don't know you. Keep your phone on you, and … wait a minute. Did I hear you mention there's a girl? She's the granddaughter, right?"

"Yes, Mom," replied Mike, thinking the conversation was now heading in the wrong direction. "I'm not going up there to see the girl."

"Is she pretty?" asked his mom.

"Drop-dead gorgeous," replied Mike, thinking of Penny with her copper skin, long black hair, and hazel eyes. "I'd be going up to see the grandfather."

"Well, just remember your biological clock is ticking," she stated.

"Good night, Mom."

"Good night, Mike."

The next two days flew by for Mike, as he chatted with the folks viewing his paintings in the Mesa Verde Room. He loved listening to other people's interpretation of his work. Often, if time permitted, they would tell him a bit about themselves. His mom was fond of saying that "every life is a story". *What is the story of Arthur White Horse?* he wondered.

By Friday evening, he had sold four of his paintings. It always hurt a little to hand them over to a stranger. But if he wanted to eat, he had to let them go. Much to his relief, he experienced no further encounters with the strange and unexplained. In fact, after thinking about it, he was ready to blame the entire incident, involving Arthur White Horse, on the stress of making his gallery exhibition a success. Perhaps, he hadn't actually seen the old man's face change after all. Thinking back to that day, he recalled he hadn't eaten anything since breakfast. He was simply the victim of low blood sugar. Relieved he'd solved the mystery, he left Nate to close as he headed for the back door. When he stepped outside, the heat closed around him like a heavy blanket. Starting his Jeep, he turned the A/C up to max and pulled out onto the busy street.

Back in his hotel room, Mike showered and changed his shirt. Not wanting to return to the heat outside, he decided to eat in the hotel's restaurant. Jake had left earlier in the afternoon for his date with Chloe and *Galactic Warriors III* and wouldn't return until sometime on Sunday afternoon. After a quick meal, Mike made his way back to his room. As he pulled his room's key card from the front pocket of his jeans, a slip of white paper drifted to the floor. There, in a flowing script, were the directions to the home of Arthur White Horse. He was just about to slide it back into his pocket when he hesitated. Was he hearing a drum? Yes! To his surprise, he discovered it was coming from inside *his* room. Sliding the key card into the slot, he shoved the door open, ready to confront the intruder. To his dismay, the sound of the drum grew louder. As he stared at the scene before him, he felt his pulse quicken.

The interior of his room had vanished, leaving in its place a desert landscape. In the far-off distance, several massive sandstone buttes shimmered in the afternoon sun. In place of his bed was an elderly Native American man. Sitting cross-legged on his black-and-red Indian blanket, his body floated just above its surface. His blue eyes stared as if in a trance, and the breeze stirred his long graying hair as it fell over his bare chest. To the man's left, a large white bird rested in the sand. It slowly turned its head to look at Mike, holding his gaze with its two small yellow eyes. To the old man's right, the symbol of the white Hopi hand covered the front of a small boulder. Suddenly, the sound of the beating drum grew louder in Mike's ears, and he wondered if the neighbors were, at that moment, complaining to the front desk.

"Excuse me," said Mike, over the beating drum. "Who are you?"

Was he hallucinating, or was the painting he'd given Arthur White Horse now coming to life in his hotel room? Taken aback, Mike quickly retreated. Pulling the door shut behind him, he leaned his back against its coolness and closed his eyes. What was happening to him? Was he putting in too many hours at the gallery? Or was Jake right, and it really *was* the heat that was now making him go crazy.

"Son, are you okay?" asked a deep male voice, breaking into his thoughts. "Are you ill?"

When Mike opened his eyes, he was looking into the face of very a tall, thin, middle-aged man resembling a hatless Abraham Lincoln. His dark three-piece suit gave Mike the impression he was either leaving for a late dinner or just returning from an earlier one. The man's deep-set brown eyes held a look of genuine concern.

"No, sir," replied Mike, stepping away from the door. "I just … thought I saw someone."

"Excellent," said the man, appearing relieved. "I'm a doctor, and I thought perhaps you were in pain the way you were gripping the sides of the doorframe. Well, if you are okay, then I'll see my way to my room. Good night, son."

"Good night, sir," replied Mike.

As the man disappeared down the hallway, Mike turned to face his room door. *Now what?* he thought, hesitating. Putting his ear to the door, he listened for the sound of the drum he heard only a moment earlier. Hearing only silence, he retrieved his key card from the floor and slipped it into the slot. When the lock's green light blinked to life, he slowly eased the door open and peered in. The wall light inside revealed the neatly made bed, a small desk, and the mahogany dresser holding a large flat-screen TV. Beyond the room's burgundy drapes, the lights of Phoenix twinkled and danced in the evening heat. Emitting a huge sigh of relief, he stepped inside and bolted the door behind him. After an hour of mindless TV, he called it quits and went to bed.

As he lay in the darkness, he thought about his earlier vision of the blue-eyed Indian. Who was this out-of-time visitor, and what could he possibly want with an artist from Michigan? He toyed with the idea of calling his mom to tell her about this latest episode; however, she really didn't have the answers either. Did the answers lie with Arthur White Horse in Dilcon? Perhaps. But his good sense told him to just forget the whole incident and concentrate on the gallery exhibition. He still had over a dozen paintings to sell. Besides, it wouldn't hurt to just lay low for a couple of days. Jake would be back on Sunday afternoon and would no doubt rebuke him for spending the weekend sitting in his hotel room, reading and watching documentaries on his smartphone. It wasn't going to be as bad as it sounded. He really did have laundry to do. With his plans for the weekend made, he turned out the light and drifted off into his favorite dream.

As he stepped out into the Huron River, he felt the chilly water against his legs through his thick green waders. In his right hand, he clutched his favorite fishing rod. Once again, he experienced that overwhelming sense of peace found only in the early morning hours. It was barely past 7:00 a.m., and the sun was just beginning to peek over the top of the dense forest surrounding him. The only sounds were those that fed his soul: the bubbling waters of the shallows as they danced over the moss-covered river rocks, the chattering of the little birds as they gathered in their breakfast, and the occasional call of a hawk as it circled overhead. He loved fishing here in this peaceful place. Lifting his rod aloft, he cast his artificial bait out into the middle of the river and slowly began to reel it back in. When the sound of a native drum broke the natural chorus around him, he stopped and listened. Where was it coming from? He glanced up just in time to see a figure step from among the trees on the opposite side of the river. He was not surprised to see it was his old friend, the blue-eyed Indian from his painting. This time, however, the man appeared anxious and in a hurry.

"You must wake up from your dream, my son," the man shouted through cupped hands. "We are expecting you. Hurry now. We've much to do. You know how to find us. Wake up!"

"I'm on my way!" Mike exclaimed, just before everything faded around him.

Sitting up in his bed, he opened his eyes. The man and the peaceful river were gone, replaced by his dark hotel room. *Ugh, it was only a dream*, he thought. Laying back down, he stared at the ceiling. It had seemed so real! Was the blue-eyed Indian now going to haunt him in his sleep? He glanced at the clock on the bedside stand—2:47 a.m. Closing his eyes, he lay quiet, willing himself back to sleep. After a few minutes, he could feel his body beginning to relax as he entered that place of peaceful solitude …

"Now, Michael!" the man shouted into his right ear. Jumping from the bed, Mike reached for the switch on the bedside lamp and looked around the room. He was alone, so where did the voice come from? When a sense of urgency swept over him, he knew where it would take him. Stepping over to the mahogany dresser, he picked up the slip of paper with the directions to Dilcon and the home of Arthur White Horse.

Dressing quickly, Mike threw a change of clothes into his backpack. After grabbing a bottle of water from the room's small refrigerator, he picked up his keys, Penny's directions, and headed for the elevator. He stopped only long enough to enter "Dilcon, Arizona" into his iPhone's GPS. When the map displayed, he learned it would take him a little over three and a half hours to get there. That would put him in Dilcon just before 7:00 a.m. Following his phone's directions, he maneuvered his Jeep through the streets of Phoenix, and headed toward the highway. He glanced down at Penny's instructions. After listing the route numbers, he was to take, she added a note saying, "At Dilcon, stop at Bashas' grocery and ask for Nick. He'll direct you to our house". He hoped it was cooler in Dilcon. At 3:15 a.m., the temperature in Phoenix was still ninety-seven degrees.

His 2015 Jeep Grand Cherokee had all the bells and whistles. When he told the salesman at the dealership in Kalamazoo, he needed something rugged, the man recommended the four-wheel-drive Jeep. It had cost him an arm and a leg but knowing the terrain he encountered during his fishing excursions into Michigan's upper backcountry, he felt his money was well spent. Now, as he sped his way toward the Navajo reservation, where the terrain was anyone's guess, he was glad to have a reliable vehicle. Pulling onto 17 North, he settled in for the 241-mile drive into the unknown.

When the elevation began to slowly rise, he opened his window. Driving through the Coconino National Forest, he breathed in the cool, fresh air. He was glad when the sun finally broke the horizon to the east and illuminated the world around him. It gave him something else to look at other than the taillights of the truck traveling in front of him. As the sun rose higher, it revealed the ancient volcanic rock field covered in towering bristlecone pines, pinion pines, and juniper woodlands. Large stands of cedar trees, white birch, and greasewood bushes teemed with birds and squirrels. Dotting the hillsides, large saguaro cacti stood with their arms uplifted like surrendering bandits. In the distance, the snow-covered mountain range of the San Francisco Peaks rose into the sky. He never grew tired of looking at the beautiful terrain of the American West. In pursuit of the inspiration for his paintings, he'd gazed at the majestic sandstone buttes of Monument Valley, eaten a sack lunch among the ancient Pueblo ruins in New Mexico, and watched an eagle circling high above the aspens on a snow-covered peak in Colorado. He felt blessed to be able to travel in search of these new ideas.

At Flagstaff, Mike picked up I-40 E. He was making great time. Just past Winona, the trees thinned, then disappeared altogether. Now the barren landscape stretched on for miles, broken only by the occasional rock formation and high flat mesa. When his stomach reminded him that he had left Phoenix without breakfast, he pulled off the highway in Winslow to search out a fast meal. Grabbing a breakfast sandwich and a large black coffee, he was back on the road in less than ten minutes.

Just outside of Winslow, he picked up 87 North. The smaller road had less traffic, and he felt more at ease. He'd driven for just a little over three hours, and his iPhone read 6:20 a.m. The rising sun warmed the air, so he rolled up his window and switched on the Jeep's A/C. By the estimated time of arrival on his iPhone's GPS, he should arrive in Dilcon in forty-two minutes. As the flat, sandy landscape slipped past his window, he hoped Arthur was awake at this early hour.

CHAPTER 3

When he thought he was nearing the border of the Navajo reservation, Mike pulled over onto the berm. In his travels throughout the Southwest, the one thing he had learned was that one entered the rez, as it was called by the locals, by invitation only. Glancing down at his iPhone for further instructions, he groaned loudly when he saw he had zero bars.

"Well, that's just peachy," he mumbled, holding his phone out the window. "Dilcon might as well be on the moon."

He was trying to decide whether he should drive on, or return to Phoenix, when a white pickup truck pulled up behind his Jeep. The situation was *not* improving. Was he about to be thrown off the rez as a trespasser? Pulling out the slip of paper with Penny White Horse's directions, he hoped it would suffice as a written invite. The owner of the pickup would no doubt demand proof he was expected by *someone* on the reservation. His palms began to sweat, as a tall man exited the pickup and started his way. He looked big. He wore a blue T-shirt, faded jeans, and a pair of scuffed cowboy boots. Sitting low across his brow, a sun-bleached ball cap hid his face in shadow. As the man neared the Jeep, Mike rolled down his window.

"You broke down?" the man asked, his voice emotionless.

"No, sir," replied Mike. "I'm headed for Dilcon. I was using GPS, but my phone lost its signal."

With the man's face shaded by his hat, his expression was unreadable.

"Dilcon is just up the road about fifteen minutes," said the man. Leaning in, he glanced into the Jeep's back seat. When he did so, Mike got a better look at his face. He was Native American—probably a local. Mike guessed he was around his own age, but with that weathered look that came from years of working out in the hot sun. "What business do you have in Dilcon?"

"I'm here to see Arthur White Horse," replied Mike, handing him Penny's directions. "I met him at an art gallery in Phoenix the other night, and he invited me up to his house for the weekend."

"So, you're the artist who gave him the painting?" the man asked, his voice taking on a lighter note.

Mike was relieved to hear it turn friendly.

"I am," he replied.

"Arthur was over the moon with your gift," the man commented. "I hung it above his fireplace myself. You touched the old man's spirit. I'm Julius, by the way. Julius George."

When the man thrust his huge hand in through the open window, Mike reached up and took it. It felt like he'd stuck his hand into a vice.

"I'm Mike Aul," he said, relieved when he got his hand back.

"Well, Mike, I'm headed up to Arthur's place now," said Julius. "I'm taking water up to his goats. You're welcome to follow me if you'd like."

"I'd like that, indeed," said Mike, relieved.

"Watch for cows on the road," Julius warned. "Out here on the rez, they free-range, so there are no fences. And, since you're not from around these parts, you'll pay dearly if you hit one. When it goes before the council, even for the sickliest cow, you'll end up paying a USDA prime choice price. Follow me."

Mike swung his Jeep back onto the road and fell in behind Julius's truck. As he drove, he found his eyes wanting to drift to the water sloshing around in the huge, round, white plastic container in the truck's bed. Recalling Julius's warning about suicidal cows, he forced his eyes to stay on the road.

Surrounding him was rock-strewn desert and the occasional one-story wooden house. After making a right turn onto Indian Route 15, it took only a few minutes for them to reach the small town of Dilcon. Since they were on the outskirts of the town, there wasn't much to see but a few sparce buildings. Making a left turn at a Sinclair gas station, he passed a True Value on the left and on the right was Bashas' Dine' supermarket. A half a mile beyond Bashas', Julius slowed his truck and turned left into a long dirt lane. When his truck disappeared in a cloud of brown dust, Mike followed the cloud. When it dissipated, a small wooden house emerged from out of the dust. Seeing no grass, Mike was unsure where the driveway ended. When Julius pulled his truck in next to a small shed, made of rough-cut boards, Mike pulled his Jeep in beside him and got out.

"Arthur is out early this morning," remarked Julius, joining Mike beside his Jeep. "He's obviously expecting you."

"Thanks for showing me the way, Julius," said Mike. Glancing over at the small house, he spotted Arthur waiting for them on the porch. Falling into step behind Julius, they headed in Arthur's direction.

"*Ya' at eeh*," said Arthur, offering his hand to Mike. "It is good. I knew you would come, Miguel. You are welcome here. Penny has prepared a meal for us. Julius, please join us when you've finished with the watering."

"Thanks, Arthur, but I can't today," said Julius. "The helicopter from the Army Corp of Engineers just dropped off another load of logs at my place." Turning to Mike, he added, "Out here, most of the families cook and heat with wood. Very few are lucky enough to have electricity like Arthur here. The army supplies the logs, but the real work starts when they fly away. It's my job to cut, split, and distribute the wood among the homes. Have a nice visit, Mike. Oh, and enjoy the food. Penny is famous for her cooking. Her specialty is lamb chops."

"Thank you, Julius," said Arthur, shaking the big man's hand. "You're a good friend. I plan on naming my next goat after you."

"I'd consider that an honor, Arthur," said Julius, laughing. "I'll see to the watering."

"Thanks again, Julius," said Mike, offering him his hand. This time he was prepared for the man's vice-like grip.

"Miguel, please come inside," said Arthur. Turning his wheelchair, he led the way into the small house.

Stepping through the door, Mike was delighted to find it was surprisingly cool inside, despite the lack of shade trees in the yard. When his eyes adjusted to the low light, he discovered the house was octagon in shape. Several small, brightly colored braided rugs added a splash of color to the dark hardwood floor. Four white walls separated the interior into two bedrooms, a small bath, and a large open area that served as a kitchen, dining room, and living room. Several pieces of Native American art dotted the walls. He smiled when he spotted his painting hanging above the fireplace in the living room. Penny greeted him as she busily set the small dining table with three place settings.

"*Ya' at eeh*," she said, giving him a warm smile. This morning she was wearing a pale-yellow sundress and brown flats. Her raven hair hung down her back in a long thick braid. He mentally kicked himself for not tossing his sketchbook into his backpack, but he'd left in such a hurry he was surprised he'd remembered to put on his boots. Why did he rush off so quickly? What urgent need brought him all the way here to Dilcon?

"Breakfast is ready, Grandfather," said Penny, placing a platter of scrambled eggs and crispy bacon in the center of the table. Beside it, she added a small plate stacked with slices of golden-brown toast. "Mr. Aul, you can freshen up through that door."

"Thank you, Miss White Horse," said Mike, making his way to the small bathroom. After splashing cold water on his face, he joined them at the table.

"Did you have a good trip, Miguel?" asked Arthur. "To arrive at this hour, you must have left Phoenix in the middle of the night."

"I left the hotel at three-fifteen," replied Mike. "I was awake, so I decided to get on the road early." He thought of telling Arthur about his dream, but thinking back on it, he decided it sounded too bazaar.

"Good idea," said Arthur. "Where did you find Julius?"

"Actually, he found me at the border of the reservation," replied Mike. "I was fortunate he came along, as my cell phone decided it no longer wanted to communicate with the mother ship. Despite the fact it's the latest iPhone, it left me stranded with no service."

"Do you have a paper map with you, Mr. Aul?" asked Penny.

"Please call me Mike," he said. "And no, I don't have a foldout map. They're considered dinosaur technology now that our smartphones have GPS. That's the wave of the future."

"Until your smartphone refuses to communicate with the mother ship," mused Penny. "Up here, we're sometimes forced to use dinosaur technology when the wave of the future fails us."

"Point taken, Miss White Horse," said Mike, giving her a warm smile.

"Please, do call me Penny," she said. "My grandfather likes to tell outsiders that up here on the reservation our methods of communication are still evolving. Some of us are slow to embrace the new technology, but we're getting better. Even the Hopi, up on Second Mesa, now have television."

"We're a traditional people," added Arthur, spooning scrambled eggs onto his plate. "Penny has a pocket phone for emergencies though. When it works, that is. And we have electricity for convenience."

"We must embrace the future, Mike," remarked Penny. "But we cannot forget our past. Therefore, we are teaching our children to speak English *and* Navajo. We're also teaching them the customs of our ancestors through songs and ceremonial dance."

"I try to honor your people's traditions in my paintings," said Mike. "It's strange. The image plays out in my mind as I paint it onto a canvas. Then it's just forgotten."

"The ancestors are speaking to you through your paintings, my son," said Arthur. "One day you will be able to decipher their message. And you may be surprised to discover just who the messenger is. We often find that our ideas come from a source outside ourselves. Perhaps it's the same for you."

"It's funny you should say this," said Mike, taking a sip of his coffee. "Not long ago, I went to see a hypnotist to quit smoking. His name was Mordecai Ruby. What I did *not* know was that he was also a psychic medium. When I stepped into Mr. Ruby's house, he kept looking from me to his front lawn, then back to me. When I assured him that I was alone, he told me the strangest thing."

"What did he tell you, Miguel?" asked Arthur, looking intrigued.

"He said, 'Do you know, Michael, that you have four Indians following you?' Well, I looked and saw no one. I know of a few people who would have immediately gone in search of a priest."

"And how do you feel about his observation?" asked Arthur.

"I'm okay with it, I guess," replied Mike, shrugging. "It does explain why my cat, Lady Bug, sits and stares at the corners of the room. Before I left Mr. Ruby's house, he told me these same four men have walked with me since birth and will continue to do so until I die. Does this sound crazy to you?"

"No, it does not," replied Arthur.

"So, you believe I really could have four Indians accompanying me through life?" asked Mike, relieved his confession didn't have his hosts showing him the door.

"I do," replied Arthur. "The unseen world is very real. Spirits have guided our people for thousands of years."

"Well, that's reassuring," said Mike. "Knowing that I have four ghosts haunting me is a bit intimidating though." *Now I may have five*, he thought, thinking of the blue-eyed Indian from his painting.

"Perhaps, they're the inspiration for your artwork," suggested Penny.

"You could be right," said Mike. "I went to this hypnotist to quit smoking, though, not to have my tea leaves read. I must say, Mr. Ruby's psychic reading left me with a few unanswered questions."

"Such as?" asked Arthur.

"Such as, why have these four Indians attached themselves to me?" asked Mike. "Who are they?"

"Perhaps, one day they'll reveal themselves to you," said Arthur, shrugging. "You are still young, with many years ahead of you."

Suddenly Mike felt the odd sensation that someone was watching him. He could actually feel their eyes boring into him. Glancing into the living room, he expected to see the eyes of a family cat watching him from its hiding place. His eyes swept the room but saw nothing.

"Did you know this Mr. Ruby before your visit?" asked Penny, breaking into his thoughts.

"What? No," he replied, shaking off his strange feeling. "For obvious reasons, he knew only my first name and no other details of my background."

"How did you find him?" asked Arthur.

"Now *that* is an odd story," replied Mike. "I was having lunch with my friend Jenna, when out of the blue she handed me this business card. She said she found it on the sidewalk, and something told her she needed to give it to me. Well, I did not tell her that I was trying to quit smoking, so why would she think I needed a hypnotist? I just labeled it a coincidence."

"I would not have done so," stated Arthur. "In my world, there is no such thing as a coincidence. Everything is connected."

"Is that so?" asked Mike. "A few of my friends *have* sought the help of a psychic. They wanted to learn what lies in their future. Frankly, I don't think I want to know."

"Our lives are but a journey, Miguel," said Arthur. "It is laid out for us at birth. Our future is only a constant continuation of that journey. But when we reach the age when we leave childhood behind us, it becomes necessary to seek the wisdom needed to complete that journey as an adult. Your friends sought the help of a psychic. The Native Americans use what is called a vision quest. I had mine when I was fourteen."

"I had no such ritual," stated Mike. "I was on my own at eighteen. When I turned twenty-one, I left Ohio and moved to Ann Arbor, Michigan. There I got a job tattooing and began my life as an artist. My Native American artwork is immortalized on the skin of more people than I care to count."

"When did you begin to paint?" asked Penny.

"Five years ago," replied Mike. "My first painting was of a deer slowly turning into an Indian warrior."

Arthur's eyes grew wide. "That, in my world, is known as a shape-shifter," he said, in a low voice. "They are evil witches. We do not speak of them out loud."

"I see," said Mike. "I had no idea it was an actual phenomenon. I just thought it was something I dreamed about, then painted."

"They have haunted my people for thousands of years," whispered Arthur.

"Have you ever seen one?" asked Mike, now intrigued.

"No," replied Arthur, his voice returning to normal. "But they're in the old stories told by my ancestors. Most are tales of great shape-shifting wolves that roamed the desert searching for victims. Come. Let us sit in comfort, and I'll tell you tales of what the Old West was really like."

"I warn you, Mike," said Penny. "My grandfather has many stories to tell."

"I have to tell them now," said Arthur. "My years are nearly spent."

"Nonsense," said Penny. "You have many years left in you. I'll have no more talk of your dying."

Cradling his coffee cup in the palm of his left hand, Arthur carefully wheeled his chair into the living room. Mike followed him and settled into the corner of a small gray sofa. When the sensation of being watched again washed over him, he sat up and looked around the room. Still, nothing caught his eye.

"Arthur, do you have a cat?" he asked.

"No, we do not!" exclaimed Arthur. "Sometimes the shape-shifter will take the guise of a cat in order to stalk its victim. For this reason, cats are bad luck. Why?"

"I just wondered," said Mike, leaning back. *I'm just being paranoid*, he thought.

"Do you still have family in Ohio, Miguel?" asked Arthur, settling back in his wheelchair.

"I have my mom," replied Mike. "She and my dad divorced when I was four, and I lived with her until my freshman year of high school. It was then I went to live with my dad, Bob Aul. At the time, he was the chief of police in a small rural town in Ohio. I was grateful for the few years I had with him as he died of cancer in the spring of 2002. I was twenty-one."

"It is always hard to lose a father so young," said Arthur, shaking his head.

"Yes, it is," said Mike. "My dad was my best friend. He taught me how to hunt, fish, and to work on cars. It's been fourteen years since his death, and I really miss him."

In the early afternoon, Penny brought them a tray of sandwiches and fresh coffee. Mike found his eyes watching her as she served the light meal. Turning his attention back to Arthur, he caught the old man's knowing smile and blushed. Once more he took in Arthur's blue eyes.

"I'm curious about your blue eyes, Arthur," said Mike. "With you being Native American, have you ever traced this unusual trait?"

"We have stories," replied Arthur. "Although odd, the blue eyes are a family trait inherited only by the first-born males. Unfortunately, we know little of where the trait originated. All we know is, it began with a girl-child named Moon Flower. My great-great-grandfather, Gray Wolf, found her abandoned in the desert when she was very small. As the spiritual leader of our Salt Clan, he took her in and raised her. That's all we know."

Joining them, Penny added, "The stories say she was incredibly beautiful and possessed a great magic. As my grandfather has told you, we know nothing of Moon Flower's family. What we *do* know is that she married a young warrior when she was twenty-four. Together they had three sons. Our line comes from the oldest son, Brave Eagle, who inherited his mother's blue eyes."

"Are blue eyes even possible if you're Native American?" asked Mike. "It sounds pretty rare."

"It's possible if you believe in magic," said Penny, raising an eyebrow.

"Now, Brave Eagle's story is a strange one," continued Arthur. "Even as a young boy, he was an accomplished healer and said to possess his mother's great magic."

"What sort of great magic?" asked Mike.

"The stuff dreams are made of, Miguel," replied Arthur, leaning forward. "It was said he had the ability to journey into the night sky and bring back great wisdom to his people. My grandfather told me that Brave Eagle learned how to time-travel on one of these journeys."

"Time travel?" asked Mike. "Okay. And what of Brave Eagle's son?"

"He was White Horse, my grandfather," replied Arthur. "And yes, he was born with blue eyes. Because of this, he, too, was taught the ancient magic. I inherited my blue eyes through my late father, Luther White Horse."

"Are *you* magical, Arthur?" asked Mike, recalling the vision he experienced at the gallery. Perhaps, he really did see Arthur's face change.

"I prefer the term "spiritually gifted"," replied Arthur. "And yes, many do come to me for healing in these troubling times."

"And the ability to travel through time?" asked Mike. "Have you ever tried it?"

Arthur just smiled and made no attempt to answer his question. Penny came to his rescue.

"What of your history, Mike?" she asked. "Do you have Native American roots?"

"A smidgen, as my mom is fond of saying," replied Mike. "I had a maternal great-great-great-grandmother who was said to be from an eastern tribe. I'm afraid my ancestry was pretty watered down by the time it reached me."

"It doesn't matter the amount," stated Arthur. "Even a smidgen is enough for you to hear the sacred earth drum. You have heard it, yes?"

Mike was taken aback. He hadn't mentioned to Arthur that he was hearing a drum. When he opened his mouth to ask how he knew this, a huge yawn escaped. Feeling embarrassed, he got to his feet. It was now after three, and his earlier flee from the city was quickly catching up with him.

"Come, Miguel," said Arthur. "Let us take a walk. I have something I'd like to show you."

"Lead the way," said Mike.

CHAPTER 4

Mike assisted Arthur in maneuvering his wheelchair across the sandy driveway and into the goat yard. The ruts in the hard-packed sand told him that Arthur's chair had passed this way on numerous occasions. When they reached the old shed, the strong, pungent odor of goat permeated the hot air. Four white Nubian goats lounged inside a small area enclosed by a high chicken wire fence. Though their water trough was full, they lay panting from the heat. Just off the path, Mike spotted a round hut with a conical top, approximately eight feet high and eight feet wide at its base. A thick layer of baked mud and leaves covered its windowless exterior. Curious, Mike walked over to examine the mud-covered structure. In the side facing him was a small four-foot-high by three-foot-wide open doorway. From the thin wheel tracks leading inside, he noted the opening was just big enough to easily accommodate Arthur and his wheelchair. Leaning down, Mike glanced into its interior. A beam of sunlight cascaded down through a small dinner plate–sized smoke hole in the hut's conical roof and highlighted a shallow pit in the center of the dirt floor. In the pit lay several cold, fire-blackened stones.

"What am I looking at here, Arthur?" asked Mike.

"This is a sweat lodge," he replied. "A *Txa Cheeh*."

"Why do you have a sweat lodge in your goat yard?" asked Mike, rising.

"It's as good a spot as any, I suppose," said Arthur, shrugging.

"Logical point," said Mike. "What's its purpose?"

"It's where we perform our purification ceremonies," replied Arthur. "We heat the rocks in the outside fire and place them into the lodge's firepit. This causes the body to sweat, ridding it of evil and dark toxins. Many of our young men returning to us from the world of alcohol use it to cleanse its toxic effects from their bodies. It also cleanses the mind. We recently had a young man return to the rez after three tours in the Middle East. It took him many hours, but he was finally able to clear his mind of all the death he'd witnessed in the war and rejoin his family."

"Amazing," said Mike. "This would definitely put the psychiatry world out of business. Instead of undergoing years of therapy, you could just spend an afternoon in a sweat lodge and achieve the same results."

"Now you see the medicine of the first people," said Arthur.

They chatted for a while, then returned to the hogan. For the rest of the afternoon, Mike listened while Arthur continued with his many stories of how the government pushed his ancestors onto the reservation and dried up their little rivers with their dams and levees. The stories that most intrigued him, though, were those involving Arthur's grandfather, White Horse, and the days when the Old West still lay untamed. When Penny announced dinner was ready, Mike was surprised to find it was after seven.

After a delicious meal of lamb chops and sweet potatoes, Mike knew he either had to stand up or fall asleep where he sat. Excusing himself, he stepped back into the living room. When he did so, the soft sound of whispering touched his ears. Stepping further into the room, he turned his head to pinpoint its origin.

When he discovered the whispers were coming from his painting, he stepped closer and leaned in to listen to the words. Sadly, they were in a language he didn't recognize. *Man, I need sleep*, he thought, shaking his head.

"What troubles you, Miguel?" asked Arthur, wheeling himself into the room.

"You wouldn't believe me if I told you," replied Mike, stepping away from the painting. "Have you always lived in Dilcon, Arthur?"

"I have," he replied.

"Is Dilcon an Indian name?" asked Mike.

"Actually, the name means "smooth black rock"," replied Arthur. "It's in the old stories that one day a huge black rock fell from the sky. It landed beside the river that flowed near the village of my great-great-grandfather. It was bad medicine, they said. It poisoned the minds of all who touched it."

"What happened to this strange rock?" asked Mike.

"I'm not sure," replied Arthur. "The story mentions something about the sky people."

"The sky people?" asked Mike. "Are you talking about Navajo aliens?"

"The sky people do not belong only to the Navajo, Miguel," said Arthur. "All native tribes have stories of how the star people came to earth to help our people in times of trouble. In the past, they brought us great wisdom. In the future, they will return to rescue us when Mother Earth sings her death song."

"Now you're talking about the end of the world," said Mike.

"Nothing is forever, Miguel," said Arthur. "Someday there will be a last moment for all of us, including Mother Earth."

"True," said Mike. He recalled how his mom had always encouraged him to live each day as if it could be his last, or the last for a loved one. As a boy, it didn't seem to matter. Now, not a day passed that he didn't wish he'd spent more time just sitting and talking with his dad when he was still alive.

"I suppose you're wondering why I invited you to the reservation, Miguel," said Arthur, breaking into his somber thoughts.

"Well, yes," said Mike. "That question has crossed my mind. I'm not in the habit of following my paintings after they've sold."

"I have brought you here at the request of an old friend," said Arthur.

"Is this the same old friend you mentioned at the gallery?" asked Mike. "The one who you say is my friend from a *past* life?"

"It is," replied Arthur.

"I don't doubt your sincerity, Arthur," said Mike, shaking his head. "I just have a hard time believing in the paranormal, whether it's sky people, traveling through time, or even a visitor from a past life."

"As you have said," stated Arthur. "But this friend will not be sent away so easily. When you dismissed him as Indian mumbo-jumbo, he found it necessary to pay a visit to your hotel room last night. When you dismissed him a second time, he pulled you from your dream as you fished in your favorite river. When you dismissed him a third, he was forced to shout into your ear!"

"Wait a minute. How could you possibly—"

"Know these things?" asked Arthur. "It's a shame that you stopped believing in magic, Miguel?"

"Truthfully, Arthur, I don't know what I believe in anymore," replied Mike. Pointing his finger at the painting above the fireplace, he continued, "That painting has turned my life into an episode of the *Twilight Zone*. Tell me, what does this friend from a past life want with me?"

"He has a very important invitation for you," replied Arthur. "You're being given the chance to go on a vision quest."

"I'm sorry, Arthur, but I haven't got the time to go on any vision quest," said Mike. "Tomorrow, I have to return to Phoenix. Perhaps, I'll do it on my next trip to Arizona."

"But *now* is the time, Miguel!" insisted Arthur.

"The time for what?" asked Mike.

"To learn the reason *why* the blue-eyed Indian has journeyed here to our time," replied Arthur. "I believe you are being called back."

"Called back? Called back to what?" asked Mike, looking confused. "Who is calling me back, Arthur?"

"Your old friend—the blue-eyed Indian, of course," replied Arthur. "He's traveled across time for *you*, Miguel. Will you now let your fear prevent you from fulfilling your destiny? You are being offered a rare opportunity to change your perception of life."

"I'm not afraid," said Mike. "And what's wrong with the way I perceive life?"

"Oh, Miguel, when you stop believing in magic, you cease to believe *anything* is possible!" replied Arthur. "You did believe once, did you not?"

"I guess," replied Mike. "If you are asking me if I once believed in Santa Claus or the Easter Bunny, well then, yes. I was five."

"And now you are thirty-five," said Arthur. "Tell me, what do you believe in now? Magic is more than believing a rabbit will bring you chocolates or colored eggs. It is believing life continues after death, and that intelligent beings exist on other worlds. It is believing our souls repeat life many times on our journey through the ages. It's believing in the unexplained, Miguel."

"Some things just defy explanation," said Mike, quoting his mom. "I see your point, Arthur. But I really don't need any magic in my life. I'm doing what I love. I have a great job at Spiral Tattoo, and in my twelve years of working for Leo Zulueta and Diane Mansfield, I have learned a skill that will support me until I die. My life is a familiar comfort zone that suits me."

"You are too young, Miguel, to confine yourself to such a small world," said Arthur, shaking his head. "Have you ever wondered how high you could fly, if you had the wings of a bird? Or what great adventures might lie *beyond* the boundaries of your familiar comfort zone?"

"I've not thought about flying since I was a kid," replied Mike. "And as for adventures, guys like me don't really take a lot of risks. We have too much to lose."

Smiling, Arthur sat back in his wheelchair and steepled his fingers.

"When I was a young boy, I found a huge nest of sticks high up on the side of a cliff," he began. "In this nest, lived a young eagle. After school each day, I would climb to a place above the nest and watch this baby eagle as he slept in the warm sun. As the days passed, his gray, downy fuzz slowly disappeared, replaced by a coat of brown feathers. Soon the young eagle moved to the edge of his nest, where he would sit and flap his sturdy wings. After a few more days, I noticed that although he possessed these powerful wings, he made no attempt to fly. His mother, however, knew it was time for him to leave, so she shoved him from the nest. Well, that young eagle tumbled like a stone toward the valley floor, and I thought for sure he was lost. Then he opened his wings, soared gracefully out across the valley, and came to rest atop a high boulder. A moment later, he flew back to his nest. For the next three days, he repeated this. He was, however, still unwilling to leave his comfort zone, Miguel, and become the great eagle he was destined to be. Each day, I would watch him leave the nest and fly in the direction of the high boulder. But one day, as he flew toward the boulder, a great wind caught him and thrust him high into the air until he was just a tiny speck against the sky. As he circled high above the desert, he quickly discovered that the world was much more than just his nest on the cliff. After a long while, he slowly made his way home. The next day, when he left the cliff, he turned his face upward, and in just minutes, was once again a tiny speck against the sky. When I returned a few days later to see my eagle friend, I found the nest abandoned. Now I ask you, Miguel, what would have become of that young eagle if the wind had not thrust him from his comfort zone and forced him to try his wings?"

"Again, I see your point," said Mike.

"Excellent," said Arthur. "Our journey through life is never a lone venture. We welcome the guidance of many friends along the way. Whether from our own time or from a time long ago, these friends come when they are most needed. Now is the time for you to welcome an old friend, Miguel. You do not know when you will return to the reservation. If you leave without hearing him out, I am afraid you will suffer a life-altering regret."

"Too late," said Mike. "I've already suffered a life-altering regret."

"When was this?" said Arthur.

"Fourteen years ago," replied Mike. "When my dad was first diagnosed with lung cancer, I regret not telling him, right then, how much he meant to me. How much I loved him. I thought we would have more time together, but I was wrong. We had no idea the cancer would take him so quickly. When the call came that he was in the hospital, I immediately left for Ohio. But, before I could complete the four-hour drive from Michigan, he slipped into a coma and died soon after I arrived at the hospital. I was too late to tell him goodbye, Arthur. And there is nothing that your vision quest, magic, or this friend from the past, can do to change that outcome."

"Perhaps, you're right, Miguel," said Arthur, softly.

When Mike heard a clock chime nine times, he yawned.

"You've been up many hours, Miguel," said Arthur. "You must be exhausted. Penny will show you where you will sleep."

"I'm much obliged," said Mike. "I'm sorry to turn down your offer of a vision quest, Arthur. I just can't spare the time right now. I guess I'll just have to fulfill my destiny some other time."

"Before you go, Miguel, I wish to leave you with one very important thought," said Arthur. "If I have learned anything in my long years, it is this: Spirit knows us better than we know ourselves. If our soul's intention is to seek out that which we will need to complete our life's journey, it will do so despite our objections. When the pupil is ready, the teacher will appear. Rest well, my son."

Mike was put in Arthur's bedroom for the night, and after a hot shower he slipped off to bed. Sifting through his backpack, he pulled out a pair of light sweatpants and slipped into them. As was his custom, his mind was already laying out his plans for the next day. After breakfast, he would head back to Phoenix. Although he was enjoying Arthur and Penny's company, he was anxious to return to the gallery and his paintings.

The room was strangely quiet as he lay staring up at the high, dark ceiling. Although he was used to the street noise of Ann Arbor, with its endless energy, he was discovering that the stillness of the high desert held its own kind of energy. Now, in the gathering twilight, the only sound was the wind blowing across the desert outside his open bedroom window.

As his mind drifted toward sleep, his last thoughts were of Arthur and his offer of a vision quest. How could a Native ritual possibly change the way he thought about his life? Or make him believe in magic again? Was it a séance? If so, he didn't need it. *I have no desire to change anything about my life or my beliefs*, he thought, just before sleep claimed him. Little did he know, by morning's light, he would find himself believing in much more than just magic. And, what he would learn about himself, would forever change his life!

CHAPTER 5

"**M**ike, wake up," called a female voice from outside his bedroom door.

"What?" he asked, pulling himself up from the bottom of a dark abyss. "Penny, is that you?"

"Yes, it is," she replied.

"What's happened? Is it Arthur?" he asked, raising up on one elbow. "Did something happen to Arthur?"

"Arthur is well," she replied through the door. "Get dressed, please. My grandfather begs you to join him outside. I'll wait for you on the front porch. Hurry, the night is fleeting."

Mike sat up on the side of his bed and switched on the small bedside lamp. The world outside his window was still dark. Glancing at the small alarm clock on the nightstand, he sighed heavily—2:30 a.m. *Why do these people insist on ignoring my need for sleep?* he wondered. This was the second night in a row, he was roused out of bed at some ungodly hour and led off into the night. He quickly shed his sweats and slipped back into his jeans and T-shirt. After lacing up his boots, he hurried through the house.

Stepping out the front door, he found Penny waiting for him. The sight of her beautiful face, illuminated in the firelight of the small handheld lantern she carried, stirred his senses.

"Come, Mike," she said, stepping off the porch. "My grandfather is waiting for you in the goat yard."

"I'm right behind you," he said, hurrying to keep up with her and the lantern. When he caught the scent of a wood fire on the air, he wondered why Arthur would be having a wiener roast at this hour. Glancing toward the eastern sky, the dark horizon told him that dawn was still hours away. The full moon, however, turned Arthur's small yard into a ghostly realm.

Just past the goat pen, the flames of a small fire reflected off the chrome piping of Arthur's empty wheelchair. Where was Arthur? When he spotted the small blue tarp draped over the entrance into the sweat lodge, he had his answer.

"What's happening here?" he asked Penny, as she set the lantern on an upturned log. "I hope this won't take long. As I said, I really have to leave in the morning."

"One never knows how long the search for magic will take," said Penny, handing him a small bundle of soft lambskin leather bound with a strip of rawhide. "My grandfather is waiting for you inside the sweat lodge."

"What's this?" asked Mike, unrolling the bundle.

"So many questions," replied Penny, grinning at him. "It's called a breechclout. It's an animal hide loin covering that dates back to mankind's beginnings. After I leave, you are to remove *all* your clothes and slip into it. Then you're to wait by the fire. When you hear a log drum and chanting, enter the sweat lodge. And, please do so without speaking, Mike. My grandfather will explain everything to you. Do you understand?"

"I do," replied Mike, holding up the twelve-by-thirty-six-inch rectangle of soft brown leather. "I'm to strip down to my birthday suit, slip into this leather thingy, and go into the sweat lodge. Oh, and I am to do so without asking any questions. Correct?"

"Correct," replied Penny. "If you have any objections, Mike, now is the time to voice them."

"No objections, I guess," he replied. "Actually, I did this very thing just last week."

"I'm sure you did," said Penny, with a soft laugh. "I'll leave you to your business. Seriously, Mike, whatever happens this night, my grandfather has your complete safety in mind. He will see that you come to no harm."

"Now I ask you, Miss White Horse," said Mike, with a look of serious humor, "what can possibly happen to me in a goat yard? Especially, with your grandfather in charge of the fun? Good night, Penny."

"Good night, Mike."

A moment later, she was gone.

When Mike heard Penny enter the house, he followed through with her instructions. In his paintings, he had often drawn his warriors wearing a breechclout, so he knew how to put it on. Removing his clothes, he slipped into the soft leather. Passing it between his thighs, he secured it around his waist with the long strip of rawhide. Unlike the fancy ones he'd seen in the gift shops, this breechclout was plain and unadorned. Adjusting the two flaps over his nakedness, it reminded him of the way the Indians had dressed in the old westerns he'd enjoyed as a boy. Standing tall, he placed his hands on his hips and raised his chin.

"I feel 'em like Tonto," he said, softly. Relaxing, he looked down at himself. The skimpiness of the soft leather revealed his slim waist and muscular thighs, and he wondered if Arthur would let him keep it. It fit great. *Sort of one size fits Aul,* he thought, snickering at the old family joke. He had to admit, it *was* a great way to show off his body tattoos. He paused when a far-off memory suddenly touched his senses. In his mind's eye, he saw himself riding bareback across the open desert atop a great black horse.

"Impossible," he muttered, as the memory faded. He hadn't ridden since he was a child, and then it was a small brown Shetland pony.

With every minute, his curiosity grew, and he longed to ask Arthur what came next. But Penny was explicit in her instructions. He wasn't concerned about what awaited him in the sweat lodge, as Arthur had explained its purpose earlier in the day. He said it was used to "rid the body of evil and dark toxins". Penny, on the other hand, had just told him it was used to search for magic. Was this just more Indian mumbo-jumbo? He hoped that whatever was about to happen, wouldn't take all night. He was leaving for the city in the morning, period. He did feel a twinge of guilt, though, over refusing Arthur's offer of a vision quest. Was this middle-of-the-night purging in the sweat lodge, Arthur's way of letting him know he was not taking his refusal personally?

Finding a nearby log, Mike sat down to wait. Above him, the stars appeared to barely hang on to the night, and he imagined if he could shake the sky, they would all tumble to the ground. *Only in the desert can one see this kind of a light show,* he thought, as a shooting star traced a white line across the heavens. The surrounding night was alive with the sounds of the high desert, and he strained his ears to listen over the crackling of the fire. Nearby, the goats stirred in their beds of straw. Farther out, he caught the deep, two-toned hoot of an owl, followed by the far-off warning bark of a dog. When he heard the mournful cry of a coyote, he scooted his log closer to the fire.

When the rhythmic sound of a drum drifted in from somewhere beyond the firelight, he rose to his feet. A moment later, the song of chanting joined in, and he knew this was his cue to join Arthur in the sweat lodge. Although he didn't understand the words, he knew they were inviting him into Arthur's world. Taking a deep breath to steady his nerves, he stepped over to the small doorway of the clay hut and slipped inside.

The heat caught him off guard, and he gasped. *It must be one hundred degrees in here*, he thought. The heat came from the dozen or so fist-sized stones filling the shallow pit in the center of the dirt floor. On the other side of the pit, the translucent shaft of moonlight drifting in through the hole in the roof, revealed Arthur sitting cross-legged on a fur rug. He, too, wore only a leather breechclout that exposed his bare chest and thin, bony legs.

"Welcome, Miguel," he said, above the soft chanting and rhythmic pounding of the earth drum. "Please sit cross-legged and place your hands on your knees."

Mike felt only a sense of intrigue as he lowered himself onto his own fur rug. Placing his hands on his knees, he could feel the beads of sweat forming on his bare skin. He watched in silent fascination as Arthur picked up a small earthen jar and poured water over the hot rocks in the pit. Steam rose upward and slipped out through the opening in the roof like a ghost fleeing captivity. From a small leather pouch, he then withdrew a portion of white powder with his fingers and sprinkled it over the steaming rocks. Immediately, a strong earthy smell permeated the hot humid air and Mike breathed it in, trying to place its scent.

"Close your eyes, Miguel," instructed Arthur. "Allow the rhythmic beating of the drum to fill your mind."

Mike closed his eyes and listened to the drum as he filled his lungs with the earthy scent. The heat penetrated his muscles, and his body finally began to relax.

"Feel your spirit leave your body," said Arthur. "Let it rise up, into the night sky."

At these words, a feeling of total weightlessness swept over Mike, and like the escaping steam, his spirit drifted up and out through the hole in the roof of the sweat lodge. Once outside, he immediately shot skyward, as a sense of total freedom filled him. When he finally halted in his ascent, he turned and gazed down on the moonlit desert below.

"Above you, my son, is a great white bird circling beneath the stars," continued Arthur, his voice smooth and steady. "He is White Raven. Rise and allow your spirit to join with his. When you are one, open your wings and fly!"

Mike rose upward to meet the white bird. The moment he felt his spirit come alive within its rapidly beating heart, his voice cried out in a loud, birdlike screech. He thought of his childhood wish to fly, and the desire took control of him. Flapping his great wings, he shot skyward toward the canopy of stars. As he soared, time ceased to exist. Then he caught the sound of Arthur's voice, and he turned his great bird's head to listen.

"You must return, Miguel," said Arthur. "Break free of the White Raven and allow him to guide your spirit back to the sweat lodge."

After feeling his spirit separate from the great bird, Mike turned his gaze toward the huge, pockmarked face of the full moon. The sheer knowledge that he could now indulge in his childhood fantasy of landing on the moon to explore its secrets, filled him with absolute wonder. Above him, the white bird stilled its great wings and began to spiral downward, toward the earth. Breaking his gaze on the moon, Mike turned and followed it.

Descending like a mist, his spirit floated down through the smoke hole and settled onto his rug. When he felt the softness of the fur against the backs of his legs, he relaxed into it. Rejoining his body, however, left him with a heavy, awkward feeling, and he quickly longed for the freedom his spirit had just experienced. In the moonlight, he saw Arthur still sitting, unmoved, on his fur rug.

Suddenly, the overwhelming sensation that he was somehow different swept over him. Glancing down, he felt his heart skip a beat. He *was* different! Cascading locks of straight, jet-black hair fell past his shoulders to his waist. Lifting his arms, his tattoos had vanished leaving his skin clear but darkly tanned. Confused, he looked to Arthur for an explanation. A serene smile curved the old man's mouth.

"Arthur!" he exclaimed. "What … is happening to me?"

"You will come to no harm, Miguel," replied Arthur. "You are being called back into the past. There, you will gain the wisdom needed to complete your life's journey. While there, you will discover your courage in the heart of a young warrior. Hurry now. Your blue-eyed friend awaits you."

Mike's heart raced wildly as he felt his consciousness begin to slip slowly away. Just before his world turned black, he heard the far-off words of Arthur White Horse touch his ears.

"Awaken, Two Ponies," he said. "You have returned!"

CHAPTER 6

Arizona—1830

Two Ponies opened his eyes and stretched. Sunlight drifted in through the hole in the conical top of the sweat lodge, ending his night of prayers. Since he wore only a leather breechclout, the cool air touched his bare skin, and he shivered. Across from him, Gray Wolf, the old shaman, sat watching him through intense blue eyes. His head of long graying hair framed his thin face, and a smile touched the edges of his mouth.

"How do you feel, my son?" asked Gray Wolf.

"Refreshed," replied Two Ponies. "You were right, Gray Wolf. A night in the sweat lodge was just what I needed to settle my scattered thoughts. But I awake hungry."

"As always," mused Gray Wolf. "We'll both feel better once we've filled our bellies."

"I agree," laughed Two Ponies. Rising, he stepped over the now cold firepit and helped the old man to his feet. Sweeping aside the hide covering the doorway, he allowed Gray Wolf to leave the lodge first. The old man's years had earned him this show of respect. After parting ways with Gray Wolf, Two Ponies made his way across his village. Around him, his people were out enjoying the early summer morning.

His small, isolated Dine' village, made up of a dozen domed earthen houses called hogans, lay east of the massive sandstone buttes that dotted the high western desert. At the southern edge of the village, a brush-lined path led to a small river that supplied them with fresh water. Along this river, cedar and birch trees shaded the thick patches of deer grass and greasewood thickets. Nearby, a small flock of white sheep grazed on the tufts of wild grasses. This was the land Two Ponies had called home for all his twenty-seven winters.

As he made his way to his hogan, he smiled at the handful of giggling children as they ate their morning meal in front of their homes. Two small brown-and-white dogs wandered among them, begging for scraps.

Arriving home, he swept aside the sheepskin hide that covered the doorway, and slipped inside. It was a simple but comfortable dwelling. The frame consisted of five large, forked saplings interlaced at the top. Covering this frame were woven bundles of long deer grass. These bundles were then covered in thick layers of river clay and allowed to bake hard in the hot sun. This made for a sturdy dwelling that sheltered him in all seasons. Its location near the western edge of the village provided him a good view of the desert yet allowed him access to all the daily activities among the hogans. He lived alone and relished in his privacy.

Two Ponies settled his tall frame onto his sheepskin rug and fed his hunger from a pouch of dried corn. He felt safe in his home, as his longbow and quiver of arrows hung beside the door. Next to his bow, was his knife and sheath. Scattered around the inside walls, were several charcoal pictures drawn on the inside surface of birch bark. Most were of the deer, elk, and small animals that lived in the desert surrounding his village. Others told the story of his people. He had discovered his talent for drawing when he was a small child, and over the years, he had worked hard to perfect it. In the center of his hogan, the small firepit smoldered from the previous night's fire, and he stirred it, bringing the coals to the surface. Tossing on a handful of sticks, it quickly sprang to life, and the rising smoke drifted out through the hole in the center of the domed roof.

In the warmth of his fire, Two Ponies removed his breechclout and stretched his stiff muscles. Hunting kept him in shape and his broad shoulders and muscular chest, tapered down to a slim waist and powerful thighs. He swept back his waist-length black hair and pulled on a thin gray woolen shirt. He was proud of his long hair as it gave him the gift of intuition and kept him connected to Spirit. He then pulled on a pair of leather pants, before slipping his feet into his sturdy moccasins. As he strapped his knife and sheath onto his woven belt, something nagged at his thoughts. Why didn't he have any memory of the previous night? Why wasn't he able to now recall any of the prayers he'd sent to the

Sacred Creator? Odd. He was contemplating this question when he heard someone stirring outside.

"Two Ponies, are you here?" asked a young man. "Chief Tall Bull bids you to join him in his hogan. There is to be a council. Two Ponies, are you here?"

"I am here, Yellow Rabbit," replied Two Ponies. Pushing aside the sheepskin hide, he stepped out into the sunshine. Standing before him was a tall boy of thirteen. His ebony hair fell well past his shoulders, and his young body easily filled out his gray woolen shirt and leather pants.

"May I walk with you?" the boy asked.

"I'd like that," replied Two Ponies. As the two made their way across the village, he listened to Yellow Rabbit's boyish chatter.

"My father, Dark Bear, is out with the scouting party," he said. "He and the others search for the wild horses that live in the canyons to the west. When he returns, I'm allowed to choose one for myself."

"Is that so?" asked Two Ponies, smiling. "I was around your age when I was given my first horse. It's a great responsibility."

"I'm hoping for a black stallion with plenty of fire in his blood," stated Yellow Rabbit.

"Whoa there," said Two Ponies, catching the young boy by the shoulders. "I think you'd better start out with a horse with a bit less spunk. Perhaps a nice paint mare would suffice until you're older."

"That sounds much too boring," said Yellow Rabbit, looking disappointed. "How will I prove I'm a man if I cannot command a spirited horse beneath me?"

"First you must become that man," stated Two Ponies, as they continued their walk. "Until then—"

"I'm ready now," insisted Yellow Rabbit. "Soon I'll go on my vision quest and seek my life's vision. But until then, I wish to seek adventure. And for that, I will need a good horse."

"Aren't you putting the horse before the man, Yellow Rabbit?" asked Two Ponies, as they approached the chief's hogan. "If you grow up too fast, you'll miss out on being a boy. Thank you for walking with me."

"You're welcome, Two Ponies," said Yellow Rabbit. "Someday they will call on *me* to join the council meeting."

"I'm sure they will," said Two Ponies, reaching out to pat the boy on the back.

Leaving Yellow Rabbit outside, Two Ponies entered his chief's hogan. It was a great honor to be included among those invited to a council meeting. He entered in silence and lowered himself onto one of the woolen rugs surrounding the central firepit. Here a crackling fire warmed the cool air. Across from him, Chief Tall Bull sat quietly drawing on his clay pipe, his eyes squinting from the smoke rising from the blackened bowl. Nearing sixty winters, his long black hair held streaks of gray as it fell over his yellow woolen shirt. Across his lap, he'd draped a colorful woven blanket. To his left, sat Gray Wolf. He, too, had exchanged his breechclout for a woolen shirt, leather pants, and sturdy moccasins. As he smoked his long pipe, he appeared to be deep in thought.

The sound of men's voices drifting in from outside, alerted Two Ponies that the others had arrived. The first to enter was Winter Bird, who greeted everyone with a nod of his head before quietly taking his place to the left of Two Ponies. A family man, he had a wife and two small children. The mighty warrior, with his long ebony hair, was a great defender of his people when called upon to fight. But with the surrounding desert enjoying a much-welcomed season of peace, his fifty-three winters now permitted him more pipe smoking than fighting. Of course, he was never short on stories of his glory days and needed little prompting to share them around the village fires.

The second through the doorway was a tall, thin man, who sat on Two Ponies' right. He was Sky Feather, the man who had raised him after the Spanish raiders killed his parents. He and his wife, Blue Corn, had taken him in as a small seven-year-old orphan, and Two Ponies thought of the gentle man of fifty-six, as his father.

The last to arrive was Three Feathers, a tall, well-built man whose very presence demanded everyone's attention. At thirty winters, his fighting skills were already well known across the region. The three black eagle feathers tied to the mane of his waist-length, jet-black hair, informed his enemies he'd cheated death three times in battle. His stories of conquest thrilled the younger boys; however, Two Ponies had long ago grown weary of hearing them. Once seated, Three Feathers sat watching the others in silence.

With everyone now present, Tall Bull laid aside his pipe.

"Welcome," he said. "As you know, my son Long Bow is not here this morning. He and seven others are still out searching for the wild horses that live in the canyons to the west. With him is Red Otter, our best tracker. Although we are in great need of the horses, they'll bring home, they are still outside the protection of our village."

"They're warriors," remarked Sky Feather. "They'll look after each other. Hopefully, they'll return with a few young horses to replace those that are aging."

"I hope so, Sky Feather," said Tall Bull. "I have just returned from the Red River, where I attended a very important meeting with several other tribal leaders. While there, I learned that the White Fathers in Washington have signed an agreement known as the Indian Removal Act, and it will do as its name suggests. This new law gives the white President, Andrew Jackson, the power to remove our eastern brothers from their ancestral homes and relocate them to the lands west of the Mississippi. I have also learned that the eastern settlers, in their ox-drawn wagons, are pushing further and further west. The plains will soon be covered with their wooden lodges and long wire fences."

"Can we stop them?" asked Winter Bird.

"No," replied Tall Bull. "They claim the White Fathers gave them this land, and we no longer have any right to it."

"How can they do this?" asked Winter Bird. "We have lived here since the melting of the great ice mountains to the north. How can they now tell us we have no right to our homeland?"

"Winter Bird is right," said Sky Feather. "When our ancestors fell under the harsh rule of the soldiers in their iron helmets, we fought back and regained our freedom. Is this simply another invasion?"

"These settlers have white skin and yellow hair," said Tall Bull. "I'm told they are different from the iron helmets."

"Their intentions are the same," stated Winter Bird.

"This is true," said Sky Feather. "It cost our ancestors many lives to keep our lands free from outsiders. That's why we are now so few. How can we fight this new invader?"

"I see no one *to* fight, Sky Feather," said Tall Bull. "These settlers are not warriors. They are soft men with women and children. They are also under the protection of the White Fathers' soldiers."

"I see trouble ahead," said Winter Bird, shaking his head.

"So do I," said Tall Bull. "This is why the White Fathers have asked for a council meeting with the tribes of the plains. I left three of our men there to discuss terms with them."

"I say we offer them no terms!" exclaimed Three Feathers. "If we allow a few to come, many more will follow."

"What can we do?" asked Tall Bull. "If we fight the settlers, we also fight against the white soldiers who protect them."

"I still say we fight!" said Three Feathers. "We cannot stand idly by and let them take what belongs to us. This time we may not get it back. Then where will we be?"

Everyone looked at Gray Wolf, anxious to see his reaction to Three Feathers' outburst.

"I agree with Tall Bull," he said, his blue eyes sweeping the circle of faces. "We are too few to pick a fight we cannot hope to win."

"You will ignore my words at your own peril," muttered Three Feathers.

"These are not the days of our fathers, Three Feathers," said Tall Bull. "We have no idea how these white soldiers fight or what weapons they possess. No, the white soldiers are not to be underestimated. I think we should—"

A sudden commotion from outside interrupted him.

"It's Red Otter!" a woman shouted. "He's been attacked!"

"What is this?" asked Tall Bull, getting to his feet. As the others did the same, the hide covering the door flew open, and a young man staggered in and fell to his knees. His labored breathing told them he'd ridden fast and hard for many miles.

"They attacked the scouting party," he gasped. "They came just before dawn."

His wild and terrified eyes swept the faces around him. In the center of his bare chest, he bore a large, blackened wound that oozed a greenish-brown substance.

"Red Otter, who attacked you?" asked Winter Bird.

"It was a snake that walked upright, like a man," he replied. "Dark Bear and Little Hawk tried to kill it with their arrows, but the walking snake spit its venom into their faces. I jumped onto the snake's back and tried to kill it with my knife, but before I could strike, it turned and spit its burning venom on me."

Tall Bull knelt in front of the injured man. "Red Otter, what of my son Long Bow?"

"I cannot say," replied Red Otter. "With the snake, was a great wolf who carried a shining weapon that shoots bolts of lightning."

"What happened to the others?" asked Sky Feather.

"They ran for their lives," replied Red Otter. "But the wolf chased after them with his strange weapon."

"Red Otter is mistaken!" exclaimed Three Feathers. "Listen to his words. He's telling us he was attacked by a snake that walks upright, like a man. That is impossible! He was simply startled by a wolf and fell into the fire. This must be how he got the burn on his chest."

"No, Three Feathers," said Gray Wolf, kneeling to peer into Red Otter's face. "Whatever it was, it's frightened him nearly to death. You do not shake uncontrollably from the sight of a wolf!"

"A walking snake?" asked Sky Feather. "What are we dealing with here?"

"We'll answer that question later, Sky Feather," said Gray Wolf. "Take Red Otter to my hogan. And take care to avoid the seeping wound on his chest. This is no burn! I'll meet you there."

"I'll help you, Father," offered Two Ponies.

While Gray Wolf saw to Red Otter's wounds, Tall Bull assembled a small rescue party.

Inside his hogan, Gray Wolf knelt beside Red Otter and worked feverishly with his healing medicines. When his best herbs failed to ease Red Otter's pain, he shook his head in confusion. Why was nothing working? Never had he felt so helpless! Of course, having never seen such an unusual wound, he was now unsure of just how to treat it. It was actually dissolving Red Otter's flesh! He feared for the young man's life when his breathing grew more labored. Desperate, Gray Wolf packed the open wound with healing moss only to watch it, moments later, disintegrate before his eyes. He thought of having his daughter, Moon Flower, treat the wound with her magic healing light, but quickly decided against this idea. The last thing he wanted, was to expose her to this flesh-eating horror! When Red Otter suddenly sat up, Gray Wolf stepped back.

"My son, how are you able to move?" he exclaimed. "Your wounds are severe."

"I must return to the others," gasped Red Otter.

Two Ponies, hearing Red Otter cry out, rushed inside only to stand amazed at his friend's tenaciousness.

"Please let me go, Gray Wolf!" Red Otter begged, as he struggled to his feet. Two Ponies was shocked by his appearance. Pain contorted his face as the oozing wound crept slowly up his chest toward his neck.

"Two Ponies, get my horse, I beg you," cried Red Otter.

"My son, your wound worsens," said Gray Wolf. "But, I won't stop you from leaving if you insist."

"He can't go out like this," said Two Ponies. "He'll frighten the women and children. I'll give him my shirt. Gray Wolf, will you help me?"

Together the two men slid Two Ponies' woolen shirt down over Red Otter's shoulders. Both were careful to avoid touching the greenish-brown ooze. Though desperately concerned for the young man, Gray Wolf carefully led him outside where Winter Bird waited.

"Gray Wolf, what of his wound?" he asked.

"I cannot say," replied Gray Wolf, shaking his head. "I have tried everything to stop ... whatever this is. I have never seen anything like this in all my years. It's as if this walking snake's venom is eating away his flesh."

"We must hurry," urged Red Otter, his face etched in pain. "You cannot waste time looking for the camp, so I must lead you to it."

"Walks Far, go and locate Red Otter's horse," Two Ponies instructed a young boy of fourteen. "When you find it, come and tell me. Do not touch it!"

After the boy ran off, Two Ponies and the others hurried to prepare their own horses. When Walks Far returned, he was shaking.

"Two Ponies, I located Red Otter's horse," he reported, breathless. "He is out near the sheep. He's limping, and his head hangs low."

"I'll see to him," replied Two Ponies, tethering his horse to a post. After sending Walks Far to fetch Sky Feather, he hurried out to where the sheep grazed south of the village.

Red Otter's horse was suffering. Two Ponies approached it with soothing words. He felt sickened when he saw the damage the venom had done. The greenish-brown ooze had eaten through the flesh of the horse's neck, and its withers rippled with the pain. He took up the reins and gently ran his hand down its long face.

"Rest easy, my friend," he said, softly. The horse looked at him through eyes wide with fear. "Your pain will be swiftly dealt with, I promise. Soon you will be flying among the stars on great wings. The grandfathers will be pleased to welcome such a fine horse as you."

"We're here, Two Ponies," said Sky Feather. Winter Bird stood beside him. "What can we do to help?"

"There is no hope, I'm afraid," said Two Ponies. "Red Otter's horse must be taken out into the desert and put down. Such a shame."

"We'll see to Red Otter's horse, Two Ponies," said Winter Bird, taking the reins. "You go and see to Red Otter. We'll be along soon."

Leaving the two men to their unpleasant task, Two Ponies returned to the village.

After grabbing a fresh shirt from his hogan, he went to find Red Otter another horse. It was not an easy task. He knew whichever one he chose, would no doubt suffer the same fate as the one Winter Bird now led into the desert. Making his tough choice, he led the brown mare from the corral. As a precaution, he slid a thick yellow blanket over her back to protect her.

Leading the mare and his own black stallion, he went in search of Red Otter. He found his friend leaning against the back of Gray Wolf's hogan, his head bent low in pain. Gray Wolf stood beside him. The snake's venom had now eaten through the front of Red Otter's wool shirt, exposing again his severe chest wound.

"I thought it best to hide him from the children," said Gray Wolf, holding the reins to his own horse. "We must hurry, Two Ponies. I suspect the others at the scout camp will be in worse condition than Red Otter, by the time we reach them."

Two Ponies carefully took Red Otter by the arm and helped him onto the mare's back.

"My time is short," said Red Otter. "We must hurry."

"We'll follow your lead," said Two Ponies. Swinging up onto the back of his black horse, he and Gray Wolf led Red Otter out to join the others.

"Sky Feather and Winter Bird will ride with us," announced Tall Bull, from atop his horse. "Three Feathers, you'll remain to protect the village."

"No, Tall Bull!" exclaimed Three Feathers, swinging onto his large brown horse. "I beg to come with you!"

"He should come," said Winter Bird. "Standing Deer has returned from hunting in the northern hills. I've alerted him to what has happened. He's willing to guard the village."

"You will need me, Tall Bull," insisted Three Feathers. "Should this walking snake return I will be there to fight it. You are the chief of our people. Will you depend on only these few men to save you?"

"You're right, Three Feathers," said Tall Bull. "Let's ride!"

The small group of men followed Red Otter out of the village. Much to their surprise, he urged his horse into a full gallop and shot out across the open country to the west. The others struggled to keep up with him.

Riding behind Red Otter, Two Ponies marveled at the man's stamina. How could his friend ride so hard when he was obviously in extreme pain? And, what was this snake that walks upright, like a man, and spits venom. *Whatever it is*, he thought, *it's killing Red Otter.*

CHAPTER 7

As the six men rode westward, the sun beat down on their backs. After a while, Red Otter brought his horse to a stop.

"Here!" he shouted. Steering his horse to the right, he led them toward a huge, dark gray sandstone boulder. Two Ponies was relieved to see no vultures circling overhead. This gave him hope that the men were still alive.

Steering their horses around the boulder, they made their way into its shadow where they found a small clearing surrounded by sparce cedar trees and sagebrush. Slowing their horses to a walk, the riders cautiously approached the camp. They were surprised to find it deserted. Chaos, however, lay all around them. Blankets, crumpled and covered in bits of dirt and leaves, lay among the scattered rocks and burnt wood from the small firepit. Sky Feather knelt and examined the ground.

"A great struggle occurred here," he said. "Something attacked them while they slept."

"Look at the size of these paw prints," said Two Ponies, kneeling nearby. "The pads are huge! Along with the snake, Red Otter did say they were attacked by a *great* wolf. If these are its tracks, then these men didn't stand a chance."

"So, what happened to the scouts?" asked Sky Feather.

"Over here," shouted Winter Bird, from a row of sagebrush, twenty strides from the camp. "I found *one* of them. Prepare yourselves."

When the others reached him, they looked down in shocked horror at a body, lying face up on the sand.

"This is Little Hawk," said Tall Bull. "That is his bow and quiver beside him."

"Look at his face!" said Sky Feather. "It's been eaten away by the same greenish-brown substance that covered Red Otter's wound."

"Don't touch him," warned Two Ponies. "Red Otter said Little Hawk was hit by the venom of the walking snake."

"Come see this," said Winter Bird, standing a short distance away. There on the sand lay a second body. His face, too, was unrecognizable and oozing the same greenish-brown substance.

"Who is this?" asked Gray Wolf.

"It has to be Dark Bear," replied Sky Feather. "Red Otter said he, too, was spit on by the snake."

Nearby lay the carcass of a large, black vulture. The flesh of its head and neck were eaten away, exposing its bloodstained skull.

"What do you make of this?" asked Two Ponies, looking down on the dead bird.

"This is why we see no vultures," said Gray Wolf, glancing skyward. "This one foolishly approached Dark Bear, and when the others saw what happened, they flew away. I don't blame them."

"These boys are disappearing before our eyes," said Winter Bird. "This is the blackest of conjuring magic!"

"Red Otter tried to save them," said Sky Feather. "He said he jumped onto the back of the snake and tried to kill it with his knife. He only survived to tell us because his face was above its mouth when it twisted around and spewed its venom. It missed his face and hit him in the chest."

"Still, he will die like Dark Bear and Little Hawk," said Two Ponies, trying to hold his emotions in check. "My friend used the last of his strength to warn the rest of us. How can we ever repay such courage?"

"Come look at *these* strange tracks!" exclaimed Winter Bird. "Whatever left these, has a long narrow foot with sharp claws that dig deep into the sand. Could they have been left by Red Otter's walking snake?"

"Perhaps," said Sky Feather. "I learned how to track from my grandfather, and I must say, this particular track was not part of the lesson."

"These are my thoughts," said Three Feathers, hesitating until he had everyone's attention. "I believe you are all misreading the signs here. I see no sign of any snake. In my opinion, these men died at the hands of the White Fathers' soldiers."

"What are you saying?" asked Sky Feather. "If you think Red Otter is lying about the snake, then how do you explain the faces of these men?"

"The soldiers must have done this with their knives," replied Three Feathers. "What better way to dishonor our dead? And as for this *great* wolf, even you, Sky Feather, must admit that in the light of a campfire, even the average wolf can appear larger than life."

"Stop this chatter!" exclaimed Gray Wolf. "Let's keep to the truth, not to what we think *may* have happened. Now, besides Red Otter, there were seven others. I count only two. Where are the other five?"

"Everyone, spread out and search," commanded Winter Bird.

"I think we should return to the camp, Winter Bird," said Two Ponies. "That *is* where the attack first occurred. From there, we may pick up their trail."

Returning to the camp, both men knelt to reexamine the strange animal tracks.

"Such an odd track for a wolf," said Two Ponies, placing his hand beside it. "Next to it, my hand is like that of a child's. And look—here are the same tracks we saw around Dark Bear and Little Hawk. The long, narrow foot with deadly claws."

"I have no idea what it could be," said Winter Bird. "Look, I think Three Feathers is right. Snakes do not walk. Red Otter must be mistaken. After all, it was dark."

"Red Otter is no fool!" exclaimed Two Ponies. "He knows the difference between a snake that crawls on its belly and one that walks on two legs. Now, we need to find the others. I think the remainder of the scout party took their horses and fled."

"If that were so, then why didn't they return to the village?" asked Winter Bird. "They had enough time. Red Otter said they were attacked just before dawn. Even he, with his severe wound, returned to warn us."

"I cannot say," said Two Ponies. "Perhaps, we only need to call out to them and—"

A sudden cry of alarm brought both men to their feet.

"That's Tall Bull!" exclaimed Winter Bird, pulling his long knife from the sheath on his belt. "Come!"

Leaving the campsite, they spotted the others a short distance away. When they reached them, Two Ponies and Winter Bird stood transfixed in horror as they looked down on the scouting party. All that remained were five mounds of gray-colored ashes atop the scorched and burnt sand. Nearby, a small cedar tree, torn from the ground, lay smoldering. Tall Bull knelt beside one of the ash piles.

"This is my son," he said, in anguish. "They killed Long Bow. This is his weapon beside him."

Beside each mound of ashes, indeed, lay their bows and quivers. Several loose and broken arrows lay scattered about them on the sand.

"I am speechless," said Sky Feather, glancing around at the macabre gray mounds. "If we are identifying them by their weapons, then this is Black Star and Lone Eagle. Why are they only ... ashes?"

"What is this evil?" exclaimed Winter Bird, kneeling between two gray mounds. "This is Brave Turtle! And, this is Red Wind! What will we tell their families? Surely we cannot tell them the truth!"

"What *is* the truth?" asked Sky Feather. "Gray Wolf, what do you think?"

"I have never seen anything like this in all my years," he replied, shaking his head.

Winter Bird stood up. "What burned these men?" he asked, glancing around him.

"What about the wolf?" asked Two Ponies. "Red Otter told us it shot fire at them with a silver weapon."

"So he says," replied Winter Bird. "It is a great wolf, indeed, if it can wield a weapon that turns its victims to ashes."

"This is indeed a mystery," muttered Gray Wolf.

"There is *no* mystery here!" exclaimed Three Feathers. "What is this talk of walking snakes and wolves that can shoot fire? I tell you; this was done by the White Fathers' soldiers! They, too, have strange weapons. They have no regard for human life. I said as much this morning. I say we ride out and confront them. They can't have traveled far."

"And do what, Three Feathers?" demanded Gray Wolf, angrily. "Expose ourselves to a weapon that can burn a man so quickly, he's reduced to a pile of ash? These men fought this enemy with their bow and arrows—*we* carry only knives. Look around you, Three Feathers. Do you see the bodies of the soldiers? Or the snake and wolf? No, you do not. If the arrows of the scouting party couldn't kill them, what chance do you think we have?"

"I agree with Gray Wolf," said Tall Bull.

"I wonder," said Winter Bird, glancing around, "What happened to their horses?"

"I suspect they've run into the desert," said Sky Feather. "If they will shy away from a snake on the ground, there's no telling what they did when confronted by one that walks upright and spits."

"It's no use searching for their horses," said Three Feathers. "I believe the white soldiers took them. They killed these brave men for the sake of seven horses! I warned you they were without honor."

"We must not pass judgment on the soldiers, without proof," said Gray Wolf. "Red Otter said nothing about being attacked by soldiers."

"Wait," said Sky Feather. "Two Ponies, where *is* Red Otter?"

"In our haste to find the scouting party, we left him behind!" he replied. "I should have stayed with him. I'll go and find him."

Making his way back to where they'd tethered the horses, Two Ponies saw that Red Otter's was not among them. Knowing that his friend hadn't followed them into the camp, he walked in the opposite direction. Thirty paces out, he spotted Red Otter's brown mare. Red Otter sat nearby with his back against a large rock, his head leaning to the right. Smears of blood covered his long black hair as the flesh-eating venom opened his throat. Kneeling, Two Ponies looked into the face of his childhood friend, whose eyes held a look of terror.

"I am here, Red Otter," he said, softly.

"Did you find the others?" Red Otter asked, his voice sounding hopeful.

"We did," replied Two Ponies.

"Are they ... dead?"

"They are," said Two Ponies. Placing his hand on Red Otter's shoulder, he was careful to avoid the greenish-brown substance that covered his neck and chest. He could feel Red Otter's muscles quiver beneath his hand. "Two are dead from the venom, as you said, and the remaining five were burned to ashes. Red Otter, who was it that attacked you? Three Feathers thinks it was the soldiers of the White Fathers."

"It was a walking snake, Two Ponies!" gasped Red Otter, blood tinging his teeth red. "Please believe me! It walked into our camp, hissing. With it was a great wolf."

"We *did* see the tracks of the wolf," said Two Ponies.

"It was huge!" exclaimed Red Otter, before coughing up blood. "When it attacked, we shot at it with our arrows, but they just bounced off. It was wearing a thick black shield over its chest and carried a silver weapon that shot fire at us. When I saw it, I told the others to run for their lives. When they did, the wolf turned and ran after them."

"Try not to speak," said Two Ponies. "You must rest now."

For a long moment, his friend was still, and Two Ponies thought he had finally breathed his last. Then Red Otter sat up.

"Did you see the snake?" he asked.

"No," Two Ponies replied. "We saw no sign of it."

"It was here!" exclaimed Red Otter, his efforts costing him precious breath. "Little Hawk and Dark Bear stayed to help me fight it, but it moved too fast for us. After it spit on me, I told them to run but the snake turned on them. Now you say they're all dead?"

"We found them just beyond the camp," replied Two Ponies. "Red Otter, you must explain to me how a snake can walk on two legs."

"Two Ponies, listen to me," said Red Otter, gasping. "You must all leave this evil place, or you will surely die here like the others."

Struggling to his feet, he pushed past Two Ponies and lunged for his horse, stomping nervously nearby. Sliding onto its back, he looked down on Two Ponies.

"I am your brother, Two Ponies," he said, placing his closed fist just above the ugly open wound on his chest.

"And I am yours, Red Otter," said Two Ponies, doing the same. "Please wait. I'll get my horse and take you home."

"It is too late for me, Two Ponies," said Red Otter, taking up his reins. "Please, I want to be alone. Now I bid you and the others to go, or it will be too late for you as well!"

"Red Otter, wait!" shouted Two Ponies. But his friend was no longer listening. He urged his horse into a gallop and fled east, into the desert.

When Two Ponies returned to the camp, he found the others waiting for him.

"Did you find Red Otter?" asked Sky Feather.

"I did," replied Two Ponies. "He grew panicked and rode off."

"We must go after him!" exclaimed Sky Feather. "If he reaches the village, he could endanger everyone."

"That, I'm afraid, will not happen," said Two Ponies. "When I found him, his wound had reached his throat. He'll die before he reaches the village."

"Then our prayers go with him," said Sky Feather.

"Did you speak to him?" asked Three Feathers. "Did he tell you it was the soldiers?"

"No, he did not!" replied Two Ponies. "He still insists they were attacked by a walking snake and a large wolf."

"Well, he's wrong!" exclaimed Three Feathers. "And the soldiers who did this are riding further and further away while we stand here discussing it!"

"What if you *are* right, Three Feathers?" asked Gray Wolf, stepping forward. "What if this *is* the work of the white soldiers? If they can do what we found here today, then we are smart not to provoke them."

"Provoke *them*?" asked Sky Feather, his hand sweeping the camp. "Red Otter and the others were sleeping when they were attacked. These men were searching for horses, not looking for a fight. But I, too, am not yet ready to blame the soldiers. My instincts are telling me that something else slithers in the grass. Something totally unknown to us."

"Are we going to warn the villagers?" asked Two Ponies.

"Not yet," replied Sky Feather. "What name do we give to this warning? Do we call it a fire-breathing wolf or a walking venomous snake?"

"What about the dead?" asked Three Feathers. "Are we taking them home for burial?"

"No," replied Gray Wolf. "I know it sounds crazy, Three Feathers. But I think we should take precautions. I say we avoid even touching the bodies of those who have the flesh-eating wounds."

"We can't just leave them here for the vultures!" exclaimed Three Feathers. "Come sundown, the scavengers will drag them off into the desert."

"That won't happen," Two Ponies insisted. "What's eating the flesh of these men spreads when it's touched. I believe the dead vulture alone will be enough of a deterrent."

"I agree," said Gray Wolf. "If you look closer, you'll see that even the insects avoid going near the bodies."

"What about those burned to ash?" asked Tall Bull. "I have to take my son back to his mother."

"What will you carry back to her, Tall Bull?" asked Sky Feather, softly. "He's only ashes. How will you explain his death? I believe our only option here, is to return only their weapons to the families."

When all agreed, they returned to the dead and gathered the bows and quivers.

"What will I tell Long Bow's mother?" asked Tall Bull. "She has now lost both her sons."

"What will I tell the son of Dark Bear?" asked Two Ponies. "Yellow Rabbit will be crushed. He thinks his father is bringing him home a horse."

"This quiver still contains many arrows," said Gray Wolf, picking up Brave Turtle's beaded quiver. "These boys were helpless against these creatures."

"This is true," said Winter Bird. "This tells me the enemy killed them so quickly they didn't have a chance to defend themselves."

"What arrows they did manage to shoot are scattered and broken on the ground," added Sky Feather. "This tells *me* their arrows hit something so tough skinned they failed to penetrate."

"The soldiers could have worn an iron shield," remarked Three Feathers. "Cowards. I will find them and kill them myself."

"You speak through your anger, Three Feathers," said Tall Bull, shouldering his son's quiver and bow.

"Wait," said Two Ponies. "Red Otter did say this wolf wore a type of thick black shield over its chest."

"A shield?" asked Sky Feather. "What animal wears a shield?"

"What am I to do with my son's ashes?" asked Tall Bull.

"Let me think a moment," said Gray Wolf. "If we cannot take the ashes home, then we'll scatter them to the wind and free their spirits. My hope is they won't become trapped in this place of unimaginable evil."

As they stood among the dead, Gray Wolf sang their ancient death song. His words sent a prayer to the grandfathers above, asking them to welcome the spirits of their fallen sons into the next world. Using the lower limbs cut from a cedar tree, they scattered the ashes to the wind. All that remained were five blackened and scorched marks on the sand.

"Let's return to the village," said Tall Bull, when the last of the ashes disappeared on the wind. "Without bodies, how will we give their families closure? Perhaps kind words if we can utter them."

"Kind words, Tall Bull?" exclaimed Three Feathers, stepping forward. "We should be on the warpath! Why do you now ask us to ride back to our hogans like whipped dogs with our tails between our legs? We should be gathering up a war party to hunt down these soldiers and make them pay for what they have done here today."

"And bring this evil upon our women and children?" asked Tall Bull, pointing to one of the scorched areas. "We don't know if this is the work of the White Fathers' soldiers. If we simply kill them, unsure of their guilt, then we're no better than they are."

"We need to think before we act, Three Feathers," offered Gray Wolf. "If it was the soldiers then we'll deal with them. If not, we need to search out Red Otter's snake and its wolf."

"I don't know how the rest of you feel," said Sky Feather, glancing up at the sun, "but I don't want to be here when darkness falls."

"No wiser words were spoken, Sky Feather," said Gray Wolf, hurrying past him. "Where's my horse?"

As the men rode east across the open desert, they did so in silence. Two Ponies' thoughts turned to Red Otter. He knew his friend was in deep trouble when he rode out earlier. The venom had nearly eaten through his throat by the time he'd stumbled to his horse. *Surely, he must be dead by now*, he thought.

"What of Red Otter?" Sky Feather asked him, as if reading his thoughts. "We need to find him."

"I know," said Two Ponies. "I should have followed him. Because of me, he's died alone."

"Don't blame yourself, Two Ponies," said Sky Feather. "Red Otter knew his fate when he rode away from the camp. Death is seldom a public spectacle, and not all seek the company of others when it comes."

"He told me as much," said Two Ponies. "Still, I—"

"Stop!" called Gray Wolf, bringing his horse up short. "I believe that's Red Otter's horse over near that small mound of stones?"

"I'll see to Red Otter," offered Two Ponies. "The rest of you wait here." Turning his horse, he rode over to check on his friend.

Approaching the pile of stones, Two Ponies slid from his horse and walked slowly up to the old brown mare. He was relieved to find her free of the snake's venom. Just beyond the horse, he found Red Otter lying on his back in the sand. Two Ponies felt sick. The flesh-eating venom had eaten away his face, leaving the front of his skull exposed. Beneath his head, a dark reddish-brown slime coated the sand. Kneeling, Two Ponies watched the exposed bones of his chest for any movement. Finding none, he knew that Red Otter was dead. Tipping back his head, he sang to the grandfathers, now asking them to welcome one more spirit into their ancestral home. When he finished, he stood and looked down on Red Otter. Though the flesh was gone, in his mind, he could still picture the face of his childhood friend, with his laughing brown eyes and crooked grin.

"May your spirit find safe travels on your journey home," he said.

He and Red Otter had grown up together. They had shared the ceremony of becoming a man and had found their visions within hours of each other. He had great affection for his friend, which only deepened as they grew into manhood. Now he was dead. No more would they race their horses in friendly competition or hunt together in the hills for deer and rabbits. Sky Feather rode up and slid from his horse.

"Red Otter was a good man," he said, wincing when he saw his condition.

"Yes, he was," agreed Two Ponies, feeling his emotions falter. "I'll miss him. His family will know he died bravely; however, his mother doesn't need to know *how* he died. Do you agree, Father?"

"I do," replied Sky Feather. "Come. There's nothing more we can do for him. I know losing Red Otter is like losing a brother, Two Ponies. Mourn him. Grieve for what you have lost. And if you ever need to talk, you know where to find me."

Taking the reins of Red Otter's mare, Two Ponies led her back to where the others waited.

"What of Red Otter?" asked Gray Wolf.

"He's dead," replied Two Ponies. "He fought bravely."

"So, he did," said Gray Wolf. "Winter Bird has located the horses of the scouting party. He and Three Feathers went to bring them in from the desert."

When Winter Bird and Three Feathers returned, they led only four of the seven horses.

"Where are the others?" asked Gray Wolf.

".We found only these few," replied Three Feathers.

"We were lucky to find these," said Winter Bird. "It seems the three missing horses were led off into the west by the same wolf that left the tracks at the scout camp."

"A wolf does not lead its prey!" declared Three Feathers. "I saw only the hoof prints of our horses as the soldiers led them away."

"I saw no sign of any soldiers, Three Feathers," Winter Bird insisted. "What I *did* see were wolf tracks—huge ones."

"The tracks only tell me that a wolf followed their scent," said Three Feathers.

"Come, let's keep moving," said Gray Wolf. "Whether it's a wolf or the soldiers, I do not want to meet them here in the open."

CHAPTER 8

When the men rode into the village, the two small, brown-and-white dogs barked incessantly, announcing their arrival. The sun hung low in the west as evening approached. Those in the village stopped what they were doing to watch the men ride in. All knew the reason for the empty horses they led behind them. They were returning *without* the scouting party.

"What of my son?" asked a tall, thin woman approaching Winter Bird's horse. "What of Little Hawk? Did you find him? That's his horse you're leading behind you." -

"In time, your questions will have answers, woman," said Winter Bird, softly.

Tall Bull led them back to his hogan. Only Three Feathers rode on, and Two Ponies worried what he would tell the people if confronted. Standing Deer approached them as they dismounted. From out of nowhere, Walks Far appeared and gathered their horses.

"You lead empty horses, Tall Bull," said Standing Deer. "Where is the scouting party?"

"Give me a moment, Standing Deer," said Tall Bull. "I beg you to hold your questions for now."

Over his shoulder, Tall Bull carried his son's bow and quiver. Dancing Star, hearing her husband outside, stepped out to greet him. When she saw that Long Bow wasn't with him, she reached up and pulled the delicate yellow cactus flower from her dark hair and tossed it onto the sand. Her hope was gone. She quietly took her son's weapons from her husband, held them against her chest, and walked slowly back into their hogan. Two Ponies felt bad for her. Long Bow was her last remaining son. Her firstborn, Dream Walker, had been killed five winters earlier in a skirmish with the

Spanish raiders. Three days later, he and his fellow Dine' warriors attacked their camp to avenge the death of the chief's son. Long Bow, however, was killed by an unknown enemy leaving no one to answer for his death.

"Tall Bull, the people will be here soon," cautioned Winter Bird. "They'll want to know what happened to the scout party."

"*I* want to know what happened!" demanded Standing Deer. A man in his early forties, he stood tall and lean, with wide muscular shoulders and long black hair that fell to his waist. His massive chest bore a long white scar running from his right shoulder to his navel. A wound suffered in battle, that he now displayed proudly. Standing Deer, a man to be reckoned with, was now being ignored, and he did *not* like it.

Gray Wolf issued Winter Bird a quiet warning. "Tell the people only enough to make them cautious," he said. "Say nothing of how the scouting party died. We don't want a panic on our hands."

"What should I say?" asked Winter Bird. "Panic will find us sooner or later, I'm afraid. Three Feathers is still not convinced that we should even use caution. He's most likely, at this moment, telling everyone of what we found in the scout camp, and blaming it on the White Fathers' soldiers."

"Surely he'll use more sense than that," said Tall Bull. Turning, he addressed Standing Deer. "I left you to watch over our people, Standing Deer. Did you see anything strange around the village while we were gone?"

"No," he replied. "All is quiet. What *did* you find at the scout camp?"

Seeing the weariness in Tall Bull's eyes, Gray Wolf stepped forward.

"We're not sure yet, Standing Deer," said Gray Wolf, lowering his voice. "But they're all dead."

"All dead?" exclaimed Standing Deer, in disbelief.

"Yes," replied Gray Wolf. "Unfortunately, we had to leave them behind."

"You left them for the scavengers?" asked Standing Deer, loudly.

"Lower your voice," demanded Winter Bird. "We'll attempt to explain."

After hearing Gray Wolf and Winter Bird's account of the fate of the scouting party, Standing Deer fell silent.

"Now do you see why we cannot tell their families how they died?" asked Winter Bird.

"I do," replied Standing Deer. "I think we should continue to keep vigilance over our village until we know more. I'll take the first watch."

When Two Ponies spotted Yellow Rabbit, he steeled himself against the news he had to tell this proud young man who idolized his father.

"Two Ponies, where's my father?" the boy asked, glancing around.

"I'm sorry, Yellow Rabbit," said Two Ponies. "He didn't return with us."

"Then he still searches for my horse?" asked Yellow Rabbit, sounding hopeful. "I'll go and tell my mother. She's worried about him after hearing of Red Otter's injuries."

"Yellow Rabbit, your father is dead," said Two Ponies, taking the boy by the shoulders.

"What ... happened?" asked Yellow Rabbit, his shoulders slumping.

"I cannot say," replied Two Ponies. "I can tell you, though, he died bravely."

"I will go and inform my mother," said Yellow Rabbit, his voice rough with emotion. Pulling himself up tall, the young man turned and walked away. Two Ponies felt the boy's pain. Even after twenty winters, the loss of his own parents still brought him nights of loneliness.

Just as Two Ponies suspected, the villagers gathered around their chief and demanded answers. Tall Bull struggled with how much to tell them. Since their village was small, only sixteen people stood before him. With the death of those in the scout camp, and the three men still attending the Red River Council, those present were women, children, and the elderly.

"I have sad news to tell you," Tall Bull began. "All members of our horse scouting party are dead. At this time, we do not know who killed them."

"Red Otter said it was a walking snake," declared the elderly Red Shirt, as he leaned on his cedar staff for support. "He also said a great wolf is running with this snake. My grandson Brave Turtle is one of the fallen! Why aren't you gathering up a war party to go after this enemy?"

"Yes!" exclaimed Gray Stone, the grandfather of Red Wind. "This snake must pay for what it has done. I will ride out and kill it myself if I must. I fear no snake, nor do I fear any wolf!"

"What of my son, Red Otter?" demanded Singing Waters, tossing her long black braids over her shoulders. "He was alive when he rode out. Why didn't he return with you?"

"He, too, is dead," replied Tall Bull.

With these words, angry voices erupted from the people, and all demanded that Tall Bull do something.

"What will you have me do?" he asked. "You are asking me to hunt down a snake that walks upright, like a man. We encountered no such creature at the scout camp."

"Why didn't you bring home the bodies of our sons?" asked the mother of Little Hawk.

"I cannot say at this time," replied Tall Bull, softly. "You must trust me."

To ease the crowd, Gray Wolf stepped forward. "This was not a decision Tall Bull made on his own," he said. "As your spiritual leader, I also bear the responsibility for leaving them behind."

"Why don't you send Three Feathers to kill this walking snake?" asked one of the elderly women. "He's a mighty warrior. He will avenge the death of our sons."

Three Feathers, as if hearing his name spoken, rode his horse to the edge of the discontented crowd and dismounted. Knowing the people thought of him as a great warrior, he walked tall and proud into the midst of them.

"Here is Three Feathers," said Red Shirt. "What did you see at the scout camp, Three Feathers?"

"I saw only death," he replied, his hands resting on his slim hips. "I saw no sign of any snake. I say it was the soldiers of the White Fathers who killed your sons. I urged the others to ride out and face them, but I was outnumbered."

"Use caution, Three Feathers," warned Winter Bird, from behind him.

"You urge me to use caution, Winter Bird?" asked Three Feathers, spinning around to face the older man. "I say caution is for old men who can no longer hold a bow or ride a horse. As we speak, the soldiers are laughing at us as they sit around their fires. They could even be planning to attack our village now that they know we won't fight to defend ourselves. I think—"

"*We* don't care what you think!" exclaimed Winter Bird, just before his fist shot out and caught Three Feathers squarely on the chin. As if in slow motion, the mighty warrior fell backward. As he landed on his back in the sand, a cloud of brown dust drifted upward. When he didn't move, everyone stepped back, shocked that someone would dare to strike the mighty Three Feathers!

"Go back to your hogans and mourn your sons," said Tall Bull. "Three Feathers has no idea what he is saying. No one can say for sure it was the soldiers who killed the scouting party. If we attack without proof, we bring the wrath of the White Fathers down upon *our* heads. When we have answers, we will give them to you. Now, we'll honor our fallen sons around a ceremonial fire and return their weapons to you."

Amid murmurs, the crowd dispersed.

"Nice work, Winter Bird," said Sky Feather, stepping over the unconscious man lying in the dirt. "Should we wake him up?"

"No," replied Winter Bird, rubbing his fist. "Let the crowing rooster sleep. If these people knew their sons were burned to ashes or eaten alive by snake venom, we would have sheer panic on our hands! They might even try to leave the area. I say the less they know, the better off they are."

"I agree," said Sky Feather. "By the way, I hope I never find myself facing your right fist."

Someone lit the central firepit and the sound of drums filled the village. The mournful sounds of chanting filled the air as the people sang their prayers to the Sacred Creator. After the weapons of the dead were cleansed and returned to their families, Tall Bull issued his warnings. No one was to venture alone into the hills to hunt. And since the river was a good sixty paces from the safety of the village, they were to go for water only during the daylight hours. Out of fear of the unknown, no one argued these new restrictions.

The following morning, a solemn mood hung over the people as each family felt their loss. Two Ponies spent the morning with Yellow Rabbit, helping the young boy to work through his grief. Gray Wolf spent his morning in quiet conversation with Red Shirt and Black Crow, the two old and wizened Dine' Elders. After filling them in on the fate of the scouting party, together they searched the old stories for the origins of Red Otter's walking snake, as well as any tales of the great wolf.

"It is unfortunate that we are being visited by the snake," said Black Crow. "It is a bad omen. The snake is held sacred among our clans. But, there are those who believe the snake is the earthly manifestation of the lightning people. As we all know, they're an ancient foe who kills by shooting fire from their eyes."

"I have also heard of these creatures," said Gray Wolf. "They're known as the Binaye Ahani."

"According to legend, they can be killed with salt," said Red Shirt. "This is good news."

"It is indeed!" stated Black Crow, using his staff to slowly rise to his feet. "I'll send our women out to gather salt from the salt deposits in the north. I'll see to this immediately."

"Black Crow, stay a moment," said Gray Wolf, motioning for him to sit back down. "We have no proof it is the lightning people we're dealing with here. Besides, Red Otter said it was the great wolf that killed with the burning fire, not the snake. The snake killed with a flesh-eating venom."

"This is all so confusing, Gray Wolf," said Black Crow, lowering himself back to his mat. "But this great wolf could still be one of the Binaye Ahani."

"We mustn't rush to any conclusions until we know more," said Gray Wolf. "And we certainly cannot send our women out into the desert after salt!"

"Very well, Gray Wolf," said Black Crow. "I will wait. As a precaution, though, I think we should place a Spirit Pole in the center of the village to ward off evil."

"Good idea," said Gray Wolf, grateful to give them something, anything, to do that would help ease their fears.

As evening approached, Two Ponies took his turn watching over the village. After walking its perimeter, he stopped to chat with the children as they ate their dinner in front of their hogans. The two small brown-and-white dogs romped among them. The little female, he noted, was showing the early signs of an impending litter of pups. Leaving the children, and the dogs, Two Ponies made his way to the large flat rock that overlooked the sheep. Below him, they grazed in the dying sunlight.

"Are you sleeping, Two Ponies?" asked Winter Bird, stepping up from behind to slap him good naturedly on the back.

"Perhaps, he's counting sheep," said Sky Feather, squatting beside his son.

"As a matter of fact, I *am* counting sheep," replied Two Ponies.

"Although we have several new lambs, the number of fully grown sheep is growing smaller."

"Are you sure?" asked Winter Bird. Sitting down on the rock, he rested his elbows on his knees. "No one has spotted any daylight predators so they must be disappearing after dark."

"This concerns me," said Sky Feather. "The scout camp was attacked during the night. I suggest we start taking extra precautions after sundown."

As the stars came to life above them, the three men sat in silence, each listening to the night sounds of the high desert.

"The stars fill the sky tonight," said Sky Feather. Leaning back on his elbows, he gazed upward. "What strange magic holds them suspended above the earth? When I was a small boy, my grandfather told me that if I see a shooting star, I'm to blow on it and say a prayer for its safe journey across the night sky. Failing to do so meant trouble would find me."

"My grandfather told me that very same story when I was six," said Two Ponies. "He would take me out into the desert, where we'd sleep beneath the night sky. I'd lay on my mat and watch for shooting stars until I fell asleep. I'd often grow breathless just trying to keep up with them."

As they gazed upward, a star suddenly shot across the sky. Sky Feather released a loud puff of air and uttered a soft prayer under his breath. They laughed. It felt good after the sadness of the last two days.

"I have the next one," stated Two Ponies. When his shooting star appeared, he, too, let out a loud puff of air as it streaked past. Traveling north, it left only a short faint white line in its wake. Softly, he uttered his short prayer.

"Oh, star so bright, may your journey this night, be unhindered and straight as the arrow," he said, softly. "Winter Bird, you have the next star. Try not to miss it."

Instead of joining in the fun, Winter Bird grew serious.

"I have something to tell you," he said. "Two nights before the killing of our scouting party, I watched a strange star shoot across the night sky. I was so amazed by its long glowing tail that I failed to blow on it or to even say a prayer for its safe journey. *I* may have brought this dark evil upon us."

"How can this be?" asked Sky Feather. "The story of the shooting star is only a tale told to us by our grandfathers. It was meant to entertain us when we were children. Nothing more."

"Perhaps you're right," said Winter Bird, falling silent.

"Tell us about your star, Winter Bird," urged Sky Feather.

"It was very odd," he said, sitting up. "This shooting star was not like the ones we saw as children. It shot out of the southern sky as a huge ball of fire and its long tail was a great red streak. I expected this star to cross the great blackness and continue its northerly journey. Instead, it seemed to slow. When it did, it lost its great red tail and—"

"And what?" asked Sky Feather.

"I thought I saw it fall to the ground out near the western bluffs," replied Winter Bird. "In only a moment, it was out of sight."

"Your star *was* odd," remarked Sky Feather.

"Indeed, it was," said Winter Bird, again falling into silence.

"I'm sure it continued on its journey, Winter Bird," said Sky Feather, trying to ease his friend's concern. "The night sky *can* play tricks on you."

"I agree," said Two Ponies. "Stars do not just fall from the sky."

When the far-off cry of a wolf drifted in from the western desert, all three took notice.

"That is a wolf," said Winter Bird.

"So it is," said Sky Feather. "It's most likely a female who's ventured down from the mountains. This time of year, she'll be looking for a birthing den somewhere away from predators."

"Or we've just found our sheep thief," said Two Ponies.

"Could it be Red Otter's great wolf?" asked Winter Bird.

"Perhaps," said Sky Feather. "Tonight, we'll pay close attention to our sheep. If it is Red Otter's wolf, we may catch a glimpse of it."

"Catch a glimpse of it?" asked Winter Bird. "I say we deal with it here and now. I have my long knife."

"Let's not get ahead of ourselves," said Sky Feather. "It could still be only a female."

"Well, I hope you're right," said Winter Bird. "I find myself unable to sleep, so I'll keep watch over the village. Both of you get some rest. I'll see you in the morning."

Two Ponies walked his father to his hogan, then made his way to his own small home. As he lay on his sleeping mat, he thought about Winter Bird's strange falling star and wondered what it could mean.

At sunrise, Two Ponies stirred from a restless sleep. As he ate his breakfast, he caught the sound of something scratching in the dirt directly behind his hogan. Curious, he unsheathed his knife, stepped out, and made his way around to the back. Squatting down, he peeked beneath the patch of tall grass and bushes. There he found the little brown-and-white female dog, cowering in fear.

"Hey, girl, what are you doing back here?" he asked, softly. Returning his knife to its sheath, he knelt and patted his knee. When the little dog refused to come to him, he wondered what could have frightened her into hiding. "The children are eating their breakfast, and you're missing out on the scraps. You'll need your strength if you're to feed your coming litter of pups. Come out."

The little dog only cowered deeper into the bushes.

Hearing excited voices out front, Two Ponies left the dog and made his way into the village. He saw several of the people hurrying in the direction of the brush-lined path leading to the river. When Yellow Rabbit ran past, he stopped him.

"What is it, Yellow Rabbit?" he asked. "What's happening?"

"The village has been given a wonderful gift from the Sacred Creator!" the boy replied. "It rests beside the river."

Two Ponies, his curiosity now piqued, went to investigate. On the way, he ran into Sky Feather.

"Where's everyone going?" asked Sky Feather, stepping away from his hogan.

"Yellow Rabbit said something about a gift from the Sacred Creator," replied Two Ponies. "Whatever it is, it's at the river."

"Let's go and have a look," said Sky Feather. "Gifts are always welcome."

When the two men reached the small clearing beside the river, they stopped in their tracks. Sticking out of the ground was an eight-foot-high rectangle-shaped block of polished black stone. Its thickness was the length of a man's leg. Etched into its smooth surface was a strange symbol of a snake's eye within a triangle. Two Ponies knew in his gut that this was no idle gift. The handful of people milling around it all talked excitingly as they discussed their good fortune.

"It's black obsidian, I say," said the elderly Dark Badger, as he stooped over his walking cane. "It'll provide many tips for our arrows."

"I agree," said Walks Far, the young horseman. "I'll have enough to last me until I'm your age, old man." They both laughed.

"Everyone, stand clear!" shouted Winter Bird, stepping in between the crowd and the stone. "We don't know what this is."

"Nonsense," said Dark Badger. "We're being compensated for the loss of our sons with this wonderful gift. Think of the tools we can make from this great stone."

Standing Deer stepped up beside Winter Bird.

"And how do you think this great stone got here, Dark Badger?" asked Standing Deer. "There are no rocky slopes near the river. Do you think the Sacred Creator just dropped it from the sky for you to divide amongst yourselves?"

"He can do whatever he chooses, Standing Deer," said Dark Badger. "He *is* the Creator."

"Here comes Gray Wolf," said Singing Waters. "He'll tell Winter Bird and Standing Deer to step aside."

"Yes, he will," said Walks Far. "Gray Wolf is no fool. He'll see this great gift and no doubt take a huge piece for himself." Laughter again swept over the crowd.

As Gray Wolf approached, all chatter ceased when they saw the look on his face. Instead of finding the situation amusing, Gray Wolf's blue eyes were wide with horror.

"Everyone, get back!" he shouted, waving his arms as if he were swatting at a swarm of angry bees. "This is no gift from the heavens, you fools! Can't you see the strange symbol etched into its surface? This is a contrivance of the enemy."

Dark Badger stepped forward.

"If the rock is not a gift from the Sacred Creator, then who do you think placed it here, Gray Wolf?" he asked.

"I have no answers," Gray Wolf replied, in frustration. "But I fear the worst."

At that moment, Three Feathers strode into the crowd. "I know who placed this great stone here!" he exclaimed. "There's no mystery. The White Fathers are testing us."

"In what way, Three Feathers?" asked Dark Badger.

Two Ponies, sensing the man's foul mood, quickly stepped in behind him.

"Be careful what you say, Three Feathers," he warned.

Grunting, Three Feathers ignored him.

"They want to know how keen are the eyes of our watchman," stated Three Feathers, nearly spitting his words. "Wait. Wasn't Winter Bird on watch last night?"

It was obvious Three Feathers still held hard feelings over the way Winter Bird chose to silence him days earlier.

"So he was," said Two Ponies. "What's your point? He sees in the dark like an owl."

"Is that right?" spat Three Feathers. Turning to face the crowd, he showed no signs of backing down. "Perhaps you should ask yourselves how this large heavy stone came to be resting here so close to your sleeping children. How was it placed here without Winter Bird's knowledge?"

"What are you crowing about, Three Feathers?" asked Winter Bird. "I walked around the village all night. I didn't hear a sound. Where were you? Asleep on your mat?"

"You heard no sound?" Three Feathers asked with a snort. "Look at the size of this rock! I'm sure it took an army of soldiers to move it here from the bluffs. And you didn't hear them? If I were on watch and an enemy came this close to our village, I would have sounded the alarm. Perhaps you *were* sleeping, Winter Bird, when the rest of us were depending on you to alert us to any danger!"

"Stop this, both of you!" shouted Gray Wolf, stepping between them. "You weary my ears. Three Feathers, you are just as big a fool as those who want to hammer this ... thing ... into arrow points. I say we fear it until we know what it is."

"Fear is for old men," exclaimed Three Feathers, his ego stinging from having just been publicly labeled a fool. "I do not fear a piece of stone. I will prove it!"

"No, Three Feathers!" shouted Gray Wolf. "Do not go near it!"

Gray Wolf was too late with his warning. To save face, Three Feathers spun around and placed both his palms flat against the surface of the huge black stone. Everyone held their breath as they waited for him to turn around and laugh at Gray Wolf for being such an alarmist. What they saw, however, caused the mothers to cover the eyes of their children.

CHAPTER 9

The moment Three Feathers came in contact with the stone; his body stiffened as rigid as a tree. In slow motion, his head rolled back, and his mouth opened in a long silent scream. Frightened, the crowd stepped back. Two Ponies, not knowing what else to do, reached out and encircled Three Feathers around the waist, hoping to pull him from the stone. When their bodies met, a myriad of colors flashed in Two Ponies' mind. Swirls of vivid purples, reds, and greens danced behind his eyes followed by a thick gray mist. When the mist cleared, he found himself standing inside a large, dimly lit room. Several tiny white orbs embedded in the gray metallic walls winked at him. Releasing his breath, he drew in much-needed air, only to find it filled with a strong, pungent stench. His heart raced as he glanced around at his strange surroundings. Then his eyes fell on a large oval-shaped opening in the far wall, and he quickly made his way toward it.

Through a crystal-clear barrier, he peered out at a star field, and he felt his legs go weak. He was floating in the night sky! *How can this be?* he thought, his mind struggling to make sense of it all. Below him, floated an enormous glowing blue ball covered in great swirls of wispy white smoke. Beneath the smoke, two large brown masses stood out against a sparkling blue background. *Where am I?* he wondered in amazement. He thought he must be in the belly of some great iron beast, as he could feel its deep guttural voice vibrating against the bottoms of his moccasins. Unsure of what to do, he continued to stare down on the scene below him, his heart pounding in his ears.

Suddenly, over the steady rumble of the beast, he caught a new sound. From behind him, a low and menacing hiss filled the room. Two Ponies slowly turned. Beyond a high doorway, something watched him from the shadows. Fear gripped his heart as the creature began to sway back and forth, its hiss growing louder. He slid his knife free of its sheath and held it against his leg.

"Show yourself!" he demanded, loudly. "Who are you?"

When the shadow halted its movement, Two Ponies swallowed hard. Was it preparing to attack? He stepped backward, only to find his back against the wall. He was trapped! His only defense was his knife. Would it be enough? Holding it out in front of him, he waited for the creature to make a move. Suddenly it leaped at him from the shadows. But, before his mind could identify what it was, he felt his body suddenly go airborne. As he slammed against the hard ground, the air was forced from his lungs. He heard Three Feathers fall beside him with a loud grunt.

Sky Feather was the first to reach the men. Kneeling, he peered into the face of his son.

"Two Ponies!" he exclaimed. "Speak to me!"

"I don't think he's injured," said Winter Bird, sighing in relief. "Stand back. He's waking up."

"What ... what happened?" asked Two Ponies, struggling to sit up.

"You were stung by the black stone," replied Sky Feather.

"How is Three Feathers?" asked Two Ponies, glancing in the big man's direction.

"I'm not concerned about that crowing rooster!" declared Sky Feather. "He nearly killed you with his arrogance."

"I'll be fine, Father," said Two Ponies, although his head was spinning, and his stomach felt queasy.

"Three Feathers still breathes," announced Gray Wolf. "But he's not moving. I fear he is badly hurt. We must get him back to the village. I can do nothing for him here. Standing Deer, I want a watcher on this stone at all times. Obviously, this is no ordinary rock. I knew it was evil the moment I laid eyes on it."

"Yes, Gray Wolf," replied Standing Deer. "Walks Far, can you get me a travois to carry Three Feathers back to the village?"

"I can," replied the young horseman, now giving the evil black stone a wide berth.

"Until I figure out why this stone is here, no one goes near it!" Gray

Wolf barked at the cringing and frightened crowd. Turning, he hurried back to the village to prepare a place for the unconscious man.

"What are your wishes, Gray Wolf?" asked Standing Deer, as he lowered the travois holding Three Feathers to the ground in front of Gray Wolf's hogan.

"Help me to get him into the sweat lodge," Gray Wolf replied. "Two Ponies, you will enter it as well."

Gray Wolf filled the lodge's firepit with hot stones and began the arduous task of preparing his healing herbs. Two Ponies lay on his back in the hot air, feeling sick to his stomach. The hole in the mud roof above him spun in circles, so he closed his eyes.

"Three Feathers is in a deep sleep," said Gray Wolf.

"Can you heal him?" asked Two Ponies.

"I'll do my best," replied Gray Wolf. Sighing heavily, he added, "Despite all my efforts, I was unable to save Red Otter."

Two Ponies slept until early afternoon. Stirring awake, he sat up. Beside him, Gray Wolf stood silently watching the unconscious Three Feathers.

"How is he?" asked Two Ponies.

"I am unsure," replied Gray Wolf. "I've used the healing herbs and burned the sweet sage. Still Three Feathers sleeps."

"Perhaps it's time to ask Moon Flower for help," suggested Two Ponies.

"I'm hesitant to expose her to any of this," replied Gray Wolf. "Many years ago, when I fell ill with a sleeping sickness, she used her magic to save my life. She reached into my sleeping mind and brought me back to the waking world. My reward for surviving are my blue eyes. Mine was a fever though. Three Feathers was touched by evil magic. You saved his life, Two Ponies. If you hadn't pulled him from the black stone, it would have surely killed him."

"Yes, and in saving his life, my actions nearly cost me my own," said Two Ponies.

"Now I ask, how are *you*?" asked Gray Wolf, turning to face him.

"I'm ... better," replied Two Ponies. "I just need some fresh air."

"Sky Feather is concerned about you," said Gray Wolf. "If you are able, perhaps you should go and see him."

Taking the old man's advice, Two Ponies rose and left the sweat lodge.

Once outside, he drew in several deep breaths as he made his way to his father's hogan. The fresh air helped to clear his head.

"My son, how are you?" asked Sky Feather, rising from his mat as Two Ponies entered. "Blue Corn and I were concerned for you."

"I'll live," replied Two Ponies, giving his father a strained smile. "I slept for many hours."

"How is Three Feathers?" asked Blue Corn.

"He still sleeps," replied Two Ponies. "Perhaps because he actually touched the black stone, it may take him longer to shake off its poison."

"That stone is evil!" exclaimed Blue Corn. "It must be taken out into the desert."

"How?" asked Sky Feather. "Obviously, no one can touch it."

"Who's watching over the stone now?" asked Two Ponies.

"Winter Bird and Standing Deer are there," replied Sky Feather.

"I'll go and talk with them," said Two Ponies. Reaching into his mother's food basket, he withdrew a handful of small yellow corn cakes. "I think better on a full stomach," he added with a grin.

As Two Ponies made his way to the river, he felt as if something watched him from the desert. Reaching for the knife on his belt, he groaned when he felt the empty sheath. Then he recalled drawing it when confronted by the black shadow in the belly of the beast. He must have dropped it when it lunged at him. He felt naked without it. He treasured the knife as it was the last gift his grandfather gave to him. He hated to think that it was now in the hands of the dark hissing shadow.

"Well, look who's arrived just in time to take the next watch!" exclaimed Winter Bird, grinning. "How are you, my brother? We were concerned about you."

"I'm doing better than Three Feathers," replied Two Ponies. "He's still asleep."

"I'm glad you weren't hurt by the black stone," said Standing Deer, pulling his hand from behind his back. "Look what I found in the grass. A weapon with no warrior."

"My knife!" exclaimed Two Ponies. "Thank you. Losing it would have been a terrible loss to me." He thought about telling them about the black shadow he'd encountered while in the belly of the iron beast; however, he still wasn't exactly sure *what* it was he'd seen. When the abrupt cries of the sheep broke the stillness of the afternoon, all three took notice.

"Something disturbs the sheep," exclaimed Standing Deer. "Follow me."

Shaking off his earlier fatigue, Two Ponies followed his friends as they ran to inspect the flock.

The nervous bleating of the sheep grew louder as they approached, and several of the young lambs hid beneath their mothers.

"Are they sensing our wolf?" asked Two Ponies. Curious, he quickly counted their numbers. "We now have only twenty-nine sheep."

"We've lost two more since yesterday!" exclaimed Winter Bird.

"Look over there," said Two Ponies, pointing to the edge of the mob. "That ewe has blood on her face and hip."

As Two Ponies approached the ewe, she nervously bolted away. Her injuries, however, allowed him to easily catch her. Beneath her right eye, he discovered a deep gash, with two more long, deep cuts marring her right hip.

"Something attacked her," said Winter Bird.

"Do you think it's our mother wolf?" asked Two Ponies. "It's unusual for a wolf to come so close to our village, and in broad daylight no less." Shielding his eyes with his hand, he looked out across the open sunbaked land. Heat waves danced above the hot sand. Scanning the trees lining the river, he looked for any movement. Was the wolf still nearby?

"Look at the size of these tracks!" exclaimed Standing Deer. "They're much too big to belong to any female wolf."

"Why are we still assuming our wolf is a female?" asked Winter Bird. Squatting, he laid his hand over the track. "Judging from the size of this paw print, I'd say it's an extremely large *male*."

"Look at them more closely," said Two Ponies. "Where did we see tracks resembling these before, Winter Bird?"

"At the scout camp," he replied.

"Our wolf still managed to take one of our sheep," said Two Ponies. "Look at the drag marks in the sand."

"The tracks lead off to the west," stated Standing Deer. "He's dragging his prize toward the bluffs. Come, let's see where he's leading us."

The line of tracks continued for about thirty paces before suddenly changing their pattern.

"Stop a moment," said Winter Bird, leaning down to examine the sand. "The tracks have changed their gait. It's as if our wolf has suddenly lost his front legs."

"That's impossible," said Two Ponies. "Let's continue on. The tracks lead us in the direction of that small stand of trees in the distance."

After only a few steps forward, Winter Bird again hesitated.

"What now?" asked Two Ponies.

"Where are the drag marks?" asked Winter Bird, examining the ground at his feet. "If our wolf is still dragging away his prize, then where are the marks to prove it?"

"He's right!" said Standing Deer. "The drag marks stop here. He must have dropped his sheep."

"I don't think so," said Winter Bird. "If that were true, then why are there no tracks showing the sheep returned to the mob? Surely it would have wanted to escape its captor. Or if the sheep were injured or dead, wouldn't we at least find blood or proof that our wolf ate it here?"

"Look how deep the tracks press into the sand," said Standing Deer. "Either our wolf has suddenly grown fat, or he carries something very heavy."

"Well, at least we know *how* the sheep are disappearing," said Winter Bird. "This wolf has been dragging them off, one by one, for days. Come, let's continue our search."

When they reached the stand of trees, the wolf's tracks disappeared into the thorny greasewood thicket covering the ground. Dangling from one of the inch-long thorns, a small clump of long, thick gray hair fluttered in the breeze.

"We've lost the trail," said Winter Bird. Plucking the clump of hair off the bush, he grinned. "But here is our proof that what we seek is indeed a wolf."

"The tracks continue over here," said Two Ponies, from the far side of the stand. "From here, they lead us further to the west."

"Should we follow them?" asked Winter Bird, joining him.

"I'd say no," warned Two Ponies. "If this *is* Red Otter's great wolf, we could find ourselves facing him *and* the snake creature."

"I see no sign of any snake," said Winter Bird, glancing at the ground. "I say we follow the wolf's tracks and see where he's taking shelter."

"To what end?" asked Two Ponies. "If it is a large male wolf, are you willing to face one mighty enough to carry a fully grown sheep in its mouth? We've only knives to defend ourselves."

"I'd say our wolf is not a loner," said Standing Deer. "He has to be part of a larger pack. One wolf, even a large one, cannot eat two fully grown sheep in two days."

"We'll abandon our search for now," said Winter Bird. "At least we know in what direction our wolf lives."

When the three men returned to their village, Standing Deer and Winter Bird returned to the river to watch over the great stone. Two Ponies went to inform Sky Feather of what they'd found.

"You'll take your meal with us," said Blue Corn. "I've made a rabbit stew."

"This rabbit is a rare find," added Sky Feather. "Once there were many; now they're hard to come by."

"We have a wolf hunting near the village," said Two Ponies. "Perhaps it's catching them before you do. It's also stealing our sheep."

"Could this wolf be the one that attacked the scout camp?" asked Sky Feather.

"I'm not sure," replied Two Ponies. "Winter Bird thinks it could be. My concern is the whereabouts of the snake creature. A wolf we can handle."

As evening fell, Two Ponies sat quietly talking with Sky Feather. He grew more restless as the light faded outside the hogan.

"I think I'll go and check on the sheep," he said, getting to his feet. "Someone should be there to—"

His words were interrupted by the sudden outburst of panicking sheep at the edge of the village. Both men hurried outside just in time to meet Yellow Rabbit as he ran in from the south.

"What is it?" asked Two Ponies, catching the boy by the shoulders.

"Many Horses and I were out by the sheep, when we saw a wolf!" he exclaimed.

"We know about the wolf, Yellow Rabbit," said Two Ponies, releasing the boy. "We'll take care of it."

"But this wolf is not like the ones we see howling on the cliffs," said Yellow Rabbit. "This wolf was like ... a man. He had the face and hair of a wolf, but he walked toward us like a man. He picked up a small lamb and ran off on his two hind legs."

"What's this?" asked Sky Feather. "A wolf who looks like a man, you say?"

"I saw him!" declared Yellow Rabbit.

By now, the panicked cries of the sheep were taking on an almost human quality.

"Where is Many Horses now?" asked Two Ponies. "Is he still out with the sheep?"

"No," replied Yellow Rabbit. "He returned to his hogan."

"Go and join your mother," said Two Ponies. "And, Yellow Rabbit, until we know more, we'll keep the last part of your story to ourselves. Do you understand?"

"Yes, Two Ponies," replied the boy.

"What have we here?" asked Sky Feather, as they hurried in the direction of the sheep. "Yellow Rabbit has to be mistaken. No wolf walks only on its hind legs."

"None that we know of anyway," said Two Ponies.

"These are strange times," said Sky Feather. "Here comes Winter Bird and Standing Deer."

"We were on watch near the river!" exclaimed Standing Deer, out of breath. "We heard the sheep and came right over. What's happening?"

"It would seem our wolf has returned for another sheep," said Two Ponies.

"And I was not here!" exclaimed Winter Bird, lowering his long knife. "I should've been with the sheep, but I thought I saw a wolf drinking from the river."

Around them, the sheep moved erratically. A few nearly knocked the men off their feet in their attempt to hide behind each other.

"Our wolf only managed to steal one small lamb this time, Winter Bird," said Two Ponies. "Yellow Rabbit saw this wolf and claims it walked upright, like a man."

"Is that so?" asked Winter Bird.

"I know this is hard to believe," said Two Ponies. "But he insisted the wolf picked up a lamb before running off on his two hind legs."

"Those were his exact words?" asked Standing Deer. "His story sounds a little crazy to me."

"No crazier than Red Otter's walking snake," replied Two Ponies. Lowering his voice to a loud whisper, he added, "I would hate to think we have a shape-shifter in our midst."

"Do not name it!" exclaimed Sky Feather. "Your very words could put us all in great danger!"

"Forgive me, Father," said Two Ponies, lowering his eyes.

"Well, it *does* explain the strange tracks we saw earlier," said Standing Deer. "Winter Bird said they appeared as if the wolf suddenly lost his front legs. It makes more sense than saying he carried off a fully grown sheep in his mouth."

"Where are those mangy dogs?" asked Sky Feather. "Why aren't they here watching over the sheep? They could have warned us about the wolf."

"The small female is hiding behind my hogan," replied Two Ponies. "Where her companion is, I don't know."

The long-drawn-out call of a wolf drifted in on the night breeze.

"Our wolf is counting coup," remarked Standing Deer. "Tonight, I'll stay with the sheep. I'll catch our thief!"

"I'll stay with you," said Two Ponies. "You may need my eyes. Winter Bird, go and get some rest. Father, you should rest as well."

"It is my turn to gather wood for the hogans," said Winter Bird. "I'll be up early should you need me."

"I'll help you," stated Sky Feather. "So, I, too, will be awake before dawn."

CHAPTER 10

Two Ponies stayed with Standing Deer until well into the night. When nothing stirred, he, too, was sent to get some rest. Now as he lay on his mat, he thought of Yellow Rabbit's tale of the wolf that walked on its hind legs. Surely it was just the ramblings of a frightened boy. The snake creature, on the other hand, left him confused. Red Otter described it as a large snake that *walked* into their camp. If Yellow Rabbit's walking wolf *was* this same great wolf Red Otter spoke of, then it, too, fell into that realm of the strange and unexplained. Closing his eyes, his mind fell into a deep and troubled sleep.

Once again, he stood in the small, gray, metallic room. A horrible stench filled his nostrils and he tried not to breath too deeply. Beneath his feet, the floor throbbed like the steady hum of a great beehive. He groaned when he realized he was, once again, in the belly of the great iron beast. Knowing what came next, he waited for the sound of the low hiss. When it came, he slowly turned to face it. Just as before, the tall, dark shadow creature swayed back and forth, menacingly. Was it waiting for him to make the first move? When he stood his ground, the creature's hiss grew louder.

"Show yourself!" he demanded. "I am Two Ponies, a warrior of the Dine' nation! I do *not* fear you."

When the shadow creature stepped into the light, Two Ponies gasped. It was a snake. No, a snake *woman*! She stood as tall as a young sapling, with muscular arms and legs. Two small scaly breasts protruded through holes in the front of the black breastplate covering her chest. In the center of this breastplate was the symbol of a snake's eye within a triangle. As the she-snake swayed back and forth, her thick greenish-black lizard scales undulated even in the low light. Her very appearance spoke loudly of her deadly nature. It was her face, however, that made his blood run cold. It was indeed the face of a large snake. She stared at him through black vertical slits, that sliced through her yellow, unblinking eyes. Two holes served as a nose, and her wide, lipless mouth was stretched into an evil sneer. *This must be Red Otter's walking snake*, he thought. *It is real!*

Without warning, the snake woman swiftly advanced on him. Two Ponies found his feet stuck to the floor. As she drew closer, her lipless mouth opened and spewed forth a stream of greenish-brown venom. The air left it steaming as it flew toward his face, and his mind screamed with fear. Waking abruptly from his dream, Two Ponies sat straight up on his sleeping mat. Panic seized his mind, and a sheen of sweat covered his body. Now he knew what had killed Red Otter and the others. Dressing quickly, he stepped out into the pre-dawn and went in search of Sky Feather. He found him and Winter Bird stacking firewood outside one of the hogans.

"What is it, son?" asked Sky Feather.

"I know what killed Red Otter," replied Two Ponies. "I saw it in a dream. I must tell Gray Wolf."

"Despite the early hour, he's in Tall Bull's hogan," said Winter Bird, stacking the last of the wood. "Come, there you can tell us your story."

When they entered Tall Bull's hogan, they found the two men smoking their pipes and chatting quietly.

"What is it?" asked Tall Bull. "It's not yet daylight."

"Two Ponies has something important to share with us," said Sky Feather.

"Sit," Tall Bull bid them.

"The stone beside the river does indeed possess an evil magic," said Two Ponies. "It revealed to me the great iron beast that floats in the sky above us. I just had a dream of coming face-to-face with the snake creature that dwells in its belly. I tell you, it's real!"

"So, this is what we are up against," stated Tall Bull. "I wonder if it's this snake creature that is responsible for bringing the black stone into our midst. If so, for what purpose?"

"What is this ... great iron sky beast you speak of?" asked Winter Bird. "How is it able to float above our heads, and we cannot see it?"

"I don't know," replied Two Ponies. "But I can tell you this: the snake creature I encountered is a woman."

"A woman, you say?" asked Tall Bull, with surprise. "This is good news! Why should we fear a woman?"

"This is *not* good news!" exclaimed Two Ponies. "This snake woman is deadly. And it is as Red Otter said. She doesn't slither on the ground but walks upright, like a man. She's nothing like our women, who cook and tend to their children. This female is immensely powerful and carries herself like a warrior."

"What of Three Feathers, Gray Wolf?" asked Tall Bull. "Was he injured when he touched the black stone?"

"I won't know until he awakens," replied Gray Wolf, pulling a twig from the fire to relight his small pipe. "I've covered him in the puma skin, smoked him with sage, and still nothing I've done has helped him. Even Moon Flower cannot reach him. I am afraid he's like a cocoon without its butterfly. Empty."

"I'm told we have a wolf hunting near the village," said Tall Bull. "Yellow Rabbit saw it among the sheep last night. Is this true?"

"It is," replied Winter Bird.

"Well, we must deal with this wolf!" demanded Tall Bull. "Standing Deer said he watched for it during the night, but it didn't return. Our sheep must be kept safe. If this wolf is allowed to take what it wants, by winter we'll have nothing to feed and clothe our children."

"Where *is* Standing Deer?" asked Sky Feather.

"I sent him back to the river," replied Tall Bull. "The sun will rise soon, and the women will need protection when they fetch fresh water."

"About this wolf," said Two Ponies. "It, too, is different than an ordinary wolf."

"A wolf is a wolf," said Tall Bull, with a dismissing wave of his hand. "At least we now know *he* is real. At this time, he is more of an immediate threat than this snake woman only you have seen—in a dream."

Two Ponies sat forward.

"Tall Bull, he said this wolf ... walked upright, like a man," said Two Ponies. Without warning, Gray Wolf gasped and fell backward.

"Gray Wolf!" shouted Sky Feather, reaching for him.

After carefully setting Gray Wolf to rights on his rug, Sky Feather retrieved the old man's pipe and placed it into his shaking hands. Gray

Wolf took the time to relight it, allowing himself a moment to steady his hands. Taking a long draw, he released the smoke upward.

"What is it, Gray Wolf?" asked Sky Feather, looking concerned. The old man looked at them with a strange expression, his blue eyes wide with fear.

"I have seen my death!" he replied.

"What is this?" asked Winter Bird. "Explain."

"When I was a boy, I was sent into the desert in search of my vision," said Gray Wolf. "That vision still haunts me to this day. For days I wandered in the wilderness, waiting for the ancestors to speak. On the fourth day, I finally saw my vision."

"And what was this vision?" asked Winter Bird.

"I saw a large gray wolf step from the shadow of a huge round rock," he replied. "I stood and faced it. Although fear gripped me, I did not run away. Because of my bravery, I was given the name Gray Wolf. That, however, is not the whole story."

"Tell us more," urged Sky Feather.

"I am ashamed to say, my heart held much fear at that moment," said Gray Wolf, with a short nervous laugh. When his hands began to shake again, he gripped his pipe tighter. "The truth is, this mighty wolf did not step from *behind* the large rock but from an open door in the side of it. As I stared at the wolf, he stared back at me through blood-red eyes."

"And?" urged Sky Feather.

"The large wolf in my vision … walked upright, like a man," replied Gray Wolf.

"Then Yellow Rabbit's tale is true?" asked Tall Bull, with concern.

"It is, indeed," said Gray Wolf, his blue eyes wide. "At first, I couldn't believe what I was seeing! Although my wolf was covered in black and gray hair, and his muzzle bared his canine teeth, he stood on his hind legs. His hands, though, were wide hairy paws with thick pads and deadly claws."

"Is that all?" asked Sky Feather.

"No," replied Gray Wolf. "The memory is now returning to me. As a boy, I thought it strange that this wolf would be wearing a thick black breastplate over his chest. One with a symbol etched on it."

"What symbol?" asked Two Ponies. In his mind, he already knew what the old man was about to say.

"As I recall now, it was the eye of a snake within a triangle," replied Gray Wolf. "The same symbol etched into the black stone. I knew I'd seen that symbol before! At last, my boyhood vision makes sense to me."

"What makes you think you now see your death?" asked Winter Bird.

"This wolf-man told me that someday I would face him, and die at his hand," replied Gray Wolf.

"Gray Wolf's story makes sense," said Two Ponies. "I saw that same symbol etched into the breastplate worn by the snake woman."

"What does all of this mean?" exclaimed Tall Bull, in frustration.

Everyone looked up when Walks Far stuck his head into the hogan.

"What is it?" asked Tall Bull.

"It's Three Feathers," replied the boy. "He's awake."

"The rest of you go and tend to him," said Tall Bull. "I'll wait for Standing Deer to return. I'm sure, he, too, will find this recent news unbelievable."

When they arrived at the sweat lodge, the sun was cresting in the east. Three Feathers stood outside the door; his hands clenched at his side. Even in the low light, Two Ponies was shocked at his appearance. His long black hair lay stringy and tangled with small bits of leaf and twig. The three black eagle feathers he wore so proudly, hung frayed and broken, and his shirt and leather pants were stained with soot from the firepit. In silence, the once proud rooster made his way across the village to his hogan. Without a backward glance, he dropped the hide over the doorway, shutting out the world.

"We must help him!" exclaimed Two Ponies.

"You three go inside with him," said Gray Wolf. "I'll go and fetch him food and water."

They found Three Feathers sitting on the dirt floor beside his cold firepit. His face wore a look of total devastation and his eyes were dull and lifeless. Gray Wolf was right. He was a cocoon without its butterfly. Two Ponies knelt and placed his hand on Three Feathers' shoulder.

"Three Feathers, it's me," he said, softly. "I know your pain, my brother. I, too, felt the sting of the black stone."

Three Fathers continued to stare at the wall in silence.

"It's like he's in a waking sleep!" exclaimed Sky Feather.

"Let's give him a chance to fully awaken," said Winter Bird.

When Gray Wolf arrived, he carried a flat basket containing strips of dried meat, and several small corn cakes. In his other hand, he held a crock of fresh water. He managed to get Three Feathers to eat a few bites of meat and several sips from the crock, before he, once again, turned his face to the wall. When the sudden outburst of bleating sheep erupted right outside the door, Two Ponies got to his feet!

"What now?" he mumbled. "These sheep are becoming quite a nuisance."

Hurrying outside, he nearly tripped over one of the old ewes standing in his path. Sky Feather and Winter Bird, rushing out behind him, nearly ran into the back of him.

"What are the sheep doing inside the village?" cried Sky Feather.

"I'm not sure," replied Two Ponies. Glancing around him, he noticed several of the sheep were now milling around the front his own hogan. The rest of the flock tumbled in from the grazing land, pushing and shoving each other in their haste to escape whatever had them in a panic.

"Well, something's chased them in from the desert," said Winter Bird.

When the screams of a young girl reached them over the cacophony of bleating sheep, they turned and headed in her direction. Near the river path, a mother was attempting to console her young sobbing daughter. The front of the young girl's tan doe-skin dress was covered in smears of dirt. The villagers gathered nearby, all talking at once. Not one, however, was willing to venture down the river path to see what had frightened the girl.

"What's happened?" asked Two Ponies, as he approached the mother. "What's happened to Little Doe?"

"I'm … not sure," her mother replied. "What she's telling me makes no sense. She says she went to the river to fetch water, and a snake tried to grab her. Oh, this is all my fault! I should have never sent her alone. But I was told Standing Deer would be there to protect her!"

"Where *is* Standing Deer?" asked Winter Bird, his eyes scanning the crowd. "He was on watch at the river. Has anyone seen him?"

Everyone shook their heads as they glanced around.

"I have a bad feeling," said Two Ponies.

"Forget the sheep," said Winter Bird. "Let's you and I go and see what frightened the girl. Stay alert! Little Doe doesn't frighten easily."

"I'll stay with Little Doe and her mother," offered Sky Feather. "You two go and find Standing Deer."

Two Ponies and Winter Bird pulled their knives and hurried down the brush-lined path toward the river, each searching their side of the path as they moved. They were nearly to the river when Winter Bird halted and let out a low cry. Just off the path, they found the still body of Standing Deer, lying on his back among the high grass. The greenish-brown venom of the she-snake spattered his face and filled his open mouth and nose. The steaming venom was already at work, eating at the flesh around his mouth and covering his dark hair with a thick slime. Winter Bird knelt and carefully laid his hand on his chest.

"He's still alive, but he won't be for long," he said, shaking his head. "Like the others, he took a direct hit to the face! At least he won't suffer as long as Red Otter suffered."

"What can we do for him?" asked Two Ponies, feeling helpless.

Winter Bird leaned over his dying friend. "We are here, Standing Deer! What can we do to help you?"

When Standing Deer opened his eyes, they held a look of pure terror. Shuddering, he swallowed the mouthful of venom, took in two gulps of air, then fell still.

"He's dead," said Winter Bird, his voice rough with emotion.

"I will kill this enemy with my bare hands!" exclaimed Two Ponies. "It must be stopped!"

"Two Ponies, listen to me!" exclaimed Winter Bird, getting to his feet. "Standing Deer was spit on only moments ago. This tells me the she-snake is nearby. Here comes Gray Wolf."

"I was told something has happened near the river," said Gray Wolf, hurrying toward the two men. "And why are the sheep in the—" Coming to a halt, he moaned loudly when he saw the latest victim of the she-snake. "We must deal with her now! She's killing within the village. And, after the sun has crested."

"Standing Deer must have run into her when he attempted to save Little Doe," said Two Ponies.

"Hear my words," said Gray Wolf. "The time has come to tell our people what it is that we face. We must use our words wisely, though. What we say could cause them to panic."

"No, Gray Wolf," said Two Ponies. "They are Dine'. They will stand and fight!"

Sky Feather arrived just in time to help Two Ponies and Winter Bird carry the body of Standing Deer out into the desert. There they hid him in the cleft of a large rock, away from prying eyes.

Returning to the village, Two Ponies went to break the news to Standing Deer's wife that he was dead. As he expected, she took it extremely hard. Gray Wolf gathered the people together and told them about the she-snake. It didn't cause the panic he feared. As Two Ponies predicted, they rallied together and vowed to fight. The women gathered in their children and tried their best to explain the danger without frightening them too badly.

"What of Three Feathers?" asked Winter Bird. "Surely he'll now join our fight. Without Standing Deer, we'll need him."

"He still sits in his hogan," replied Gray Wolf, shaking his head. "I'll go and speak with him. Two Ponies, will you come with me? You know some of what he's going through."

They found Three Feathers lying on his mat. Beside him, someone had built a small fire in his firepit. When Two Ponies saw that Three Feathers was awake, he carefully helped him to sit up. His face held no expression and dark circles shaded the skin beneath his eyes.

"Three Feathers, you must return to yourself," he said, softly. "We need you."

Getting no response, he rose and stepped away. Gray Wolf, however, was less accommodating.

"Three Feathers, on your feet!" he exclaimed. "The enemy is here, and we need your fighting skills."

Suddenly Three Feathers cried out. "The she-snake is inside my head, Gray Wolf!" he exclaimed, turning his face toward the old shaman.

"She is also in the village," said Gray Wolf. "She just killed Standing Deer with her vile flesh-eating venom."

"Standing Deer is dead?" asked Three Feathers, in a tone of disbelief.

"He is," replied Two Ponies. "He was just killed on the river path."

"Standing Deer was a good man," stated Three Feathers, now sounding more like himself.

"Yes, he was. Now on your feet, boy!" exclaimed Gray Wolf. "We've work to do!"

Tall Bull bid the men to meet him in his Hogan to discuss Standing Deer's death. As they sat planning their next move, Three Feathers joined them. Everyone was genuinely glad to see him up and about. Freshly bathed and wearing clean leathers, he now resembled the warrior they had all come to respect. Once more his mane of black hair fell shimmering to his waist. On the side of his head, three fresh eagle feathers dangled from a strand of braided leather. His weight, however, had dropped, giving his muscles a more defined appearance. After a wash and a good meal, even the dark circles beneath his eyes were beginning to fade. Now the question on everyone's mind was who sat before them—the crowing rooster or the warrior?

"Welcome, Three Feathers," said Tall Bull. "I am pleased to see that you've recovered from your ordeal."

"What have you done with Standing Deer?" asked Three Feathers.

"All we could do," replied Gray Wolf. "I prayed over him, and we hid his body in the desert. He must remain concealed. Although his death was extremely hard on his wife and daughter, they must never see the way in which he died. Gruesome! Because of this, the people are more frightened now than ever."

"That will prove useful," said Sky Feather. "It will, I hope, keep them from wandering off alone to fetch water from the river."

"What are we to do?" asked Tall Bull. "If this illusive she-snake can kill Standing Deer, a grown man, then she can surely kill a child."

"She's already made an attempt to do just that," said Sky Feather. "Little Doe claims a snake tried to grab her on the river path. Three Feathers, what are your thoughts?"

Two Ponies was sure Three Feathers was about to suggest they mount their horses and engage in a full-on attack. All waited for him to speak.

"This she-snake is real, I assure you," he said. "She held me captive for days inside a dark room with no door. She probed me with questions. How many are we? What weapons do we possess?"

"What did you tell her?" asked Sky Feather.

"I told her nothing," replied Three Feathers. "She is full of hate and would have eventually killed me. But my mind revolted, and I awoke in the sweat lodge. I can tell you this: the stone beside the river is here to lead others of her kind into our land."

"She's not our only threat, Three Feathers," said Winter Bird. "We're also dealing with Red Otter's wolf that walks on its hind legs. He's the one helping himself to our sheep."

If Winter Bird thought his statement would be challenged, he was wrong.

"Yes, it is as Red Otter said," stated Three Feathers. "In my opinion, our weapons are useless against them both. We need to come up with a better way to fight them."

"Welcome back, Three Feathers," said Winter Bird, smiling. "I'm pleased to see it's the warrior who joins us. By the way, I'm sorry about the other day when I—"

"You had no choice," said Three Feathers. "I acted stupidly."

When Red Shirt pulled back the hide covering the door, everyone looked up.

"My chief, I'm sorry to interrupt," he said. "But we've spotted three riders approaching the village. They are Hopi, and one of them is their spiritual leader, Black Fox."

"What are the Hopi doing here?" asked Winter Bird.

"I cannot say," replied Red Shirt. "Should I have Walks Far send them on their way?"

"No," replied Gray Wolf. "The Hopi are no fools. They wouldn't send their shaman out into the desert unless the need were dire. Have Walks Far ride out and escort them in, Red Shirt, then bring them to us."

"Yes, Gray Wolf," replied Red Shirt, dropping the hide back over the door.

CHAPTER 11

Tall Bull glanced at the faces around him and quickly issued a warning. "Black Fox is as cunning as his name," he said. "I suspect he's only here to find out how we feel about the White Fathers sending others to live among us. Speak nothing of the walking wolf or of the she-snake. We'll deal with them on our own."

"Should we at least warn the Hopi?" asked Winter Bird. "What if the wolf and snake find their way to the mesas?"

"We'll see," said Tall Bull. "The Hopi only visit us when something has made them unhappy. What is it this time, I wonder?"

"Tall Bull, this is wrong," said Three Feathers. "The Hopi are a peaceful people. If the wolf or she-snake should—"

He was interrupted when Red Shirt stepped into the hogan.

"My chief, they're here," he said, stepping aside. When the Hopi shaman entered, he smiled down on everyone. Two Ponies knew then that he was not here to confront but to converse.

"Ah, here is Black Fox," said Gray Wolf. "I have not seen you in a very long time. You are brave to have lived for so many winters, my friend."

"As have you, Gray Wolf," said Black Fox. "I see your hair is now as gray as my own."

"Black Fox, please sit with us," said Tall Bull. "We'll smoke a pipe of greeting."

"May I bring in my two companions?" asked Black Fox.

"You may," replied Tall Bull, nodding to Red Shirt, who quickly slipped out to retrieve the two remaining Hopi.

"Here are my brothers," stated Black Fox, as the two men entered. "This is Spotted Dog and Painted Hair."

"Join us," said Tall Bull, motioning for the men to sit.

As the Hopi found a place within the circle, Two Ponies was pleased to discover that he knew the one called Painted Hair. He recognized the long, three-finger-wide streak of white that ran down through the man's ebony waist-length hair. He was dressed in freshly tanned leathers and fringed high moccasins. Seeing him now, Two Ponies recalled meeting the Hopi when they were both young boys and about to shoot the same large buck deer. The younger Painted Hair had graciously stepped aside and allowed him to have the kill. When their eyes met, Painted Hair's knowing smile assured Two Ponies that he, too, recalled their youthful encounter near the red sandstone bluffs.

The one called Spotted Dog, however, was a stranger to him. Shorter then Painted Hair, he was dressed in a long brown shirt tunic, drawn in at the waist with a red sash. A pair of well-worn leather pants fit into fringed knee-high leather moccasins, and over his shoulder he carried a dark, worn leather bag. His black hair, falling only inches past his shoulders, was secured with a headband of yellow and red beads. Two Ponies could see how he achieved his name. Across the right side of his face and neck were several small bright red birthmarks that stood out against his copper skin. Spotted Dog didn't greet them with the friendliness of Black Fox and Painted Hair. And his fidgeting now made him appear on edge, as his dark eyes scanned the Dine' with suspicion. Two Ponies decided to give him a wide berth.

Gray Wolf, always prepared, pulled the sacred pipe from its leather sheath. Holding it aloft, he said a prayer to the four directions. Packing it with tobacco, he lit it and pulled in a mouthful of smoke. When he released it, it drifted upward to mingle with the smoke from the fire. Nodding to Black Fox, seated to his left, he handed him the pipe, and the Hopi shaman took a pull.

As the sacred pipe made its rounds, Two Ponies watched the Hopi. Having had little contact with them, he knew only that they were a peaceful people who lived to the northeast on the high flat mesas. Black Fox, he noticed, sat watching the Dine' with keen interest. His long graying hair fell over his thin shoulders, and Two Ponies guessed the old man's age to be around seventy winters. His leather shirt and pants hung loose over his bony frame, and Two Ponies was sure his battered moccasins had walked more miles than he cared to guess.

After each man took his turn at the pipe, Gray Wolf emptied it and placed it back into its leather sheath. All were silent, until Tall Bull spoke.

"Black Fox, what brings you to the camp of the Dine'?" he asked. "You were never one to travel."

"I do agree I'm too old for much adventure these days," said Black Fox. "That is why I have brought my two companions with me. They are also of the Bear Clan."

"You are welcome here," said Tall Bull, nodding in their direction. "Now, what can we do for you, Black Fox?"

"I have come to speak with you on a very important matter," replied Black Fox. "One that involves both our clans."

"I see," said Tall Bull. "If this is regarding the agreement known as the Indian Removal Act, I am already aware of this decree. I left three of my people up at the Red River Council to hear what the White Fathers have to say."

"The Hopi also know of this decree," said Black Fox. "That is not why we're here."

"Are you saying this matter doesn't cause you concern?" asked Gray Wolf.

"Oh, it concerns us a great deal," replied Black Fox. "We are aware of their plans to send the Creek to live among the western tribes."

"And you don't see this as trouble?" asked Winter Bird.

"I do, indeed," replied Black Fox.

"Will the Hopi honor the white man's treaty?" asked Gray Wolf.

"Gray Wolf, you and I are old experts when it comes to the white man and his worthless treaties," replied Black Fox. "And we both know what we think matters little to the White Fathers in Washington. That said, we can be sure the Creek will not be the last newcomers thrust into our midst. There are dark times ahead, my old friend—not only for the Dine' and Hopi but for all tribes and clans that live west of the great muddy river."

"Black Fox speaks the truth," said Painted Hair. "To prevent the white settlers from grazing their cattle on our sacred burial grounds, we must join our clans. It takes many small streams to make a mighty, raging river."

"Wise words, Painted Hair," said Tall Bull. "The Dine' will hold council on this matter and discuss what is best for us. We'll let you know of our decision. Now that we have settled this matter, Red Shirt will show you to your horses."

The three Hopi glanced at one another in confusion. Were they being dismissed? Black Fox leaned forward so he could look Tall Bull in the eye.

"Tall Bull, we are not here to discuss the white settlers nor the White Fathers' decree," he said. "We're here on another matter more dire than even a useless treaty."

"As you have already stated," replied Tall Bull. "If the White Fathers are not your reason for coming here, then it must be to get provisions. We did have a good growing season last year. Perhaps we can even spare a couple of our sheep. You know we will always help our Hopi neighbors if you are in need. We can give you—"

"We have not come for food!" exclaimed Black Fox, his raised voice startling everyone. "We've come to warn you of the snake that walks upright, like a man."

"A what?" asked Tall Bull, snickering. "Black Fox, you have been listening to too many children's tales. A *walking* snake, you say?"

"Does this amuse you, Tall Bull?" asked Painted Hair, with a look of disdain. "It has already killed eight of your best warriors. I fail to find *that* amusing."

"Nor do we, Painted Hair," said Gray Wolf, solemnly. "How is it that you know about the she-snake?"

"Now this is more like it," said Black Fox. "We know of it because it killed near our mesa. It is a vicious enemy who kills for no reason. Have you seen it?"

"Why do you wish to know, Black Fox?" asked Tall Bull, with suspicion. "You were never a warring people."

"We wish to help you in your hour of need!" stated Black Fox.

"Why would the Dine' need the help of the Hopi?" asked Tall Bull. "What makes you think we cannot defeat this enemy on our own?"

"Because it is not an enemy from *this* world," stated Black Fox, in frustration. "If you think the White Fathers are your greatest threat, then you're wrong!"

"This snake is not alone, Black Fox," stated Sky Feather. "With it travels a great wolf that kills with a spear of fire. This wolf reduced five members of our clan to ashes. And *four* have now died when the she-snake spit its—"

"Venom into their faces?" asked Black Fox, interrupting him. "We've seen what its greenish-brown venom can do. It consumes all the flesh in just one day. Only days ago, this snake killed two of our young women. They were working the soil below our mesa when it attacked them."

"This is a dangerous enemy," added Painted Hair.

"Wait. We know of no wolf," said Spotted Dog. "We only know of the snake. What is this wolf?"

"We're told that a great wolf runs with the snake," said Sky Feather. "One of our young boys saw it. He claims it walks on its hind legs like a man."

"Is this so?" asked Spotted Dog. "These are strange times."

"I believe the snake comes from the east," said Tall Bull. "If we band together, we can send it back to the White Fathers and let *them* deal with this menace."

"You think it comes from the eastern lands?" asked Black Fox. "It is obvious you know very little about this enemy. I'll show you where this she-snake comes from, Tall Bull. Spotted Dog, I'll take the sacred scroll."

Spotted Dog pulled a rolled-up piece of dark leather from his shoulder bag and handed it to Black Fox. The elderly shaman spread it out on the floor in front of him, and all leaned forward to view it. The thick hide, as wide and as long as a man's forearm, was darkened with great age. Painted on its surface were three faded star patterns as seen in the night sky. A faint white line encircled the largest of these constellations.

"This is the star map passed down to us by our ancestors," stated Black Fox. Pointing to the circled constellation, he added, "We believe this cluster of stars is the home of this snake."

"How do you know this?" asked Tall Bull, shaking his head with skepticism.

"I know this because our old stories tell us that our people have dealt with this enemy before," stated Black Fox. "Our ancient ancestors spoke of a time when the walking snakes filled the skies."

"It was a time of great sorrow," continued Spotted Dog. "One day, in ages past, the giant snakes invaded our world. They brought with them a great weapon that burned the earth with a light like a thousand suns. This light left a mysterious energy in the air that killed the crops, poisoned the survivors, and ruined the soil for many years. Our ancestors managed to defeat the snakes, but at a great price. We have an ancient drawing of what it was our ancestors fought against."

On cue, Black Fox picked up the age-worn hide, flipped it over, and held it aloft for all to see. The image was barely visible against the darkness of the leather, but Two Ponies was able to make out its faint outline. Although the image was very crude, he recognized its tall stature and snake-like features. In the lower right-hand corner, was the faint outline of a serpent's eye within a triangle. He gasped.

"You have seen the image of this creature before, my son?" asked Black Fox.

"No," replied Two Ponies. "I mean, yes, I've seen this creature."

"Where?" asked Spotted Dog. "As far as we know, this is the only likeness that exists."

"I didn't see it as an image on leather," said Two Ponies, now wondering if he'd said too much. "When Three Feathers and I touched the black stone, this is what we faced."

"What stone do you speak of, Two Ponies?" asked Spotted Dog.

"The one near the river," he replied. He glanced at Tall Bull, whose face now wore a sour look.

"I must see this stone!" exclaimed Black Fox, rolling up the leather image. "It may tell us more about this walking snake."

"It's not necessary for you to see the stone," said Tall Bull. "We'll describe it to you and leave it at that. It is nothing."

"Tall Bull, you do not know what you are dealing with here!" exclaimed Black Fox. "We must learn why the walking snake has returned at this time and what its intentions are. Together we may be able to defeat it."

"I know why the snake has returned at this time, Black Fox," said Tall Bull. "It wishes to destroy our race. It wants us out of the way so the white settlers can move in and take the land that *our* ancestors have lived on since the great migrations. They have—"

He fell silent when Three Feathers suddenly jumped to his feet.

"You think this snake creature is here for our land?" he exclaimed, his sudden outburst startling everyone. "I am here to tell you, Tall Bull, that this creature cares nothing for the ground beneath your feet! And it has *not* come to destroy only our race. It is here to destroy *all* peoples of the earth. I've seen visions in my mind that would make your heart grow faint!"

"What visions, Three Feathers?" asked Sky Feather.

"I will say no more," he replied, falling silent.

"You must believe us now, Tall Bull," demanded Black Fox. "And I must see this stone."

"I'll take you to see it," said Three Feathers.

"I will come as well," said Gray Wolf. "Winter Bird, help me to my feet."

As the small group assembled before the large black stone, the three Hopi walked around it in silence. The early morning sun glistened off its shiny surface and illuminated their faces.

"This disturbs me greatly," said Black Fox. Stepping forward, he held his hand just above its smooth black surface.

"Black Fox, do not touch it!" warned Gray Wolf. "It will poison your mind."

"It pulsates from within," said Black Fox. "This is no ordinary stone. Do you see this? The serpent's eye within a triangle. This is their symbol."

"Black Fox, where in the night sky is the home of this she-snake?" asked Sky Feather.

"According to the old tales, it is a dark world that lies far into our northern skies," replied Black Fox. "They say the land of the snakes never drops below the northern horizon. In this way, they can watch our world. Other than a couple of crude images on aged leather, I'm afraid we've little else to go on."

"Which leaves us at a disadvantage," remarked Sky Feather. "We know what they look like and the location of their world, but not how to stop it from killing again. And it *will* kill again."

"I've seen the she-snake up close," announced Two Ponies.

"How?" asked Spotted Dog, turning to face him. "It killed our women very quickly. The mother watched as it spit its venom into the faces of her two daughters. She ran to us for help, but by the time we got to the women, they were unable to speak and died soon after. How is it that you were able to get close to the snake and live to talk about it?"

"I saw it in a vision," said Two Ponies.

"In a vision!" exclaimed Spotted Dog. "Are we now to fear a vision?"

"It showed itself to me when I pulled Three Feathers from this stone," explained Two Ponies.

"Three Feathers, what did *you* see when you touched the stone?" asked Black Fox.

"The same creature as Two Ponies," he replied. "This she-snake is more than a mere vision, I assure you. She held me captive in a dark room until I nearly died. I can tell you this: At this time, there is only the one she-snake. If we wait, more of her kind will come."

"The Hopi have long known ours is not the only world that harbors life," explained Black Fox. "And, we're very much aware that not all those worlds are peaceful."

"I, too, have heard this," said Gray Wolf. "I must say, the world of the snake must be dark indeed to have spawned such a violent creature as the one who now stalks us."

"This is true," said Painted Hair. "But, among those violent worlds, exists our peaceful ancestral home. It lies among the stars of the Pleiades and is the home of the blue star people. We know this because the Hopi are their descendants. We are the people of the Katsinas, the sky gods."

"This is so," said Black Fox. "The old stories say the sky gods brought us here to live on this world back in the mists of time. To ensure our survival, our grandfathers would consult with them when they had great need."

"Tell me," said Three Feathers, "do you think these sky gods would help us to defeat this she-snake?"

"We could ask them," replied Black Fox. "My grandfather told me of how the ancestors would call these sky gods down from the stars with a blue crystal."

"Do you have such a crystal?" asked Gray Wolf.

"I do," replied Black Fox. "It was passed down to me from the grandfathers of old. I carry it in this pouch." He illustrated by lifting a small leather bag hanging from a braided sash around his waist.

"Then we must try and contact this sky god," said Gray Wolf. "Do you know the words that will call him down to us?"

"I learned them at my grandfather's knee," replied Black Fox, proudly. "Growing up, I was taught the ways of the crystal and it came into my possession when he died. I am to carry it with me always, as it will protect my life."

"Then what are we waiting for?" asked Sky Feather. "What must we do?"

"We need to travel to the great sacred mountain," replied Black Fox. "There lies the place where the sky god visits earth."

"Are you speaking of the mountain we call *Doko'oo'sliid?*" asked Gray Wolf. "We call it the Summit That Never Melts."

"To us, it is *Nuvatukya'ovi*," said Spotted Dog. "Place of High Snows."

"It seems this mountain is sacred to both our peoples," stated Gray Wolf. "There we will be on common ground."

"I agree," said Black Fox. "Gray Wolf, will you and the others accompany us to this mountain?"

"I knew you would need my help," said Gray Wolf, smiling. "Wisdom is a terrible gift to waste. Now, what must we do?"

"You need only to follow our lead," replied Spotted Dog. "I suggest you leave someone here to guard this stone. It possesses a great power and is extremely dangerous."

"I will remain to watch over the stone *and* our people," said Three Feathers, stepping forward. "I'm well aware of the dangers."

"Make it so," said Gray Wolf. "The rest of us must prepare for our journey to the sacred mountain."

Two Ponies returned to his hogan and changed into clothes more suitable for the desert at night. Knowing it would cool off once the sun set, he pulled on a long-sleeved leather shirt and his deerskin pants. He also collected the leather bag containing his fire drill and stones. If they were going to be there overnight, they would need a fire. Strapping his knife and sheath to his waist belt, he hoped it would be sufficient to protect his life. With this new enemy, however, he was unsure of his weapon's capability, and he hated the feeling of uncertainty.

As the sun continued its climb in the east, the three Hopi and the five Dine' men mounted their horses for the long trek to the meeting place of the sky god.

"Let us ride," said Tall Bull. "The sun will be above us soon, and we have many miles to cover. If we ride hard, we can reach the mountain just before nightfall."

With the sun following at their heels, the men rode their horses westward toward the mountain. Tall Bull, with his eyes alert for the slightest movement, led the way. Gray Wolf and Black Fox rode behind him. Spotted Dog and Painted Hair followed their spiritual leader, their war lances ready to defend him at any cost. Winter Bird followed next; his long knife strapped to his leg. Bringing up the rear was Sky Feather and Two Ponies. Each carried their own personal knife. Two Ponies hoped it would be powerful enough to pierce the thick skin of the she-snake, should the long two-sided blades of the war lances fail. Regardless, in his heart, he vowed to protect, to the death, all those who rode with him.

It was evening when they finally reached their destination. Other than a short stop to water and rest their horses, the journey had taken them the entire day.

"This is where Earth meets heaven, Two Ponies," said Sky Feather, bringing his horse to a slow trot. "My grandfather told me of the creation story when I was a boy. He said the Sacred Creator himself placed the Dine' between these four sacred mountains. They represent the four directions of our world."

"Then we're on sacred ground," said Two Ponies.

Black Fox motioned for all to come to a halt, and everyone dismounted. Around them the thick trees over-shadowed the thorny greasewood thickets.

"We are about to enter a sacred place," said Black Fox. "All weapons must be left here."

"Now this concerns me!" said Winter Bird. "We still have an unknown enemy out there."

"The enemy will not dare enter where we're going," said Black Fox. "I was shown this place by my father. For generations, it has been known among my people as the doorway to the stars. It is sacred ground; therefore, no weapons are permitted."

"Very well," said Winter Bird. He was obviously not happy about being so far from the protection of their village and now being asked to disarm completely. Placing his long knife into the cleft of a large gray rock, he stepped back to allow the others to do the same. Two Ponies, though apprehensive, placed his own knife on a small rocky ledge above the cleft. He then followed the others as they led their horses along a narrow path leading into a large clearing roughly fifty paces across. In its center lay a large pile of small rocks. Thick trees and brush surrounded the clearing on three sides, leaving the fading sky to the west open all the way to the distant bluffs.

"What happens next, Black Fox?" asked Winter Bird.

"We'll need a fire set in the center of the clearing," he replied. "The rest of you, gather in a generous amount of firewood before the light fades. Two Ponies, I see you've brought your fire drill. Will you see to the fire?"

"I will," he replied.

"And bring the horses in close," added Black Fox. "They, too, will need protected."

"I'll see to the horses," offered Winter Bird. Gathering several thick fallen limbs, he drove each deep into the sand with a rock. One by one, he tethered the reins of each horse to a limb.

Two Ponies, having his own task to accomplish, gathered kindling from among the trees beyond the clearing. He was glad to be doing something to take his mind off the fact they were now without any means to defend themselves. That alone could spell disaster. Glancing in the direction of the rock that held their weapons, he mentally paced off the steps it would take to retrieve them. He decided it would take an eternity to reach them if the attack came after nightfall. And he thought it best not to mention that most of their party was over fifty winters old. *So much for our survival if it comes down to hand-to-hand combat*, he thought.

By the time he returned to the clearing, the others had arranged most of the large pile of rocks into a wide circle that defined the edges of the clearing. The remainder of the rocks were used to create a firepit in its center. Two Ponies leaned down on one knee and dug out a shallow hole in the center of the pit. Pulling his fire drill and stones from their leather pouch, he dropped in the small pieces of kindling and dried moss and set about building the fire. He knew this type of fire making dated back to the great migration, and no Dine' male, or female, reached adulthood without mastering the skill. In no time, he had a warming blaze.

On the western edge of the circle of stones, Gray Wolf and the three Hopi spread woven ceremonial blankets out on the sand.

Two Ponies, Winter Bird, and Sky Feather lounged around the fire, awaiting further instructions. Tall Bull sat off by himself, smoking his pipe. The only sounds were the wind in the trees and the restless stomping of the horses tethered nearby.

"What watches us from beyond the firelight?" asked Sky Feather, his eyes sweeping the shadowed trees.

"I don't know," said Winter Bird. "But whatever the threat, Black Fox has assured us that his sky god will protect us. He holds great faith in this friend he calls a blue star Katsina."

"I wonder," said Sky Feather. "Has Black Fox ever summoned this being before?"

"Again, I don't know," replied Winter Bird. "I suppose we'll just have to trust our Hopi friends on this one."

Two Ponies, feeling restless, got to his feet and stretched. As he stood watching Gray Wolf and the three Hopi, he was eager for things to gets started. Earlier, Black Fox had announced that nothing would begin until nightfall and the waiting game had himself, and those around the fire, on edge.

Against the rapidly dropping sun, Painted Hair and Spotted Dog sat facing each other on their red-and-black ceremonial blanket. Talking quietly, they, too, waited for nightfall. Between them, sat a small log drum. To their left, Black Fox sat on his own blanket, with his face upturned to the sky. Eyes closed; his lips moved in quiet prayer. Next to Black Fox, sat Gray Wolf. With his back to the west, he sat cross-legged on his own black-and-red blanket. In his lap, his gnarled hands rested on his knees as he, too, prayed to the ancestors. Behind his right ear, a single black eagle's feather danced in the hot breezes. In the background, the setting sun hung just above the gray sandstone bluffs. Two Ponies was just about to turn away, when the scene suddenly changed right before his eyes!

He stood transfixed as Gray Wolf's body slowly floated upward until it hovered a foot above his blanket. As if in a trance, the old shaman's unblinking blue eyes stared forward. To Gray Wolf's right sat the three Hopi. To his left, the ghostly image of a white raven rested on the sand beside him. Two Ponies shook his head. Was he seeing a vision? If so, what did it mean? Looking away, he tapped Sky Feather on the shoulder.

"Father, look at Gray Wolf!" he whispered. When he turned back, to his disappointment, the vison was gone and Gray Wolf once more rested on his blanket, his eyes closed in prayer. The white raven, too, had vanished.

"Gray Wolf is praying to the ancestors for wisdom," said Sky Feather. "Black Fox does the same."

Two Ponies knew, at that moment, that the vision of Gray Wolf floating above his blanket, was one meant for his eyes only. Joining the others at the fire, he decided to keep it to himself. Someone produced a woven sack filled with strips of jerked deer meat and they ate to pass the time.

Above them, *Doko'oo'sliid*, the Summit That Never Melts, still wore its glistening, snow-covered crown. Below the mountain, all lay quiet, except for the crackling of the fire.

Winter Bird reached out and stoked the flames higher with a stick. "I've heard that snakes and wolves hate fire," he told the others, flashing a knowing smile. From somewhere in the trees, a large owl announced the coming of night.

The moment the last sliver of sun disappeared, Black Fox began to chant softly, breaking the silence. As Two Ponies listened, the words soothed his unease. Spotted Dog joined in his leader's song while Painted Hair beat on the small drum.

"The Hopi summon their sky god," remarked Sky Feather, his long, gray-streaked hair fanning out in the hot breezes. "I cannot guess just who will answer their call."

"We shall see," added Two Ponies. Glancing skyward, the stars were beginning to blink into existence. "The stars are out. How will they be able to *see* this help when it *does* arrive?"

"*If* it arrives," remarked Winter Bird. "The sun has already set. If this help doesn't come soon, it'll be stumbling around in the darkness. Along with the night comes my uneasiness. We still have an enemy out there *and* no weapons with which to defend ourselves."

As the Hopi continued to chant, Two Ponies walked over to check on his horse.

"Rest easy, my friend," he said, running his hand down the long black face of his stallion. "Whatever this night holds, you and I will face it together. May we both have the eyes of the mighty owl and the sure-footedness of the puma. Will your courage stay strong?" His answer came in the form of a soft neigh. Two Ponies gave his horse one final reassuring pat on his great neck before rejoining the others around the fire.

When the chanting finally ceased, and the drum fell silent, Spotted

Dog helped Black Fox to his feet. Painted Hair assisted Gray Wolf and the old shaman joined his companions around the fire.

"What is happening, Gray Wolf?" asked Two Ponies.

"The Hopi are about to summon our help," he replied. "And Black Fox bids us to prepare ourselves."

"For what?" asked Sky Feather.

"That, he did not say," replied Gray Wolf. "I hold no concerns though. The Hopi are an ancient people who possess an immensely powerful magic."

"I hope they'll use that powerful magic to now protect us," said Sky Feather. "Anything can happen in the blackness of night."

"Black Fox gives us another warning," said Gray Wolf, as Winter Bird lowered him onto the sand beside the fire. "His words were plain enough. "Whatever happens, do not leave the protection of the circle of stones"."

As the others looked on, Black Fox stepped away from his two companions and faced the western sky. Withdrawing the palm-sized crystal from the worn leather pouch at his waist, he blew on it until it gave off a bright blue glow. When he held it aloft, a beam of brilliant blue light, emanating from the crystal's center, shot skyward like a long fiery arrow. Within seconds, it was swallowed up by the night sky. Placing the crystal back into its leather pouch, the Hopi shaman turned to face the others.

"Now we wait," he said. "Spotted Dog, place my blanket beside the fire and help me to sit."

"What was the blue arrow of fire you shot into the sky?" asked Winter Bird.

"It is our means of contact," replied Black Fox, as he was lowered to the ground.

"Have you ever done this before?" asked Winter Bird.

"No, I have not," the old man admitted with a long sigh. "Only in the old stories do they tell of summoning down one of the blue star Katsinas."

"Then how do you know this will work?" asked Winter Bird.

"It will work," Black Fox assured him. "The knowledge of the blue crystal was passed down to the Hopi from ancient times. Now, after many generations, *I* am being called on to use it. I'm excited to do so!"

"This doesn't mean we have not kept in touch with the sky gods," said Spotted Dog. "Our Hopi elders speak to our sky ancestors from time to time. They teach us many things about the world around us. To deal with this walking snake, however, we find it necessary to contact someone with a *higher* knowledge."

"The being I summoned is a chief among the blue star Katsinas," said Black Fox. "Our stories say we have not called on him since the invasion of the iron helmets over three hundred winters ago. At that time, when the iron helmets came into our lands seeking gold, they unknowingly brought with them a great sickness that killed many of our people. Burning fevers and bloody sores ravaged their bodies before death finally released them from their pain. When the dead outnumbered the living, the old shaman contacted the great sky god and asked him to send us a healer."

"Did he?" asked Winter Bird.

"The old stories say he did," replied Black Fox. "This helper gave us a healing magic that freed us from the sickness before our people were no more. Of course, even my grandfather, who passed this knowledge down to me, had only stories." ·

Winter Bird appeared less than convinced. "And you're sure this message will reach into the sky and summon this sky god down to us?" he asked.

"I do," replied Black Fox. "The power of the crystal must work, or the knowledge would not have survived for many thousands of years."

"That's good enough for me," declared Sky Feather. "I suggest we stay alert. We are unarmed men with only a small fire between us and the enemy."

With their backs to the fire, they talked quietly among themselves while all eyes watched the darkness beyond. From the desert, came the sound of a coyote calling to its mate. As the minutes ticked by, they all fidgeted in anticipation of what was to come. Finally, Black Fox spoke.

"Relax, my brothers," he said. "The prayer we said was for our protection. According to my grandfather, the enemy cannot harm us *if* we remain within the circle of stones. This clearing is where the heart of the sky god, So'tuknang, speaks to the people."

"I, for one, am anxious to meet this sky god," stated Winter Bird. "It'll be something to tell my—"

Before Winter Bird could finish his sentence, a great breeze began to sway the boughs of the trees surrounding the clearing. Sparks, stirred from the fire, leapt high into the air like fiery demons. The horses, tied to their tethers, whinnied and grew restless.

"Something approaches our circle," said Sky Feather, getting to his feet.

CHAPTER 12

"What's happening?" asked Winter Bird, rising.

"I believe our help has arrived," said Black Fox, motioning for Spotted Dog to help him to his feet. "It didn't take as long as I thought it would."

"What brings the great wind, Gray Wolf?" asked Tall Bull, his eyes searching the surrounding trees.

"Relax, Tall Bull," said Gray Wolf, as Winter Bird pulled him from the sand. "The being Black Fox summoned is an old friend to us. He and his people have watched over our race since our arrival on this world way back in the dim and distant past. I consider meeting him face-to-face an old man's last wish!"

The trees continued to sway as the great wind moved through them.

"Something moves in the trees!" declared Winter Bird.

"Not *in* the trees," said Sky Feather. "It moves *above* the trees. Look to the sky!"

All watched in amazement as the stars to the west began to wink out as if a great dark blanket were slowly being drawn across the sky in their direction.

"What is it?" asked Winter Bird, retreating a couple of steps backward. "It's as big as our village!"

"I see a round cloud," said Sky Feather.

"What cloud is perfectly round?" asked Winter Bird.

"What cloud is as black as the night?" asked Sky Feather. "It appears as solid as the mountain."

As they looked on, a large, dark, circular craft drifted silently in over the clearing. When all forward motion ceased, the wind died down, and all went silent. Two Ponies wondered if this was the great iron beast that floated in the sky above his head. Was the she-snake now watching them from inside its belly?

"How does the cloud stop moving?" asked Tall Bull. "It's as if a great hand holds it in place."

"This is an old man's dream!" exclaimed Black Fox. "Our help, I admit, is not quite what I expected."

A great blue eye slowly opened in the black underbelly of the craft, and a beam of light so bright it illuminated the surrounding area, descended to the ground. All waited in anticipation. From out of the beam stepped a tall, thin man dressed in a light blue breechclout, blue leggings, and an unadorned blue shirt. On his feet, he wore white calf-high boots. From his head of snow-white, waist-length hair, a ceremonial headdress of white feathers cascaded down his back, stopping inches from the ground. His body and face glowed from within as if an internal light burned inside him. He gazed at them through shining blue eyes.

"Behold," Black Fox told the others, "I give you a sky god."

Two Ponies was speechless. *So, this is one of the ancient ones?* he thought, relieved to see it didn't resemble a snake.

"My old eyes are opened!" exclaimed Black Fox, obviously pleased. "Now, we must listen to his words. This opportunity is rare for us mortals! Not for many, many winters has this particular sky god visited this land."

Stepping forward, Black Fox bowed his head in reverence. "Welcome," he said. "I am Black Fox, spiritual leader to the Hopi."

"I am Tarus, a blue star Katsina," stated the tall being, his voice strong yet friendly.

Black Fox motioned them all forward. "Come, we must all voice our concerns."

"Why have you summoned me here?" asked Tarus.

"For council," said Black Fox. "I am the one who called you down from the stars. We are in desperate need of your help. Our stories tell us that three hundred winters ago, you brought aid to my ancestors when a fever invaded our land. You sent someone wise in the ways of powerful medicine, and he healed our people of the sickness brought to us by the iron helmets. Our need, at this time, is just as dire. A female walking snake is killing our people. We are seeking your help and wisdom to defeat her."

"I know of this enemy you speak of," said Tarus. "It is one that plagues us all."

Sensing an opportunity, Sky Feather stepped forward.

"I am Sky Feather, of the Dine'," he said. "I wish to know *who* it is we are dealing with?"

"Their ancient race is known as the Reptoids," replied Tarus. "They come from a dark world at the edge of your galaxy known as Alpha Draconis."

Tall Bull now stepped forward, wishing to address the sky god.

"I am Tall Bull, Chief of the Dine'," he said. "Can you tell us why this Reptoid is here? For what purpose does she kill my people?"

"The Reptoids are a race of warmongers," replied Tarus, "with little regard for the well-being of their galactic neighbors. They conquer through fear. It is obvious they have now set their sights on your world. If you show them fear, you will fall."

"We are helpless against them," said Tall Bull.

"So you are," said Tarus. "But, we are now aware of your plight and will monitor the ship that orbits your planet. As to why this female Reptoid is here? She was most likely sent to reconnoiter your planet."

Curious, Two Ponies approached Tarus.

"I am Two Ponies, of the Dine'," he said. "Three Feathers and I have seen this walking she-snake. We encountered her when we touched the black stone that rests beside the river. This stone poisoned our minds."

"Do not touch this stone!" warned Tarus "It is a communications device used to instruct a landing party. If you touch it, you may be pulled into their link, and this could prove harmful to your primitive minds. For this reason, this stone must be dealt with immediately."

"I've more to tell," said Two Ponies. "Accompanying this snake is a wolf that also walks upright, like a man."

"It is as I feared," said Tarus, shaking his feathered head. "These wolf-like creatures are a vicious race known as the Wolfen. They lack the intelligent coordination to conquer on their own, so they work alongside the Reptoids. They are the bullies of the universe. I must warn you, the Wolfen have developed the ability to manipulate their DNA. In other words, they can change their appearance to mimic the inhabitants on your planet. They are—"

"Shape-shifters!" exclaimed Gray Wolf. Everyone gasped and stepped back in fear. To explain, Gray Wolf now stepped forward to address Tarus. "I am Gray Wolf, spiritual leader to the Dine'. Our ancestors gave us stories of these evil skinwalkers who possessed the ability to change their appearance."

"It seems the Wolfen have visited your world in the past," said Tarus. "Those curious few are likely why the Reptoid queen is now taking a closer look at your planet. I suspect she's in need of your natural resources."

"How do we fight this she-snake and her Wolfen dog?" asked Black Fox. "We have only the bow and knife."

"We're aware of your primitive weaponry, Black Fox," said Tarus. "As a planet, your defenses are still in the early stages of development; therefore, we must proceed with great caution. Any use of force at this time, may forever alter the timeline of that development."

"Will you leave us defenseless?" asked Black Fox.

"This is not the first time your world has faced the Reptoids, Black Fox," stated Tarus. "Around twelve thousand earth years ago, they swept into your solar system and surrounded your planet with their great sky ships."

"We have stories of when the snakes came to our world!" exclaimed Black Fox. "The Hopi lived on a great island then. It is said the snakes used a mighty weapon that churned the sea and leveled the great mountains of the continents."

"Yes, their weapons were very destructive," said Tarus. "And this island you speak of, was known as Aztlan."

"Did you come to our aid then?" asked Black Fox.

"We did. We had no choice," replied Tarus. "The queen sent thousands of her best warriors with orders to conquer and enslave your world's inhabitants. We could not allow this to happen, as your world must continue to evolve on its own. Then, as now, you possessed only a primitive defense system. To aid you at that time, the Pleiadians brought to the fight, an advanced proton weapon. When engaged, it sent forth a burst of powerful energy that destroyed the battle cruisers of the queen and sent her fleeing back into the stars."

"Your words give us hope," said Black Fox. "If we had this mighty weapon now, we could again send the enemy back to the stars."

"Therein lies our dilemma," said Tarus, sighing. "After the great war, we foolishly left this proton weapon in the hands of your men of science. How were we supposed to know you would foolishly use it against each other? In the vacuum of space, this proton weapon was a focused and directed energy beam. When the leaders on your island of Aztlan engaged it on the planet's surface, it scorched vast areas of your earth and poisoned its soil for many years. It unleashed a powerful explosion that caused your island of Aztlan to sink beneath the waves."

"Yes, we have stories," said Black Fox. "At that time, many perished from this lost island home. The Hopi survived only because the ant people took us into their underground world and cared for us until Mother Earth healed herself. During the Age of Emergence, the first people crawled out of the great Kiva and made a new life for themselves, here on this desert land."

"The Dine', too, have stories of the ant people," Gray Wolf pointed out.

"This story belongs to more than the Hopi and the Dine'," said Tarus. "The subterranean world of these beings is vast. In this way, they were able to save *many* that would have otherwise perished. As for *your* ancestors, those the Pleiadians originally placed on Aztlan, we asked that you be brought here, to the northern and southern continents. Here they cared for you in their underground world until the surface was once more deemed habitable. At that time, they returned you to the surface and taught you how to live with the land. You have done well."

"Where are these beings now, Tarus?" asked Black Fox.

"I suppose they've returned to their home world," replied Tarus. "They were known as the Silents, and they came here millennia ago to study your planet's thermal dynamics. After the great war, these benevolent beings agreed to stay and assist in the survival of its inhabitants. When they were no longer needed, they moved on. We have not heard from them in a very long time."

"Too bad," said Black Fox. "I would very much like to meet with them and hear their story."

"As would I," said Gray Wolf. "At the moment, though, we have a snake to deal with. Tarus, what is your council?"

"Once more we will come to your aid," replied Tarus. "It is in the best interest of all that these murderous beasts be kept out of this quadrant of space. But this is not an invasion, so great force is *not* required here. At this time, my friends, there are more of you than there are of them."

"True," said Black Fox. "But we've only light weapons. How do you propose we fight them?"

"You must outsmart them," replied Tarus. "Though the Reptoid and the Wolfen possess weapons of mass destruction, they will not use them at this time. They won't risk destroying the natural resources they now covet."

Winter Bird stepped forward to add his voice to the conversation.

"I am Winter Bird, of the Dine'," he said. "How do you suggest we outsmart this enemy?"

"The Reptoid and the Wolfen are great fighters, but only if they're called into aerial combat," replied Tarus. "They are not surface-dwelling creatures and therefore cannot comprehend the art of hand-to-hand fighting."

"We are not a violent people," said Black Fox. "When pressed, however, we *will* defend ourselves. One of our women, when confronted, hit the she-snake in the back of the head with a digging tool."

"Then you already possess that which is required," said Tarus. "You also have the resources of Gaia—your Earth. I suggest you use them as well."

"Will it be you that returns to help us?" asked Winter Bird.

"Not I," said Tarus. "Only those who hold the ancient knowledge know of our existence. We must keep it this way, as the time of the great disclosure is still many years into your future."

"I am Sky Feather, of the Dine'," said Sky Feather, now stepping forward. "What of the white man? I'm sure they won't help us, even though the threat is theirs as well."

"Those of the white race are concerned only with their needs at this time," said Tarus. "Therefore, Sky Feather, the task of saving them, as well as yourselves, will now fall upon the Dine' and the Hopi. The enemy is here now, so there is no time to gather others to help you. We must act immediately. The few, I'm afraid, will have to fight for the many. I will send two sky helpers to assist you. They are Arcturians—wise in the ways of both the Reptoid and the Wolfen."

"When can we expect these helpers?" asked Black Fox.

"When your star returns to your eastern sky," replied Tarus.

"Your help is appreciated, Tarus," said Black Fox. "The Hopi have kept your memory alive so our children's children will recognize you when you return someday to take us to our true home among the stars. We have remained peaceful."

"We are aware of your loyalty," said Tarus. "But there is a time for peace and a time when one must take a stand to keep that peace. Now is the time, Black Fox, for the Hopi to fight, or peace will cease to exist for all who dwell on your world."

"I am Spotted Dog, of the Hopi," said Spotted Dog, stepping forward. "We have kept sacred the secrets of our ancestors."

"Which is why you still remain *Hopituh Shi-nu-mu*," replied Tarus. "Far back in the mists of time, we brought you to this planet to ensure the survival of our race."

"Our stories tell us this," said Black Fox.

"Then you still carry the memory," said Tarus. "I am pleased. You have all persevered in times of great hardship and adapted well to the changes in the world we have given you. The fact that you haven't forgotten how to contact us is proof enough that you've successfully passed on the knowledge of the blue crystal. But the time has come for you to share this knowledge with your brothers, the Dine'. You must work together to defeat this enemy."

"The Hopi *will* fight beside the Dine'!" exclaimed Black Fox. "Even if it means we also fight for those who wish to do us harm. I have seen the prophecies written on the great stone bluffs. Sadly, they tell us that the White Fathers' *will* eventually harness the strength of our race and reduce our great numbers. How ironic, they will never know that it is those they consider worthless savages, who will now step forward and save *them* from certain death."

"And, they must *never* know," warned Tarus. "If the white race knew what the Wolfen are capable of, they may seek to join with them in an effort to clear the path ahead. By using the Wolfen against *you*, they would unknowingly condemn themselves, and this world, to slavery or worse. Now I will depart."

"We thank you for your wisdom, Tarus," said Black Fox. "We have always sought to protect our Mother Earth. We will not fail her now. Farewell, my friend."

"Farewell to you all," said Tarus. "I leave you with these words: you are not alone in your fight."

"I have one last question," said Sky Feather. "We left our weapons in the desert. Without them how will we defend ourselves now that night has fallen? Surely the enemy now knows we are here."

"I've placed a force field around you that will resist the enemy as long as you are here," replied Tarus. "Nothing can penetrate the sacred clearing. You'll be safe as long as you remain within the circle of stones."

"As I have told you all," remarked Black Fox.

With a final nod of his feathered head, the sky god from the Pleiades stepped back into the beam of brilliant white light and retreated up into his floating craft. A moment later, the great disc moved off to the west and was quickly swallowed up by the night. The clearing, now devoid of the sky god's light, was plunged into darkness. Two Ponies hurried to pile more wood onto the fire, and everyone gathered around its flames.

"That was interesting," said Black Fox, as he was lowered onto his red-and-black blanket. "Now, I suggest we all get some sleep."

"I agree," stated Gray Wolf, as Winter Bird lowered him to his blanket.

"Tell me, Black Fox," said Winter Bird. "What magic made it possible to summon this Tarus down from the stars? He bid you to share this knowledge."

"He did," said Black Fox. "This knowledge of the Hopi was given to us by the ancient ones. Before they carved the pictures into the great rock faces, they passed the knowledge of our beginnings down to their children through stories."

"And the blue crystal?" asked Two Ponies.

"Belongs only to the Hopi," stated Spotted Dog, giving him a stern look. "The sacred crystal has survived only because the Hopi have valued it above all other possessions."

"Relax, Spotted Dog," said Black Fox. "The secret of the crystal is safe, I'm sure." Turning to Two Ponies he continued, "When the blue crystal was given to our people, we still lived on our great island in the eastern sea. The stories passed down to us by the ancient ones tell us that our island was destroyed by a great fire and sank beneath the waves. And I now learn from Tarus, that it did so because we misused a great fiery weapon."

"And this was the island Tarus called Aztlan?" asked Two Ponies.

"It was," replied Black Fox. "But the name of the island was lost long ago. I shall now restore it to the old story."

"Your children will thank you," said Sky Feather. "And will you also include the part about your having blown yourselves up?"

"Well, I may have to think about including *that* part of the tale," replied Black Fox, with a short laugh. "It doesn't quite fit with our being known as the Wisdom Keepers, now does it?"

Spotted Dog produced a thin woolen cape and draped it over the old man's shoulders.

"What happens now, Black Fox?" asked Sky Feather.

"In the morning, we'll return to your village and welcome the two star helpers," he replied. "They'll know how to defeat the Wolfen and this Reptoid snake. I must say, I fear greatly that not all of us will survive the fight that lies ahead."

"Listen to your words, Black Fox," said Sky Feather, shaking his head. "When this is over, will we not have great stories to tell our grandchildren? Up until now, we had only the tales of how our ancestors fought in the Spanish wars, as well as the coming of the white man. Now we can tell them tales of how *we* fought the invaders from the stars. My grandchildren are in for a treat!"

When they heard the far-off call of a wolf, Winter Bird sat up. "That is our wolf," he said. "No doubt he's about to feast on fresh sheep."

"I don't believe that's our wolf," said Gray Wolf. "He's too far north to concern us."

"I hope you're right," said Winter Bird. "After what we've just learned, though, any wolf should concern us greatly." Yawning, he curled up on the sand to sleep.

"Rest, my brothers," said Gray Wolf, doing the same. "Tomorrow will be a busy day."

Two Ponies envied the confidence of those who now slept around him. He felt too anxious to lay down or to even close his eyes. Above him, the moon cast everything beyond the firelight in a ghostly pale shadow. As he sat watching the surrounding trees and brush for any movement, his mind attempted to make sense of all he had just witnessed. He actually spoke to a star being from another world! One who promised to help them fight Red Otter's she-snake and its great wolf. He would not have believed any of it, had he not seen it with his own eyes. And then there was the vision of Gray Wolf floating above his ceremonial blanket! Again, he wondered what it meant. What was the magic that allowed Gray Wolf to—" His thoughts were interrupted by the sound of the horses suddenly stirring to life.

His eyes swept the surrounding trees but detected no movement. *What is it the horses are sensing?* he wondered. When the sound of heavy rustling reached his ears, he pulled himself up onto his knees. He dropped a log into the hot coals, and the growing flames now revealed a dark shadow passing slowly in front of a large rock. *Is it a deer attracted by the firelight?* he wondered. The horses didn't seem to think so. When the shadow stepped forward and into the firelight, two red glowing eyes peered at him, and the low growl of a feral animal made his heart quicken.

CHAPTER 13

Two Ponies reached over and tapped his father on the shoulder.

"I see it," said Sky Feather, sitting up.

"Should we wake the others?" asked Two Ponies.

"I'm already awake," said Tall Bull, rising. "What are we looking at?"

"Out there," replied Two Ponies, pointing to the two menacing eyes. "In front of that large rock."

"Blood eyes!" declared Tall Bull. His sudden outburst brought everyone to their feet.

"What is it?" asked Winter Bird.

"Do not panic!" exclaimed Black Fox. "Whatever it is, it cannot harm us. Need I remind you of the protective force Tarus placed around us?"

Sensing the new arrival, the horses grew panicked and pulled on their tethers.

"See to the horses!" exclaimed Gray Wolf. "If they bolt, we'll lose them!"

Spotted Dog hurried over to secure the horses. Black Fox stepped forward and waved his arms in the air.

"Be gone with you!" he shouted.

The creature, knowing it was exposed, pulled himself up to his full height, and stared menacingly at them. He stood at least a foot taller than a grown man, and thick, matted gray-and-black hair covered his body. Over his chest, he wore the now familiar black breastplate. Hanging from a belt encircling his thick waist was a long silver weapon the length of a man's forearm. When no one moved, he raised a huge paw and beat twice against his chest.

"This has to be Red Otter's great wolf!" declared Sky Feather. "Look! He wears the silver weapon that burned our brothers to ash."

125

"You cannot harm us here!" Black Fox shouted bravely. "We are protected by the sky god Tarus. Be gone with you, I say!"

The creature displayed no fear. Leaning forward, it bared its large canine teeth in a further attempt to intimidate them. When even this tactic failed, he let go with a long, vicious, drawn-out snarl.

"Look on his breastplate," said Sky Feather. "It's the same symbol that's etched into the black stone beside the river. The snake's eye within a triangle."

"This is no doubt our sheep thief," said Winter Bird. "Yellow Rabbit will be happy to know we've seen proof of his wolf that walks upright, like a man."

Two Ponies stared in awe at the creature. A thought struck him, and he knew he had to preserve its image. Retrieving a section of birch bark from the pile of firewood, he brushed the underside clean of debris. Fumbling in the coals at the edge of the fire, he picked up a cool piece of charcoal and began to draw the wolf-like being. As the charcoal flew across the smooth bark, a perfect likeness of the Wolfen emerged.

"Well done, son," said Sky Feather. "We'll need your likeness to identify him to our people."

"He has a damaged right ear," stated Two Ponies. "I will call him Broken Ear."

"My vision has come to life before me!" stated Gray Wolf, his blue eyes wide. "I'm sure this is the same creature I confronted when I was a boy."

"Why are you here, wolf dog?" Sky Feather asked in a loud, intimidating voice.

In reply, the creature's head fell backward, and a long, mournful howl filled the night.

From out of the darkness, three more creatures answered his call.

"He is not alone!" exclaimed Painted Hair. "I feared as much."

"I knew there had to be more than one," stated Winter Bird. "One lone wolf, even one that walks like a man, cannot eat so many sheep on his own! They were waiting for us to fall asleep before attacking us. I imagine, they did the same to the scouting party. Two Ponies, unable to sleep, exposed that plan."

Tall Bull groaned as the firelight illuminated three more sets of blood-red eyes.

When Broken Ear barked, two of his companions brazenly stepped forward. Both were just as large as he and just as powerfully built. Covering their hairy chests were identical dark breastplates emblazoned with the symbol of the snake's eye within a triangle. Two Ponies noticed that the fourth creature, who remained in the background, was slightly smaller than the others. Although he, too, possessed the bloodred eyes and black breastplate, he hung slightly back, less emboldened than his companions. Looking closer, Two Ponies noticed the silver nose ring hanging from the flesh between his black nostrils.

"They can smell our fear," stated Winter Bird, in a low voice. "They're waiting for us to show weakness. If we do so, we embolden them even more."

"Hold your ground," urged Black Fox.

Sky Feather pulled a burning stick from the fire. "I say we treat these Wolfen dogs just as we do any feral animal," he said. "We show them that if a fight is what they want, then a fight is what they will get." Stepping forward, he waved his burning stick in the direction of one of Broken Ear's companions. Two Ponies was not surprised when it, too, held its position.

"Be careful, Father," he warned. "There is no fear in them. This makes them even more dangerous."

"I can see this," said Sky Feather, lowering his stick. "All my life I've heard stories of strange creatures that terrorized the people. Now one of those stories has come to life before my very eyes. Why does it have to be the wolf?"

Two Ponies thought back to another confrontation he had with a wolf. He was twelve the day he came upon it in the desert. In the act of stalking a large rabbit, he quietly crept around the side of a large rock. In his right hand, he held a fist-sized stone ready to make the killing shot. Instead of finding the rabbit, he found himself facing down a large gray-and-black male wolf who fiercely guarded *his* fresh kill. Two Ponies stood his ground, although his knees shook. In an attempt to intimidate him, the wolf held him in his gaze and bared his large canine teeth. Two Ponies saw no escape. When he felt the rock clenched in his fist, he let it fly, hitting the wolf in the face. The wolf yelped in pain and shook its massive head. The pause was all Two Ponies needed to escape back out into the open and to safety. Once again, he was being challenged by a wolf.

"What do we do?" asked Tall Bull. "We've no weapons."

"We'll use the rocks as our weapons," said Two Ponies, leaning down to pick up a fist-sized stone from around the edge of the firepit. "Tarus said nothing can *enter* his barrier; he didn't say something couldn't go out. Even a great wolf will feel pain if he's struck in the face."

"Excellent idea," said Sky Feather, picking up a rock.

Soon everyone held a rock. Even the peaceful Hopi now filled their hands.

"Now fight!" shouted Two Ponies, throwing his rock at the smaller Wolfen with the silver nose ring. The well-aimed rock struck him in the face, and he howled in pain. When Broken Ear advanced on them, he, too, was bombarded with rocks. Although they bounced off his thick hair and dark breastplate, it still gave him pause and he took a step backward.

"He didn't think we'd challenge him!" exclaimed Winter Bird.

"I imagine he's not used to it," said Black Fox. Turning, he threw his rock at the Wolfen sneaking around to his left. It cried out with a painful "yelp" and put his paw to his head.

"Tarus did say they were bullies," said Two Ponies.

"Leave our land!" shouted Painted Hair. "If you do not go, you will die like the dogs that you are!"

Broken Ear snarled with rage and dropped his large paw to the silver weapon at his waist.

"Beware!" shouted Sky Feather. "Broken Ear is reaching for his weapon!"

When the Wolfen leader raised his paw, he clutched the silver tube in his sharp claw-like fingers.

"We are doomed!" exclaimed Tall Bull. "Surely this is the burning spear that killed my son."

"Remember the magic of the sky god," Black Fox reminded them. "His weapon is no threat to us here."

"Black Fox," whispered Tall Bull. "I certainly hope your sky god is as powerful as you say he is. If he's not, we'll all soon be ashes."

"Just remain within the circle, Tall Bull," warned Black Fox.

No one dared to move, as all waited for the Wolfen leader to make his next move. Emboldened by their silence, Broken Ear raised his weapon and fired. From its muzzle came a brilliant white fireball.

When the shot came, everyone jumped. The fireball, however, harmlessly bounced off the air just shy of the circle of stones, sending a shower of white sparks raining down on the surrounding area. The look of utter confusion on the Wolfen leader's face was almost comical.

"You missed, dog!" shouted Two Ponies.

Broken Ear, seeing his weapon fail to hit its mark, tipped back his head and howled with the viciousness of a wounded animal. Undeterred, he raised his weapon and fired again. Once more, the fireball bounced off the invisible barrier. This shot, however, ricocheted sideways and struck a nearby cedar tree, turning its bole into burning ash. In slow motion, the tree crumpled into a smoldering heap on the sand. Hot sparks rained down on his Wolfen companions, and they beat their thick hair with their great paws. Two Ponies caught the smell of singed hair on the wind.

"Unbelievable," stated Painted Hair.

"The magic holds!" exclaimed Sky Feather, allowing his taut nerves to relax a little. "Beware. Broken Ear will not take his failure to kill us lightly."

Curious, the large Wolfen stepped up within three paces of the stone circle. Reaching out with his right paw, he touched the air. A flash of blue light and a loud snap made everyone jump. The Wolfen leader yelped loudly and quickly withdrew his paw. A low guttural sound filled his chest and throat. In his left paw, the silver weapon still smoked from its last ill-effective shot. The Wolfen stood, legs apart, his body quivering with pent-up rage. Two Ponies, transfixed by the strange and powerful creature, took two steps forward. Broken Ear, intrigued by the young man's boldness, did the same.

"Two Ponies, go no closer!" warned Sky Feather.

"I only wish to know this enemy," said Two Ponies. "Though he wears the face and body of a wolf, I sense a powerful warrior. He is like no other enemy we've ever faced. Animal or man."

As man and wolf stared at each another, Two Ponies studied the Wolfen's face. Short, thick facial hair surrounded two oval eyes that glowed red in the firelight. When Broken Ear parted his thick black lips to emit a low snarl, he revealed a row of white incisors flanked by two long, sharp fangs. His hot, steaming breath smelled of rotted meat. When Two Ponies caught movement just over Broken Ear's right shoulder, his eyes drifted in that direction. Something tall and black swayed menacingly back and forth beyond the fire's light. Following Two Ponies' gaze, Broken Ear turned and peered at the shadow. Its low hiss could be heard, even over the crackling of the fire. Two Ponies recognized the sound and felt a chill run through him. Broken Ear, with a show of obvious fear, barked loudly, then bolted off into the night. His three companions turned and followed him.

"Well, what do you suppose scared them away?" asked Winter Bird.

"Whatever it is, it has to be meaner than they are," stated Sky Feather.

Two Ponies continued to stare into the darkness, his nerves taut.

"What is it, Two Ponies?" asked Winter Bird, stepping up beside him.

"It's the walking snake," he replied.

"There's a Reptoid out there?" asked Tall Bull, backing away from the circle's edge. "Where?"

"There—twenty paces out," replied Two Ponies, pointing at the tall shadowy figure swaying back and forth in the moonlight. "It hissed at the Wolfen and they fled into the night. Even Broken Ear showed great fear of it."

"He's the alpha!" said Gray Wolf. "If something exists that can frighten that beast, it is evil indeed! I'll build up the fire."

Two Ponies continued to stare at the Reptoid. He pitied a creature who only knew how to hate. When the fire suddenly flared up, the brighter light illuminated the swaying figure, and it stepped closer to the circle. He was not surprised to see it was the female from his dreams. Did she recognize him from their short encounter inside the belly of the iron beast? Without breaking eye contact, the she-snake ran a long lizard-like claw slowly down the bole of a thick tree. He could hear the steady grating sound as her long razor-sharp nail tore at the tree's bark. When he showed no reaction to her taunt, she leaned forward, her yellow eyes boring into his. He did the same. Beside him, the others gasped. Two Ponies addressed her.

"You will rue the day you came to *my* world, she-snake!" he warned her menacingly. "We are the Dine', and we are not conquered easily. Know this—*I* do not fear you! *We* do not fear you. We will fight you to the death! Leave here and take your dogs with you!"

Slowly, the Reptoid rose to her full height, opened her wide black lips, and hissed loudly. When they still showed no fear, she turned and fled into the night.

"I have never seen a being so full of hate," his father stated. "She even scares the Wolfen!"

"Come," said Black Fox. "Let's rest for a while. They won't return tonight."

As the others slept, Two Ponies lay on his back, watching the night sky. Growing up, he had always looked upon the stars as friendly nighttime companions that watched over him as he slept. Now he gazed up at them in fear. Could there be other worlds out there, harboring creatures even more deadly than the she-snake or her Wolfen dogs? He was now sure of only one thing: he would never again look upon the stars as friendly.

CHAPTER 14

arkness still covered the sacred mountain when Black Fox stirred them awake. Near the edge of the clearing, the horses stood in quiet repose on their tethers. Two Ponies stood and gazed up at the stars. They appeared brighter now that the moon had moved on. He hadn't meant to sleep, but pure exhaustion had forced him to close his eyes. In silence, the men gathered in the rocks from the perimeter of the sacred clearing and piled them in its center. After smothering their fire with sand, they mounted their horses and nervously left the clearing. They stopped only long enough to collect their weapons from the cleft of the rock, then set out on their long journey back to their village.

As they swiftly rode across the open country, no one spoke. Two Ponies felt uneasy in the total darkness. The female snake he'd faced in his dreams was only a trick of the mind—a specter incapable of doing him harm. The one he'd faced earlier, however, was flesh and bone, and he fully sensed her hatred for him and his companions. When the sun finally broke in the east, Two Ponies relaxed. With the coming of morning, he could now scan the surrounding land for the enemy.

It was midafternoon when they finally reached home. As the small party dismounted, Walks Far was there to take their horses. Red Shirt, leaning on his staff, informed Tall Bull that two men awaited him in his hogan.

"Ah, our sky helpers have arrived," Tall Bull exclaimed. "Come, everyone, we'll greet them together."

Sky Feather handed the reins of his horse to Walks Far. "Go find Three Feathers and have him join us," he said. "Will you take our horses and see to their needs? We've important guests to welcome."

"I will, Sky Feather," replied the young horseman.

As they entered Tall Bull's hogan, each found a place around the burning firepit. Two Ponies took his seat beside Sky Feather and both men nodded a greeting at the two strangers seated across the fire.

"Welcome," said Gray Wolf, addressing the two strangers. "I am Gray Wolf, the spiritual leader of the Dine'. My companions are Two Ponies, Sky Feather, and Winter Bird. This is Tall Bull, the chief of our Salt Clan."

"And I am Hopi," said Black Fox. "I'm the spiritual leader of the Bear Clan. My name is Black Fox and my companions are Painted Hair and Spotted Dog."

"I am Vonn," said the first of the two strangers.

"And I am Jin," replied the other.

Dancing Star, slipping in quietly, carried a flat woven basket filled with chunks of steaming meat and vegetables. Everyone paused and looked at the two visitors.

"Please, enjoy your meal," said Vonn. "We know you've spent a restless night in the mountains. We'll talk after you've eaten."

As Two Ponies ate, he studied the two newcomers. The one called Vonn was very tall and thin, with long silver hair that hung loose and flowing well past his shoulders. Although he looked to be in his late forties, the silver hair made him appear much older. He wore a thin silver shirt, silver pants, and calf-high silver boots. Draped across his chest was the strap of a square, cream-colored bag. His light skin bore no signs of battle, and Two Ponies wondered if he was a warrior or a chief.

Turning his gaze on the other man, Two Ponies smiled. *Now this is a warrior*, he thought. The man called Jin was stouter than his companion. His silver hair fell over his chest in two thick braids. His manner of dress, though similar to that of Vonn, was more suited for fighting. He wore a thick short-sleeved shirt of grayish material, with matching pants and short dark gray boots. Draped across his chest was a thick black belt holding a string of egg-sized red beads. Each bead carried the strange pattern of two jagged lightning bolts etched into its exterior. Unlike Vonn's smooth, unblemished skin, Jin's hands and arms bore several small scars. Two Ponies made a mental note to stick close to Jin when the fighting began.

When the hide covering the hogan's door lifted, all heads turned as Three Feathers stepped inside and took his place next to Two Ponies.

"Welcome, Three Feathers," said Tall Bull. "Prepare yourself, my brother. Much has happened since we departed for the sacred mountain."

Three Feathers listened in silence as the others filled him in on the strange meeting with Tarus, their encounter with the Wolfen and female Reptoid, and why two strangers now sat in Tall Bull's hogan. Finally, Tall Bull turned to address the newcomers.

"You were sent by Tarus to help us, Vonn," he stated. "How will you do so?"

"We are knowledgeable in the art of fighting the very creatures that you now face," Vonn replied, his voice smooth and steady.

"I see," said Tall Bull, hesitantly. "And you now wish to teach us these fighting skills?"

"We *are* here to instruct you, yes," replied Vonn. "We're also under strict orders not to interfere with the progress of your species. But we will step in, should the need arise. We cannot have your world overthrown by these most aggressive creatures."

"I see," Tall Bull said a second time. "And what of your companion? Is he, too, knowledgeable in the art of fighting these creatures?"

"He is, indeed," replied Vonn. "But I am the strategist; therefore, it will be me who decides what plan of action must be taken."

"I see," Tall Bull repeated for the third time. Two Ponies could tell by Tall Bull's reaction that, so far, he wasn't too sure about the "help" Tarus sent them.

As Tall Bull contemplated his next question, Two Ponies glanced over at Jin. He couldn't begin to imagine the exciting battle stories this man from the stars could tell. Jin, as if sensing he was being pondered over, turned and looked at Two Ponies. When their eyes met, it was as if they suddenly connected on a spiritual level. As they gazed at each other, words seemed to fly into Two Ponies' mind, though Jin did not open his mouth to speak his words aloud.

I have come to help you in your hour of need, Two Ponies, said Jin.

Two Ponies nodded slightly.

Again, he heard Jin's words, but only in his mind.

Great! You can hear me. Don't be afraid. I'm using a mind tool known as telepathy to speak to you.

Amazed at their strange conversation, Two Ponies nodded in acknowledgment.

Jin smiled. *Stick by my side, Two Ponies. I will teach you the ways of my people, for the Arcturians are mighty warriors. Together we will free your lands of this enemy. Please do not tell your companions of my gift. This must remain our secret.*

Two Ponies nodded a third time and turned away. Yes, he would definitely follow this man into battle.

"What fighting skills do you possess, Vonn?" asked Tall Bull. "How will you defeat this Reptoid and its Wolfen companions? Did you bring us a mighty weapon?"

"No. I must first assess the situation," replied Vonn. "Then I will lay out a plan of operation."

"And we will follow it, Vonn," said Black Fox. "But we are up against an enemy *we* have heard about only in the old stories. We simply wish to know *if* it can be defeated."

"I'm curious about this as well," said Gray Wolf. "The Wolfen proved their viciousness last night."

"And I faced off with the Reptoid," added Two Ponies. "I sense it is even more deadly than the Wolfen. I can see no way to approach it without becoming its next victim."

"Jin and I are Arcturians," stated Vonn. "We are soldiers of the Galactic Ninth Realm, a mighty force that defends the weak and keeps the peace in the universe—our corner of it anyway. Our race has fought alongside the Pleiadians for many thousands of years. Tarus, the one you call a sky god, is a great leader among these light-beings."

"Have you fought against these Wolfen before?" asked Tall Bull.

"More times than I wish to recall," replied Vonn. "The Arcturians have seen the destruction left by these renegades, Tall Bull. And like any good soldier, we've studied their ways, searching for anything that will give us an edge. In doing so, we have perfected one of the skills they possess. Jin, will you demonstrate?"

"I will, sir," replied Jin.

As they looked on, Jin's gray boots were replaced by the narrow, webbed feet and sharp claws of a lizard. Quickly, the transformation moved upward as Jin's gray pants turned into two dark, scaly, muscular legs and sturdy hips. A moment later, his gray shirt darkened into a black breastplate, and his face changed into the male counterpart of the walking snake from the night before. Leaning forward, the snake glared at them through two hard yellow eyes, each split down the middle by black vertical pupils. Below its eyes, two dark holes emitted a loud snort. Three Feathers moaned loudly and leaned back when the snake opened its lipless mouth and emitted a long, drawn-out hiss. Two Ponies, knowing what came next, felt the meat and vegetables sour in his stomach. He closed his eyes and waited for the stream of hot venom. When nothing happened, he slowly opened his eyes again. A coy smile parted the snake's hard lips, as it turned its gaze on him.

What do you think of my little trick, Two Ponies? asked the voice of Jin, his words flying into Two Ponies' mind.

Two Ponies could only give him a slight smile, as his "little trick" had nearly scared him into throwing up his meal.

When Winter Bird reached for his knife, Vonn stayed his hand.

"Obviously, this is the creature you encountered last night in the mountains," he stated. "Jin, you'd better change back, and quickly!"

In a matter of seconds, the Reptoid's hard, scaly body disappeared, leaving in its place the young sky helper named Jin.

"Very impressive!" said Gray Wolf, smiling.

"Perhaps for you, Gray Wolf," exclaimed Tall Bull. "I see a shape-shifter, the scourge of our people."

"You are wrong, Tall Bull," said Black Fox, letting out a hearty laugh. "I see an ally who has mastered the tricks of his enemy. Jin will be able to approach the Wolfen without being recognized. This is an asset, indeed. Tarus was wise to send him!"

"What other skills do you possess, Jin?" asked Tall Bull. "It will take more than changing your appearance to combat this enemy. They have a weapon that burns its victims into ash, as well as the flesh-eating venom."

"We saw the burning weapon demonstrated last night," said Winter Bird. "Fortunately for our sake, its only victim was a tree and not flesh and bone. I wouldn't want to face it without the protecting magic of Tarus."

"I understand," said Vonn. "Jin will tell you some of the history of *who* you are dealing with."

"The Reptoids are a very ancient race," Jin explained. "The fact that several of your young people died from the flesh-eating venom tells me that your Reptoid is a female. Am I correct?"

"You are," replied Two Ponies. "How do you know this?"

"Genetics," replied Jin. "Only the female of the species carries the venom. And I give you this warning. On your world, the female is the weaker of the gender. Not so among the Reptoids. Do not underestimate *this* female, for she is deadly."

"We've seen her," said Winter Bird. "Our women should be so bold!"

"This female warrior is here for only one reason," Jin continued. "She seeks a world for her queen to conquer."

"Yes, we've learned this from Tarus," stated Black Fox. "We have an image of one of these Reptoids." Spotted Dog pulled the age-darkened animal hide from his shoulder bag and handed it to Vonn to examine.

"Ah yes," said Vonn, his eyes taking in the drawing of the snake creature. "This is a bit crude, but sufficient, Black Fox. The last time your world faced this enemy was during the great space war twelve thousand years ago. At that time, it was the Galactic Ninth Realm that assisted the Pleiadians in driving the Reptoids out of this part of the galaxy. Your race lived on an island then if I read my history correctly."

"We did," replied Black Fox, offering no further details.

"Yes," said Vonn. "I recall that it sank in a day and a night, killing millions."

"It did, indeed," replied Black Fox, still offering no further details.

"Yes," Vonn repeated a second time. "But I don't recall *why* it sank. Do you know?"

After a long moment Black Fox smiled. "Outside forces," he replied. "Let's just leave it at that."

"Very well," said Vonn, returning the aged piece of hide to Spotted Dog. "Jin, continue with your report."

"Yes sir," replied Jin. "As you have learned, the Alpha Draconis Reptoids are a warring race of lizard-like creatures. Their history tells us why. Once they were ruled by a king named Lokk who terrorized his galactic neighbors by taking over the lesser worlds and enslaving the inhabitants. He used these slaves to colonize other worlds. By putting his own people in charge of those planets, he expanded his kingdom. But Lokk was old so he no longer ventured out very far in his conquests. As a result, the rest of the galaxy considered him harmless. For many thousands of your earth years, his queen, Gorra, stood by his side and gave him many powerful sons as well as many beautiful daughters. In my opinion, though, beauty is in the eye of the beholder when it comes to lizards. Then again, I'm not a good judge of—"

"Jin, you digress," interrupted Vonn. "Move on."

"Sorry, sir," said Jin. "As I was saying, Queen Gorra was a loyal and obedient wife. But after a few thousand years, she saw her kingdom begin to grow smaller as the king grew older. She thought she could do a better job of ruling her species, so she began to devise a plan to replace Lokk as ruler of Alpha Draconis."

"It was a well-planned coup," remarked Vonn. "To use one of your earth expressions."

"Vonn is correct," said Jin. "Behind the king's back, his docile and obedient queen was turning her females from meek and mild midwives into fierce and deadly warriors. One night, she made her move and beheaded the king while he slept. Three days later, when the warriors prepared to leave for yet another conquest, she stepped forward and announced that the king had "died in his sleep". Therefore, it would be her, and her army of female warriors, that would now lead them into battle. Anyone who opposed her daring move was swiftly put to death. Thus, she assumed control of Alpha Draconis. But unlike her king, who kept his conquests within close range of his home world, Gorra greedily set her sights on worlds in the far reaches of space."

"Well said, Jin," said Vonn. "I will add this. The queen is extremely old and immensely powerful, and she has ruled with an iron fist for millennia."

"What became of the remaining males on their world, Jin?" asked Sky Feather, swallowing hard.

"The queen turned them into slave warriors and breeding stock," replied Jin. "She is ruthless and has expanded her kingdom by using her great power to the detriment of millions of innocent lives."

Spotted Dog just shook his head. "Fortunately for the Hopi, we are a peaceful people," he said. "We do not possess such an ambitious need for domination, nor do we possess any powerful weapons in which to kill our enemies."

"And *that* is precisely why she has again chosen your world," said

Jin. "Your species is still barely past its primitive state. Your people use a weapon made from the wood of a young sapling, strung with a length of animal tendon. Using this primitive weapon, you kill your enemy with a stone blade attached to the end of a feathered stick."

"We've studied your weaponry," said Vonn. "I found it most inadequate, to say the least."

"I, on the other hand, found it extremely interesting," said Jin. Turning to look at Two Ponies, he added, "Although the weaponry of the Arcturians is light-years ahead of your own, Two Ponies, I do like the looks of that knife you have strapped to your belt. As a warrior, I'm a firm believer in hand-to-hand combat."

"Indeed, Jin," said Vonn. "I prefer aerial combat to surface fighting. To take unnecessary chances with one's life is not logical."

"That is where bravery enters in, Vonn," said Jin. "Without the use of advanced firepower, or the technology needed for aerial combat, these people of earth are forced to fight on the planet's surface, with what weapons are at their disposal. Inadequate, yes, but add brawn and bravery into the mix and it proves most effective. As I stated, nothing introduces you to an enemy better than engaging him in hand-to-hand combat."

"Bravery leads to hasty decisions, in my opinion," said Vonn. "Please continue, Jin."

"We have learned that in other parts of your world, the people are only slightly better equipped," said Jin. "They defend themselves with a fire-belching cannon filled with gunpowder. The blast hurls an iron ball at their enemy when massive firepower is needed. For smaller skirmishes, they use a primitive weapon known as a musket. It is a smoothbore firearm made of wood and iron, that fires from the shoulder. This musket shoots a small lead ball by creating a flint and steel spark that ignites a small amount of gunpowder in a pan."

"We do not yet possess these weapons!" stated Tall Bull, his eyes lighting up. "We could defend our homeland if we had them."

"This is true," said Jin. "But we have studied the recent wars fought on your world, Tall Bull. Although these weapons *are* most effective against similarly armed combatants, neither the cannon, or the musket, will slay these creatures."

"I agree," said Vonn. "You might as well be throwing rocks at them.

Fortunately, at this time in your evolution, earth's inhabitants do not possess any weapons or skills that the queen can use to expand her kingdom."

"Then why does she bother with us?" asked Black Fox. "If we have nothing to offer her that will benefit her rise in power, then why does she send her warriors here to harm us?"

"I remember the words of Tarus, Vonn," said Winter Bird. "He said she is only interested in our natural resources. I take this to be our gold and silver. After all, these are our most valuable minerals. Perhaps if we give her a gift, she'll go away. Will this work?"

For a moment, Jin and Vonn exchanged glances as if weighing out the answer to Winter Bird's question. When Vonn nodded, Jin cleared his throat.

"The natural resources she needs are *not* your metallic minerals, Winter Bird," replied Jin. "I'm afraid she is after your planet's inhabitants. She plans on turning your world's population into nourishment for her Wolfen army. And since you have no way of fighting back, your world will quickly fall to her."

Jin hesitated, allowing his words to sink in.

"We are to be their food?" exclaimed Tall Bull, his eyes wide. "This cannot be!"

"This Gorra sounds like a woman to be admired," said Sky Feather, attempting to soften the dire news. "Of course, that part about her feeding us to her friends disturbs me a little. But other than that, I like her."

"Now do you see why you must fight the Reptoid?" asked Jin. "Your world *must* be allowed to remain intact and continue to evolve on its own."

"Are you speaking of only our race?" asked Three Feathers, joining the conversation.

"I'm speaking of your species as a whole," replied Jin. "All races who share your world. The black man, the white man, and the yellow man."

"I ask only because we are now in danger of disappearing," said Three Feathers. "The White Fathers are removing us from our homelands. If they have their way, their soldiers will wipe us off the face of Mother Earth and laugh as they kill the last Dine' child. What are we to do?"

"We've been made aware of your predicament, Three Feathers," replied Vonn. "But at this time, you must put your skirmish with the white man aside and concentrate all your efforts on ridding yourself of *this* enemy. Your world is at stake here!"

"Listen to me," said Jin. "Vonn and I realize that what we're telling you is beyond any knowledge you have of your surroundings. Your world is so much more than what you see with your eyes. Beyond the boundaries of your small village are vast bodies of blue water called oceans. These oceans surround massive continents filled with thousands and thousands of people of many different cultures. *This* is what is at stake here. The Wolfen will care little what color their meal is if they are hungry enough. And in my experience, they can eat their weight in no time."

"So far they've eaten more than their weight in sheep," remarked Winter Bird. "Our small flock is disappearing like spring snow."

"So, we have come to this," muttered Gray Wolf, shaking his gray head. "We're to become food for an enemy who strikes out at us in the black of night. One we have no defenses against."

"Unfortunately, this is true," said Jin. "And you've no time to gather help from your neighbors. By the time you alert others, the enemy will have discovered your weaknesses and returned with a full invasion force. If this happens, we're still capable of defending you, but with great cost to your evolutionary timeline, as well as your world's population."

"Jin is right," said Vonn. "The queen has many allies that will come to her aid, especially if she offers to share the spoils. Even with our help, we could not guarantee your species, or your animal kingdom, would survive such an onslaught. The queen lost the fight once; she will not lose again."

Two Ponies felt sick. He now feared the female Reptoid even more. Jin was right. He and his people knew nothing of what lay beyond their small desert world with its sacred mountains and little painted canyons. What more could there be? Suddenly he knew what it was he'd seen from the belly of the great iron beast. His mind's eye saw again the huge blue ball with its dark brown masses beneath thick smoky clouds. Was this his world? He looked at Jin for his answer. In his mind, he heard Jin's unspoken words.

This is what you fight for, Two Ponies, he said. *This is Gaia, your Mother Earth.*

Two Ponies felt a sense of determination envelop him. Suddenly his fear fell away, and he knew he would fight this Reptoid and her Wolfen dogs, to save his blue world.

"We are all willing to join you, Vonn," said Sky Feather. "Now, perhaps you can tell us a little about *your* world."

"As I stated earlier, Jin and I are Arcturians," said Vonn. "Our world is not unlike your Earth, which orbits your star you call Sol or sun. Our home world orbits a red giant star we call Arcturus. We're a highly advanced civilization and a member of the Galactic Ninth Realm, which includes the Pleiadians and the Sirians. It is at the request of the Pleiadians, however, that we've come to assist you. Because this is not an invasion force, at this time, they feel we can do this without a lot of … fuss and firepower."

"Your presence is an old man's dream come true," said Gray Wolf. "The Dine' have long awaited the return of our ancestors from the stars. And after meeting you, I will not look at the night sky through the same blue eyes."

"I thank you," said Jin. "Now, we have no time to lose. We cannot allow the Reptoid queen to gain a strategic foothold on Earth. From here, she can launch her battle fleets in all directions and claim vast sections of your spiral galaxy. Surrounding your solar system are many other worlds, not unlike your own, that orbit their own central star. These will also be in danger. The unwritten law of the universe is that it is beneficial to the whole that the few, or the one, not be permitted to rule everything. Have you any more questions?"

"Yes, Jin," replied Sky Feather. "Why would you and Vonn risk your lives to save our world? What do the Arcturians take from this?"

"It's simple," replied Jin. "Your world is extremely important to us because you are a species of fighters. Your history proves this. The Arcturians have watched over your development for thousands of years. It is our hope that one day the people of Earth will join the Galactic Ninth Realm in defending those on other worlds, who suffer tyranny and oppression. *This* is why Vonn, and I are here."

"Well, that's reason enough for me to join you," said Winter Bird. "I can tell my grandchildren that I saved the world. My name will be revered for generations to come, and my image will be etched into the great stone bluffs. I will certainly be a legend!"

"Or a myth," stated Gray Wolf, smiling.

"Don't listen to him, Winter Bird," said Black Fox. "To become even a myth, you must do great deeds. You continue to dream big, my brother."

"Let us concentrate on what we are faced with, at this moment," said Vonn. "We have several ways to help you. Our main objective, however, is to not violate the Prime Directive. That is, whatever methods we choose to share with you, cannot remain with you. They would, I'm afraid, change your world forever."

"Are you speaking of the red eggs that Jin wears on his chest?" asked Black Fox. "Is this your weapon?"

"What weapon?" asked Three Feathers. "I cannot see how throwing an egg at the situation can be of much help."

"Oh, this is no egg," said Jin, pointing to one of the red objects strung on his chest. "Their function will amaze you. They're a very powerful weapon that uses the combination of electrons and protons with a little cold nuclear fusion to stir them up. This makes for a very controlled explosion. I don't leave home without them."

"Jin, I believe that is *too* much information," said Vonn, raising an eyebrow.

"Sorry, sir," said Jin, with a sheepish look.

"What other ideas do you have?" asked Black Fox.

"Yes," said Tall Bull. "Our village population is smaller as we've just lost eight of our best young warriors to this enemy. As you pointed out, there is little time to gather help from beyond our village. How will we fight with so few men?"

"This will sound strange to you, I'm sure," warned Jin. "We will employ a method called bioregeneration."

Every man but Vonn looked at Jin with a look of bewilderment.

"I see this confuses you," Jin remarked. "It's understandable, given your primitive knowledge. I'll attempt to explain *without* giving you too much information. Since we have learned the art of DNA manipulation, we are able to regenerate the life force of those lost to the female Reptoid's flesh-eating venom."

"What are you saying?" asked Tall Bull, leaning forward. "What is this bio—"

"Bioregeneration," repeated Jin. "We can restore the life force, and flesh, to those who are now only bones."

"And what of those who were burned to ash?" asked Tall Bull, hopefully. "Can you give them life as well? Can you make my son live again?"

"I'm afraid not, Tall Bull," replied Jin, sadly. "Since there are no skeletal remains of your son, we would have to create something out of nothing. Even the highly advanced Arcturians are incapable of that feat. I'm afraid, he is sadly beyond our help."

"Then my son Long Bow, is truly lost forever?" asked Tall Bull, softly.

"I'm afraid so," replied Jin. "And even those who are given new flesh will only live for a short time. Eventually, they, too, will slowly return to bones and be no more. While they are here, however, we will harness their strength! They will be our most important warriors as they will now be immune to the Reptoid's venom."

"How will the rest of us face her?" asked Winter Bird. "She is powerful!"

"That she is," replied Vonn. "And she possesses powerful arms and legs that can crush a man to death. But on your planet, she has one weakness."

"I knew it!" exclaimed Winter Bird. "You can defeat even the fiercest enemy if you can find his weak spot. What is this weakness?"

"Your sun," replied Vonn. "The heat and light generated by your sun is known as solar radiation. Our Reptoid is a cold-blooded creature. Therefore, she must either remain aboard her sky ship during your planet's daylight hours or retreat underground into the darkness."

"She's a nocturnal hunter," added Jin. "We'll use this fact to our advantage."

"How can the Hopi help?" asked Painted Hair. "We're not a warring people."

"Your job will be to support the Dine'," replied Jin.

"Do the Wolfen possess any weaknesses?" asked Two Ponies.

"They do, indeed," replied Jin. "They are big dumb brutes with the mentality of your earth dog. And since they have no real leader among them, the queen uses them to do her dirty work."

"Now, we must locate the Wolfen pack," said Vonn. "Beware. You have already seen their weapon at work, so do not approach them on your own. Remember, the Wolfen can alter their DNA. But they are unfamiliar with your human genetic make-up, as well as that of your animal population.

Because of this, they'll have trouble mimicking them at first. They'll learn fast, though, so we must move quickly."

"Do we look for a den?" asked Sky Feather. "Our wolves live in holes dug into the hillside."

"I do not know this word *den*," said Jin. "What I can tell you is this; the Wolfen most likely entered your world inside a large rock. It would have appeared to you as a boulder that fell from the sky. Examine your landscape for one that looks out of place. This will be their stronghold."

"This must be our first priority," added Vonn. "This rock won't be hard to find if you know what you're looking for."

"A rock that fell from the sky?" asked Tall Bull. "We have no such thing."

"Oh yes, we do!" announced Sky Feather, looking over at Two Ponies. "Winter Bird's falling star."

"I warned you trouble would find us," said Winter Bird, shaking his head.

"What are you saying, Sky Feather?" asked Tall Bull.

"I'm saying that we may know of such a rock," he replied. "Winter Bird saw it fall from the sky the day before the raid on the scout camp."

"Well, then you may already be aware of what we seek," said Jin. "We locate this rock, and we locate the Wolfen."

"What do these Wolfen look like?" asked Three Feathers.

"Two Ponies made a likeness of one of them," said Sky Feather. "Show him, son."

Two Ponies reached behind his back and retrieved the piece of birch bark with the sketched image of Broken Ear, and handed it to Three Feathers.

"This is a very good likeness, Two Ponies," said Three Feathers, studying it. "They look vicious, indeed."

"Vonn, I have a question," said Black Fox. "You told us the Wolfen can change into an animal. How is this a weakness? How are we to know that what we are looking at is truly a coyote, or a Wolfen shape-shifter?"

"Excellent question," replied Vonn. "The Wolfen are not acclimated to your earth's gravity; therefore, they will be unable to maintain the animal's likeness for long. This means they will appear larger than normal and clumsy when they walk. Also look for their red eyes. They have very keen eyesight so approach them as a shadow."

"May I point something out, Vonn?" asked Sky Feather. "You will make a poor shadow with your silver hair and clothing. The Wolfen will see you coming in the dark."

When Vonn failed to laugh, everyone held their breath. Did he see Sky Feather's comment as an insult? In answer to the taunt, Vonn's silver boots darkened into a pair of sturdy knee-high moccasins, and rich golden-brown leather replaced the thin silver fabric of his pants and shirt. The last to change was his long white hair. It now flowed over his shoulders, black and glistening. When his pale skin darkened to a rich copper color, Sky Feather looked on in amazement. The sky helper now looked no different than himself.

"Will this do?" asked Vonn.

"It will, indeed," laughed Sky Feather. "Now if you can convince your gray friend here to do the same, we can get on with our mission."

In the blink of an eye, Jin's gray boots became a pair of high-top leather moccasins with sturdy soles. His gray shirt and pants changed into rich golden-brown leather, and his silver braids darkened into two shiny black ropes. As he smiled at his audience, his light skin darkened to match their own. His only difference from Vonn's appearance, was the single black eagle's feather that dangled from a strip of leather behind his right ear.

"Jin, for what purpose do you wear a bird's feather in your hair?" demanded Vonn, looking displeased.

"You are the strategist on this mission, Vonn," replied Jin. "Therefore, you are unadorned. I, on the other hand, am a skilled Arcturian warrior of the Galactic Ninth Realm. Besides, I like the image of the eagle's feather. It gives my character a certain … fierceness."

"And you wear it well, my friend," stated Sky Feather, getting to his feet. "Shall we take that first step in our long battle?"

"We shall," said Gray Wolf. "Winter Bird, help me to my feet. Our first task is to set Jin and Vonn to a horse."

"To a what?" asked Vonn, looking alarmed. "Set me to a what?"

"To a horse," replied Jin. Getting to *his* feet, he looked down on his

Superior. "A large, domesticated, plant-eating mammal with a solid hoof. They are used for riding and for pulling small loads."

"Am I going to like this … horse?" Vonn asked Jin.

"Probably not," replied Jin. Breaking into a huge grin, he turned and strode from the hogan.

CHAPTER 15

Near the edge of the village, Vonn and Jin joined Walks Far for a quick riding lesson. Jin mastered his brown-and-white paint in no time. Vonn, however, was given a rather feisty young black horse. Dealing with such spunk, his training took a bit longer. In his attempt to master the unfamiliar beast, Vonn suffered two rather painful tumbles.

"Are you injured, Vonn?" asked Jin, coming to his aid. He did little to hide his obvious amusement as Vonn picked himself up from the ground for the second time. "I see that you are unharmed. Excellent. I will, of course, enjoy informing our comrades back home of your newly acquired horse skills."

"If you even think about it, Jin, I will personally hand you over to the Reptoid queen myself," Vonn growled, brushing the sand from his backside. Mounting the horse for the third time, he finally managed to stay on its back. When the others joined them, they smiled at Vonn and Jin's success.

"You have trained them well, Walks Far," said Sky Feather, praising the young man. "Our star helpers are now ready to follow us into the desert."

"We are, indeed, Sky Feather," said Jin. "We have both successfully *set a horse*. Well, one of us has anyway."

"What comes next?" asked Vonn. When his horse decided to turn a full circle, he leaned down to address it. "Listen to me, domesticated horse creature. Are we to walk in circles until we both tire from the effort?"

"You must use the reins to guide your horse," instructed Walks Far. "They will steer him. If he is running, you pull back on the reins. This will slow him down or bring him to a stop."

"Use my what?" asked Vonn, throwing up his hands. "I don't understand! Jin!"

Smiling, Jin reached over and gave Vonn his horse's reins.

"These rawhide cords are used to change your horse's trajectory," he said. "Once your horse is motion, you'll use these same cords to make any minor adjustments to its navigational course. To slow the horse's velocity, pull back on the cords, and this will throttle down its thrust to desired speed or terminate all forward movement. Do you understand now?"

"I do," replied Vonn, settling the reins into his hands. "In what direction do I wish to go?"

"First we're heading to the river," said Sky Feather. "We need to show you the black stone."

"When did it arrive?" asked Jin, sliding from his horse.

"Right after our young men were killed," replied Sky Feather. "We awoke to find it in the clearing beside the river. It has strange writing on it. Come. For this leg of our journey, we walk."

"Excellent," exclaimed Vonn. Hastily sliding from his horse, he handed the reins to Walks Far. "This beast is slow to obey my orders, young man. Have him retrained."

"Have him what?" asked a confused Walks Far.

"Vonn doesn't mean his words," said Jin, patting the boy on the back. "Even the beasts on our home world won't listen to him. It's his superior attitude."

When the people first laid eyes on the star visitors, they hid in their hogans in fear. The strangers, with their silver hair and pale clothing, were immediately mistaken for the dreaded White Fathers from the east. But now that they looked just like them, they quickly relaxed and emerged to welcome them to their village. Curious as to whom the visitors were, they followed the two strangers to the river.

"These are the helpers from the stars," said Tall Bull, introducing them to his people. "They are Vonn and Jin. Welcome them."

"You are welcome among the Dine'," said Red Shirt. Stepping forward to greet the strangers, he stood leaning heavily on his staff. Beside him, the equally stooped Black Crow awaited his turn to speak. He, too, leaned heavily on an ornately carved walking stick.

"I also welcome you," said Black Crow. "I must confess that neither Red Shirt nor I know much about fighting this new enemy. But we *are* deeply knowledgeable in the old stories of our people, should you wish to hear them."

"Thank you," said Vonn, giving the two old men a slight bow. "Your chief, Tall Bull, and his companions, have asked for our help in doing battle with those who killed your sons. We are willing to fight alongside you to rid your world of this enemy."

"This is good news!" stated Red Shirt, brightening.

"Good news, indeed," added Black Crow. "And if I were fifty winters younger, I, too, would fight at your side. But I am now old and no longer of any use."

"Nonsense," said Jin. "You know all the old stories of your people. Passing on one's history not only teaches your youth what traditions have served you well for generations, but it gives them a sense of family unity. It tells them, no one walks alone. I, myself, would love to hear a few of your stories."

"Then we are at your service," replied Black Crow, bowing slightly.

After the introductions, Jin and Vonn slowly walked around the black stone, examining it closely. Those watching stood in silence awaiting their verdict.

"This is a highly advanced system, Jin," stated Vonn. "One I'm not familiar with."

"I believe I know what we're dealing with here," said Jin. "It's crude but effective. It's brilliant, actually. By using obsidian, which is a volcanic rock, their threshold of conduction will be higher yet untraceable by our multidimensional scanners."

"Which means?" asked Winter Bird.

"We did *not* see this thing coming," replied Jin, with a grin.

"Tarus called it a device for talking," said Sky Feather.

"It *is* used for communication purposes," replied Vonn. "The female Reptoid is using it to coordinate her Wolfen companions while she remains in her sky ship. You must never touch it!"

"Three Feathers touched it," said Tall Bull. "It sent his mind into a deep sleep."

"And, I pulled Three Feathers from the stone," added Two Ponies.

"What did you see, Three Feathers?" asked Vonn.

"I saw the she-snake in my mind," he replied. "She held me in a room with no door. Without using her mouth, she demanded I tell her about my people. How did she do that anyway?"

"We'll explain later," replied Vonn. "Go on."

"She wanted to know what weapons we use to hunt our food," continued Three Feathers. "She asked me how many people lived in our land. Soon, however, I grew hungry and thirsty, and I couldn't think clearly anymore. It was then my mind returned me to my village."

"You should be glad she failed to feed you," said Jin. "When your mind grew weak, she couldn't telepathically hold you any longer. In answer to your question about how she could speak *without* using her mouth, she used an advanced skill called telepathy. Her mind spoke directly into your mind. You should be all right now."

"But I am still her prisoner!" Three Feathers insisted. "Her voice is constantly in my head, bombarding me with more questions. This she-snake haunts my thoughts, begging me for answers."

"And you, Two Ponies?" asked Vonn. "What did you see?"

"I found myself in the belly of a great iron beast that floats above my blue world," he replied, his arm pointing upward. "There I came face-to-face with the she-snake. Before she could do me harm, though, my body was thrust onto the sand at my father's feet. I don't hear her words in my mind, as Three Feathers does, but I feel her eyes watching me."

"You are both most fortunate," said Vonn. "Apparently, she learned very little from either of you. This is why she approached you at the mountain. She's still after information. I say we keep her guessing."

"She allowed her dogs to attack us," said Tall Bull. "Broken Ear used his weapon of fire. But we were protected by the magic of Tarus."

"That clearing is an ancient space portal," said Jin. "It's been used for thousands of years as a place where the Pleiadians can come and go without detection. Unfortunate for us, the female Reptoid is now aware of its location as well. Now let's see what we can do with this stone."

Stepping closer, Vonn held his hand just inches away from its surface.

"Do not touch the stone!" warned Gray Wolf.

"Vonn is able read the stone without touching it," said Jin. "You're wise to keep your people away from it, Gray Wolf. It holds a message not meant for those with a primitive mind."

When Vonn finally lowered his hand, the others fell silent, awaiting what he had to say.

"This stone is not the work of the Reptoid *or* the Wolfen, Jin," he said. "Oh, the technology is, but the stonework is definitely of Shetu origin."

"You're right!" exclaimed Jin. "How could I have missed this?"

"Who is this … Shetu?" asked Gray Wolf. "Are we to fight them as well?"

"I don't think so," replied Jin. "The Shetu and the Wolfen are both master stonecutters. And I can see both of their warrior emblems on this stone. The insignia of Wolfen, as well as the Reptoid, is the snake's eye within a triangle. The insignia of the Shetu is a bright red spiral within a green six-sided star."

"I see no such symbol," stated Gray Wolf, stepping forward. "I see only the symbol of the snake's eye."

"You have to use pure thought to find the Shetu insignia," said Vonn. "They do not want their presence known."

Once more, Vonn placed his open palm near the surface of the stone. Suddenly the glowing bright green outline of a six-sided star appeared against the blackness of the surface. In its center was the illuminated image of a red spiral.

"I am speechless," said Sky Feather. "Powerful is the mind of the Arcturians!"

"Are the Shetu great warriors?" asked Winter Bird.

"No," replied Jin. "They're actually a race of peaceful followers. The queen enslaved their young males only to bolster her numbers in battle. As a result, thousands of them have died needlessly. We're attempting to ally several federations to help free them from her iron fist."

"They resemble the Wolfen but are smaller in stature," added Vonn. "But do not let their smaller size fool you. They, too, can deliver a vicious bite when cornered."

"I believe I saw one of these Shetu last night," said Two Ponies. "He was with the Wolfen at the sacred mountain."

"A Shetu is running *with* the Wolfen?" asked Jin.

"Yes," replied Two Ponies. "He was smaller than the other three and more timid. He wore a silver ring in his nose."

"Keen are the eyes of the young," said Gray Wolf. "I saw none of these things."

"The nose ring is important," remarked Jin. "It's a sign that this particular Shetu is being forced to fight with them. This knowledge could prove useful to us."

"All four wore a breastplate bearing the symbol of the snake's eye within a triangle," continued Two Ponies. "Gray Wolf told us that he saw this very same symbol when he was young. Tell Jin of your vision, Gray Wolf."

"This is true," said Gray Wolf. "I saw it when I was a boy. It was on the breastplate worn by a wolf that walked upright, like a man."

"You've seen one of the Wolfen before now?" asked Vonn, stepping away from the stone.

"I believe so," replied Gray Wolf. "But this was many winters ago. I saw the creature while on my vision quest. This is a ritual we perform when a boy becomes a man. In my vision, the wolf stepped from a door in the side of a huge, blackened boulder."

"Why do you think this encounter was only a vision?" asked Vonn.

"Within a day or two, I returned to the place where I saw this strange wolf and his great rock," replied Gray Wolf. "Both were gone."

"That makes sense," said Vonn. "Once seen, he probably hightailed it out of here. He didn't want attention drawn to him."

"I see," said Gray Wolf. "Another reason I thought my encounter with the wolf was a vision was that he spoke to me!"

"Odd," said Jin. "I've never known them to speak in any other language but their native grunts and barks. What did he say to you?"

"He threatened to return someday and end my life," replied Gray Wolf. "If he was truly an enemy, then why didn't he kill me then?"

"Simple," replied Vonn. "He didn't harm you because he was not supposed to *be* here. They are not permitted to be loners. This particular Wolfen was simply curious about what lived on the blue planet."

"Is that so?" asked Gray Wolf. "After seeing the Wolfen leader last night, I'm now certain he is this same wolf from my boyhood."

"You may be right," said Jin.

"What makes these Wolfen so evil?" asked Painted Hair.

"The Wolfen were a warrior race long before the queen joined forces

153

with them," replied Vonn. "They're fierce fighters. When the Reptoid queen attempted to take over their world, they viciously killed many of her warriors. She did not take this defeat lightly. Realizing she would be unable to control the Wolfen, she made a pact with them."

"What sort of pact?" asked Gray Wolf.

"One of convenience only, I'm sure," replied Vonn. "The queen needed to harness the Wolfen's thirst for ruthless killing. The Wolfen, on the other hand, needed the queen to supply them with food for their growing population. For thousands of years, this union has worked mutually for them both. But the Wolfen will never be her slaves, nor will she ever allow them to become her equal."

"Then your words are true?" asked Winter Bird. "The people of my world really *are* to become food for these Wolfen dogs?"

"Not if we can help it," said Jin.

"Wait until the queen discovers our sheep," remarked Winter Bird. "Then they really will disappear!"

"What of this talking stone?" asked Black Fox, motioning to the black rock.

"It must be destroyed immediately," replied Vonn.

"How?" asked Black Fox. "We have no weapon that will shatter such a large solid stone."

"I *do* have such a weapon," said Jin. "I will, in the words of Three Feathers, "throw an egg at it"."

"Everyone, stand back!" exclaimed Tall Bull, taking several steps back himself. All, except for the two star helpers, followed his lead. Once everyone was clear, Jin stepped forward and sized up the huge rectangle-shaped stone.

Two Ponies stood mesmerized. How strange that Jin should appear so much like himself yet possess powers beyond any imagination. He now watched as Jin plucked one of the red beads from the black belt draped across his chest, and placed it against the stone. Like a dollop of wet river mud, the red bead flattened out across its smooth surface. When Jin stepped back, so did Two Ponies. A moment later, the stone disappeared in a bright flash of brilliant green light, leaving behind a deep smoking hole in the sandy earth. For several moments, no one moved.

Grinning, Jin turned and took a low bow. "And that is how to destroy a stone with an egg," he said.

Suddenly Two Ponies felt an intense pain in his head, and a myriad of colors burst into his mind. Purples, reds, and greens flashed through his brain, and he clutched his head in his hands. Then his mind filled with the image of an angry, hissing, female Reptoid. He felt his heart race, and his knees buckled. Sky Feather, seeing his son's distress, managed to catch him before he hit the ground.

"Two Ponies!" he exclaimed. Turning to Vonn, he demanded, "What is happening to my son?"

At the same time, Three Feathers cried out and staggered backward.

"Three Feathers!" exclaimed Winter Bird, reaching out to hold the man steady. "What is happening to them, Vonn?"

"Do not panic!" replied Vonn, holding his hands up to calm everyone. "They're not injured. By destroying the stone, Jin also destroyed their mental connection to the Reptoid. They will recover and be much better for it."

"Talk to me, Three Feathers," said Winter Bird, peering into the big man's face.

"I am ... well," replied Three Feathers, swaying slightly. Suddenly his mouth broke into a huge grin. "The she-snake is gone from my mind. She speaks to me no longer! I am grateful to you, Jin, for freeing me of her."

"I am your servant," said Jin, bowing low to the mighty warrior.

"And what about you, Two Ponies?" asked Vonn.

"I, fortunately, was not forced to listen to her endless words," he replied. "But when the stone was destroyed, my mind saw an incredibly angry snake! She is not happy with what you've done here."

"Once more you gave my heart a scare, my son," said Sky Feather, smiling in relief. "I'm not sure how much more I can take."

"I am unhurt, Father," said Two Ponies, giving Sky Feather a weak grin.

"You will both recover from your ordeal, my friends," stated Vonn. "The female Reptoid will just have to get her answers some other way. This I hope, will slow down her progress. The queen is no doubt expecting a report, very soon, on whether or not the way is clear to send more of her warriors."

"The queen hates delays," added Jin. "Also, by destroying the stone, we force our female to return to the surface if she wishes to communicate with the Wolfen. Here, we can deal with her. She can't take the direct sunlight, so it'll be after dark. This should buy us some time. We must use that precious time to search for the Wolfen. Once we locate their base camp, we can decide how best to approach them. That alone could prove ugly. The Wolfen hate the Arcturians more then they hate the Reptoids."

"And we have given them good reason to hate us," added Vonn. "We have pursued them across the cosmos, thwarting their malicious conquests whenever possible. This time, however, we have the advantage as they do not yet know *we* are here. They still think they're facing a primitive people who offer no resistance."

"They have not yet felt the mighty wrath of the Dine'," said Sky Feather. "Nor have they tangled with the Apache, the Comanche, or the Kiowa. They best not venture out too far in their search for victims. We are a race of warriors who will fight to the death to defend our people and our sacred lands."

"I'm happy to hear this," said Vonn. "Now, where do we go to find your fallen star?"

"We need to ride toward the western bluffs," replied Winter Bird.

"Are we going to use the horse?" asked Vonn, looking concerned.

"We are," replied Winter Bird. "It's many miles to where I saw the star fall to earth."

"Argh," mumbled Vonn. "Why must I endure the company of a beast that will not listen to me? My time would be better spent walking across the galaxy!"

Returning to the village, the men rejoined Walks Far and their waiting horses.

Winter Bird moved his horse out in front of the group as they mounted their horses.

"Let's ride!" he exclaimed. Urging his horse into a gallop, he led them toward the west. When Two Ponies noticed that Vonn was still having trouble with his horse, he turned and went back to him.

"My horse creature is still not obeying my orders!" exclaimed Vonn, as he and his horse took three steps backward. "This is insubordination, I say!"

"You have to show your horse who is the master," said Two Ponies, trying to hide his smile. "Once he understands *you* are in charge, he'll gladly take you to the ends of the earth and back. Of course, a few sweet words never hurt."

"We shall see," muttered Vonn. Taking up the slack in the reins, he gave them a slight shake as he added, "Go forward, beast. If you take me to where I wish to go, I will reward you with a nutritious meal and a comfortable place in which to lay your head."

He smiled in triumph when his horse turned and galloped out to join the others.

"Works every time," said Two Ponies, urging his own horse forward.

CHAPTER 16

When they reached the large boulder where the scouting party was killed, Winter Bird led them into its shade.

"Jin, over there, among those trees, lies the clearing where the Reptoid and her Wolfen attacked our scouting party," he said. "We lost eight of our best warriors that day. They were killed for no reason."

"This enemy needs no reason to kill," replied Jin.

Tall Bull, refusing to even look in the direction of the clearing, sat staring down at his hands.

Two Ponies dismounted and pulled out his waterskin. After giving his horse a cool drink, he drank deeply himself. Sky Feather steered his horse over to stand next to Jin's.

"Jin, what exactly are we searching for?" he asked.

"As we've told you, the Wolfen are master stonecutters," Jin replied. "They are also masters' of disguise. Knowing that a shiny metallic ship would be noticed as it maneuvered through a planet's atmosphere, the Wolfen learned to utilize the great rocks that float around in space. We call these rocks asteroids, and your galaxy offers them an unlimited supply. The size of the asteroid required, depends on the size of the Wolfen force. They hollow out the interior and install a command center and living quarters."

"The asteroid we seek will be hard to locate, I'm afraid," added Vonn. "Due to your rocky terrain, it will blend in with its surroundings. Because of this, the Wolfens' arrival would have gone virtually undetected."

"This makes sense," stated Winter Bird. "It was only by chance that I saw them arrive."

"Actually, it's quite a brilliant move on their part," said Jin. "Your people wouldn't be alarmed to see a rock fall from the sky as they've done so since your planet's early beginnings."

"We do have stories," said Sky Feather. "Vonn, what do we do once we locate this Wolfen asteroid?"

"Wait for my instructions," replied Vonn. Glancing at the sky, he added, "Now is a good time to search for it as your sun is high. The Wolfen will take refuge within it to avoid the heat. As for the Reptoid, she'll be aboard her ship."

Jin nodded in agreement and turned to face Black Fox. "You have asked us here to assist your people, Black Fox," he said. "Vonn and I are familiar with the enemy, but not with the layout of the land. Therefore, we must rely on the clever tracking skills of your people."

"The Dine' know this land better than anyone," said Black Fox. "Their tracking skills are well known."

"They are, indeed, Black Fox," said Winter Bird. "We need only to know what we're searching for."

"Then we'll follow your lead, Winter Bird," said Jin. "When you spot the Wolfen asteroid, you'll then know what is meant by, "out of place"."

"Here's my plan," said Vonn, calling for everyone's attention. "Jin, you will lead a group further west to search for the asteroid. Three Feathers, you will accompany myself, Gray Wolf and the three Hopi. Herein lies the bones of two of those killed by the flesh-eating venom. I will execute bioregeneration. Gray Wolf, you will then lead us to the remains of your Standing Deer and Red Otter. They, too, will undergo bioregeneration. Your task, Three Feathers, is to see that we are not disturbed."

"I can do this," replied Three Feathers, swelling with pride.

"Tall Bull?" asked Jin.

"I wish to go with you, Jin," he replied. "This place holds only sorrow for me."

"Then it's settled," said Jin. "You'll come with me. Two Ponies, Winter Bird, and Sky Feather, you'll come with me, as well."

Leaving Vonn and the others to seek out the dead, Jin and his small party left the shade and rode back out into the hot sun.

"My falling star fell to the ground out near that massive reddish-gray boulder," remarked Winter Bird, pointing to the west. "We'll head in that direction."

When they drew within a mile of the boulder, Jin held up his hand, and they brought their horses to a halt.

"From here, we must proceed with caution," he said. "Never assume the Wolfen will do as predicted. We'll take refuge in that small stand of trees over there to the left. That should give us a good view of the area while providing us with ample cover."

When they reached the small grove of trees, they steered their horses into the shade. The only sounds were the steady falling of their horses' hooves in the soft sand, and the rustle of the wind through the leaves above their heads. Dismounting, they tethered their horses to the lower limbs. Quietly making their way to the edge of the trees, they peered out at the landscape. The hot sand shimmered in the heat as the sun's intense rays baked the land.

"Now let's see what fell," said Jin, quietly.

The others gathered around him. Approximately one hundred-fifty yards beyond the trees, loomed the massive reddish-gray boulder. At its base, lay a large, round rock; its exterior burnt and pockmarked.

"Notice that large rock in front of the boulder," said Jin, pointing in its direction. "See how it appears blackened as if it's been through the flames of a hot fire. If I'm not mistaken, that should be our asteroid."

"You could be right," said Winter Bird. "But, as a boy, my father would bring me deer hunting here among the stone bluffs. Often, I'd see great chunks of rock dislodged from above by time and wind. That rock could be just another one of time's victims."

"Or it could be what we seek," suggested Jin. "There's only one way to be sure. We must get closer. This endeavor, however, will require someone much younger than me."

"I'm only twenty-seven winters," said Two Ponies, stepping forward. "I'll go."

Knowing that he was again putting his life in danger, he dared a glance at Sky Feather. The look on his father's face was a mixture of rage and pride.

"Our people will know of your bravery," said Tall Bull. With a smile he added, "Today I am finally grateful of my graying hair."

"This *will* be an act of bravery, Two Ponies," said Jin. "Now, to go in undetected, I'm afraid you're going to have to crawl on your belly. Once you're close enough to get a good look at the rock, don't signal to us. Simply crawl back here. If it *is* the Wolfen camp, we'll rejoin the others and decide our next move."

"I'm curious, Jin," said Winter Bird. "How old are you?"

"I'm too old to crawl that far on my belly, I can assure you," replied Jin, smiling. "Actually, I'm seven hundred-thirty-three in earth years."

"Incredible!" exclaimed Winter Bird. "I'm approaching forty-five winters, and yet you appear so much younger than I."

"Yes, it is incredible, Winter Bird," said Sky Feather. "If you were to live to that great age, you could become that legend you spoke of."

Two Ponies smiled at his father's joke. Being able to find anything amusing when they were quite possibly looking down the throat of the beast, eased his mind a bit. Turning his attention back to the large, blackened rock, he wondered what he'd gotten himself into. Closing his eyes, he took a moment to mentally prepare himself for what lay ahead. After a silent prayer, he stepped forward.

"I'm ready," he announced. He removed his knife sheath and belt and handed them to his father.

"Keep your head down, Two Ponies," said Sky Feather.

"I will, Father," said Two Ponies. "I won't fail you."

"You could never fail me, Two Ponies," said Sky Feather, looking him in the eye. "I'm immensely proud of you. Now, remember the lessons I taught you growing up. You always loved best, the games of stealth."

"We'll await your return, Two Ponies," said Jin. "Just be careful to keep as low as possible. The Wolfen possess excellent eyesight. But they don't see well in the harsh sunlight, so this is to our advantage. If they *should* see you—"

"I am a Dine' warrior," stated Two Ponies, proudly. "Death will be an honor I will embrace one day. Today, I hope, is *not* that day," he added, with a nervous smile.

Two Ponies lowered himself onto his belly and roughly gauged the distance to the great blackened rock. From the protection of the trees, it lay roughly one hundred-seventy paces across the hot, barren sand. Another ten paces beyond the rock, loomed the face of the massive reddish-gray boulder. Could the smaller rock *be* the Wolfen asteroid? There was only one way to find out. Drawing in a deep breath, he released it slowly and began his long arduous trek forward. As he pulled himself along with his elbows, the intense rays of the sun beat down on his back and legs. He was now grateful he'd chosen a leather shirt and pants when he'd dressed the previous night, as they now protected his body from the hot sand.

When he was roughly forty paces from the blackened rock, he paused. Close up, he now marveled at its great size. It was as tall as six grown men! Seeing nothing move ahead of him, he raised up onto his elbows and allowed his eyes to scan the surrounding landscape. To the south, he could just make out the edges of a wide, deep crater where something huge had slammed into the desert with such force, it scattered sand for a great distance. From this crater, a long, shallow trough ran across the sand, and disappeared beneath the blackened rock in front of him. *This must be the Wolfen asteroid!* he thought. To his right, he caught the sudden movement as something scampered across the ground, and he quickly lowered to the sand. He released his breath when a long-eared jackrabbit scurried past him and disappeared beneath a small deergrass bush near the base of the great blackened rock. *Only a rabbit*, he thought.

Convinced the rock was indeed the Wolfen stronghold, Two Ponies knew he had to tell the others. He was in the process of turning his body for the return journey when his ears caught the distinct sound of rock sliding against rock. Just beyond the asteroid, movement drew his eyes to a spot in the lower face of the massive boulder. In fascination, he watched as a section of rock slowly slid aside, revealing a dark passageway beyond.

Pressing himself into the sand, Two Ponies willed his heart to slow down. How could a door open in solid rock? He raised his eyes just as one of the Wolfen creatures stepped from the dark doorway. It was Broken Ear, the Wolfen leader, and in the light of day he looked even more intimidating.

Although Broken Ear still wore his black breastplate, the silver weapon no longer hung from the grimy black belt around his thick waist. Turning, the Wolfen leader squinted against the harsh sunlight as his bloodred eyes scanned the open desert in front of him. When they hesitated on the very spot where Two Ponies lay, he stopped and stared. Two Ponies held his breath as fear gripped his heart. Was his body visible above the sand? If the Wolfen leader attacked, would he be able to outrun him? These questions tumbled through his mind as he waited for what came next. When Broken Ear looked away, Two Ponies sucked in a much-needed breath.

Broken Ear, sensing no danger, gave off a short bark and two of his companions stepped from the dark doorway, into the light. Behind them, the slab of rock slowly slid shut and disappeared. Two Ponies looked on in wonder, as the bodies of the two lesser Wolfen bent forward, changed into two fat coyotes, and lumbered off in a northerly direction.

After seeing his companions off, Broken Ear turned and approached the blackened asteroid. Suddenly his ears perked up, and his head jerked to his left. Dropping his sharp claws into the deergrass bush, he pulled up the helpless jackrabbit. With a deep, guttural sound, he opened his mouth and tore the squirming rabbit in half with his great canine teeth. Blood ran down his chin and pooled in the dark gray hair above his breastplate. A moment later, he ate the remaining half of the dead jackrabbit and wiped his bloody mouth on his hairy arm. With a satisfied grunt, he reached out and pressed his paw against a four-inch diameter silver disc on the outside of the asteroid. Immediately, a large rock door slid aside with a loud hiss. After one final glance at his surroundings, the Wolfen leader stepped inside, and the door hissed shut behind him.

Two Ponies was sickened by the Wolfen's horrendous act. His mission complete, he maneuvered his body around in the sand, and began the long and arduous crawl back to where the others waited. In his haste to reach the safety of the cedar trees, he barely felt the hot sand against his body. When he was only a few paces out, he jumped to his feet and closed the distance. As he ran into the shadows, the others surrounded him, anxious to know what he'd discovered.

"Two Ponies, I'm happy you're back!" exclaimed Sky Feather, pulling him into a quick embrace. "That was a long, hot crawl in the open."

"What did you see, Two Ponies?" asked Jin.

"Winter Bird's falling star *is* indeed the Wolfen's asteroid!" exclaimed Two Ponies, reaching for his waterskin. "To the south, I saw the great hole where it slammed into the earth. It left a deep track in the sand as it rolled to where it now rests."

"As I suspected," said Jin. "Did you see any sign of the Wolfen?"

"I did," replied Two Ponies. "I saw Broken Ear and two of his companions. The smaller one wasn't with them."

"Why would they leave their asteroid?" asked Jin, rubbing his chin. "Your sun is still too high."

Two Ponies drank deep from his waterskin before answering Jin's question. "I'm not sure how, Jin, but I watched them walk out of the boulder *not* the asteroid."

"What are you saying?" asked Winter Bird. "There's no hole in the face of that boulder. I've hunted here all my life, and I would have known about any cave."

"It's not a cave as we know it, Winter Bird," insisted Two Ponies. "The face of the rock slid away to reveal an opening *into* the boulder. After the Wolfen stepped out, this strange opening closed."

"So, the Wolfen have retreated underground," said Jin, stepping over to peer out at the blackened asteroid.

"Are you saying that Two Ponies speaks the truth?" asked Winter Bird.

"I am," replied Jin, turning. "It seems our Wolfen friends have discovered the abandoned underground passageways that run beneath the desert. They must have scanned the surface and located the closest entrance. That's how they knew where to position their asteroid. Very clever."

"I also watched Broken Ear walk into the side of his asteroid," said Two Ponies. "He touched its surface, and a door slid open. It's magic!"

"It's not magic, Two Ponies," said Jin. "It's technology. The Wolfen are very clever, indeed."

"They're also vile creatures," said Two Ponies, in disgust. "Broken Ear ate a jackrabbit—alive!"

"The Wolfen are known for that," said Jin. "But it's not just the wildlife they have a taste for. Remember the warning Vonn and I gave you earlier? The queen needs your planet's people to feed her armies."

"It sickens me just to think about that," said Sky Feather.

"I've more to tell you," said Two Ponies. "I watched Broken Ear's companions change into two fat coyotes and run off toward the north."

"Then our time is short," said Jin. "The Reptoid female is sending her scouts farther and farther out, expanding her search."

"The she-snake has already discovered the Hopi," said Sky Feather. "They live on a great high mesa to the north. She killed two of their women."

"With her venom," added Winter Bird. "What happens if she discovers there are others besides us?"

"Plenty," replied Jin. "At the moment she sees only a few servings of bony flesh on a bed of hot sand and rocks. If she should discover that this world is a plump feast on a bed of lush greens, she'll ring the dinner bell!"

"What's our next move?" asked Sky Feather.

"We'll rejoin the others," replied Jin, sliding onto his horse. The mare immediately began to do a fancy sidestep, and Jin stiffened. After taking three steps backward, it finally settled.

"You need to tighten up on the reins, Jin," said Winter Bird. "You and the horse must become one. Only then will it know what you want it to do."

"On my world, our means of transportation is mechanical and operated by our minds," said Jin, reaching down to rub the horse's ears. "I simply make a wish, and it responds to fulfill that wish."

"Is that so?" asked Sky Feather, sliding onto his own horse. "Does that work on your women, as well?"

"Unfortunately, no," replied Jin, with a grin. "Even with our advanced technology, we've yet to accomplish that feat. I am curious about the horse though. How can you control something that obviously has a mind of its own?"

"Logic, my friend," replied Sky Feather. "In my opinion, horses are much like women. You have to make them believe what *you* wish for them to do, is actually *their* idea."

"Fascinating," remarked Jin, "That's the same strategy I use on Vonn."

"Does it work?" asked Sky Feather.

"Actually, it does," replied Jin. "But don't tell him!"

Turning his horse, he led the others from the trees.

CHAPTER 17

When Jin and his search party rode into the village, Walks Far was there to collect their horses and to inform them that Vonn and the others had not yet returned.

"Will you eat with us in our hogan, Jin?" asked Sky Feather.

"I could use a good meal," said Jin. "Winter Bird, we'll need a watchman until Vonn and the others return."

"I'll watch over the village," said Winter Bird.

"Two Ponies?" asked Sky Feather.

"I'll walk with Winter Bird for a while, Father," he replied. "Then I'll join you."

As the two men walked near the river, Two Ponies voiced his concerns. "The she-snake has already killed within the village, Winter Bird," he said. "What's stopping her and her Wolfen from attacking us? I hate this game of waiting."

"As do I," said Winter Bird, scanning the horizon. "Remember the words of Vonn. He said neither the she-snake nor the Wolfen will come out of hiding while the sun burns hot. Even Standing Deer died just as the sun was rising. I never thought I'd be grateful for the blistering heat of the desert sun."

When Morning Song joined Winter Bird with his meal, Two Ponies made his way to his parents' hogan. Before entering, he glanced around the village. Several of the children played quietly in front of their hogans while their mothers hovered nearby. He knew they would take no chances with their children's safety. The sheep still sought refuge around the central firepit. Remembering what the Wolfen leader did to the jackrabbit, he couldn't blame them.

Slipping into his parents' hogan, Two Ponies quietly settled himself near the fire. Sky Feather smoked his pipe while Jin lounged on a sheepskin rug. Nearby, Blue Corn quietly prepared their meal.

"Welcome, son," said Sky Feather. "I take it all is quiet in the village?"

"For the moment," replied Two Ponies. "The stillness has me on edge though. I'm anxious to deal with this menace once and for all."

"Don't be too anxious, Two Ponies," warned Jin. "When the time comes, it'll get extremely ugly. The Wolfen will fight dirty."

"I don't doubt they will," said Sky Feather, shaking his head. "If the Wolfen were native to this area, I'd give their leader the name Fights Without Honor. How appropriate."

"I'm curious, Sky Feather," said Jin. "How does one acquire their name among your people? Sky. Feather. Odd."

"I was given my name by the old shaman, Ghost Dancer," replied Sky Feather. "At fourteen winters, my father prepared me for my vision quest and sent me out into the desert to the south. I walked for three days until I found myself sitting on a small outcropping of stone that overlooked the little valley of the painted rocks. I was tired, hungry, and worried that if I didn't have my vision soon, I was going to die of starvation. I'm not one to skip a meal. Anyway, I was sitting and thinking of my mother's corn cakes, when a white feather floated down from the sky and landed in the palm of my left hand. I quickly closed my fingers around it and sent a prayer to the grandfathers, thanking them for this wonderful gift. When I opened my fingers to look at the feather, a gust of wind caught it up and took it out over the little painted valley, and in moments it was gone."

"What did you do?" asked Jin.

"What do you think I did?" asked Sky Feather, smiling. "I headed for my home and its comforts. I did nothing until I had a full belly. When I told the old shaman of the feather that came from the sky, he gave me the name of Sky Feather."

"That's quite a story," said Jin.

"Speaking of stories," said Two Ponies. "I would truly love to hear one about the great battles you've fought among the stars."

"Well, I might have one I can tell you," said Jin, looking up to think. "I guess I could tell you why I fight the Reptoids. I entered the Galactic Federation Academy when I was only two hundred of your earth years. I was the youngest to ever serve in the Ninth Realm. But I had an uncle who knew someone in the upper echelon, so I was accepted. I had large boots to fill."

"You were only two hundred, huh?" asked Sky Feather, smiling. "That's nearly three times our life span."

"At that age, I was barely considered a man," said Jin. "At what age do you reach manhood?"

"Fourteen," replied Two Ponies.

"For real?" asked Jin, in disbelief. "At that age, I wasn't even weaned."

"At what age did you learn to fight?" asked Two Ponies. "I learned to shoot the bow and arrow when I was six."

"I was brought up on a world where you begin your combat training soon after you've learned to walk," replied Jin. "After entering the Academy, I excelled quickly as I loved the challenge. I got along well enough with my peers, as well as all my teachers. In my final year at the academy, however, I had a combat instructor named Klack—big brute of a man. He had gills and breathed pure argon gas. It gave him the worst breath in the morning. He was the instructor you hoped you *didn't* get; however, he was the best teacher of the old arts. He could fling projectiles at you at hyper-speed. Either you deflected them, or you went home with a black eye and a demerit. I quickly learned to deflect them."

"My first father gave me my long bow when I was six," said Two Ponies. "But it was Sky Feather who taught me to fight."

"Is that so?" asked Jin. "My father spent my entire childhood in space, working aboard a science vessel. I barely knew him. Anyway, after cadet training, I was given my first assignment. My fellow recruit, Wika, and I, were issued a small observation scout ship and sent to observe a mining planet in the Gamma Quadrant called Dresdan IV. It was home to about four thousand mine workers and support crew. There was an outbreak of deadly Serin fever on the surface, and the Federation placed it under quarantine to prevent it from spreading to other worlds. Our job was to see that no one left Dresdan IV until the fever had burned itself out. Our strategy was simple: We surrounded the planet with a force field that could detect any organic life-forms attempting to leave the surface. You could go in, but you couldn't leave—just your standard stop-gap to prevent anyone in an escape pod from slipping out undetected. If someone attempted to leave the planet, the force field would cause the kinetic energy in their body to heat up their organs to very painful levels. Essentially, it was a cheap but remarkably effective guard bot."

"A guard bot?" asked Sky Feather. "Can I assume this is the equivalent of a good warrior?"

"One worth his weight in Cyconian crystals!" exclaimed Jin. Suddenly his smile faded, and he looked at them in all seriousness. "Please, I beg you, you must never breathe a word of what I'm telling you to Vonn. He would be very unhappy. He's all about protecting the Prime Directive and not revealing our advanced technology to the primitives."

"Your story is safe with us," said Sky Feather. "As we have no idea what you are saying, how will we ever hope to repeat your words?"

"Point taken," said Jin, relaxing back onto his elbows. "Anyway, there we were, three days into our assignment, when Wika detected a slight fluctuation in our Ion Detection System."

"Your what?" asked Sky Feather.

"Ion Detection System," replied Jin. "We smelled something. So, I did a quick perimeter scan but saw nothing. Probably just a spark of black matter, I deduced. Nasty stuff, that black matter. We'd just resumed our game of Quark, I was winning for once, when something rocked our ship, nearly throwing us out of our seats. We both flew to our consoles just in time to see them light up like a thousand suns. This time, when I scanned the thermosphere, what do you think I saw on my monitor?"

"I'm at a loss for words, Jin," stated Sky Feather, laughing.

"Well, I'll tell you what I saw," continued Jin. "I saw a massive Alpha Draconian battle cruiser. And, it was looking right down our throat. Well, I felt like a Calloyian Thwort Beetle under a magnifier. I could not believe I didn't see this thing coming! I was sure they'd used some kind of a cloaking device to sneak up on us."

"Is that so?" asked Two Ponies. "A well-trained Dine' warrior would never allow the enemy to sneak up on him. If he did, he would never admit it to anyone," he added, with a smile.

"Well, it wasn't my fault," said Jin. "Our small scout ship wasn't equipped to read fluctuations in interstellar space."

"Well, then you are forgiven," said Two Ponies. "Please go on."

"Well, I'd learned of these cloaking devices while in the academy, but never actually witnessed one in action," continued Jin. "Plasma Stealth isn't taught to new recruits. As a result, I was now getting a crash course in identifying ionized plasma radiation. When the captain hailed me on the communication screen, I felt my feet melt out from beneath me. It was Slagg."

"Slagg?" chorused Two Ponies and Sky Feather.

"In the flesh!" exclaimed Jin. "He's only the meanest, most vile Reptoid to ever pilot a battle cruiser. He was the queen's most loyal fighter, so he had her ear. I've no doubt it's how he's stayed alive all these years. Well, he immediately started barking questions at me. Why was I here? How many men were aboard our ship? Were we armed? Well, I wasn't about to tell him it was just Wika and myself—bad strategy there. So, I informed him that we were a squad of fifteen and that our ship was armed with four thermite high-velocity missiles. Actually, we were running light, as it was only a surveillance mission. I've always been good at handling the truth carelessly. You have to be when you're in my line of work. Well, Slagg then informed me that he was on a recovery mission, and if I didn't get out of his way, he would blast me out of existence. At that point, I wondered just what he wished to recover. With just a few inquiries on the Cybernetic Stream, I discovered just why he was there. Three days before the outbreak, the Union had delivered a payload of Cyconian crystals to the surface, and he was there to help himself to them."

"What are these Cy … conian crystals?" asked Sky Feather, with a look of confusion.

"It's a material used by the miners on Dresdan IV," replied Jin. "It can turn sunlight into a particle beam, which revolutionized the process of cutter-ray mining. But the crystals can also be used to manipulate a quantum accelerator. If you know how, you can create a wormhole anywhere in space. Don't ask—I'd be here all night explaining that one. Anyway, these crystals are extremely valuable on the black market. Old Slagg must have figured he could sweep in undetected and claim them for himself."

"Then what happened?" asked Two Ponies.

"I informed Slagg there was an epidemic of Serin fever on the surface," replied Jin. "He foolishly ignored me, which was his style. No Reptoid captain, if he has any common sense, would expose his men to Serin fever.

It's a nasty microbe that, in just a few hours, can turn a Reptoid into a terrestrial gastropod."

"Now what is that?" asked Two Ponies.

"Basically, your average earth slug," replied Jin. "Well, after this bit of news, I was sure Slagg would hightail it out of there. Instead, he broke off all communications and immediately took a small transport down to the surface. When I contacted the Draconian ship, Slagg's first officer, Borr, informed me that it was Slagg himself leading the small band of ten thieves down to the surface. Now we had four thousand and eleven souls to watch over."

"So, was that the end of old Slagg?" asked Sky Feather.

"I wish!" exclaimed Jin. "It wasn't long before he was again hailing my ship and demanding that I turn off the force field. He and his men wanted off the plant as there were sick people everywhere. 'Yeah, well, I tried to tell you that,' I told him. I refused to do his bidding, and joyfully informed him that he was now stranded there until the Federation lifted the quarantine. Somewhere in his ranting and raving, I was given a choice: if I didn't allow him and his thieves to leave, he was going to have his fully armed battle cruiser destroy me *and* the force field."

"Amazing," said Sky Feather. "I certainly wouldn't want to be faced with such a choice."

"Well, neither did I," replied Jin. "I could either let Slagg spread the fever throughout the galaxy, thus failing my very first mission, or go out in a blaze of glory. I decided to do neither. I was just about to contact Borr and to try to reason with him, when the unthinkable happened."

"Now you have my attention, Jin," remarked Blue Corn, coming to sit beside her husband. "What happened?"

"The Draconian battle cruiser began to pull away, and in seconds it was only a vapor trail," he replied.

"They just abandoned their chief on a dying world?" asked Two Ponies. "What loyalty is this?"

"You must understand the Reptoids, my friend," said Jin. "One doesn't serve under them willingly. Those men were given a simple choice: serve or die. Slagg was a cruel and deadly taskmaster. Borr's loyalty to his captain was never an issue here, I assure you. I have deduced that Slagg's crew were monitoring the exchange between their captain and me. And when they realized Slagg was unable to return to his ship, they saw their chance at freedom and fled."

"And is this the end of your tale?" asked Two Ponies.

"Not quite," replied Jin. When I informed the Federation that I had the notorious Slagg as a prisoner on Dresdan IV, they immediately sent me back-up. They'd been searching for him for over two-thousand of your earth years. For our bravery and quick thinking, Wika and I received five Excellence of Merit points in our permanent records. Of course, as Wika's superior by three weeks, I claimed all bragging rights when the girls began to gather in clusters to hear of our bravery."

"So, what became of Slagg?" asked Blue Corn.

"He got just what he deserved," replied Jin. "Somehow, he managed to survive the fever, and when the quarantine was lifted the Federation took him into custody. I must say, the miners were ready to rid themselves of him. Apparently, he'd made quite a nuisance of himself. Despite his association with the queen, he was sentenced to a life of hard labor in a hot, high-security penal colony, located on a remote planet in the Vesta Star System. And since a Reptoid can live up to thirty-six thousand earth years, he'll be toiling away for a very long time."

"That was indeed a story of courage," said Sky Feather. "I understood very little of your words, but you used them well."

"Someday I'll return and tell you why I fight the beings from Zeta Reticuli," said Jin. "They're known as the Grays. Dirty little fighters, the Grays."

Jin sat up when Winter Bird entered the hogan.

"The others have returned," said Winter Bird.

"Who's on watch?" asked Jin.

"Three Feathers," replied Winter Bird.

When Vonn stepped in, Jin fell silent.

"I've come to inform you of our success in bioregenerating the bones of your fallen warriors," Vonn stated, finding a place beside Jin.

"Where are they now?" asked Winter Bird. "I would very much like to see them."

"Bioregeneration is not an instant process," replied Vonn. "It'll take some time to complete. We have, however, set the process in motion. Now we wait."

"I've prepared food," said Blue Corn. "Vonn, will you eat sheep and vegetables with us?"

Vonn's face took on a look of confusion. Leaning toward Jin, he questioned him.

"*Will* we eat sheep and vegetables?" he asked. "And what is this ... sheep?"

"Sheep?" replied Jin, shrugging his shoulders. "I believe it's the fluffy white mammals pushing and shoving each other in the center of this village."

"The four-legged beasts making that horrible whining noise?" asked Vonn. "They show no sense in their actions!"

"I believe, Blue Corn, Vonn will eat the vegetables only," said Jin. "I'll take a portion of the sheep though. I'm curious."

"It's the staple of our people," said Blue Corn, passing him the wooden platter holding the meat and vegetables.

Jin picked up a small piece of meat and placed it in his mouth. "It's very good!" he said, choosing a larger piece. "Yes, I could get used to eating this sheep very quickly."

"Unfortunately for our flock, Broken Ear thinks the same way you do," said Sky Feather, shaking his head. "He's eaten enough for ten wolves!"

Gray Wolf entered just as they were finishing their meal. "Vonn, after your long day, you must be in need of rest," he said. "Our Hopi friends bid you to share their hogan."

"Thank you, Gray Wolf," said Vonn, getting to his feet. "I have my own accommodations. But I would very much like to speak with you on an urgent matter."

"Then we'll go to my hogan," stated Gray Wolf.

"Excellent," said Vonn. Turning to Winter Bird, he added, "We'll need to set at least two watchman this evening. The Wolfen are close. I don't understand why they haven't shown themselves or attacked the village. Odd. Very odd."

"That's my concern," stated Two Ponies.

"Mine as well," said Jin, rising. "Vonn, I'm going to check the perimeter of the village before sunset."

"Very well," said Vonn. "I'll await your report."

Two Ponies felt uneasy as he joined Jin on his walk. According to

Vonn, the Wolfen would be venturing out of their asteroid soon, and he did not want to run into them in the dark.

As he and Jin made their way to the river, Jin talked of his home planet that orbited the giant red star called Arcturus. Two Ponies listened with rapt attention and wished he could visit this marvelous world.

"See that star constellation to your north?" asked Jin, pointing to the northern sky. "Your astronomers call it the Big Dipper."

"To us it's known as the Great Drinking Gourd," said Two Ponies, gazing upward.

"Well, just off the curve of the handle lies my home world," said Jin.

"Is it far?" asked Two Ponies.

"It would be for you, my friend," replied Jin. "To reach my home, you would need an immensely powerful starship to span the vast distances of space. Come, I want to show you something that will utterly amaze you. Something that, again, must remain our secret."

Jin led Two Ponies east, along the river. Not far from the edge of the village, they came to a halt in the middle of nowhere. Before them lay open desert.

"Jin, I've walked this desert all my life," remarked Two Ponies, glancing around. "If something amazing lay in my world, the Dine' would already know about it."

"Oh, what I have to show you is not of *your* world, Two Ponies," said Jin. "It's actually of *mine*."

Stepping forward, Jin touched a small device on his belt, and a large dark gray object materialized out of thin air. Two Ponies looked on in total amazement.

"Out of nothing, appears something," he said.

CHAPTER 18

Two Ponies gazed up in wonder at the long dark gray object. Its long metallic body, stretching across the sand for fifty paces, rested on four short sturdy legs. It reminded him of one of the dark beetles that scurried about atop the sand. Protruding from its sides were two short, black, V-shaped wings. In the face of this great beetle, two small eyes were set ablaze by the setting sun. Curious, he reached out his hand to touch its surface. His mind, however, recalled what happened when Three Feathers touched the black stone, and he withdrew his hand.

"What is it?" he asked Jin. "It looks like a great winged beetle."

"This, my friend, is the XRV-330," replied Jin, proudly. "It's a sturdy little scout ship, only used when a short trip through space is required. These wings, as you call them, are two sub-light engines capable of reaching impulse velocity."

"Is that fast?" asked Two Ponies, thinking of his horse running at a full gallop.

"It's not bad," replied Jin. "I've seen them run faster, though. I have a Serian friend who is a master at modifying a sub-light engine. The XRV-330 is capable of hosting a crew of eight but will comfortably accommodate only two."

"It still looks like a huge bug," commented Two Ponies.

"So, it does," said Jin, smiling. "This "bug", however, can travel 190 kilometers per second when you open her up. I know, as I've had her at top speed a few times. It makes Vonn nauseous. That fact alone makes it worth the risk."

"So, your world is only a short trip from here?" asked Two Ponies.

"No. Allow me to explain," said Jin. "The XCV-330 is only a scout ship. Our main galaxy-class cruiser is parked on the back side of your moon."

"You've been to the moon!" exclaimed Two Ponies, in awe.

"Of course," replied Jin. "It's amazing. There's a huge spaceport located there. It's like a village, but many, many times larger than yours. Oh, Two Ponies, I wish I could show you just a portion of the wonders I've seen in outer space. Your night sky is so much bigger than you can ever imagine."

"Is this "outer space" larger than the desert?" asked Two Ponies, trying to put it all into prospective.

"See that rock formation in the distance?" asked Jin, pointing toward the east. "It would take you roughly seven earth days to reach it on foot. In outer space, vast distances stretch out so far that you could walk for millions and millions of *years* and still not reach the closest star that shines in your night sky. Your great-great-great-grandchildren, Two Ponies, will someday build their own starships, much like this one. They'll use them to fly up to your moon and visit the great spaceport that exists on its far side. From there, they'll travel to other worlds, other star systems. Perhaps, one day, they might even visit my home world."

"Amazing!" exclaimed Two Ponies, looking up at Jin's scout ship. "When I pulled Three Feathers from the black stone, I found myself inside a great iron beast. When I looked out the large hole in its wall, I saw below me the glowing blue ball you say is my world. I was floating in the night sky, Jin! Is your beast similar to that belonging to the female Reptoid?"

"No. Her ship is much larger than this one," replied Jin. "My smaller ship was built to withstand the force of entering your planet's atmosphere. Its outer hull is 40 layers of Terrilium-grade ceramic fibers, gamma welded into a hard deflector shield. In other words, I can land my ship on Earth; she cannot."

"How does she get from her sky ship to the desert?" asked Two Ponies.

"It's a process called teleportation," replied Jin. "She can turn her body into energy and transfer it to Earth without traversing the physical space in which—never mind, my friend. Let's just say, she comes down in a bolt of lightning."

"Amazing," repeated Two Ponies, trying to imagine riding on a lightning bolt. "I hope your beast smells better than hers. Hers smells like a dead sheep!"

"Vonn is thinking of me," said Jin, glancing back in the direction of the village.

"How do you know?" asked Two Ponies.

"Telepathy, my friend," replied Jin. "If he's thinking about me, he's wondering where I am. We must return immediately. Now, as I said, this must remain our secret, Two Ponies. If Vonn found out I revealed our ship to you, he'd hand me my backside."

"Your secret is safe with me," said Two Ponies, once more gazing up at Jin's ship. Feeling more confident now, he placed his palm against its dark exterior. It surprisingly felt cool to the touch. Stepping back, he knew he would remember this day for the rest of his life.

"I think we'll go back along the river," said Jin.

"What about your ship?" asked Two Ponies. "The others will see it."

"I'll just make it disappear," said Jin, touching the small device on his belt. "It has a cloaking device that—never mind. Let's go."

Two Ponies watched in awe as Jin's ship faded away, leaving only the open desert.

"Amazing," he muttered again as they turned and headed back down river.

Returning to the village, Two Ponies and Jin parted ways. To the east, the moon was rising fast, and Two Ponies stopped to gaze at it. He thought of Jin's scout ship and its ability to fly there. Was there truly a village on its backside? He found himself wishing he could live in that far-off distant time when his grandchildren's grandchildren would build such an amazing thing as a spaceship. If he lived in that future time, he would definitely fly one to the moon to explore its pockmarked face. What wonders would he find there?

Shaking himself free from his dream, Two Ponies went to feed the small female dog. On his waist belt, he carried a woven reed pouch containing a small handful of meat scraps from his dinner. Slipping behind his hogan, he called the small dog from her hiding place in the shadows. As she ate, he gently stroked her soft fur. After she fell asleep, he crawled from the bushes and went to check on the sheep milling among the hogans. With the flock now staying virtually within the village, it was hunger that now fueled their stressful bleating. Even though the open lands to the south held large patches of tall deer grass, the sheep still refused to venture out to feed. Kneeling, he rubbed the head of a large ewe to soothe her.

"Rest easy, old girl," he said, softly. "We'll soon send these Wolfen dogs back to their own world. Then you can return to your grazing land. I'll go and gather some grass for you."

Leaving the sheep, he made his way down the path leading to the river. When he neared the spot where Standing Deer was killed, he hesitated. The memory of his friend's horrible death still angered him. When nothing stirred, he continued. At the river, he spotted a large patch of long deer grass. Using his knife, he soon harvested an armload. When he caught the sound of rustling in the tall grass behind him, he halted. Something large was approaching the clearing. Dropping the armload, he turned and drew his knife. He held his breath as the tall grass slowly parted and a large buck deer stepped out. He released his breath in a short nervous laugh.

"Phew!" he exclaimed, sheathing his knife. "You're lucky, my friend. I nearly dealt you a hard blow. Now go and seek cover among the hills."

He expected the deer to bolt in fear; however, it just stood watching him with its large brown eyes. Two Ponies took a small step forward, and still the deer did not bolt. What happened next stunned him to his core. The deer's two black rear hooves and thin hair-covered legs slowly faded into a pair of light brown moccasins and worn leather pants. A moment later, the deer's thick hairy body curved upward, and its white chest darkened into a brown woolen shirt and a pair of crossed arms. Two Ponies stared in disbelief as the deer's short brown hair grew out into two waist-length locks of ebony hair, and its muzzle flattened into the copper-skinned face of a man. The last to disappear were the deer's two large antlers. Two Ponies smiled broadly as he stared into the serious face of his childhood friend, Red Otter. He was just about to step forward when a thought struck him. Was this truly Red Otter, or was he staring into the face of a Wolfen shape-shifter? Then Red Otter's face broke into the familiar crooked grin he'd worn since childhood.

"Well, are you just going to stand there and stare?" he asked. "Or are you going to tell me how much you've missed me?"

His words shook Two Ponies' free of his fear. "My friend, how can this be?" he asked, through a tight throat. "I stood over your dead body."

"Bioregeneration," replied Red Otter. "I've met the sky helper, Vonn.

And I'm not sure how, but he's given me new life. You wouldn't believe where I've been!"

"Well, I'm glad you're back!" exclaimed Two Ponies, pulling his friend into a tight embrace. "I'll fight well with you by my side."

"You will, indeed," remarked Red Otter. "I will again have your back, Two Ponies. Just like old times."

"I'm sorry, Red Otter, that I wasn't there when you—"

"No apology needed, my brother," said Red Otter. "It was as it should be. I have renewed an old friendship, Two Ponies. After my grandfather died, I would often sit in his empty hogan and tell his spirit all about my day. As the years passed, the boy inside me never stopped missing him. It was my grandfather who found me and led me away from the pain of my wounds. Now it is he who sits and tells me of *his* day."

"This comforts me," said Two Ponies.

"Let's not think about that now," said Red Otter. "So, what's happened since my demise?"

The two friends settled beside the river, and Two Ponies filled Red Otter in on all that had transpired since the killings at the scout camp. Time, for them, slipped away as the sun dropped below the western horizon. For Two Ponies, the world in shadow no longer felt as intimidating now that Red Otter was back. But one thing still intrigued him.

"How were you able to approach me as a deer?" he asked.

"It must be Vonn's bioregeneration," replied Red Otter. "I made a silent wish to surprise you as a deer, and a moment later, I had antlers. It was amazing!"

When Two Ponies spotted Sky Feather coming down the river path, he motioned him over.

"Father, come see who lives again!" he exclaimed.

"Red Otter! You'll be a sight for your old mother's eyes," said Sky Feather, with obvious delight. "Singing Waters has mourned you with a broken heart."

"I'm not going to see her," said Red Otter, sadly. "She will only have to face my death all over again when my time is over. Vonn warned us that our new life will be short lived."

"You're right in your decision, of course," said Sky Feather.

"What of Dark Bear and Little Hawk?" asked Two Ponies.

"They, too, live again," replied Red Otter. "But like me, they've made the decision not to reveal themselves to their families. We have returned for only one purpose, Two Ponies. And that is to help you fight the she-snake and her Wolfen dogs. As I've said, our time is short."

"Then we'll put all else aside and teach this enemy a well-earned lesson," exclaimed Sky Feather. "If you mess with the Dine', you'll receive a good sting!"

"Well said," said Two Ponies.

"What happens next, Sky Feather?" asked Red Otter.

"At sunrise we'll begin preparations to confront the Wolfen," he replied.

"I'm ready to start this fight now!" declared Red Otter. "Vonn's plan, however, will take time to unfold."

"Did they tell you Standing Deer is dead?" asked Sky Feather. "He was also killed by the Reptoid's venom. He was a good man."

"Yes, he was," said Red Otter.

"He, too, is missed by his family," added Sky Feather. "I have to admit, I, too, miss him."

"That's nice to know, my friend!" said a familiar voice behind him. "And, I've missed you too!"

"Standing Deer!" shouted Sky Feather, turning. "My old friend, how are you?"

"Much better than I was the morning I faced that murdering she-snake!" he said, stepping forward. "It *is* a female, by the way. But fear not, I've returned to free my people from her venomous wrath."

"Have you now?" asked Sky Feather, embracing him. "Do we now have a new crowing rooster to contend with?"

"For a short time, yes," said Standing Deer. "Sky Feather, how are my wife and daughter?"

"They miss you," he replied. "But our people are caring for them."

"I'm pleased," he said, sadly. "I won't return to them. It's a hard decision, I assure you."

"It's for the best," said Red Otter.

"And how is Little Doe?" asked Standing Deer.

"She's coping," replied Sky Feather. "She had quite a fright. What happened?"

"I was returning to the river, when I met her running back up the path," he replied. "The poor girl was terrified! She told me a snake tried to grab her. I was taking her back to the village when I heard something behind me. When I turned, the she-snake stepped out of the tall grass. Before I could unsheathe my knife, she opened her mouth and hit me right between the eyes with her hot venom. I didn't suffer long."

"You saved the life of Little Doe," said Sky Feather.

"Then my death was not in vain," said Standing Deer.

"Nor was mine," said Red Otter. "I was able to warn my people of her and her wolf. Now, since I no longer require sleep, I'll watch over the village tonight. Standing Deer, perhaps you'll stay with me while these brave warriors sleep?"

"I will, my friend," replied Standing Deer. "We've much to share."

All turned their heads at the far-off howl of a wolf.

"Do you hear the Wolfen leader?" asked Sky Feather. "I wonder: Where are his companions?"

His question was answered only a moment later when their answering howls drifted in from the north.

"Rest well, my friends," said Standing Deer. "We'll watch for them."

"Night approaches," said Sky Feather. "The female Reptoid may be with them."

"She's no longer a threat to us, Sky Feather," said Standing Deer. "Vonn has assured us that we're now immune to her venom."

Two Ponies, remembering what brought him to the river, gathered up his armload of cut grass. After seeing Sky Feather to his hogan, he spread his armload on the ground for the sheep. After one final glance around the village, he slipped into his hogan and dropped the woolen hide over the door. Stirring his fire to clear the chill from the air, he undressed and stretched out on his sleeping mat. As he lay on his side, watching the flames, he wondered what strange magic now brought his childhood friend back to him from the land of the dead. Rolling to his back, he fell asleep to the quiet crackling of the fire.

His dream was a memory of Red Otter, and himself, as boys. The day was hot, and the two of them were cooling off in the river. Their happy boyhood laughter sounded carefree as they floated on the gently moving water. He loved the feeling of the coolness on his back while the sun's heat warmed his face and chest. Suddenly the loud bleating of sheep broke the serene moment, and the scene vanished. Two Ponies startled awake and sat up. *Something is disturbing the sheep*, he thought, jumping to his feet.

"Two Ponies, are you awake?" asked a disembodied voice. "Two Ponies?"

"I'm awake," he replied. "Is that you, Red Otter?"

"It is. I'm behind your hogan. We have an enemy among us. Come out this way so you don't spook it."

Two Ponies quickly pulled on his woolen shirt and leather pants. Slipping his knife and sheath into his leather belt, he slid his feet into his moccasins and stepped to the back of his hogan. Pushing aside the wooden box containing his eating dishes and extra food, he removed a section of the back wall just big enough for his body to slip through. This was his secret door, cut there to insure a quick escape. During the long-ago night when the Spanish raiders attacked his village, his parents were killed just inside the door, trapped like rabbits in a hole. With no way to escape, they were helpless. A soldier, finding his way inside, cut them down with his long knife. He'd survived only because his father used his tomahawk to quickly chop a small hole in the rear wall and push his tiny body out into the night. When he returned to his parents' hogan after his vision quest, he enlarged the small hole that same day. Only Red Otter knew of this secret door. Now, slipping through it, he closed it quietly behind him. The little female dog, huddling nearby, whimpered softly, and Two Ponies reached out to scratch her on the ears.

"Guard my hogan well, my friend," he whispered, softly. Giving off a soft whine, the small dog shrank back into the shadows. Continuing through the low brush, he found Red Otter squatted on one knee, his knife drawn.

"What's happening?" asked Two Ponies, squatting down beside him on the sand.

"Follow me," whispered Red Otter.

Bending low, the two quietly made their way between the hogans. The sheep, bunched up near the central firepit, moved nervously in a mob. The moon overhead bathed everything in ghostly shadows.

"What has you concerned?" asked Two Ponies, his eyes straining. "I see nothing beyond the sheep."

"Don't look *beyond* the sheep, Two Ponies," whispered Red Otter.

"Look *among* them, in front of Black Crow's hogan. Do you see that odd-looking sheep slowly making its way toward that ewe and her lamb? I think we have a shape-shifter among the flock."

"I see it," whispered Two Ponies. "It could be one of the Wolfen. Jin told us they often have trouble maintaining the shape of the animal they're trying to mimic. He warned us they may appear misshapen and unsteady on their feet."

The sheep in question was indeed having difficulty walking. Its head appeared too large for its body, and it stumbled several times in its attempt to walk on all fours. The closer it got to the mother sheep, the more it struggled to move forward. It was just about to pounce on the tiny helpless lamb, when a man suddenly jumped from out of the shadows and struck the faltering sheep on the back of the head with a small war club. The sheep immediately fell to its belly and grew still. Two Ponies and Red Otter hurried over.

"Good job, Standing Deer," said Red Otter. "We've taken our first enemy prisoner."

"How can we be sure it's one of the Wolfen?" asked Two Ponies.

As the three friends looked down at the motionless sheep at their feet, its curly woolen coat slowly darkened into the thick gray-and-black hair of a wolf. Red Otter, using his foot, turned the creature over onto its back. The bright moonlight overhead sparkled off the silver ring in his nose.

"It's Jin's Shetu," said Two Ponies. "See his silver nose ring? He was with the others at the sacred mountain."

"Is that so?" asked Standing Deer. "We need to drag him away from the sheep. Their ruckus will awaken the children."

"Wait," said Red Otter. "I think we should bind our Silver Ring's hands and feet to prevent his escape when he awakens."

"Good idea," said Two Ponies. "I'll fetch a rope.

It took all three men to drag the heavy Shetu over to the river path.

"We'll take it from here, Two Ponies," said Standing Deer. "We'll conceal him in that small cave near the river. Little Hawk and I will watch over him."

"Little Hawk is with you?" asked Two Ponies.

"He is," replied Standing Deer. "Dark Bear is there as well."

"I look forward to seeing them again," said Two Ponies. "What happens now that we've captured one of the Wolfen?"

"Hopefully, Vonn and Jin will have the answer to that question," said Standing Deer. "We'll be in the cave."

Two Ponies glanced toward the eastern horizon, where the impending sunrise was just tinting the sky a soft yellow. "It's nearly dawn," he said. "I'll go and wake the others and we'll join you at the river."

Two Ponies waited at the central firepit for the others to join him. Around him, the sheep still stirred restlessly but their frantic bleating had quieted. When Sky Feather, Winter Bird, and Three Feathers emerged from their hogans, the four quickly made their way to the river. Jin and Vonn were already there, and Vonn's face wore a dark scowl.

"I wasn't sure how to contact you," said Two Ponies. "A lot has happened. Just before dawn we—"

"Captured the Shetu?" asked Vonn, glaring at him.

He was obviously not happy with their brave deed. Before he could voice his displeasure, Tall Bull, Gray Wolf, and the three Hopi arrived.

"What has happened?" asked Black Fox, stepping from the path.

"We captured an enemy," said Two Ponies. "Just before dawn he entered our village disguised as one of the sheep. We caught him attempting to steal a lamb. Our clumsy thief turned out to be the Wolfen dog I call Silver Ring. Standing Deer, Red Otter, and I managed to subdue him and take him prisoner. Now we hold the advantage."

"You're wrong," stated Vonn. "Holding the Shetu will only make the Wolfen more aggressive."

"Vonn is right," said Jin. "Your prisoner is the personal slave of the one you call Broken Ear. He wears the ring in his nose to prove this."

"Then we saved him from his fate," said Two Ponies.

"I'm afraid he won't see it that way," said Jin. "He'd rather live as a Wolfen slave then be held captive on a strange planet by an unknown race. He'll be killed if they find him here."

"Why would they kill their own kind?" asked Gray Wolf.

"Actually, the Shetu are not kin to the Wolfen," replied Jin. "Though they are similar in species, they're nothing alike. In fact, they should be pitied. As slaves, they're treated by their masters with disdain and utter contempt."

"What a shame," said Sky Feather. "Perhaps they, too, could use a couple of star helpers such as yourselves."

"We're working on that very thing," said Jin.

"It seems the Shetu is the one feeding the others," said Vonn. "That's why he was after your sheep."

"That's all the more reason to hold him," said Sky Feather. "We'll save our dwindling flock."

"That may be true," said Jin. "But, it could get messy if the Wolfen attempt to retrieve him."

"What will you have us do, Jin?" asked Winter Bird. "Release him to rejoin his pack? I say we keep him and reduce their numbers by one."

"Where is the Shetu now?" asked Vonn.

"He's in that small cave over there," replied Two Ponies, pointing to the deep hollow fissure in the side of a huge rock. "He can't escape. We've bound his legs and wrists."

"Well, use caution," said Jin. "Beware of his bite. The Shetu carry a nasty microbe in their saliva that causes inflammation and infection. Their victims die of septic shock."

"Standing Deer and Little Hawk are with him," said Winter Bird. "I thought they were immune to his bite?"

"They are," replied Jin. "But the rest of you are not. So, give the young Shetu a wide berth."

"What of the female Reptoid?" asked Two Ponies. "What are we to do about her?"

"She won't pose a problem until nightfall," replied Jin. "Even then, we'll leave her to those who are now immune to her venom. The Wolfen, too, will stay hidden until sunset. We must use the daylight hours to prepare ourselves for tonight when we face off with them."

"How are we to fight them?" asked Tall Bull. "Do you still refuse to give us any star weapons?"

"I do," insisted Vonn. "This fight won't require anything more than light weapons, Tall Bull."

"Light weapons won't kill these murderous dogs!" exclaimed Tall Bull. "I must avenge the death of my son. A life for a life!"

"I understand your pain, Tall Bull," said Vonn. "But killing the Wolfen or their Reptoid leader will only bring the wrath of the queen down upon your world. My plan is to drive them away, *not* to kill them."

"Now you see the Hopi way," said Black Fox. "We are peaceful; however, that doesn't mean we won't help you to persuade the enemy to leave."

"How will we do that?" asked Painted Hair. "They are too powerful."

"I have an idea," said Two Ponies. "The sky god Tarus suggested we use the resources of Gaia, our Mother Earth. Last night Sky Feather said we should teach the enemy a "stinging" lesson. Near our village is a nest of scorpions."

"Are these scorpions deadly?" asked Vonn.

"No," replied Gray Wolf. "But their sting will make you yearn for death. It causes painful swelling, muscle spasms, and difficulty breathing."

"This sounds like my kind of weapon," remarked Jin. "What do you have in mind, Two Ponies?"

"I suggest we gather up a few of our thin-shelled friends and introduce them to the Wolfen," replied Two Ponies. "In what manner, I'm not yet sure. But I'll think of something. I may have another little nasty we could use as well."

"I like the way you think, Two Ponies," said Jin, smiling. "What do you say, Tall Bull?"

"Well, if we cannot kill them, we can at least make their time among us unpleasant," he replied.

"Then it's settled," said Vonn. "Two Ponies, you and Jin gather your cave dwellers, and I'll go and check on our Shetu friend. I may be able to learn what the Wolfen have planned—that is, with a bit of persuasion."

"Excellent," said Gray Wolf. "I and my Hopi brothers will go and see the women. Perhaps we can find suitable food for this Shetu. I suppose anything we'd feed a dog would do."

After the group dispersed, Two Ponies returned to his hogan to collect two large woven sacks, two strips of leather, and a small hatchet. Hearing the small dog scratching in the dirt behind his hogan, he filled an earthen crock with fresh water and made his way to the shaded area. Squatting down, he slid the crock in, and the pup began lapping up the water. With her thirst quenched, she came over and licked him on the hand. She was now only a shadow of the playful pup that had only days earlier romped among the children, begging for scraps from their plates. She looked up at Two Ponies through eyes filled with longing.

"You are wise to hide, my friend," he said, softly. "This enemy is one more vicious than even your brave heart can handle. I suspect he has already taken your mate. When we remove this enemy from our land, you and your pups will live in peace." Rising, he went in search of Jin.

The sun was directly overhead when Jin and Two Ponies mounted their horses and rode into the desert in search of their ultimate weapons. A short distance from the village, Two Ponies halted.

"Here's where we'll find our first nasty," he said, sliding from his horse.

"What is this "nasty" you speak of?" asked Jin.

"It's what I call something that is so painful, so unpleasant, that its kiss will make you cry like a baby," replied Two Ponies, with a smile.

"I like this nasty!" exclaimed Jin, rubbing his hands together. "Where do we search first?"

"Do you see that small opening at the base of that pile of large stones?" asked Two Ponies. "That's where we'll find our scorpions."

Taking a woven sack, Two Ponies knelt and used his knife to scoop out the small creatures. When he stood up, the bottom of the sack squirmed as if it were alive. Securing the bag with a strip of leather, he dropped it at Jin's feet.

"I'll put you in charge of nasty number one," he said, pulling the second woven sack from his belt. "Wait here. I'll return with nasty number two."

On foot, Two Ponies made his way in the direction of a tall cedar tree that stood like a lone soldier in the sand. His eyes searched the overhead branches until he spotted his prize. Suspended from a medium-sized branch, a large gray paper nest swayed in the hot breeze. A cloud of black-faced hornets buzzed around its small opening. Shimmying up the tree's trunk, Two Ponies cautiously approached the humming mass from behind. Holding the sack open, he quickly pulled it up and over the nest and secured it with a strip of leather. Using the small hatchet, he chopped the limb free. His easy capture, however, cost him dearly. Pain shot through him as several of the stragglers nailed him on the scalp, legs, and back. Attempting to outrun their onslaught, he quickly retreated to the ground. Grinning through his pain, he held up his prize.

"And what is this?" asked Jin, quickly distancing himself from the noisy, pulsating bag. When a large black bee buzzed his head, Jin raised his hand and swatted at it.

"Jin, stop!" shouted Two Ponies. His warning came too late. The angry bee buried its stinger deep into the exposed flesh of Jin's right arm.

"Ah!" Jin shouted in pain. Before he could swat the hornet, it brazenly buzzed his head and flew away. "What is this creature that bites with the burn of a laser beam?"

"It's called a bee," said Two Ponies. "A hornet, actually. Although you now feel as though you've been struck by lightning, its sting won't kill you."

"Well, it hurts nonetheless!" exclaimed Jin, rubbing his arm. "Is this what you have in store for the Wolfen?"

"It is," replied Two Ponies, grinning. "And inside this bag are a thousand more just like it."

"How can something so small deliver such a painful sting?" asked Jin, examining the red welt forming on his arm.

"The sting of the scorpion is even more painful than the hornet," stated Two Ponies.

"I can't wait," muttered Jin, as he mounted his horse.

After securing the sack of scorpions to the cedar branch, Two Ponies carefully slid onto his own horse. "Now, if you'll take the other end of the branch, we take our angry weapons back to the village."

As they rode in, the children ran to see what they carried in the two large sacks. Vonn and the others were just returning from their visit to see Silver Ring.

"Jin, what's that you're carrying?" asked Vonn, leaning in to examine the sack containing the hornets.

"A weapon more powerful than a quasar!" exclaimed Jin, dismounting. "It's called a hornet. See what just one did to my arm. If I were you, Vonn, I'd stay back!"

"Point taken!" exclaimed Vonn, backing away.

"What of the Shetu?" asked Jin. "He's not injured, I hope."

"No, he's unharmed," replied Vonn. "He's angry though. He's quickly mastered the language of these people and has verbally threatened to have us all annihilated."

"Excellent," said Jin. "This means he's not timid. Was he willing to tell you anything?"

"No," said Vonn. "But I was able to glean all I need to know from his ranting. I might add, he is planning to inform the Shetu Hierarchy of the abuse he's endured. He says he is the son of a Shetu High Chancellor. A lot of good that did him when the Wolfen took him captive."

"We still can't allow him to rejoin the others," said Jin.

"I agree," said Vonn, sighing. "Dark Bear and Little Hawk are willing to watch over him until we have need of him. Though they say he wearies their ears. Here are Gray Wolf and the Hopi. Black Fox and his two companions are willing to help us as long as they aren't forced to kill anything. I'm satisfied with their request."

"What happens next, Vonn?" asked Black Fox, approaching.

"Tonight, we'll deal with the Wolfen," he replied. "We've waited long enough. After your sun sets, Jin and Two Ponies have a surprise for our lupine friends."

"We do," said Jin. "I hope to find them in their asteroid. If they're in the underground tunnel, it could prove a problem for us."

"I have a request," said Black Fox. "I wish to learn what is behind the door that leads into the rock face. It could be the very kiva in which the ant people brought our ancestors to the surface at the end of the First World."

"I understand your curiosity," said Vonn. "But the Wolfen will kill you before you get close to its entrance."

"This is true, Black Fox," said Gray Wolf. "I, too, am curious as to what lies beneath the desert. But I can see no way past the Wolfen. Sadly, we may never learn of the door's secrets."

"I may know of a way to get in," said Two Ponies. "Jin, would Silver Ring know how to open this door leading into the rock?"

"You could ask him," replied Jin. "The most he can do is tell you no, then threaten to have you killed."

"He'd never help us," muttered Black Fox. "He hates us."

"All is not lost, Black Fox," said Two Ponies. "Vonn, how well do *you* know Silver Ring?"

"I know his species," replied Vonn. "I *can* tell you that the Shetu are not aggressive in nature. The Wolfen have forced them to be so. They were once a very peaceful race, not unlike your domestic earth dog. They hate the Wolfen because of this."

"Could the Shetu be persuaded to help us?" asked Two Ponies, looking from Vonn to Jin. "Using his hatred of the Wolfen perhaps we can get him to turn on his captors."

"Impossible!" exclaimed Vonn. "That will never happen."

"Let's listen to his plan, Vonn," said Jin. "Who knows? It may be something even we haven't thought of."

"I'll tell you at the cave," said Two Ponies. "First, I must retrieve the means to set my plan into motion. I'll only be a moment."

"Oh, very well," said Vonn. "Hurry. We've little time to waste."

"May I come with you, Two Ponies?" asked Jin. "I'm curious to see what you have in mind."

Two Ponies led Jin to the rear of his hogan. "Wait here," he said. "I have someone I'd like you to meet."

"Is it part of your plan?" asked Jin.

"It is," replied Two Ponies. Dropping to his knees, he crawled into the brush and retrieved the small brown-and-white dog.

"What's this?" asked Jin. "Why didn't I see this creature before?"

"Because the Wolfen sent her into hiding," replied Two Ponies, handing him the little dog. "She had a companion, but unfortunately he was unable to outrun them."

Accepting the wiggling dog, Jin pulled it against his chest and stroked its short dusty fur. The pup resisted for only a moment, then sensing no danger, began to lick his chin.

"This earth dog is a friendly sort, isn't it?" said Jin. Lifting the small dog, he stared into its face for a long moment. "I'm having difficulty communicating with this species. Its brain is unlike any I've ever encountered. Its only purpose is to eat, sleep, and procreate. It's like holding a Wolfen child, except this species feels no hostility toward me. I sense only affection and a small amount of fear. Odd. How do you converse with it?"

"In my world, Jin, dogs only bark," replied Two Ponies. "We do not talk *with* them; we talk *at* them."

"Odd," Jin said, again. "I must tell you, Two Ponies, I did learn that this dog contains five exact replicas of itself within its body. Did you know this?"

"I did," replied Two Ponies, taking the dog from Jin and cradling it in his arms.

"Wait. You're not going to harm her, are you?" asked Jin.

"No," replied Two Ponies. "I'm actually going to use her to persuade Silver Ring to help us."

"Are you serious?" asked Jin, with a look of surprise. "What makes you so sure the Shetu won't just kill the creature and be done with it?"

"I'm not," replied Two Ponies. "My plan is to use the pup to appeal to his kindred spirit."

Jin fell silent for a long moment, then smiled.

"You know, Two Ponies, this just might work," he said. "Come. Let's go and inform Vonn of your plan. Of course, we may have to choose our words carefully—you know, make him believe this plan will succeed only if we consult his high intellect. How would it look if a primitive species like yourself came up with all the good ideas?"

CHAPTER 19

"You want to what?" exclaimed Vonn, after hearing their plan. "The Shetu boy will not go along with this, I assure you!"

"Perhaps not," said Jin. "But can we at least try Two Ponies' plan?"

"Well, give me a moment to deduce the risks involved in such an endeavor," stated Vonn. "Yes. Yes, I believe the demeanor of the Shetu could be reasoned with, if united with a docile creature similar to his own species."

"Brilliant deduction!" exclaimed Jin. "Vonn, once more you prove your superior intellect. This is, without a doubt, why the Galactic Alliance chose *you* to lead this most important mission."

"It was the most logical conclusion," replied Vonn, looking pleased. "Of course, I also believe the odds are highly against its success."

"Let them try, Vonn," said Black Fox. "Who knows, it just may work."

"Proceed then," he said. "But I will not be responsible for the life of that poor innocent creature."

Jin aimed a knowing smile at Two Ponies.

"I'll come with you," said Black Fox.

"I, too, will come," said Gray Wolf. "This I must see!"

Cradling the pup in his arms, Two Ponies made his way down the river path to the cave. He could hear Silver Ring venting his anger at his captors. Hearing this, the pup snuggled closer to his chest.

"It'll be all right," Two Ponies whispered into the dog's ear. "I'll see that you come to no harm. I promise."

As he neared the cave entrance, the pup suddenly perked up and barked three times. Within the cave, Silver Ring's snarling ceased, and he barked three times in response.

"I don't believe it!" exclaimed Vonn.

"Come. Bring the dog!" said Black Fox, hurrying inside.

Two Ponies hesitated. Suddenly he was having second thoughts on what he was about to do. Did he have the right to endanger the innocent mother-to-be and her unborn pups?

"We're with you, my brother," said Painted Hair. "Neither Spotted Dog, nor I, will allow the dog to come to any harm."

Finding confidence in their words, Two Ponies approached the cave's entrance. Two men stood guard just inside.

"Dark Bear! Little Hawk!" exclaimed Two Ponies, breaking into a huge grin. "You *do* live again."

"We do," said Dark Bear. "Little Hawk and I have been waiting for you."

"How are you, Two Ponies?" asked Little Hawk, his youthful face lighting up. "How is my mother? With my father attending the White Fathers' council at the Red River, I worry about her being alone now that I am dead to her."

"She is well," replied Two Ponies. "The others are caring for her until your father returns."

"And my family?" asked Dark Bear. "How are my wife and my son, Yellow Rabbit?"

"They, too, are being cared for," replied Two Ponies.

"I am glad to hear this," said Dark Bear. "I asked to accompany the others on the scouting party, you know. I was going to bring Yellow Rabbit his first horse."

"He told me," said Two Ponies. "He has his heart set on a stallion with fire in its blood."

"Even I know better than to grant that wish!" exclaimed Dark Bear. "Why are you carrying one of the dogs?"

"It's a gift for our Shetu friend," replied Two Ponies. "I hope it'll make him more agreeable to our needs."

"I wish you well," said Little Hawk, rolling his eyes. "He wearies our ears. He "hates all who live and breathe on this pitiful spinning rock". Dark Bear and I grow tired of his endless threats."

"Come," said Two Ponies. "Let's see if a dog will soothe the savage beast."

Stepping into the cave, he hesitated a moment to allow his eyes to adjust to the low light of the small burning torch, before moving further inside.

As soon as the little dog saw Silver Ring, she squirmed anxiously, and her excited barking echoed off the walls of the cave. Silver Ring, sitting on the stone floor with his back to the wall, tilted back his head and answered the pup's barking with several loud thunderclaps of his own. Straining against the ropes that bound his hands behind his back, he yipped at the small dog excitedly. Unafraid, the pup jumped from Two Ponies' arms and ran straight into the Shetu's lap. There, she licked at his chin. Lowering his head, the angry and desperate Silver Ring suddenly grew docile and calm. A soft moan escaped him as he and the dog bonded.

"I am without words," said Black Fox, shaking his head. "Our Silver Ring seems to have turned from a roaring puma into a purring kitten."

Realizing that he was being discussed, the Shetu stiffened and glared up at his captors.

"I am not this Silver Ring!" he declared, snarling at them in his gruff voice. "I am Aten, son of Atu. I warn you, earth life-forms, my father is a Shetu High Chancellor on my world of Colladron. He will not be pleased to know his only son was abused!"

His outburst surprised Black Fox and Gray Wolf.

"He speaks our tongue well!" exclaimed Black Fox, with surprise.

"I told you so," whispered Dark Bear. "He learns fast! Wait. Now he will threaten to have his father "wipe out our race of hairless primitives and destroy our pitiful world"."

"My father, Atu, will wipe out your race of hairless primitives and destroy your pitiful world!" growled Aten.

"We know who you are, Aten, son of Atu," said Jin, stepping forward.

"Then I demand you release me at once!" Aten exclaimed, straining against his ropes. "At least the Wolfen didn't restrain my hands and feet and force me to sit in a hole in the ground." In his lap, the little dog buried her head under his arm.

"You're correct, Aten," said Jin. "They restrained you with cruelty and violence when you failed to obey them, didn't they? You are *not* our prisoner. You're simply being detained."

"If your plan is to kill me, Jin of the Arcturians, I give you this warning," spat Aten, in his gruff voice. "My father will put a price on your head. Your race has always been one of warmongering and sticking your nose in where you have no calling! I will not forget the ill treatment I've endured at the hands of this race of—"

When Vonn stepped forward, Aten ceased his ranting.

"We are not going to kill you, Aten," said Vonn. "We're here to appeal to your good sense. We simply need you to help us fight the Wolfen, and the female Reptoid who leads them."

"Why should I help you?" spat Aten, his eyes narrowing to mere slits. "I have no allegiance to you."

"No, you don't," replied Vonn. "And neither do you have an allegiance to the Wolfen—one not forced on you anyway. I am offering you a mutual exchange. If you help us, we will help you."

"Help me? How?" demanded Aten, in his rough voice. "The Wolfen are here on a reconnaissance mission. Soon others will come to enslave the primitive species that dwell on this planet." He then added quietly, "Like they did to my world of Colladron."

"Aten, hear me out," requested Jin. "We are aware of what the Wolfen did to your world. Unfortunately, we found out too late to help you. We are, however, working with our allies in this sector to come to the aid of your people."

"You're too late!" growled Aten. "The Reptoid queen has already done her damage. For eons, my world saw death only as an end to a long and fruitful life. Now we see it before we have a chance to even live that life. Too many have died too young."

"We know what the Wolfen did to you," said Jin. "Once your people were as this earth dog in your lap, content in your existence. You made your homes beneath the towering cota trees. Your young romped in the open meadows and grew strong in the nourishing light of your star. It is most unfortunate the queen found your peaceful world. Now your race lives in fear, and your heart is black with a rage you cannot understand."

"My rage is justified!" exclaimed Aten, causing the small dog to whimper and burrow deeper into his hair. "The Wolfen came to my home world in search of new recruits. I was barely past adolescence when I was forced into servitude to the Reptoid queen. My father was attending the high council the day the Wolfen swept in from beyond the boundaries of our world and stripped it of its sons. They left only women, small children, and the elderly to protect Colladron. Even my father has seen too many years to fight."

To get control of his rage, Aten dropped his hairy face onto the little dog's head and grew silent. Gray Wolf, sensing an opportunity, stepped forward.

"Now you see the plight of my people, Aten," he said. "We are also helpless against this enemy. You say they turned the sons of your world into slaves. They killed ours. Their mothers still mourn for them."

"Is this so?" Aten asked, his face contorting into a mask of rage. "My mother was off gathering food when the Wolfen came. I never saw her again. Now my parents can only mourn my loss."

"Now hear me, Aten," said Vonn. "I make you this solemn vow. If you will help us to rid the earth of the Reptoid and her Wolfen, I will liberate you from their grasp and take you back to your world. There you can raise an army of fighters."

"With what?" exclaimed Aten. "With women and children?"

Dark Bear stepped forward to address the Shetu.

"You can teach *them* to fight!" he exclaimed. "Our women are certainly not afraid to take up a weapon and defend their homeland and their people. When the Spanish soldiers attacked our village, my grandmother picked up the war lance of a fallen brother and killed four Spanish soldiers before she was struck down. Our children are taught how to use the bow and arrow when they are quite young. Men are not the only fighters on my world, Aten. Your women and children can be taught to be warriors!"

Aten's red eyes slowly panned the faces in front of him. "You say you will not harm me?" he asked, his gaze turning into a menacing glare. "I don't believe you."

Having heard enough, Two Ponies approached Aten. Without a word, he slid his knife from his sheath.

"Two Ponies, beware!" warned Sky Feather. "He's an unpredictable enemy!"

Nodding, Two Ponies knelt and looked into the eyes of the Shetu. Without breaking eye contact, he leaned forward and cut the rope that bound Aten's arms behind his back. At first Aten remained still. Then, as if in slow motion, he pulled his hairy arms forward and rubbed his wrists.

"You're the one who hit me in the face with a rock," he said.

"I am," said Two Ponies. "*That* was your first lesson in becoming a warrior—hand-to-hand combat."

"Then I will not have you annihilated," said Aten.

Two Ponies swung his body to the left and cut the remaining rope binding the Shetu's hairy ankles. When the dog in Aten's lap whimpered softly, he lowered his gaze and pulled it into his arms.

Two Ponies stood and returned his knife to its sheath. "Aten, you have the solemn oath of my people," he said. "If you will help us to send the Wolfen and the she-snake back to the stars, you will no longer be considered our enemy. You will walk among us as a brother."

"I agree," said Gray Wolf.

"As do I," added Tall Bull.

"And you have the word of the Hopi," said Black Fox.

"As well as the promise of the Arcturians," added Jin, stepping up beside Two Ponies. "Vonn and I *will* return you to your world. Will you help us?"

The small cave grew silent as everyone awaited the young Shetu's reply.

"I *will* help you," he said, after a long moment. "But I have one condition that *must* be met."

"You have only to name it," said Gray Wolf.

"I wish to keep this earth dog," said Aten, cradling the dog in his arms. "She soothes my pain and reminds me of my home world."

"Done," announced Gray Wolf.

With the matter settled, Two Ponies offered Aten his hand and pulled the young Shetu to his feet. "We've much to discuss, my friend," he said.

"Heed my words, Gray Wolf," said Vonn. "Aten must only leave the cave under the cloak of darkness. If the Wolfen see him leave without restraint, they will know his loyalty has turned, and his life will be in grave danger. Jin, are we in agreement?"

"We are, sir," Jin replied. "Once again, you demonstrate your superior intellect. The Shetu will remain in hiding."

"Well, see that he does," said Vonn, glancing around him. "Prepare yourselves. Tonight, we deal with the Wolfen. Jin and Two Ponies, you have the next watch."

When a loud grunt filled the cave, all eyes turned to look at Aten.

"Watch over your children closely," he warned in his rough voice. "The queen has demanded a human specimen as proof that your world has … edible resources. The Reptoid female ordered us to capture one of your children, as they are easier to control than a full-grown adult."

"We'll heed your warning, Aten," said Two Ponies. "Rest now, my friend. Someone will see that you have meat to eat."

"Make sure it is raw this time," remarked Aten, laying his hand over his hairy stomach. "The Shetu do not eat cooked meat. And I wish to have meat for my earth dog as well. And water."

"Done," announced Gray Wolf, for the second time.

Stepping outside the cave, Vonn stopped Jin. "I have my reservations about the Shetu keeping the dog, Jin," he said, hesitantly. "This will, I'm sure, violate the Prime Directive. We'd be introducing an unknown species of mammal to his planet. This could prove disastrous to the population. What if this dog attempts to conquer the Shetu when it grows up!"

"I hear your concerns, Vonn," said Jin. "But this is a primitive-thinking animal. It cannot communicate with anyone but its own kind. I've attempted to do so and find it possesses only limited skills. It will grow no bigger than its current size, and since it has no mate, it will be a short-lived guest. It will prove no more than an oddity."

"We shall see," said Vonn.

As the sun lowered in the west, Jin, Two Ponies, and Painted Hair walked the perimeter of the village. When nothing stirred, they retreated to a flat log in front of Two Ponies' hogan. Lounging, they sat discussing the best way to approach the Wolfen asteroid after nightfall. Above them, the blue sky faded to gray, and a few of the brighter stars were winking into existence. Jin smiled as he observed the children at play. Earlier in the day, they accompanied the women and children as they gathered armloads of the tall grasses to feed the sheep, who now grazed quietly. A few of the mothers shooed the sheep away from their hogans, only to have them circle around and return to stand in the same spot.

Jin chuckled. "If this situation were not so dire, I would find these sheep quite amusing," he said. "I must say, they have little sense and are afraid of their own shadow."

"That they are," said Painted Hair.

"Jin, what can we expect from the Wolfen?" asked Two Ponies. "I'm guessing they aren't like these sheep nor are they like the young Shetu."

"No, they are not," replied Jin. "They're a most formidable foe."

"As you have told us," said Two Ponies. "I really don't mind facing the Wolfen, even though they possess a weapon that can reduce me to ashes. It's the Reptoid female that gives me pause. I felt her extreme hatred toward me when I faced her at the sacred mountain. Is she as brutal as she appears?"

"More so," replied Jin. "She's the chosen daughter of the Reptoid queen herself and is in line to replace her mother one day."

"So, she holds a high place in her clan," remarked Painted Hair. "I care not. I see her only as a threat to my people. I'll deal with her in the same manner I will deal with the Wolfen."

"The queen will retaliate viciously if the heir to her throne suffers any harm," warned Jin. "It may prove dangerous for your world. There are no winners, my friend, in a war fought with that royal she-snake. If you resist, she'll simply send her drones to deal with you."

"Then what are we to do?" asked Two Ponies, sitting forward. "We're doomed either way."

"As Tarus suggested, we'll have to outsmart them," replied Jin. "Our *plan* is to run them off your world without their human specimen. Our *hope* is they will be too afraid to admit their failure to the queen and take the long road home. The queen will not tolerate any inept behavior."

"Not even from her chosen daughter?" asked Painted Hair.

"Especially from her chosen daughter," replied Jin. "As the future queen of Alpha Draconas, the daughter must prove her worthiness as a leader. The Reptoids are a race of selfish creatures who have no love for even their own kind, my friend. Make no mistake, the queen will get what she wants, and those who get in her way will pay a heavy price."

All three men looked up, as a small boy approached them. In his hand he held a tiny bow and one arrow. His short, cropped black hair glistened in the setting sun, and his small breechclout came to just above his dirty knees. Jin smiled down at his small, equally dirty bare feet.

"Are you really from the stars?" the boy asked him.

"I am," replied Jin. "My name is Jin. What's your name?"

"Little Owl," the boy replied. "My father is Winter Bird, a mighty warrior."

"Is he now?" asked Jin, smiling.

"Yes," replied Little Owl. "I'm five winters old, and I wish to become a great warrior like my father. I've come to offer you my help to fight this enemy."

"Well, I wish I could use you, Little Owl," replied Jin, amused. "I have all the warriors I need right now. But, if I find I have need of one more, I know where you live."

"Are you a mighty warrior like Winter Bird?" asked Little Owl.

"Well, not on your world, little one," replied Jin. Pointing to the sky, he added, "Out there among the stars, however, I fight alongside the mighty warriors of the Galactic Ninth Realm. As a member of the advanced guard, I defend the little guy, like yourself."

"Have you ever been to the moon?" asked Little Owl, pointing toward the rising moon. "There is a magic rabbit that lives there. He opens and closes his great eye. Tonight, his eye is open."

"Yes, I guess the craters on the moon's surface do resemble a rabbit," said Jin. "And the closing of his eye has to do with the movements of the moon and the earth. Well, I won't go into that right now. And yes, I have been to visit the moon."

"Did you see the rabbit who lives there?" asked Little Owl, with a look of delight.

"I did," replied Jin. "He watches over you as you sleep."

"Even when his eye is closed?" asked Little Owl.

"Even when his eye is closed," replied Jin, grinning.

"Here, Little Owl," cooed a beautiful young woman as she approached them. Her long ebony braid fell over the front of her yellow woolen dress. "You must come and have your evening meal. Your mother will be searching for you."

Jin immediately jumped to his feet. Two Ponies, wondering why, blindly did the same. Painted Hair just stared at them both in confusion.

"Yes, Moon Flower," said the boy. "I was just telling the star man about the great rabbit that lives in the moon."

"Well, you come along now," said Moon Flower. Turning her bright blue eyes on Two Ponies, she smiled. "How are you, Two Ponies? You wear the red welts of the black hornet."

"I do," said Two Ponies. "I disturbed their nest and was rewarded for my foolish bravery."

"Wait, you were stung by the black-faced bees?" asked Jin. "How many times did they get you?"

"Five," replied Two Ponies, wincing.

"Five stings!" exclaimed Jin, shaking his head in wonder. "How did you not cry out in pain? I suffered only one, and I'm still whimpering like a child. You earth people amaze me."

"We often amaze ourselves," said Moon Flower, smiling. As her beautiful face lit up, Two Ponies felt his insides quiver. "I've brought you both some jewel weed to soothe the burning and itching of your stings."

"I'm pleased," said Two Ponies, accepting the small clay cup of salve.

"I'm relieved!" exclaimed Jin, accepting his own small cup. "The sting of your bee still plagues me." Holding up his arm, he proudly displayed the red and swollen welt on his arm.

Suddenly Moon Flower grew serious, and her blue eyes swept the faces of the three men. "Please be careful when you face the Wolfen tonight," she said. "I've heard their howls in the night. They are a vicious enemy who kills for no reason. Just keep in mind that they're in a strange land and a long way from home. They are as unsure of you as you are of them. This makes them very unpredictable."

"We'll be vigilant," said Two Ponies, softly.

"Moon Flower, I have a warning for you," said Jin. "The Shetu told us the Reptoid queen is demanding a human specimen. He says the Wolfen will try for a child."

"Vonn has already given us this warning," replied Moon Flower. "We've taken precautions. Our children are our future, Jin."

"I'm sure they are," he said. "Please keep them under close protection, especially our little warrior here."

Lowering her gaze, she turned and walked off, holding on to the hand of Little Owl, who dragged his tiny bow through the dirt behind him. Two Ponies stared after her. He was suddenly taken aback at the way she now stirred his heart. *Could this be love?* he thought.

"*That* is a beautiful woman," said Jin, breaking into his thoughts. "She's Pleiadian, you know."

"What's this?" asked Two Ponies.

"She's Pleiadian," Jin repeated. "She does well in disguising the light body within her. I've known a few of their women in my time. They are extremely kind and possess a healing light that calms the soul and heals the wounded heart. Is your Moon Flower alone?"

"She is," replied Two Ponies. "Gray Wolf found her in the desert as a small child. She showed no fear of him when he approached her."

"You don't say?" asked Jin. "I can't imagine how she would have gotten separated from her people. They often send small groups here to your planet to meet with the chosen ones. The children are brought along to enhance their training, which begins at birth. Because your planet's consciousness is asleep at the moment, they rarely make contact with the populous. As I have said, only a chosen few ever see them."

"Odd," said Painted Hair. "My grandfather used those same words. He said our people would one day awaken from their long sleep and gain the wisdom needed to travel to the stars. He claims we were brought here as star seeds long ago. He called himself one of these "chosen ones" and would spend much time in the desert in council with the sky people."

"Your grandfather was obviously a contact," said Jin. "Many of the descendants of those original people still seek the wisdom needed to adapt to this changing world. Does your grandfather still venture into the desert?"

"No. He's dead," replied Painted Hair. "He died five winters ago. When he knew his time was near, he prayed to the dying sun, then walked out into the desert. He was never seen again."

"Well, here's what I think," said Jin, settling back onto the log. "The reason he was never seen again, is that the Pleiadians, your sky people, came to retrieve him."

"That's amazing," stated Two Ponies, his eyes still watching Moon Flower, as she made her way across the village.

"It's good to hear he still lives!" exclaimed Painted Hair. "The Hopi know our true home is in the stars, and someday they'll return for us."

"Well, actually, your entire race of people is from the stars," stated Jin. "Many thousands of years ago, the Pleiadians colonized your planet by seeding a great island with those brave souls wishing to begin a new world.

The chosen ones are those who have strived to maintain a connection to the home world. By dedicating their very lives to keeping the ancient knowledge alive, their hope is that you will not forget who you are nor where you came from. Your grandfather must have been a guardian of that knowledge. His mission was to pass it on to the next generation. When the old guardian's mission on earth is complete, each are given a choice. They can either allow their spirit to remain here on this earthly plane or return to their home star system. Your grandfather obviously made the choice to leave. The fact that your Black Fox was able to contact the Pleiadians is indeed proof you've kept in touch with home."

"I'm curious," said Two Ponies, turning his attention to Jin. "If we are all descended from the Pleiadians, why don't we all have blue eyes like Moon Flower?"

"Because your people have been here too long, basking under a white star," replied Jin. "Moon Flower has only been on your planet for a few short years. She actually comes from the same star system as your sky god, Tarus. Their home planet lies among a cluster of blue stars formed roughly one hundred billion earth years ago. Her people are constantly bathed in this blue light, giving them the blue eyes. I see she is draped in the copper skin of your people. She can reveal her light body if she so chooses."

"Yes, Gray Wolf has seen her do this," said Two Ponies. "He also has the blue eyes, as years ago he was healed by her magic."

"Yes, it can work that way," said Jin. "If she chooses to find a mate here on your planet, her male descendants will inherit her trait of blue eyes. With each generation, though, it will fade and eventually disappear."

"I hope she chooses to stay," said Two Ponies, softly.

"Here comes Winter Bird," said Jin, getting to his feet.

"Everyone is to meet by the river," said Winter Bird. "There we'll finalize our plan of attack. Hurry, night approaches."

CHAPTER 20

At the river, preparations to confront the Wolfen were well underway. Jin and Two Ponies looked on as Three Feathers busily deepened the hole left by the black stone.

"This will be a fine trap," said Three Feathers. Tossing the wooden scoop up to Two Ponies, he climbed from the hole.

When Vonn and Winter Bird stepped from the cave, Vonn was shaking his head.

"We've just come from talking with our young Shetu," he said. "For someone who possesses a peaceful nature, he's filled with much anger. For the opportunity to return home, he's now willing to take on the Wolfen single-handedly."

"He wants to become a warrior!" declared Winter Bird, proudly.

"Well, he'll soon get his wish," said Jin.

"Where are the others?" asked Vonn.

"We are here," said Tall Bull, as he, Gray Wolf and Sky Feather stepped from the river path. Right behind them strode the three Hopi.

"We are here, as well," said Red Otter, as he led Standing Deer, Little Hawk, and Dark Bear from the tall grass.

"Excellent," said Vonn. "Now that we're all here, I'll lay out my plan."

"I'm ready," said Winter Bird, rubbing his hands together.

"It's simple," said Vonn. "We'll lay in wait and confront the Wolfen when they leave their asteroid to feed."

Everyone just looked at him in confusion.

"That's your plan?" asked Winter Bird. "That could take all night."

"I don't believe so," said Vonn. "I'm under the impression they feed right after your sun sets."

204

"Tell me, Vonn," said Winter Bird. "What do we do with them once we have their attention?"

"There are more of us than there are of them," Vonn pointed out. "I'm sure we can overpower them with your wooden clubs and a few well-aimed rocks. Our goal is to discourage them from remaining on your planet. If they are suddenly confronted by a small army, my hope is they'll climb back into their asteroid and leave."

"What about their deadly weapon of fire?" asked Gray Wolf. "Who is willing to confront it?"

"That *does* still prove a challenge," replied Vonn, sighing heavily. "I'm still working on a strategy to avoid anyone being annihilated. In the meantime, we have a few surprises up our sleeve. If you *are* pursued by the Wolfen, lead them here. Three Feathers is laying a trap for them. He has enlarged this hole and will cover it with sticks and grass. Here we'll use your scorpions, Two Ponies."

"And if your plan should fail?" asked Gray Wolf. "You must remember Vonn, a few of us are well past our "confronting" years. Let alone, outrunning a wolf that can run on his hind legs."

"My plan simply will *not* fail, Gray Wolf," Vonn insisted. "I've used my superior intellect to deduce the risk as well as the ratio of success versus failure."

"What about the angry hornets?" asked Jin.

"I'll use them to force the Wolfen back into their asteroid," said Vonn. "I'll instruct this insect to attack the Wolfen only. Remember: Our goal is to make the Wolfen *want* to leave Earth. Pain is a good way to convince them to do so."

"I already see a major problem in your plan, Vonn," said Jin. "The angry bees don't take orders very well. They sort of do their own thing. They're not as agreeable as the Shetu."

"Where *is* the Shetu?" asked Winter Bird.

"I am here," Aten replied, stepping from the cave. In his arms, the little brown-and-white dog panted from the heat. "I am pleased to be liberated from my hole in the earth."

"Our apologies," said Gray Wolf. "I can only imagine the discomfort you have experienced in such a dark and smelly place."

"Think nothing of it," said Aten. "This cave is actually quite enjoyable compared to what I'm used to. I just spent a lengthy interstellar flight trapped inside a hollowed-out asteroid with three Wolfen animals who allowed their food to spoil. This is why we required so much fresh meat. Since arriving on your planet, their main staple has been small rodents and the large and woolly creature that cries out and runs in circles when threatened."

"That would be our sheep," said Tall Bull.

"Yes. A sheep," said Aten. "This creature was easy enough to catch; however, it proved difficult to eat. Its exterior layer got stuck in our teeth and throats and was not easily swallowed."

"You ate it fleece and all?" asked Tall Bull, with a look of pure disgust. "At least we remove the woolly hide and cut the meat into manageable pieces."

"Don't forget we *kill* it first," added Two Ponies, remembering the way Broken Ear ate the unsuspecting jackrabbit.

"Our sheep are precious to us, Aten," said Gray Wolf. "We've lost several to your carnivorous appetites."

"For that I am most regretful," said Aten, in his gruff voice. "Unfortunately, I had little choice in the matter. I took my orders from my master. When I was captured by your warriors, I was attempting to acquire a sheep for his meal. I was told that if I returned without one, I would be the substitute. But before I could secure my bounty, I was discovered. How still confuses me, for I felt I'd used a sufficient disguise."

"Oh, you did," said Red Otter. "But the eyes of the Dine' are keen. Your attempt to change into a sheep was what gave you away. Your head was too big for your body and your legs wobbled worse than a newly born foal."

"Your earth gravity is to blame for that," stated Aten. "It renders us clumsy. I must tell you; your gravitational force also affects the weapon of the one you call Broken Ear. His name is actually Ogg, by the way."

"So, the beast has a name?" asked Sky Feather. "Ogg? What kind of a name is that? I—"

"Wait," said Jin, holding up his hand for silence. "Aten, in what way does the gravity affect the weapon?"

"It causes it to lose power," replied Aten, gruffly.

"Interesting," said Jin, turning to Vonn. "Yes, of course. The Wolfen weapon is a device that emits concentrated light particles through a process of optical amplification based on the stimulated emissions of high-energy radiation. The gravitational pull on this planet could, in a sense, bend the light particles enough to change the thermodynamic quantities, thus weakening the weapon's strength after only a couple of bursts!"

"This surprised Ogg," said Aten. "His weapon astonishingly went inactive after he used it to kill the five earth men right after we arrived."

"Our men at the scout camp," said Sky Feather.

"Yes," said Aten.

"Is his weapon now useless?" asked Jin.

"No," replied Aten. "Ogg discovered that it'll recharge if placed in the direct rays of the earth's sun. Even by using this method of regeneration, however, he is still only able to achieve a partial charge that allows for only two, possibly three, emission bursts."

"Interesting," said Jin, again. "And the next time he used it?"

"Ogg tried to kill the group at the mountain three days later," replied Aten. "He only managed to pull two bursts before it, again, went dead. But his attempts to kill you failed only because you were protected by a deflector shield of energy particles. Not because of Ogg's aim."

"That would be the magic shield of Tarus," said Black Fox, nodding his head.

"Yes," said Aten. "Ogg was enraged!"

"Interesting," Jin repeated for a third time. "Tell me, how long does it need to charge before it holds enough power to fire off?"

"At least three cycles of the earth's sun," replied Aten.

"Which means what?" asked Sky Feather.

"That we now hold the advantage," replied Jin, smiling broadly. "Ogg last used his weapon two days ago. If Aten is correct, the weapon won't be charged enough to fire for another day. This is why the Wolfen have not yet attacked the village to obtain their human child. They have no weapon to intimidate you. My guess is their plan was to do so sometime tomorrow night. Am I right, Aten?"

"Yes," replied Aten. "Our plan was to attack the earth people while they slept."

"That figures," muttered Winter Bird. "Cowards!"

"Aten, do they have only the one weapon?" asked Vonn.

"Yes," replied Aten. "Hatha, the female Reptoid who leads us, was afraid Ogg, in his blundering haste, would show an excessive use of force. She did not want him to prematurely alert the planet to our presence until she could discover the strengths and weaknesses of its inhabitants. The last time the queen attempted an invasion of Earth, she thought she could sweep in and claim it without a fight. Instead, she found herself facing the Galactic Ninth Realm, and her army was beaten back. She hates to lose. This time, she sent her daughter Hatha in to have a quick look around before she deploys her forces. I might add that Hatha is not afraid of you."

"Well, she should be," said Winter Bird. "I've killed a few mean snakes in my lifetime."

"Your threats mean nothing to Hatha!" stated Aten. "She laughs at your show of aggression. She *was* communicating with us from her ship that orbits your planet. But you figured out a way to destroy our com-link."

"The stone by the river?" asked Black Fox.

"Yes," replied Aten. "What you did sent her into a fit of rage! You do not want to anger Hatha."

"It was I who destroyed the stone," stated Jin. "Nice piece of Shetu handiwork, by the way."

"The stone was not supposed to be placed so close to the village," said Aten. "Ogg was to oversaw its placement, and as is his nature, he bungled the job. The plan was for Hatha to beam it down to a designated spot near the asteroid. Ogg was to be there to receive it. Of course, when Hatha engaged her transporter, he was not in his place. Instead, he was beside your river spying on a group of chattering women as they gathered water. Fortunately for them, he'd just eaten."

"Your words make me sick," muttered Gray Wolf.

"Can she still watch us from her sky ship?" asked Sky Feather.

"No," replied Aten. "Tarus intercepted her powerful surface scanner and jammed her signal. When we first arrived, though, Hatha used this scanner to search for a human life-form to capture and return to the queen. This is how she discovered the three female earth beings digging in the soil to the north."

"Our Hopi women," said Spotted Dog.

"Yes," replied Aten. "All Hatha wanted to do was capture one. When she approached the two young women, however, they refused to cooperate."

"Why did this Hatha have to kill them?" asked Spotted Dog. "They were no threat to her. They were only tilling the earth."

"The one she chose refused to come willingly," replied Aten. "This enraged Hatha so much, she spit her venom into the young woman's face. When her companion also refused to come willingly, she, too, was spit on. Seeing this, the older aggressive woman came up behind Hatha and struck her in the back of the head with a digging tool. The blow dazed the Reptoid, and by the time she recovered, the old woman had escaped. Hatha has had Ogg and his two soldiers searching for her in the lands to the north ever since. The Reptoids leave no witnesses."

"That older aggressive woman, as you call her, was the mother of the two women," said Spotted Dog, angrily. "She escaped to bring help to her daughters, but help came too late. The mother is on a high mesa where Hatha will never find her."

"Wise move," said Aten. "After Hatha's failure to capture one of your young women, she searched for another suitable specimen. It was then she discovered several male humans sleeping around a small fire. She had Ogg and his fellow Wolfen surround them. Her orders were to observe only. We were *not* to make contact until she arrived. Capturing a human was too important to her to allow Ogg to bungle it."

"Why *did* you attack the scouting party?" asked Sky Feather.

"Convenience," replied Aten. "Hatha was pleased to find she now had eight specimens to choose from. Even if they scattered, her odds of success were better than her first attempt."

"What happened?" asked Gray Wolf.

"Like I said, our orders were to observe only," replied Aten. "All was going as planned until Ogg discovered the small herd of large solid-hoofed mammals standing nearby. He has an insatiable appetite for fresh meat, you know. In the end, he did manage to grab three. The rest I scattered into the desert. Don't tell him."

"Are you speaking of the horses at the scout camp?" asked Sky Feather.

"Is that what you call them? Horses?" asked Aten.

"So, what happened then, Aten?" asked Sky Feather.

"All chaos broke loose," replied Aten. "Hatha's plan was to approach the humans and capture one. It was Ogg's job to eliminate the remaining witnesses. I must say, it did not go the way she'd planned. When Hatha grabbed a young male, the others stood up and fought her for him! They threw sand in her face and pelted her with small rocks. Seeing Hatha in danger, Ogg rushed in and fired his weapon. Fortunately, he missed his target. Your earth men turned and ran but Hatha sent Ogg to pursue them. He killed five of them with his weapon before it malfunctioned."

"My son Long Bow was among those he turned to ashes!" exclaimed Tall Bull, angrily.

"I offer you my regrets," said Aten, bowing before Tall Bull. "Hatha does not permit her victims to fight back. They fought back."

"What of those she killed with her venom?" asked Sky Feather, glancing over at Little Hawk and Dark Bear.

"When Ogg's weapon malfunctioned, this allowed three of the earth men to escape," replied Aten. "When Hatha pursued them, I followed her. Your brothers were no match for her. One foolishly attacked her with a weapon. When the other two came to his aid, she swiftly eliminated them. The one who attacked her did manage to escape, though mortally wounded."

"I am that man!" exclaimed Red Otter.

"Tell me this, Aten," said Jin. "Why didn't you warn Hatha that Red Otter had escaped?"

"I chose not to," he replied. "The senseless attack on your people was no different than the one I witnessed on my home world. Besides, the man was hit by the venom of Hatha. I knew he'd soon have little life remaining in him."

"I had enough left to warn my people of your murderous deeds," exclaimed Red Otter, angrily.

"Stand down, Red Otter," said Jin, softly. "In my opinion, Aten is just as much a victim as the rest of you."

"What about Little Doe?" asked Sky Feather.

"Hatha is still desperate to obtain her human specimen!" exclaimed Aten. "The queen demands she not leave your world without one. As I warned you, she's now decided to take a child because they won't fight back. She nearly had one near your river, but the young female hit her in the face with a water vessel. Hatha didn't spit her venom because she needed the female alive. But the child was able to escape when a man intervened. That man paid with his life."

"Our Little Doe is a warrior at heart," said Gray Wolf, proudly.

"And in giving my life, I saved hers," said Standing Deer, softly. "I would hope my brothers would do the same for my daughter."

"We would," said Winter Bird.

"Aten, where are the Wolfen now?" asked Vonn.

"After sunset, I take them a sheep, and they retreat into their asteroid to eat," he replied. "That's a real treat to watch, I assure you."

"What are your thoughts, Vonn?" asked Jin.

"I'm not sure now," said Vonn, hesitating. "My plan of strategy was to surprise them when they emerged to feed."

"Bad plan," said Aten, shaking his head. "They now have enough meat to last them well into tomorrow."

"I'd like to know where they got that!" exclaimed Winter Bird.

"No, you don't," said Aten.

"Okay. We need to rethink your plan, Vonn," said Jin. "From a strategist's point of view, your plan is *not* going to work. Sorry."

"Well, what do *you* suggest?" asked Vonn, with mild annoyance.

"It's simple," replied Jin. "Instead of looking at the situation strategically, I suggest we look at it through the eyes of a warrior."

"Now we're talking," said Three Feathers.

"But I'm not a warrior!" exclaimed Vonn.

"Precisely, sir," said Jin. "Now, allow me to show you why they sent *me* on this mission."

"Oh, very well," said Vonn, stepping back. "Tell us your plan."

"We need to *force* the Wolfen from their asteroid," replied Jin. "If this Ogg is permitted to hide until his weapon is charged, he has two, possibly three, chances to incinerate us. If we hit him now, we eliminate those chances. If we can somehow confiscate this weapon, all they have left is their brute strength."

"Brute strength we can deal with," said Three Feathers. "Well, a few of us can."

"Now listen closely," said Jin. "Under the cover of darkness, Two Ponies, Painted Hair, and I will force the Wolfen out of their asteroid with the sack of bees. This is an insect the Wolfen have no defense against, so if it affects them the same way it affected me, this should be fun to watch."

"Oh, I'm sure my bees will bring the Wolfen to their hairy knees," said Two Ponies.

"Once the Wolfen are out of the asteroid, they'll come looking for their tormentors," continued Jin. "It's my hope that Ogg brings his useless weapon with him, if only as a show of force. Our goal is to take it from him. Just how that feat will be accomplished, however, is still rolling around in my brain. But, I find that each problem often offers up its own solution."

"Still, it is a good plan," said Winter Bird, smiling broadly. "If we do take Ogg's weapon, he'll be all bark and no burn."

"That's the idea," said Jin, smiling. "Now, we'll let the scorpions deal with the Wolfen soldiers. As for Ogg, once we have his weapon, Two Ponies and I will pelt him with rocks. We'll aim for the face. I'm told that's a sensitive area. My hope is that they finally have enough of this planet and flee."

"I will gather the rocks," offered Three Feathers. "I'll be the one highlighted by the fire. I want to make sure the rocks are big enough to hurt."

"Excellent," said Jin. "Now, Sky Feather, I'll need you to come with us. Your job will be to see we have no stragglers. I want all three Wolfen to pursue us here to the river. If one lags behind, change his mind."

"I can do this," said Sky Feather. "I have a fast horse!"

Aten stood nearby, snuggling the small dog with his gray muzzle. "I will enjoy watching the Wolfen scatter in pain and confusion," he said.

"Aten, about the earth dog," said Vonn. "It would be unwise to take it into battle with you."

"I see your logic," said Aten. "How will we keep her safe?"

"I have an idea," said Jin. "I've recently had a young boy named Little Owl express a desire to help us fight the enemy. I told him if I found a way for him to do so I would contact him. I believe I've just found a way for him to be of help. Winter Bird, what are your thoughts?"

"Little Owl will enjoy caring for the dog," he said. "But my wife, Morning Song, will have to be convinced. Having Little Owl, a baby daughter, *and* a dog in the hogan may prove too noisy for her."

"I'll convince her," said Two Ponies. "Everyone likes to think they're helping to save the world."

Pulling the Shetu aside, Two Ponies and Jin gently coaxed him to surrender the dog.

"I promise that Little Owl will take good care of her, Aten," said Two Ponies, softly.

"Guard her well!" declared Aten, handing over the dog. "I've named her Yarra."

"That's a strong name," said Two Ponies. "But you must come up with five more names."

Aten looked at him in confusion for a moment, then his reddish eyes widened.

"She's carrying offspring?" he asked, in surprise.

"Shhhh," whispered Two Ponies. "She is, indeed."

"This must remain our secret, Aten," said Jin. "If Vonn is uncomfortable with you taking one dog back to Colladron, he may change his mind if he discovers that number will soon grow to six."

"*I* will say nothing," whispered Aten, in his rough voice.

"Excellent," said Jin. "Two Ponies, you deliver the dog to Little Owl. I need to get something from our ship. We'll meet back here."

Cradling the small dog, Two Ponies headed back toward the village and Winter Bird's hogan.

"Morning Song, it's Two Ponies," he said, as he stood before the door. It was Little Owl who pulled back the hide.

"Two Ponies!" he said. "Why do you have the dog?"

"Here, Little Owl, let him come in," said Morning Song. "Two Ponies, you are welcome."

"I have need of a small warrior," said Two Ponies. "I need Little Owl to care for the dog for a short time. I'll return for it soon."

"Why not just turn it loose outside?" asked Morning Song.

"Not this time," replied Two Ponies. Handing the small dog off to Little Owl, he quickly explained the dire situation to Morning Song, who nodded slowly as he spoke. "And that's why we must protect the little dog. Aten has our word that it'll be his to take back to his home planet if he helps us to fight the Wolfen," he concluded.

"We'll keep her safe for the star wolf," said Morning Song.

Two Ponies was just rejoining the others when Jin returned from upriver. He sent Two Ponies a knowing smile and patted a gray backpack slung over his shoulder.

"Everyone, gather around," said Jin, "It'll be dark soon. You all know what to do. Aten, you'll come with us. Don't worry, we'll keep you hidden. Now remember everyone, you know the desert and the Wolfen do not. Three Feathers, prepare your scorpion pit. The rest of you, stay alert. After we confront the Wolfen, they will turn most aggressive, so just stay out of their way."

"Winter Bird," said Three Feathers, slapping him playfully on the back. "Here is where your ability to see in the dark like an owl, will be most helpful."

"Are we ready?" asked Jin.

"Wait," said Gray Wolf. "What if not all of us makes it through the night? We must take a moment to ask the Sacred Creator to protect our spirits."

"I understand, Gray Wolf," said Jin. "You have until complete darkness falls."

Returning to the village, the Dine' and Hopi joined Gray Wolf in his hogan. As they surrounded the central fire, its light danced off their faces as Gray Wolf swept a smoking bundle of sage around their bodies, cleansing their spirits. It was Two Ponies who first noticed the beautiful young woman standing in the doorway of the hogan. Her unbound, waist-length hair cascaded down her back like liquid night. Because of Jin's earlier declaration of her origins, he knew why she was there. She stepped quietly inside the door and stood with her head bowed and her eyes closed in prayer. Suddenly all eyes fell on her. Tall Bull addressed her.

"Moon Flower, are you in need of help?" he asked. "If so, I will have Dancing Star attend to you."

"Allow her to speak, Tall Bull," said Painted Hair. "She has much to share with us."

Tall Bull shook his head. "No! Our women are not permitted to—"

"She will speak!" exclaimed Black Fox.

In silence, the proud young woman raised her head and allowed her eyes to touch each face before she spoke.

"I am only Moon Flower to the Dine'," she said. "On my home world, I am Kadua, Child of the Blue Star."

"You are Pleiadian?" asked Black Fox, his eyes growing large.

"I am," replied Moon Flower. "And I have come to add my own healing energy to your prayer before the fight."

"Then we welcome you, Kadua, Child of the Blue Star," said Black Fox, looking pleased.

"I don't understand her words!" exclaimed Tall Bull. "She is only Moon Flower, a young maiden of our clan."

Stepping forward, Moon Flower raised her face upward and began to sing. Her voice was as sweet as flowing water, and her strange words seemed to lift their spirits. As she sang, her copper skin faded, until her body became a shimmering blue figure that bathed the interior of the hogan with light. Her flowing ebony hair faded to silver and surrounded her body like a mist of sparkling water. Two Ponies stood gazing at her in absolute wonder.

"Black Fox, your crystal!" exclaimed Spotted Dog, pointing to the leather pouch on the old shaman's waist. Black Fox reached in and pulled forth the Hopi crystal used to call down the sky god. It, too, now glowed with the same bluish-white intensity. To everyone's astonishment, their own skin began to shimmer like the morning sun on rippling water. When Kadua ended her song, everything faded, and she once more stood before them as Moon Flower. Their own lights faded as well until all that remained was the firelight.

With a knowing smile, Gray Wolf stepped forth and prayed over each man, asking the Sacred Creator for His protection.

"If death finds you this night," he said, his arms raised, "I pray your spirits will find safe passage back to the Sacred Creator. May your feet be swift and your aim true. Go now with my blessings."

When he finished, he gazed at them with a look of great sadness on his face.

"What is it, Gray Wolf?" asked Sky Feather.

"Remember what I have told you, my sons," he replied. "With the coming of the Wolfen, so comes my death. Regardless of what the sky helpers think, I feel I may not escape the wolf that walks upright, like a man. A vision is an omen. I accept this. I ask only that you watch over my Moon Flower for she is my precious daughter."

"Nonsense, Gray Wolf," said Moon Flower. "You have many years ahead of you. I'll have no more talk of your dying."

"We *will* care for your Moon Flower, Gray Wolf," said Three Feathers, now gazing at the young girl. "She is precious to us all."

Painted Hair stepped forward. "How did you get here, Moon Flower?" he asked her. "How is it that you are now on *our* world?"

"I was three winters when I was tragically left here by my family," she replied. "When we arrived that moon-lit night, our small ship put down in the desert, just west of here. My parents were here to make contact with your grandfather, who still is one of the Wisdom Keepers. Left alone on the steps of our small ship, I grew curious over a passing rabbit, and wandered away in pursuit of it. I quickly became lost. My parents searched for me until nearly dawn but because of their urgent need to depart, they were forced to leave without me. When I finally found my way back to the landing site, they were gone. I waited beneath a bush for an entire day, but they failed to return for me. Gray Wolf found me that night as he gathered his sacred herbs beneath the full moon."

"So, that is how you came to be in the desert?" asked Gray Wolf. "You never told me your story. Are you homesick, my daughter?"

"Not really," she replied. "I've been in contact with my family many times since you found me, Gray Wolf."

Gray Wolf's old eyes misted over. "And yet you chose to stay with me?" he asked. "Why would you do this, Moon Flower? You could have returned to your home and your people long ago."

"I stayed because of my love for you and for my *new* people," replied Moon Flower. "You need me, Gray Wolf. My family understands this. They will come for me when I choose to leave. I am happy here on your world."

"You are truly from another world?" asked Two Ponies, taking her hand in his.

"I am," replied Moon Flower, her brilliant blue eyes shining. "My light body *is* my true identity."

"I feel as though I'm meeting you for the first time," he whispered to her.

"I am still Moon Flower," she said. "Now you and the others must prepare for your fight. The enemy is still out there."

"I will return to you, Moon Flower," promised Two Ponies.

"See that you do," she said, with a smile. Releasing his hand, she turned and walked from the hogan. Two Ponies was stunned at what he'd just witnessed. For the first time in his life, his mind was clear. He loved her.

"We still have our task before us, Two Ponies," said Sky Feather, breaking into his thoughts. "We still have a world to save."

"I say we go and confront these dogs," said Two Ponies, patting the knife on his belt.

"I, too, am ready to end this waiting game," exclaimed Winter Bird.

"I'll meet you at the Wolfen asteroid, Two Ponies," said Sky Feather.

"I'll be along quickly, Father," he said. "Don't start without me."

Leaving Gray Wolf's hogan, Two Ponies paused only a moment to glance around the village. The people, milling around in front of their homes, anxiously awaited what came next. Only the sheep, unaware that a fight was coming, rested peacefully in the sand around the unlit central firepit. He noticed that someone had placed several burning torches in the sand near the river path. As he walked past, he plucked one from the sand and made his way to the river.

When he arrived, he found Painted Hair and Jin waiting on him. He was surprised to find Walks Far there as well. The boy held the reins to several horses, his own included.

"Walks Far, what are you doing here?" asked Two Ponies.

"I know about the she-snake and her Wolfen, Two Ponies," stated the young horseman. "While the rest of you deal with the enemy from the stars, I'll be here to care for the horses."

"I'm proud of you," stated Two Ponies, pushing the wooden pole of his burning torch into the sand.

"As am I," added Jin. "We need a brave recruit to deal with our four-legged transportation. Where's Aten?"

"I am here," replied the Shetu, stepping from the mouth of the cave. When he stepped into the firelight, Two Ponies smiled. Aten no longer wore the objects identifying him as the Shetu slave of the Wolfen known as Ogg. To show his allegiance to his new friends, he'd removed the silver ring from his nose and shed the black breastplate emblazoned with the snake's eye within the triangle. To show his willingness to join the battle, he'd tied a single black eagle's feather to the gray hair behind his left ear. A sheath containing a long knife hung from a red-and-black sash tied around his thick waist. As he made his way toward the group, the timid young citizen of Colladron, now moved with a sense of renewed purpose. Two Ponies knew he was witnessing the birth of a new warrior—one determined to learn the art of fighting so he could return to his own world and liberate his people.

"Walks Far, this is Aten, a Shetu warrior," said Two Ponies, proudly.

"We've met," said Walks Far, handing Aten the reins to a small paint with huge brown eyes. "I've brought you my horse, Aten. She's small, but she is swift."

Aten stepped over and run his hand over the horse's back.

"I am grateful to you," he said, carefully climbing onto the horse's back. "Although I found the taste of horse flesh to be most unpleasant, it *is* easier to digest than the woolly-coated sheep."

"He's not serious, Walks Far," said Jin, jovially slapping the young boy on the back. "I'll watch over the Shetu *and* your horse."

"I'm not worried," stated Walks Far, with a grin. "My horse won't obey anyone's commands but my own. This should prove interesting to watch."

Jin laughed heartily, as he swung himself up onto his horse's back. Two Ponies did the same and Walks Far handed both men their end of the limb holding the sack of angry bees.

"Are we ready?" asked Jin. When his three companions nodded, he urged his horse forward. "Then let's ride!"

CHAPTER 21

"It's about time you got here!" declared Sky Feather, as Two Ponies and Jin rode into the small stand of trees and dismounted. "Where are Painted Hair and Aten?"

"They're bringing up the rear," replied Jin. lowering his end of the limb holding the sack of bees. "It's obvious they would rather be anywhere else but here."

A moment later, Painted Hair and Aten rode in and slid from their horses.

"We're here," announced Painted Hair. "But I must tell you, we'd rather be anywhere else *but* here."

"So, I've been told," said Sky Feather. "Nothing has stirred since I arrived."

"Well, let's take a look," said Jin. Stepping over to the edge of the trees he looked out on the asteroid. The moon overhead bathed it in a pale white light, and it now cast a ghostly shadow on the sand.

"Here's the plan," said Jin. "We'll lead our horses to the asteroid. Going in on foot will make us less of a target. Painted Hair, you'll approach their asteroid and get them to open the door. Two Ponies, you know what to do."

"I wish you well," said Aten. "I'll stay behind. I'm not yet ready to alert them to my shifted allegiance."

"We understand," said Two Ponies. "You'll get your chance to fight soon enough."

"I do hope so," said Aten. "Now, the mechanism to open the asteroid is a palm-sized silver disc about shoulder high. You can't miss it in the light of your moon. You should be in no immediate danger, as their weapon won't be fully charged until tomorrow at sunset." He quickly added under his breath, "I think."

"Will they not see us coming, Aten?" asked Painted Hair.

"I doubt they'll be looking for you," replied Aten. "They think your species is lazy and greatly lacking in intellect. In fact, Ogg compares your intelligence to that of your sheep."

"Brute!" exclaimed Sky Feather. "I can assure you, Aten, we're much smarter than our sheep!"

"Excellent," said Aten, with a serious face. "Ogg hopes you will taste better, as well."

Two Ponies smiled when he heard Painted Hair swallow hard.

"Fight well, my brothers," said Sky Feather. "Stay low."

Painted Hair mumbled a soft prayer as he led his horse quietly across the open desert. Coming to a stop ten paces in front of the Wolfen asteroid, he waited. His horse, sensing his master's unease, nervously pawed at the ground. Two Ponies and Jin followed next, leading their horses and carrying the limb holding the bees. Reaching the asteroid, they brought their own horses to a halt in its shadow. Two Ponies freed the sack of bees from the limb, and both now watched Painted Hair for their cue to go into action.

"Are you ready, Two Ponies?" whispered Jin.

"I am," Two Ponies replied, holding up the sack of angry bees. Even now it hummed loudly. "And so are my friends." As an added touch, he shook the bag a couple of times just to make sure he had their full attention. In preparation, he carefully removed the strip of rawhide securing the top of the bag. Jin stepped back two steps, then three.

Painted Hair signaled to them that he was ready to begin. Taking a deep breath, he stepped forward. "Come out, you Wolfen dogs!" he shouted at the asteroid. "We have a little surprise for you! I am Painted Hair of the Hopi Bear Clan, and you are not welcome on my world. Come out and face me, you cowards!"

When door of the asteroid slid open, a bright green light spilled out and illuminated Painted Hair. He looked terrified! His horse whinnied and took two steps backward. When Two Ponies saw the large shadow on the sand, he knew it was Ogg before he heard the Wolfen's loud grunt. Seeing his cue, Two Ponies rushed forward. As he ran past the open doorway, he pitched the bag of angry black-faced hornets into the opening between Ogg's parted legs. Reaching up, he drove his hand against the silver disc, closing the door in the Wolfen's hairy face. Raising his arms, he let out a loud war whoop.

When the door slid open again, the sound of yelping dogs in pain rang out across the desert. Two Ponies reached up and again slammed his hand against the silver disc. He smiled as the door closed on them, trapping them inside with the swarming black cloud. Just for fun, he repeated the process three more times. When Jin called for them to retreat, Two Ponies jumped onto his horse and looked around for Painted Hair. He caught sight him just as his horse entered the safety of the small stand of trees.

"This way!" shouted Jin. Urging his horse forward, he, too, headed for the trees. Following him, Two Ponies rode hard on his heels. Behind them, the three Wolfen spilled from their asteroid, yelping in pain and waving their arms in a feeble attempt to ward off the swarm of angry black bees. They were failing miserably.

"That was quite a coup!" exclaimed Two Ponies, as he rode into the trees and dismounted. Painted Hair, standing beside his horse, appeared shaken.

"How are you, my friend?" asked Two Ponies, placing his hand on Painted Hair's shoulder. He could feel the Hopi's muscles quivering beneath his fingers. "You've just proven your worth as a mighty warrior."

"I have never been more frightened in my life!" Painted Hair exclaimed, with a nervous laugh. "I will never forget the moment I faced off with a Wolfen dog from the stars. And thanks to you, Two Ponies, it'll be *my* face he seeks after he licks his wounds!"

"Well, I suggest we leave Ogg and his two minions to do just that," said Aten, climbing onto his horse. "They'll come looking for us when the bees tire of them. And Ogg will not be happy."

"That's our plan," said Jin, from atop his horse. "Sky Feather, you make sure all three come to the river. There we have another surprise waiting for them."

"Stay well ahead of them, Father," said Two Ponies. "Lead them to us, don't try to fight them on your own."

"I'll be right behind you, Two Ponies," assured Sky Feather, swinging up onto his horse.

When Two Ponies, Jin, and Painted Hair rode into the clearing beside the river, the others were there to meet them. As usual, Aten brought up the rear.

"You have returned," said Gray Wolf, looking relieved. "Where's our Shetu warrior?"

"I am here," Aten announced, riding up. He looked pleased.

"Did your plan of using the hornets work?" asked Vonn.

"It did, indeed," replied Two Ponies, sliding from his horse. "We left the Wolfen yelping and rolling on the sand. Painted Hair called the dogs from their asteroid, and I handed them a gift they won't soon forget."

"I almost felt sorry for them," said Aten, smiling in satisfaction. "Almost."

"I've no doubt they're headed our way," said Gray Wolf, nervously. "Sky Feather will see to that. Three Feathers, is your trap ready?"

"It is," he replied. "As you can see, I've built a welcoming fire, and our scorpion friends are ready for some fun."

"Vonn, what of Hatha, the she-snake?" asked Gray Wolf. "Now that it's dark, will she come to their aid?"

"That, I cannot say," replied Vonn. "We *do* have our bioregenerated warriors should she choose to join the fight."

Right on cue, Dark Bear and Little Hawk stepped from the cave. On their heels were Standing Deer and Red Otter.

"What now, Jin?" asked Red Otter, as they approached the group.

"We need to surround the village," he replied. Kneeling on one knee, he drew a circle in the sand with his finger. "Although we still need to watch for Hatha, let's not forget we have three extremely angry Wolfen heading our way. So, we'll have to deal with them first. Little Hawk, Dark Bear and Spotted Dog, you three patrol the desert to the north and east of the village."

"We will do so," said Little Hawk.

"Excellent," said Jin. "I can't imagine the Wolfen circling around to attack us from either of those directions, but they *are* unpredictable. So, stay vigilant."

"Nothing will get past us," stated Dark Bear.

"Standing Deer and Winter Bird, you keep a lookout to the west," said Jin. "If Hatha does decide to help the Wolfen, she'll most likely come from that direction. Standing Deer, now that you're immune to her venom, try and lure her into the desert should she transport to the surface. Sky Feather is helping the Wolfen to find our fire, so he'll need your help."

"Red Otter and Painted Hair, you two have the desert to the south," Jin continued. "Should she approach the river, lead her off into the desert."

"What will be my task?" asked Tall Bull.

"Tall Bull, you go back to the village and see to your people," replied Jin. "They're frightened. If they see you, this may calm their fears."

"The rest of you, stay as much to the shadows as possible," warned Vonn. "Your moon is bright."

"Good advice" said Jin, rising. "Aten, you patrol this side of the river, but stay out of sight! The less contact you have with Ogg, the better. I'd like to keep you in one piece if you don't mind."

"I don't mind," said Aten, appearing anxious.

"Don't worry, Aten," said Red Otter. "Painted Hair and I will be close."

"Thank you," said Aten, looking relieved. "I'm new at this."

"As for the rest of us," said Jin, "Three Feathers will lure the Wolfen into his trap. My hope is that Ogg will send his minions in first. Once they fall in on top the scorpoins, we'll only have Ogg to deal with. Two Ponies and I will hide in the bushes behind Three Feathers. When Ogg pulls his weapon, we'll bombard him with the rocks. My hope is he'll drop his weapon to defend his face. If not, ... well ... I'll think of something. Either way, we have your back, Three Feathers."

Three Feathers, though standing tall and mighty, turned away to hide his sigh of relief.

"I will keep to the entrance of the cave," said Vonn. "If need be, I *will* step in and diffuse the situation. I *do* have the means to do so. I'll say no more. I will, however, be the last resort. Do you all agree?"

Everyone nodded.

"Black Fox and I wish to be included," announced Gray Wolf. "Our eyes still see well enough to be of some help."

"We'll need a horse, Gray Wolf," said Black Fox. "My bravery will surely outlast these old legs."

"I'll take you on my horse, Black Fox," offered Spotted Dog. "The northeast may prove quiet enough."

"May I ride with you, Red Otter?" asked Gray Wolf. "I'll try not to be a burden to you."

"If you are, you'll be a burden I will gladly bear," said Red Otter, hoisting the old man up behind him.

In the distance, their ears caught the approaching howl of a wounded animal.

"That's Ogg!" shouted Aten.

"Everyone, to your posts!" shouted Jin.

The riders mounted their horses and rode off in their designated directions. Those left behind, quickly took their places. Jin and Two Ponies concealed themselves in the high grass just off the edge of the clearing. Beside them, lay the large pile of rocks Three Feathers had gathered earlier. Jin smiled.

"This is a generous number of rocks, Three Feathers," he mused.

"Just don't miss!" exclaimed Three Feathers. Finding his log, he sat down and nervously began stirring the fire needed to lure the Wolfen into his scorpion trap.

"Are you concerned, Two Ponies?" asked Jin.

"A little," he confessed. "Not of the Wolfen. My concern is, I may have to face Hatha again. I have always seen myself as fearless, Jin. She proves to me, I am not."

"I have something for you," said Jin, removing a cord from around his neck.

"What's this?" asked Two Ponies, holding it up to examine it in the firelight. Dangling from a thin, sturdy cord was a small round silver ring slightly larger than his thumbnail. Inlaid, within the silver ring, was a dark yellow disc divided by three black broken circles.

"It's called a Q-link," replied Jin. "For you, it will relieve the negative effects of your earth's electromagnet force, by normalizing your bio-field. It will also boost your energy and give you mental clarity. Clearer thinking will help you to handle any situation in which you may find yourself."

"Earlier Gray Wolf led us through a protection ceremony," said Two Ponies.

"That was to protect your spirit," said Jin. Pointing to the device, he added, "This will protect your body. Every day your planet is bombarded with high-energy electrons that can damage your cells. This device creates a force around you that will—never mind. Just promise me this, my earthly friend, you will wear it and never take it off."

"I will make you that promise," said Two Ponies, dropping the cord holding the small disc over his head. "I will never take it off."

"Excellent," said Jin.

Three Feathers, sitting upright on his log, nervously tossed another log onto his fire. Just beyond the flames lay the large grass-covered hole containing the scorpions. When Ogg's loud grunting and snarling drew closer, everyone braced themselves.

"Vonn!" called Three Feathers, glancing around. "Where are you?"

"I am here," replied Vonn, from the mouth of the cave.

"Here they come!" said Jin.

"They're like raging bulls!" declared Two Ponies, as the Wolfen crashed into the underbrush.

"Stealth was never one of their strong suits," remarked Jin. "Are you ready, Three Feathers?"

"I am," he replied, patting the deadly looking long knife strapped to his waist. "I'm well-armed, should they miss my trap. I *pray* they do not miss it."

"Well, if they do, we have your back," Jin reminded him.

The first to emerge from out of the brush was Ogg. He drew to a halt at the edge of the firelight and stood glaring at Three Feathers through blood-red eyes. At his waist hung the silver weapon that burned with a deadly fire. Behind him, his two companions halted, awaiting his instructions.

"Jin," whispered Two Ponies. "I thought Aten said Ogg's weapon was too weak to fire. He's wearing it!"

"Only as a show of force," replied Jin.

Three Feathers stoked the fire with a stick and addressed the Wolfen leader.

"Well, well, well, if isn't Ogg," he said, nervously eyeing the weapon. "Come and join me around my fire. Bring your two friends. We'll talk over old times—tell a few stories. Come. Sit."

Ogg tipped his head back and howled with rage. Reaching behind him, he shoved one of his two companions forward and grunted a command. Obeying its leader, the lesser Wolfen shot toward Three Feathers, his teeth bared. Three strides into his attack, his feet hit the sticks and grass covering the large hole, and he disappeared from sight. His sudden cries of pain assured Two Ponies that his scorpions had found their mark. A moment later, the whimpering Wolfen climbed from the hole and ran off into the night. Ogg turned, and with another loud grunt, demanded his remaining Wolfen soldier now advance on Three Feathers. Instead of following that order, this soldier, too, fled into the darkness. Red Otter and Painted Hair, seeing them leave, slipped from the brush at the river's edge and followed after them.

"Stay here!" Jin whispered. "If Ogg advances, aim your rocks for his face." A moment later, Jin disappeared into the darkness.

Ogg's eyes took on a menacing red fire as he turned his gaze on Three Feathers. Slowly, the Wolfen leader stepped around the scorpion pit and approached the firepit. As he moved, his huge claws reached back and slipped the silver weapon free of its holder. Three Feathers, thinking he was about to die, slid to his knees and broke into his death song. Ogg halted in his advance and stared at him in confusion.

Two Ponies reached down and picked up a rock, then hesitated. Without Jin there to do the same, would only one rock cause the distraction they'd hoped for? Or, would it only enrage Ogg further? Thinking he had to do something, anything, to pull Ogg's attention off Three Feathers, Two Ponies pulled his knife and stepped from the tall grass.

"Well, Ogg, it looks as though your army has deserted you," he said, the knife shaking slightly in his hand.

With Ogg's attention now on Two Ponies, Three Feathers unsheathed his long knife and stood up.

Two Ponies stared at the weapon in Ogg's hand. Was Aten correct in thinking the weapon wasn't fully charged enough to kill? This question rushed through his mind as Ogg now turned the weapon on him. Suddenly Two Ponies felt a surge of courage sweep over him, and his hand ceased its shaking. Looking into Ogg's bloodred eyes, he spoke his mind.

"Go home, Ogg," he said, his voice low and steady. "And take your murdering she-snake with you. There's nothing for you here. Despite your belief, we are *not* as foolish as our sheep. My people will fight you *and* your dog soldiers. Leave. My. World!"

Ogg glared at him through steely eyes. His rage rumbled deep in his throat as he parted his black lips and bared his teeth. Two steaming strings of hot saliva slid down his long canines and dripped onto the sand at his feet. But before he could react to Two Ponies' threat, Aten appeared out of the darkness and rushed the Wolfen leader from behind. When their bodies collided, Ogg lost his grip on the silver weapon, and it tumbled to the ground. In one fell swoop, Aten picked it up and hurried to Two Ponies' side.

"That was a brave move!" Two Ponies exclaimed, just before Aten turned and pointed the weapon at *his* chest. Three Feathers raised his knife, but Aten gestured to him that he would shoot Two Ponies if he didn't drop it on the sand. Three Feathers, confused by Aten's turn of loyalty, did as he was told.

"Just whose side are you on, Aten?" Two Ponies demanded in a loud whisper.

"Drop your knife!" Aten demanded menacingly. Two Ponies obeyed.

Turning to Ogg, Aten let go with several yips followed by three quick barks. Two Ponies felt unbridled anger as he listened to the Shetu and the Wolfen leader converse in their strange canine language. Ogg shook his head, and holding out his hand, demanded the return of his weapon. Aten shook his head in refusal, but kept it aimed at Two Ponies' chest. Ogg, growing angrier by the second, bared his teeth and made a move toward the young Shetu. After two strides, however, he halted in his attack. He turned away when something drew his attention in the trees beside the river. When his ears perked up, Two Ponies caught the sound of a long, drawn-out hiss somewhere beyond the firelight. *Could this situation possibly get any worse?* he wondered.

When Hatha stepped into the firelight, Two Ponies felt his heart sink. What chance did they have now? When he glanced toward the mouth of the cave, Vonn was no longer there. And what of Jin's sudden disappearance? So much for the aid from their star helpers! Were Three Feathers and himself now expected to finish the fight on their own? How could they possibly win? They were outnumbered and unarmed. With Aten pointing a weapon at his chest, Ogg's brute show of uncontrollable rage, and now Hatha hissing in his face, Two Ponies knew the fight was over. He'd failed his world. Beside him, he heard Three Feathers groan.

Hatha swayed back and forth, her mouth spread into a deadly grin. Even Aten gasped at this sudden turn of events and the weapon in his hand began to shake slightly. When the she-snake turned her deadly grin in Two Ponies' direction, he closed his eyes. He knew what came next and he braced himself for her stream of hot venom.

Then he heard the voice of Jin speak within his mind.

It's me, Two Ponies, he said. *I'll handle this. Do not relax! Continue to show your fear of me.*

Despite Jin's simple request, Two Ponies nearly collapsed with relief. With much effort, however, he managed to stand his ground. Beside him, Three Feathers leaned over and picked up his knife. Two Ponies hoped he wasn't about to foolishly launch into an attack of his own. With Aten's loyalty now in question, he felt he couldn't safely warn Three Feathers of Hatha's true identity.

Ogg turned and gave Hatha his full attention. His blood-red eyes grew large as he displayed his obvious fear of her. Like an obedient dog, he waited for her next command. The situation hung in the balance as everyone waited on the other to make the first move. Then, with a loud hiss, Hatha reached out with her sharp-clawed hand and struck Ogg on the left side of the head. The blow surprised him, and he yipped in pain as his paw flew to his ear. When Hatha raised her hand a second time, Ogg had had enough. He turned and bolted into the darkness. The Reptoid let go with a long, hissing laugh, and quickly changed back into Jin. Grinning from ear to ear, he took a low bow. Two Ponies would have found the situation amusing as well, if not for the fact that Aten still had Ogg's deadly weapon pointed at his chest.

"That went surprisingly well," declared Aten, lowering the weapon. "I wasn't expecting Hatha to show up, but Jin did manage to defuse a rather tense situation, if you ask me."

"I thought you were going to shoot me, Aten!" Two Ponies exclaimed angrily.

"With what? A dead weapon?" asked Aten, pointing the weapon at a nearby tree.

"Aten, no!" shouted Jin. His warning came too late. When Aten pulled the trigger, the bole of the tree exploded in a huge fireball, and sparks rained down on everyone's head. In obvious surprise, Aten peered down at the smoking weapon in his hand.

"Who fired that weapon!" demanded Vonn, hurrying into the clearing.

"I ... a ..." stammered Aten.

"I'll take that!" Vonn demanded, plucking the weapon out of Aten's grasp. "Foolish Shetu. You could have killed someone. Even a partial charge can prove deadly."

Winter Bird ran in from the trees. "I saw the explosion!" he gasped. "Who—"

"All is well," said Vonn. "The weapon is now in *my* possession."

A moment later, the rest of the force arrived. Sky Feather rode in and dismounted. Spotted Dog followed, lowering Black Fox to the sand. On his heels, Red Otter rode in with Gray Wolf. The faces of the two old shamans were flushed with excitement.

"Has anyone been harmed?" asked Gray Wolf, as Red Otter lowered him to the ground. "I saw that the weapon was fired."

"We're all well," said Two Ponies, placing his hand on Aten's shoulder. "It was a tense situation, but Aten here, in a one-man attack, managed to disarm Ogg. He saved the day!"

"Did you now?" asked Black Fox, with surprise. "Aten, I knew you would prove yourself to be a mighty warrior!"

"As did I," added Winter Bird. "Well done, Aten!"

The young Shetu looked pleased with their praise.

Three Feathers, knowing the truth of the situation, just smiled and slipped his knife back into its sheath.

"Where's Ogg now?" asked Gray Wolf.

"Gone," replied Jin. "Hopefully, he's firing up his asteroid and preparing to leave earth."

"Dare we think he's had enough?" asked Black Fox.

"That I cannot say," replied Gray Wolf. "But after enduring a pit of scorpions and a stinging hoard of angry hornets, we can only hope the Wolfen are ready to escape us."

"What about the real Hatha?" asked Two Ponies. "She's still out there."

"I doubt if she's willing to continue the fight," offered Jin. "I hope she, too, is leaving earth's orbit."

"Come, Gray Wolf," said Black Fox. "Let's you and I return to the village. I could use a long pipe after all this excitement."

"Here, here," replied Gray Wolf. "With old Ogg on his way home, it seems I have successfully escaped death at his hand. A nice pipe sounds like a fine reward for a couple of old warriors like us."

"I'll accompany you, Black Fox," said Spotted Dog. "Unlike the others, I fear the danger has not yet passed."

"If you insist," said Black Fox.

Spotted Dog plucked a burning torch from beside the fire, and led Black Fox and Gray Wolf up the river path toward the village.

When Standing Deer walked into camp, Two Ponies was shocked by his appearance. His body was rapidly breaking down and his skin sagged on his bones. His copper skin now wore a yellowish pallor that swallowed up the long scar across his chest. Dark Bear and Little Hawk, stumbling in after him, fared no better. Two Ponies, Painted Hair, and Winter Bird rushed to help them. Jin and Vonn, seeing the three dying men, went to evaluate the situation.

"Standing Deer, I'm here for you," said Two Ponies, gently lowering him to the ground.

"Two Ponies, I fear my time is short," Standing Deer gasped. "We knew this would happen when we returned to you. But I *had* hoped to stay longer."

"I hoped you would too!" exclaimed Jin, shaking his head. "I don't understand their rapid degeneration, Vonn. These men should have had at least three to four days."

"I, too, thought so," said Vonn. "I was sure I'd identified any of the earth's harmful elements that could disrupt the bioregeneration process. I examined their anatomical make-up atmospherically, physiologically, as well as how well the human species adapts biomechanically to outside forces. Apparently, I missed something important."

"I feel my life force fading, Two Ponies," said Standing Deer. "I'm afraid the rest of the fight belongs to you, my brother."

"You have fought well, Standing Deer," said Two Ponies. "You have earned a place of honor among our people."

"Watch over my family," said Standing Deer, softly. "And tell Little Doe to always be brave."

"What of you, Dark Bear?" asked Painted Hair, lowering the older man to the sand.

"I, too, will leave this fight," he replied. "Watch over my wife and Yellow Rabbit. I was supposed to bring him back his first horse. The attack on the scouting party now seems like such a long time ago. We didn't find

Hatha; however, I do have word of Ogg's companions. They were headed back to their asteroid. One was limping and the other carried a large jackrabbit under his arm."

"No doubt for a snack on the ride home," remarked Winter Bird. "Rest now, my friend. You've earned it."

Three Feathers caught Little Hawk as he slumped to the ground. The young man's sagging skin adding many years to his otherwise boyish face.

"What of Ogg?" Three Feathers asked him.

"We saw no sign of Ogg," replied Little Hawk, his voice strained and growing weak. "And now I lack the energy to search for him. I'm sorry."

"Don't be sorry, Little Hawk," said Jin. "Your bravery helped to save your people." Peering down on the dying men, he added, "Each of you went through the process of bioregeneration for one purpose, and that was to help us to defeat the Wolfen. We have done so. Although, Vonn and I are uncertain why its effects have worn off so soon, we are all immensely proud of you. You have fought well for having returned from the dead. Go now mighty warriors, and pass through the great veil. I promise, we will not disturb your eternal rest again."

"We won't forget our star helpers," said Standing Deer. Falling silent, he closed his eyes.

"Come," Jin said to the others. "We can do nothing for them now. In a short time, their bodies will return to skeletal remains. Even now their eyes are closing."

"They were good sons," said Sky Feather, his voice emotional.

"I'm sad to see them go … again," said Three Feathers.

"Wait. Where's Red Otter?" asked Two Ponies. Glancing around him, he spotted his childhood friend sitting by the fire with Aten, and he hurried to his side. "How are you, Red Otter? Are you leaving us too?"

"Not just yet," replied Red Otter, looking up. He did, however, show the obvious signs that his death, too, was returning. Though not as prominent as the other three, his skin revealed a slight pallor around his eyes, and his cheeks were beginning to sink in. "I still have life in my bones and strength in heart. For yet a little while anyway."

"What of Ogg?" asked Aten.

"It's unsure where he is," replied Two Ponies. "Dark Bear told us that his two companions returned to their asteroid. But they saw no sign of Ogg."

"What more harm can he do?" asked Winter Bird. "He's unarmed, and his soldiers have deserted the fight."

"You must not underestimate the Wolfen leader," warned Aten. "I cannot see him just turning tail and leaving without a fight. He's much too mean."

"Aten is right," said Vonn. "Though we have Ogg's weapon, he is *anything* but harmless. He's a ruthless and cunning adversary. We'd be fools to turn our backs on him just yet. Until we see him safely aboard his asteroid, we must assume he still may have mischief up his hairy sleeve!"

When the anxious sound of a barking dog erupted in the village, Aten jumped to his feet.

"That is my Yarra!" he exclaimed. "She cries out for my help!"

"Back to the village!" exclaimed Three Feathers, plucking a burning stick from the fire. "Follow me!"

They were nearly to the village when they met Tall Bull on the path. He stumbled into Winter Bird and fell to the ground at his feet. In the light of the burning stick, Two Ponies could see the large gash just above his left eye and the blood staining the front of his woolen shirt.

"Come quickly!" cried Tall Bull. "It's Ogg. He's in the village!"

"Follow me!" exclaimed Three Feathers, disappearing up the path.

"Vonn, what will you have me do?" asked Jin.

"Get Ogg to his ship and see he leaves this planet!" exclaimed Vonn, shaking his head. "I'll help Tall Bull back to the village and see to his wound."

"Red Otter?" asked Two Ponies. "Are you still up for the fight?"

"Lead the way!" he replied.

"I'm right behind you," exclaimed Jin. "Aten, stay out of sight. One monster among the people is enough. We don't want them injuring you by mistake."

Arriving in the village, the men looked around them. Ogg was nowhere in sight. Someone had laid a match to the central firepit, and its growing flames now revealed a world in chaos. The moving mob of sheep ran to and fro pushing and shoving each other amid their frightened bleating. Armed mothers stood in the doorways of the hogans, protecting their children.

Aten's little brown-and-white dog stood in front of Winter Bird's hogan, barking at the open door. From within, came the sound of a woman's frightened screams. Gray Wolf stood facing the hogan, brandishing a war club.

"Leave the child!" he shouted. "I will smite you, Ogg, if you do not drop him!"

"Winter Bird, Ogg is in *your* hogan!" announced Aten. "He's after his human child! Hurry!"

When Ogg stepped from the doorway, he held the small, limp body of Little Owl in the cleft of his huge, hairy left arm. Gray Wolf stepped up behind him and struck the Wolfen in the back with the war club.

"Drop him, I say!" he shouted. Ogg turned and faced the old man. Raising his huge right paw, he struck Gray Wolf in the chest. The hard blow sent the body of the old shaman sailing through the air, where he struck the front of Black Crow's hogan and fell to the ground. There he lay like a broken doll on the sand.

Winter Bird rushed toward his hogan. But before he could reach the Wolfen leader, Ogg turned and fled into the night, Little Owl tucked under his arm. Aten appeared out of nowhere, swooped up his little dog, and disappeared back into the shadows. Morning Song appeared in the door, tightly holding on to her crying baby.

"Winter Bird!" she exclaimed, tears running down her cheeks. "Little Owl and I only stepped out for a moment to allow the little dog to relieve itself. The wolf monster appeared out of nowhere and chased us back inside. Oh, Winter Bird, he has our son!"

"I will bring him home, my wife," said Winter Bird, pulling her and his crying daughter into his arms.

Two Ponies shook himself out of his daze and rushed to check on the old shaman.

"Gray Wolf!" he cried, peering down into the old man's face. Gray Wolf slowly opened his eyes.

"Save ... the ... boy," was all he managed to get out before he fell silent.

"Go after Little Owl!" demanded Moon Flower, kneeling beside Gray Wolf. "I'll see to my father. Two Ponies, be safe."

Walks Far appeared at the western edge of the village, holding the reins to several horses. Two Ponies found his horse and swung up onto its back.

Winter Bird, clutching a burning torch, slipped onto his own and turned to address the gathering party.

"Ogg has taken my son, Little Owl," he said. "Now the fight is *mine*. I will ask no man to ride to his death."

"I *returned* from death to fight this enemy," said Red Otter. "Until all life leaves my bones, I will not abandon the battle."

"My son and I will fight by your side," stated Sky Feather. Two Ponies looked at his father with pride. Even though Sky Feather's winters numbered well into their fifties, he was never one to back down from a fight.

Painted Hair rode forward. "Though the ways of the Hopi are peaceful, Spotted Dog and I will not leave the fate of your child in the hands of this murderous dog. We'll ride with you."

"I'm here, as well," said Three Feathers. "I have a score to settle!"

"What about Aten?" asked Two Ponies. "Will he be riding with us?"

"He's coming," replied Jin, swinging onto his horse. Two Ponies noticed he carried the gray pack strapped to his back.

"I am here!" Aten announced, mounting his horse. "You will need your Shetu warrior."

Two Ponies was surprised to see that Aten was wearing the black breastplate of the Reptoid.

"Hear me, Aten," said Three Feathers, giving the Shetu an ominous stare. "I see you again wear the armor of the enemy. I wonder, can you still to be trusted?"

"I'll need it," stated Aten. "I won't let you down, Three Feathers."

"Aten, Ogg has taken my son captive," said Winter Bird. "Will he take him into his asteroid?"

"No," replied Aten. "Hatha refuses to enter their asteroid. Ogg will take the boy into the underground caverns until he contacts her. We must hurry. As soon as he does, she will beam herself to the surface and claim her prize. Once the child is in her possession, he will be irretrievable."

"Wait for me!" shouted Black Fox, hurrying up to the group.

"Black Fox, I am against *your* coming with us," declared Spotted Dog.

"Why, because I am too old?" asked Black Fox. "No, Spotted Dog, this may very well be my last adventure on this earth. Aten thinks Ogg took the boy into the underworld. Will you deny me a chance to venture into this most sacred of kivas? I think not! Besides, Ogg nearly killed poor Gray Wolf. Now *I* owe him one."

"You have no horse," Spotted Dog pointed out. "We have to ride fast and hard."

"He can ride with me, Spotted Dog," said Aten. "I'll bring up the rear."

"Let's ride!" exclaimed Winter Bird. Turning his horse toward the west, he led his band of warriors off into the night, his torch lighting the way.

CHAPTER 22

Arriving at the small stand of cedar trees, they dismounted and looked out on the Wolfen asteroid.

"I'm glad to see all is quiet," said Aten. "I doubt if Ogg has posted a guard. He thinks he now has the advantage."

"No guard?" asked Winter Bird. "Surely he knows I will come for my son."

"Not necessarily," said Jin. "You must understand how the Wolfen creatures think, Winter Bird. They possess no sense of kinship. To the Wolfen, the situation is simple. You once possessed the boy, and now he belongs to them. You'll accept this fact and move on."

"They have not yet faced the love of a father!" exclaimed Winter Bird.

"You're right about that," said Jin. "The Wolfen know nothing of a father's love. This is why they're such ruthless killers."

"Now you see why I must return to my home world," stated Aten, in his rough voice. "My people are still a loving and peaceful race. The Wolfen seek to change this. I know now that I must fight to save our way of life. But first I will do all I can to save the son of Winter Bird."

"Thank you, my Shetu friend," said Winter Bird. "I'm most grateful for your help."

"Let's go get Little Owl," said Jin. "We'll lead our horses west and approach the Wolfen asteroid from behind. This way, we will not alert them to our presence. No talking. Their hearing is excellent."

Two Ponies dreaded their walk across the open desert, as the moon over head revealed their every move. If Ogg did have a watchman, he already knew they were coming. Two Ponies allowed his taut nerves to relax a little when they reached the back of the asteroid without incident.

Tethering their horses to a bush, they quietly made their way around to the front. Aten stepped forward.

"I'll see if anyone remains inside the asteroid," he said. Tapping the silver disc, he waited for the door to hiss open. The light, spilling out of the asteroid, brightly illuminated the area in an unnatural green glow.

"I hope it's empty," said Sky Feather. "If not, we just shouted to Ogg, 'Hey, we're out here. Come and get us!'"

A moment later, Aten reappeared.

"The asteroid is empty," he said. Tapping the silver disc, the door hissed shut, plunging them all into darkness.

"Aten, can you open the entrance into the tunnel?" asked Jin.

"I can," he replied. "Follow me."

Moving quickly, Winter Bird and his torch led them to the front of the boulder.

"This is where I saw the doorway open," said Two Ponies, pointing to the rock face in front of him. "Here is where Ogg and the others emerged from out of rock."

"I see no doorway!" said Winter Bird, holding up his dying torch. "If my son is inside this huge boulder, how can I walk through solid rock?"

"Patience, Winter Bird," said Aten. "There's a tunnel here, I assure you."

"Wait," said Sky Feather. "How are we to see in the darkness? Surely it's pitch-black inside."

"I thought of that," replied Jin, removing the gray pack from his back. "That's why I brought you each a bit of magic to light your path."

"How will you make fire out of nothing?" asked Winter Bird. "We've no wood to make torches and mine is nearly spent."

"My magic doesn't involve fire," said Jin. "It involves water."

"Water!" asked Sky Feather. "How will water help us to see in the dark?"

Jin withdrew a white, fist-sized stone from his pack and struck it against the face of the rock. It immediately lit up, bathing his face in a bright blue light.

"This *is* magic!" exclaimed Black Fox. "It's like my crystal."

"Almost," said Jin. "Its true name is mia-zite. But we call it Aqua-lite. It's a liquid-filled mineral mined on Moon Flower's home world. It's simple to use, actually. Once activated, it'll illuminate your path. If someone approaches, and you wish to go dark, simply hide the Aqua-lite under your shirt. If it starts to lose its brightness, striking it against any hard surface will reactivate it."

"Very impressive!" exclaimed Sky Feather. "I thought Vonn was against you showing us your sky magic."

"He is," replied Jin. "And if he finds out I revealed an advanced tool to you, he will be most unhappy. But, as a soldier in the field, I often find myself in that rare situation in which bending the rules becomes necessary. *This* is one of those situations. So, just to be on the safe side, we won't tell Vonn. Got that?"

"He won't hear about it from me," said Sky Feather. "How about the rest of you?"

"No,"

"Not I,"

"I see nothing,"

"Excellent," said Jin. "Now, I have an Aqua-lite for each of you. Don't activate them until just before we enter the tunnel."

"Aten, where does this invisible tunnel go from here?" asked Winter Bird. Now under the glow of Jin's Aqua-lite, he tossed his spent torch aside. "Where are they keeping my son?"

Aten squatted down and drew a crude map in the sand.

"The tunnel goes in for about one hundred paces," he explained. "Ten paces in, on the left, lies the first guardroom. A second guardroom lies about sixty paces further in, on the right. Thirty or so paces past this second guardroom, the tunnel makes a forty-five-degree turn to the left and opens into a large room. Here, Ogg and the others spend the hottest part of your daylight hours. There are three tunnels leading further into the catacombs, but Ogg stays only in the main room. It's here he holds the boy."

"Here's my plan," said Jin. "Painted Hair and Spotted Dog, you'll watch over the Wolfen asteroid. Although Aten found it empty, that doesn't mean that all three of them are inside the tunnel. If one should return from the desert, lead them away until we emerge with the boy. Three Feathers, I need you to watch the entrance to the tunnel. This will be critical, as our only means of escape will be back up this tunnel."

"I will guard it well," said Three Feathers, holding up his war lance.

"Yeah, about the spear," said Jin. Reaching into his gray pack, he pulled out a small silver handheld device with a pistol grip. "You'll need something with a bit more bite. For this task, I'll loan you my little friend. It directs a pulsed energy beam that—well, we won't go into the details at this time. It's simple to operate. Hold it in your hand, aim, and pull the trigger. The energy beam will temporarily short circuit your opponent's brain waves, causing uncontrollable muscle activity."

"Will this be yet another secret we don't tell Vonn?" asked Sky Feather.

"Most definitely!" replied Jin. "We're not lying to him. We're merely handling the truth carelessly. As I have told you, I'm quite good at it."

"I'll keep your secret, Jin," stated Three Feathers. In the glow of Jin's Aqua-lite, no one could miss the look of sheer delight on his face as he examined this new weapon.

"Try not to use it on one of us, Three Feathers," warned Two Ponies, stepping back.

"Wise words," said Jin. "Black Fox, Sky Feather, and Red Otter, you'll wait in the first guardroom. Red Otter, since you're immune to Hatha's venom, it'll be you who must confront her should she transport herself inside the tunnel's entrance. If she does, lure her outside where Three Feathers can deal with her. Reptoid princess or not, being hit by fifty units of pulsed energy will have her crawling around in the dirt."

"I'm almost sad I'll miss that," said Two Ponies, smiling.

"Will it harm her?" asked Three Feathers.

"No," replied Jin. "But she may glow in the dark for a while. Now, Sky Feather, your job is to make sure Three Feather's knows it is *us* coming up the tunnel. You'll hear us, I'm sure. Two Ponies, you and Winter Bird will accompany me on to the second guardroom. Aten, you will—"

"No! Not I," said Aten, rising up and stepping back.

"But I need you," exclaimed Jin, getting to his feet. "You know the layout of the tunnel as well as the location of Ogg."

"I cannot go in with you," Aten insisted.

"Why not?" asked Winter Bird.

"There is ... ah ..." stammered Aten.

"There is what?" asked Winter Bird, with impatience.

"There is ... something else down there," replied Aten.

"What do you think it is?" asked Black Fox, now intrigued.

"I cannot say," replied Aten. "One day, while the others slept, I heard the sound of falling rock in one of the three tunnels leading off the main room. I decided to investigate. All I had for a light was a nearly dead beacon from the asteroid, but it provided enough illumination for me to see where I set my feet. I was only a short way in when something huge and gray blocked my path. It stood very tall, with long spindly arms and a huge gray head that stared down on me through two enormous black almond-shaped eyes. I asked it, "Who are you?""

"And what did it answer?" asked Black Fox, urging him on.

"Telepathically, it replied, "I am pain"," said Aten.

"I am pain?" asked Winter Bird. "What does that mean?"

"I don't know," replied Aten, his reddish eyes huge and fearful. "And I did not wait to find out. Whatever it was, I sensed it did not want us down there. I turned and ran back to the main room. When I told Ogg about meeting the tall gray creature in the dark, he laughed. He said he was not afraid of any earth creatures. But I sensed that whatever it was in the darkened tunnel, was not *of* this earth."

"Great," said Jin. "What other off-world entities are here that the Ninth Realm doesn't know about?"

"Aten, I may know of this creature you saw in the tunnel," said Black Fox. "It could be one of the ant people. We have no fear of them. They have watched over my people since the beginning. Back in the mists of time, they took the first people into the underground caverns and cared for them when the surface of our world proved uninhabitable. I am pleased to hear they may be still with us. Oh, I do hope I get a glimpse of one!"

"What is this talk of caverns and ant people?" exclaimed Winter Bird. "We have to get my son out of this place now! Aten, please come with us."

Aten thought a moment then relented. "Very well," he said. "I'll do it for the human child. I know what fate awaits him should you fail in your rescue. Unspeakable! But heed my warning! Do *not* go beyond the great room."

"Everyone, activate your Aqua-lites," said Jin. "Aten, get us into the tunnel."

"Yes, sir," said Aten. "No talking once you are inside. Even the softest voice can travel a great distance."

The darkness fled as the sound of stone striking rock activated the strange glowing Aqua-lites. Holding them aloft, all turned and faced the huge boulder.

"Now, Three Feathers," said Aten. "You questioned my loyalty because I again wear the breastplate of the Wolfen. Here is my answer to you."

Stepping forward, Aten placed his right paw over a raised black disc embedded in the breastplate's upper left-hand corner. Immediately, a large section of stone slid in behind the rock's face, revealing the entrance to a tunnel as black as night. In silence, they followed Jin inside.

As Three Feathers stepped past Aten, he leaned down and whispered into his hairy ear. "I will never doubt you again, my star brother."

Two Ponies raised his Aqua-lite and stepped through the stone doorway. When he did, a sense of impending doom swept over him so intense, he nearly turned and bolted back to his horse. Was it the foul air drifting up from below? Ten paces in, they approached the first guardroom and Black Fox and Sky Feather silently slipped inside. Red Otter paused only long enough to place his hand on Two Ponies' shoulder. The look in the eyes of his childhood friend told him that he, too, felt the sense of impending doom. Was it for himself? In the glow of the blue light, the gray pallor of his face was now more prominent and the corner of his left eye drooped slightly. Two Ponies nodded before falling in behind Jin and Winter Bird. As they descended into the blackness, he caught the sound of Aten's large canine pads softly slapping against the stone floor behind him.

Halfway in, they hesitated when Ogg's angry grunting met their ears. When it was followed by the sound of a child's frightened sobs, Winter Bird groaned. To calm him, Jin laid his hand on his shoulder and shook his head. In the light of the blue stone, Two Ponies could see the pain etched into Winter Bird's face as concern for his tiny son mounted.

Holding their Aqua-lites aloft, they continued down the tunnel, Aten trailing behind them. Ahead, where the tunnel curved to the left, a bright green light reflected off the rock wall. At the second guardroom, they stepped inside, and Jin motioned everyone over to the far wall.

"I'll go in first and draw their attention," he said, in a low whisper. "Once I have them looking at me, Aten, you rush in and grab the boy—"

"No! *I* will grab my son!" whispered Winter Bird. "I'll not put his welfare into the hands of someone else. No disrespect intended, Aten."

"None taken," Aten whispered, looking relieved.

"What is my task?" asked Two Ponies.

"You're to wait here," replied Jin. "You're younger than us and can run much faster. Once we're all out, you follow us up the tunnel. When the Wolfen take chase, lure them away from where we left the horses."

"How do you intend to approach them, Jin?" whispered Two Ponies. "They'll attack you the moment you enter the room."

"I've already thought of that," replied Jin, softly. Removing his gray backpack, he handed it to Two Ponies. "Bring my pack with you when you leave the tunnel."

Stepping back, Jin quickly changed into the deadly form of Hatha, the female Reptoid.

"Now they will fear me," he said, in a low and menacing voice. Releasing a soft hiss, he swayed back and forth for effect. Even though Two Ponies knew the true identity of the snake in front of him, he still stepped back. A moment later, he stood alone in the foul-smelling guardroom. Again, the feeling of impending doom closed in on him, and he shivered from more than the cold. Although his Aqua-lite glowed brightly in his hand, he tapped it against the stone wall, giving it a little extra boost.

Leaning against the far wall, Two Ponies watched the blue glow of the Aqua-lites slowly fade as Jin, Aten, and Winter Bird moved further on down the tunnel and turned the corner. Suddenly a flash of brilliant white light lit up the doorway of the guardroom, temporarily blinding him. When his eyes finally readjusted to the darkness, he raised his Aqua-lite and peered at the doorway. What he saw made his heart skip a beat. There, bathed in his blue light, stood the female Reptoid. Her dark green scales undulated in the low light, and her mouth spread into a wide, sneering grin. She gave off a low hiss as her body swayed back and forth, and her yellow-and-black eyes glared at him with contempt. Remembering Jin's plan to rescue Little Owl, he released a hard breath.

"Jin! You nearly scared the wits out of me!" he said, in a loud whisper. "I thought you were going after Little Owl. Where are the others?"

When Jin failed to answer him, even within his mind, Two Ponies took another hard look at the swaying snake in front him.

"Jin? This *is* you, isn't it?" he asked, his voice trembling. Suddenly, the intense feeling of impending doom, he'd felt when he entered the tunnel, made sense to him. Swallowing hard, he knew he was looking into the face of Hatha.

Pulling his knife from his sheath, Two Ponies held it out in front of him. If he was going to die, he was not going to go down without a fight. Knowing Red Otter's knife had missed its mark because he had jumped on her back, he quickly sized up the situation. Since he now faced the she-snake, did this ensure him a better chance? He knew he had only one shot. When Hatha opened her lipless mouth, he quickly closed the gap between them and launched himself at her face.

The instant he felt his knife bounce off the hard scales just above her black breastplate, he felt the hot liquid of her venom hit him in the chest. Helpless, he fell at her feet, his knife still clutched tightly in his hand. His attempt to wound her had failed. As he lay on his back against the cold stone floor, he heard her hissing laugh of triumph as she turned and fled back up the tunnel.

CHAPTER 23

T wo Ponies was unprepared for the hot, searing pain that now filled his chest. He could already feel the venom at work, dissolving his flesh. From somewhere beyond the boundaries of his black world, he caught the sounds of the rescuers', as each ran past his door. The first to pass was Winter Bird, and his soft cooing meant the rescue of Little Owl was a success. Next, he recognized the jingle of Jin's tool belt as he, too, hurried past. Bringing up the rear, he caught the sound of Aten's thick, rough paws as they slapped against the stone floor. Two Ponies moaned. Here was where *he* was supposed to step into the rescue. Knowing he would now fail in his task; he closed his eyes in defeat. In the room at the end of the tunnel, Ogg bark his orders at his two companions. Who would now lead them away from the rescue party?

Then his jumbled thoughts turned to Hatha, and his eyes flew open. Knowing the she-snake was in the tunnel, Two Ponies now feared for the lives of Sky Feather and the others. He lifted his head just high enough to see beyond the door of the guardroom. His Aqua-lite lay on the floor just outside, and its bright blue light illuminated the tunnel.

When Ogg ran past the door, the tunnel walls echoed with several loud thunderclaps as he barked out his rage over the loss of his human child. At his heels, ran his two companions. What came next, had Two Ponies questioning the effects of his severe pain. Following the Wolfen was a tall, thin gray creature with a huge bulbous head and large, black, almond-shaped eyes. As it moved past the door, its long willowy arms and legs gyrated off the tunnel walls. A moment later, a second and then a third creature rushed past. Each gave off no sound in their silent pursuit. *These must be Black Fox's ant people*, he thought. But who were they pursuing: Ogg and his companions, or Little Owl and his rescuers? When the sound

244

of the Wolfen's painful yelping reached his ears, Two Ponies lowered his head to the floor. He could die knowing the ant people still watched over the lives of his people. He closed his eyes against the darkness, and his wounded body lay shivering in the cold.

"Two Ponies, where are you?" Jin shouted, as he approached the door of the guardroom. Two Ponies opened his eyes as the room filled with the welcome glow of Jin's Aqua-lite. "Oh no, Two Ponies. I thought you were behind me! I didn't realize you were not, until I was halfway to the trees. I would have never left you behind, my friend."

Then Two Ponies heard the far-off voice of Sky Feather.

"Jin, where are you!" he shouted, from somewhere up the tunnel. "Where is Two Ponies?"

"He's down here," shouted Jin. "Hurry. He's injured."

"Jin, beware!" gasped Two Ponies. "Hatha is in the tunnel."

"Not anymore," said Jin. "When she lost her prize, she transported back to her ship and deserted her Wolfen soldiers."

"Aten is right," said Two Ponies, grabbing Jin's arm. "There *is* something else down here—something tall and gray. I saw three of them chase after Ogg and his companions."

"So that's what happened to them," said Jin. "When I turned to see if Ogg was pursuing us, that's when I discovered you were not behind us."

"What of the Wolfen?" asked Two Ponies.

"I found the three of them lying in an unconscious heap just outside the entrance to the tunnel," replied Jin. "Whoever these beings are, they don't tolerate uninvited guests. Rest now, Two Ponies. Your father is coming."

Two Ponies tried to call out to Sky Feather, but his chest felt heavy, and he struggled to catch his breath.

"Jin?" called Sky Feather.

"He's in here," replied Jin. Stepping to the door of the guardroom, he issued his warning. "Sky Feather, he's been injured by Hatha, so do not touch him."

"No!" cried Sky Feather, as he stepped into the room. "Not this way!"

When Two Ponies saw his father's face above him, he could read the absolute horror in his eyes.

"Everyone, get back!" demanded Red Otter, as he swept into the room. "I'll attend to him. I'm immune to Hatha's venom, you are not."

With his back against the hard stone floor, Two Ponies began to shiver. He felt someone remove his knife from his hand and slide it back into the sheath on his belt. The knife was the last thing his grandfather had given him, and he hated the thought of losing it here in the smelly darkness. Red Otter lifted him from the floor of the guardroom and carried him back up the tunnel.

When they emerged out into the fresh air, Two Ponies felt the night breezes off the desert touch his face. He drew in a breath, only to send his lungs into a fit of labored coughing.

"I know your pain," said Red Otter, softly. "I will not let you die here among this Wolfen filth, Two Ponies. I'm taking you home."

For Two Ponies, the ride back to his village was one of pure agony. When his mind could no longer take the blinding pain, he felt his spirit separate from his body and rise upward. He nearly wept when his pain stayed behind. Below him, he could see his limp body rocking against Red Otter's chest as the horse galloped across the moon-bathed desert. Sky Feather rode beside them, his anguish driving him forward.

Hearing the loud cry of a bird, Two Ponies raised his eyes. A great white raven circled above him, its mighty wings sweeping the sky. This, he knew, was a sign that someone was about to die. *Who*? he wondered, just before he fell into blackness.

When he again opened his eyes, the pain returned in a hot rush, making him gasp. A lit torch appeared, and he glanced at his surroundings. He was lying on a blanket behind Gray Wolf's hogan. Just beyond, he could see the small conical top of the sweat lodge. True to his word, Red Otter had brought him home.

His childhood friend knelt beside him and peered into his face.

"Two Ponies, I cannot enter the village," he said, his voice now raspy. "I must leave you here with your father. He'll see that you get into the sweat lodge."

In the light of the burning torch, Two Ponies could see Red Otter's progressing deterioration. His left eye had drooped shut, and his copper skin looked pale as death. Even his crooked grin now sagged considerably.

"Red Otter," said Two Ponies, placing his fist just above the gaping wound in his chest. "I am your brother."

"And I am yours, Two Ponies," said Red Otter, placing his fist against his own chest. "I will see death before you, my friend, so I will wait for you beside the river. There we'll be like children again, floating on our backs in the cool water, with the warmth of the sun on our faces."

"Go. I will … join you soon," said Two Ponies. He gasped as a new wave of pain gripped his chest and throat. Closing his eyes, he felt his body cradled within his blanket as he was carried to the doorway of the sweat lodge. Nearby, a fire burned, and the smell of the wood smoke reminded him of his mother's corn cakes.

"Two Ponies is dying, Black Fox," said Sky Feather, above him. "Please, you must save him."

"I have no magic against this kind of evil," said Black Fox, in frustration. "Oh, if Gray Wolf were not so badly injured."

"Gray Wolf would be just as helpless," stated Winter Bird. "Even with all his healing herbs, he couldn't save Red Otter."

"I'm sorry, Sky Feather," said Black Fox, in anguish. "Winter Bird is right. Two Ponies was hit with Hatha's deadly venom. There's nothing I can do for him."

"Winter Bird!" gasped Two Ponies, opening his eyes.

"I'm here, Two Ponies," said Winter Bird, kneeling beside him.

"Little Owl?"

"He's with his mother," replied Winter Bird. "He's young and will forget his ordeal in time. Oh, my brother, I regret that you were injured while trying to save him. How can I ever repay you?"

"Remove my knife and sheath from my belt," replied Two Ponies. "See that Jin gets it. He says he likes the looks of it. Tell him I will never forget my friend from the stars."

"I'll see to it," said Winter Bird, removing the knife and sheath. "Jin is making sure the Wolfen are preparing for the ride home. I must tell you, Two Ponies, Red Otter is dead."

"I know," whispered Two Ponies. He closed his eyes as a new wave of pain hit him.

When he opened them again, the sight of Sky Feather and Blue Corn filled his blurring vision. The firelight revealed the look of absolute devastation on their faces. Blue Corn wept softly as she clung tightly to his hand. When she looked into his eyes, he witnessed her pain.

"I will never wish for another son," she said, her voice heavy with grief.

She lifted one of her thick, graying braids and wiped away her tears. "You will always live within my mother's heart, Two Ponies. And I promise to tell others the story of how the star people came to save our world. Rest now, my son. I love you." A moment later, he felt her grip release his hand and she was gone. He could, however, hear her quiet weeping nearby. It was Sky Feather who now leaned forward and picked up his hand.

"My son, I am honored to have been your father, if only for a little while," he said, tears welling up in his eyes. "I've loved you like a son born to me with Blue Corn. I will say goodbye for now, Two Ponies, but know this. Death is only a temporary separation for you and me. We are destined to share this bond of father and son. Though we are separated for now, we *will* be together again someday. Here is Moon Flower." When his face moved off, Two Ponies knew he was somewhere comforting Blue Corn.

"Two Ponies, I'm here," said Moon Flower, softly. Dropping to her knees beside him, her whole body shimmered with her comforting blue light. Her blue eyes emitted a luminescent glow that turned her unshed tears into tiny uncut diamonds. "I don't know how to heal your wounds, Two Ponies."

"Gray Wolf?" he whispered.

"His body is broken beyond my ability to repair it," she said. "He's dying, Two Ponies. Oh, have I failed you both?"

"No, Moon Flower," said Two Ponies, his eyes drinking in her face.

"I wish you would stay with me," she whispered, softly.

"I, too, carry this wish," he whispered, struggling to bring her face into better focus. Two Ponies knew he would not get another chance to share his feelings with her. Gazing up into her beautiful blue eyes, he felt his heart stir.

"I love you, Moon Flower," he whispered.

"Oh, Two Ponies, I love you too!" she said, her diamond-studded tears finally spilling down her cheeks. "How will I live without my friend who draws me pictures and makes me laugh? Remember these words, Two Ponies. Be safe in your travels. Someday our paths may cross again. And when they do, our spirits will greet each other as old friends."

"It's time to take him into the sweat lodge now, Moon Flower," said Winter Bird, softly.

At the door, Black Fox leaned over Two Ponies, anguish etching his face. "You have my blessings, my son," he said. When Two Ponies felt him slip a small object into his hand, he instinctively folded his fingers around it. "I've given you something to help your spirit find strength. Take your courage with you, Two Ponies, and allow it to guide your steps in the world beyond."

"Black Fox, the ant people are—"

"I know," said Black Fox, his dark eyes shining, "Unknown to the others, I remained behind in the guard room. Tonight, these old eyes witnessed legend come to life! In the morning, I will return to my people and tell them our ancient ant friends still dwell beneath the earth, protecting our clans. I must say—they dealt a savage blow to the Wolfen. Oh, how I would love to venture into the deep and hear their ancient stories."

When the old man moved away, Two Ponies felt his blanket sway as he was carried into the sweat lodge. Before they lowered him onto the woolen rug, he looked back through the door one last time. He wanted to take with him into death, the image of his beautiful Moon Flower. She stood between Sky Feather and Blue Corn, weeping as they comforted her within their arms.

The firelight disappeared as the hide fell over the doorway. Now only the shaft of moonlight, drifting in through the hole in the lodge's roof, lit the hot interior. Once alone, Two Ponies struggled to raise himself up to a seated position. The warrior within him refused to meet death lying down. Although he could feel the venom working its way up his neck, he was surprised to find he was now able to tolerate the intense pain. *How?* he wondered. When his body began to shine with the now familiar blue glow of Moon Flower's comforting light, he smiled knowing she was still with him. Remembering Black Fox's gift, he opened his hand. In his palm lay a small bear amulet carved from a white stone. To his people, the bear symbolized spiritual protection and courage. He closed it tightly within his hand. With his other hand, he grasped Jin's Q-link and immediately felt the presence of his sky brother.

The heat radiating off the hot rocks in the center pit warmed him, and he slowly stopped shivering. It was then that he noticed Gray Wolf. The old shaman sat across from him, his bruised and broken body propped up against a soft pillow of sheep's wool. He, too, glowed from within, as Moon Flower's soothing light comforted him.

"I see I will have company on my journey into death," said Gray Wolf.

"I mocked the she-snake, Gray Wolf," said Two Ponies. When he coughed, blood spattered onto the thighs of his leather pants. "And I'm now paying for my foolishness."

"I boasted of cheating death at the hands of the wolf that walks upright, like a man," stated Gray Wolf. "I, too, am paying for my arrogance. Are you afraid, Two Ponies?"

"Strangely, I'm not," he replied. "It's as if I know what death holds for me."

"That is because you are an old soul, my son," said Gray Wolf.

"An old soul?" asked Two Ponies. "What is that?"

"It is someone who has lived many, many lives," replied Gray Wolf. "I, too, am an old soul. In between these lives, our spirits walk what our ancestors called the Passage of the Warrior Souls. It's the path you and I travel, on our long journey toward the Sacred Creator."

"I have no memory of this," remarked Two Ponies.

"Sometimes it works that way," said Gray Wolf. "Our conscience mind *can* forget our journey while in the body. But our spirits will always remember the path that lays before us."

"Are you saying that you and I have walked this Passage of the Warrior Souls *together*?" asked Two Ponies, finding the old man's words comforting.

"I am," replied Gray Wolf. "You and I are old traveling companions, Two Ponies. But every once in a long age, one of us somehow strays from the path. When this happens, the other always appears as a guiding light in the distance to lead he who is lost, home. This time, it was *you* who needed *my* help."

"Why?" asked Two Ponies.

"I lost you!" exclaimed Gray Wolf. "Not long ago, I looked up and discovered you were no longer beside me on the warrior path."

"And now you've come to show me the way back?" asked Two Ponies.

"Behold! I am that beacon in the night, my old friend," replied Gray Wolf. "I searched for you until I found you in the world of tall hogans and great flying machines. But, by that time, you'd stopped believing in the magic of the journey. I feared you would never return. I called you back to renew an old friendship, my son, in hopes that you will one day rejoin me on the Passive of the Warriors Souls."

"And Hatha?" asked Two Ponies, thinking of the sneering face of the she-snake just before she mortally wounded him with her venom.

"*She* was necessary to restore your warrior's heart," replied Gray Wolf. "Facing her, took great courage. And, although she will now bring about your death, what you have learned from your encounter, is yours to keep. When you return to your world of talking boxes, my son, nothing will have changed. You, however, will not be the same."

"Thank you for finding me, my blue-eyed friend," replied Two Ponies, now struggling to remain upright.

"I'll wait for you, Two Ponies," said Gray Wolf.

Two Ponies nodded his head.

Gray Wolf sighed heavily. "I feel the death wind blowing across my spirit, and I welcome the end of this long life," he said, softly. "Ahead of me, the path is clear."

"I, too, see ..." was all Two Ponies managed to say before his voice failed him altogether. His last thoughts were of his Moon Flower and of the love they'd just confessed to each other. He wondered what would become of her now that he and Gray Wolf were gone. Would she return to her home world and rejoin her real family? Coughing up more blood, he wiped it away with the back of his hand. Suddenly he could hear the beating of his heart as if it lay exposed outside his chest.

"Close your eyes, my son," said Gray Wolf, softly. "We'll meet death together. Above us, I hear the call of the White Raven."

When Gray Wolf began to chant softly, Two Ponies closed his eyes. In the darkness, he listened to the ancient words as the old shaman called out to the Sacred Creator to guide their spirits back to the ancient path. Above him, he, too, could hear the cry of the White Raven as it circled somewhere above him. As he listened to both, Two Ponies felt his spirit finally let go. When it separated from his body, the pain left him. Like smoke, he drifted out through the hole in the conical roof of the sweat lodge and emerged into the cool air.

Once outside, Two Ponies hovered over his tiny village. The smoke, rising from the hogans, lay like a protective shroud over his people. Glancing eastward, he was surprised to see the face of the rising sun. Three lone riders, bathed in its early light, rode out to welcome it. Their new friends, the Hopi, were returning home to their high mesa. Near the river, Jin and Vonn's long gray scout ship silently rose from its resting place and hovered above the trees. Suddenly he heard the words of Jin within his mind.

Farewell, Two Ponies! he said. *Thanks for the knife. I like the looks of it! I'll wear it proudly as a reminder of my brave earthly friend.*

Out among the western bluffs, the huge, blackened asteroid rolled southward along the desert floor. The Wolfen were leaving his world. Picking up speed, the sky rock lifted off the sand and quickly disappeared into the southern sky. Jin's scout ship accelerated and shot after it, in hot pursuit. With their mission accomplished, and Mother Earth safe once more, the two Arcturians were returning to the stars. This time, however, they carried two extra passengers, and he wished Aten and the little brown-and-white female dog, a safe journey home.

Hearing the call of the White Raven, circling high above him, Two Ponies knew it was time to move on. With one last glance at his little village home near the river, he ascended and united his spirit with the great white bird. When he was joined by a second White Raven, he recognized an old friend, and greeted Gray Wolf with a loud bird-like call. Facing the open sky, the two Ravens soared higher until the desert and its little painted valleys, fell away beneath them. From this height, Two Ponies noticed a third White Raven circling above the river and called out to his childhood friend, Red Otter. Catching his friend's far-off reply, he flapped his great wings in greeting. Then Two Ponies heard a voice on the wind.

"Return," it said. Calling out his acknowledgment, he stilled his wings and began to spiral downward, toward the desert floor. As he circled the small sweat lodge below, he felt his spirit leave the great bird and drift down through the hole in its peak. As he settled onto his fur rug, he heard the voice whisper into his ear.

"Open your eyes, Miguel," it said. "You are home."

CHAPTER 24

The Navajo Reservation
July 2016

Feeling his spirit rejoin his body, Mike opened his eyes and looked around him. The rocks in the pit had cooled, but the morning sun flooding in through the open door warmed the air. Suddenly his mind recalled the massive wound inflicted on him by Hatha, and his hand flew to his chest. When his fingers splayed over pink healthy flesh, he sighed with relief. *It was only a dream!* he thought. Across from him, Arthur sat watching him from his wheelchair.

"How do you feel?" he asked, his blue eyes reflecting the light coming in through the open door. Mike thought for a moment.

"I feel … alive," he replied. "I feel refreshed and alive. Arthur, I had the most incredible dream!"

"Did you now?" asked Arthur, smiling.

"I did," replied Mike. "Normally, my dreams fade quickly soon after I wake up. This one, I doubt I will ever forget. I can still recall every detail, every name, every face."

"Do not let it go, Miguel," said Arthur. "Your dreams, even the bad ones, have much to teach you. If you let it fade, you will lose the lesson."

"It was incredible!" said Mike. "I was a young warrior named Two Ponies, and I lived in an Indian village somewhere here in the desert. We had, believe it or not, an attack of alien wolf-men. They were led by this female snake creature who hated me. I spent nearly a week trying to—wait. How long have I been sitting here? Oh, Arthur, my gallery exhibit! Howard Goodheart probably thinks I've abandoned it. And Jake will have called my mom by now. She must be frantic! What day is this?"

"Why, it's Sunday morning," replied Arthur.

"Really?" asked Mike, amazed. "I feel as though I've been gone for days."

"Yes, it can seem that way," said Arthur.

"So, it was just last night that Penny brought me—"

"To the sweat lodge? Yes," replied Arthur.

"Amazing," said Mike, his mind trying to process his thoughts. "What a dream! Are you telling me I helped save the world from aliens in just a few short hours? Jake is gonna love this. Truly amazing."

"Sometimes truly amazing things only take a few short hours to unfold, Miguel," said Arthur.

"It was nothing short of magic," whispered Mike.

When a shadow fell over the door, Arthur broke into a smile. "Ah, that will be Penny," he said.

"I've come to collect you, Grandfather," said Penny, from outside. "Breakfast is ready."

"As always, we awake hungry. Right, Miguel?" asked Arthur.

"Right," agreed Mike.

Penny leaned down and entered the lodge. Stepping in behind Arthur's wheelchair, she gave Mike a bright smile.

"Your clothes are beside you on your rug, Mike," she said. "I'll take my grandfather to the hogan. You can dress and join us."

"I'll be along," said Mike. When he remembered he was wearing nothing but a breechclout, he blushed clear to his toes.

Penny skillfully maneuvered Arthur's chair out the small door, and a moment later Mike was alone. He dressed quickly and stepped out into the fresh air and sunshine. He truly did feel more alive than he had in years. Stepping to the edge of the goat yard, he looked out over the barren landscape. Where was the little river with its shade trees and tall grasses? How different this world was compared to the village of Two Ponies. Gone were the small patches of cedar trees and greasewood bushes. Here no grazing sheep dotted the land. Some things, however, never changed. Far off in the distance, the great sandstone boulders still jutted from the earth like uneven teeth. They were the only timeless relics that Two Ponies would recognize if he were here today. *Which of these great boulders holds the secret entrance into the world of the ant people?* he wondered. Did the gray cave dwellers still watch over the Navajo and Hopi from their doorway into the deep? When he caught the sound of a bleating goat, he turned and left the goat yard. Following the tracks left by Arthur's wheelchair, he made his way back to the small house.

Arthur was waiting for him on the small porch of his hogan. The smoke from his gray pipe circled his head before the wind whisked it away. Arthur's quaint little dwelling, he noted, was only a modern version of those existing in the village of Two Ponies.

"Come, Miguel," said Arthur. Knocking the fire from his pipe, he slipped it into his shirt pocket. "I smell bacon and eggs."

Mike heard his stomach growl as he pushed the old man into the house.

"There you are, Mike," said Penny, smiling at him from the kitchen. "By the time you wash up, breakfast will be on the table."

Splashing cold water on his face, Mike looked at his reflection in the bathroom's small mirror. He was glad to see it was his own face that now looked back at him. In his mind's eye, however, he could still picture the strong copper-tone features of Two Ponies, with his waist-length ebony hair. Looking now at the way his own dark hair barely touched his collar, he toyed with the idea of letting it grow until it reached his waist. He knew his mom would raise an eyebrow. But he could now argue with her that a man's long hair kept him connected to Spirit. She'd like that.

When he joined Arthur and Penny at their small table, the smell of food drew his attention. *Yep! Some things never change*, he mused.

"You appear well rested, Mike," stated Penny, serving up the scrambled eggs and strips of crispy bacon.

"Despite the fact, I spent most of the night in a sweat lodge?" he asked. "It's funny. I've always thought of the hours between dusk and dawn as a time when evil spirits walked the earth."

Glancing at the small clock above the stove, he was surprised to see it was only seven-thirty.

"Is that right?" asked Penny. "Did you know the star people often choose the dead of night to make contact with the chosen ones? Not all who inhabit the night, are evil. Besides, the Native Americans are protected by our amulets."

Her comment made him think of the small Q-link given to him by

Jin. His hand almost went to his neck before he remembered the entire encounter with Two Ponies was still only a dream.

"Miguel, did your time in the sweat lodge give you clarity?" asked Arthur.

"I don't know," replied Mike. "It appears I slept the entire time. Good thing, as I have a long drive back to Phoenix. I need to return to my gallery exhibition."

"And so, you shall, Miguel," said Arthur. "But no trip to the rez is complete without a visit to the Little Painted Desert. It's a sacred spot for my people."

"Is it far?" asked Mike, his mind already figuring out how long it would take him to make the drive back to his hotel.

"Not far," replied Arthur. "You can reach it in under an hour. Penny will give you the directions."

"That sounds within reason," said Mike. "Did you know it was at the Painted Desert that Sky Feather had his vision and received his adult name?"

"Who is Sky Feather?" asked Penny.

"Never mind," said Mike, softly. "Arthur, how long will I retain the details of this dream?"

"As long as you need them," replied Arthur. "We all have dreams that can change the outlook of our morning, Miguel. Upon waking, we roll the details over in our mind while we enjoy our coffee and toast. But as the morning fades, so does the dream. A chosen few of us, however, are fortunate enough to have that one dream that changes how we look at *life*. That, Miguel, is called a vision quest."

"So, you managed to slip one in on me anyway," said Mike, shaking his head.

"Are you angry with me, Miguel?" asked Arthur, looking serious.

"No," replied Mike. "I'm actually grateful to you, Arthur. I'll never forget my vision quest nor what it helped me to discover."

"What *did* you discover?" asked Arthur.

"Well, my courage, for one thing," Mike replied without thinking. *Now where did that come from?* he wondered. *Why would I say such a thing? Did I lack courage before my dream?*

"Then the vision quest was a success," said Arthur.

"I guess it was," said Mike. "After last night, I know my future paintings will take on a whole new life. Arthur, am I allowed to share this dream with anyone?"

"If you wish," replied Arthur. "It *is* your own."

"Good," said Mike. "I want to share it with my mom. I told her I would try to bring her back a strange story. She'll no doubt turn this one into a book."

"Will you let me know if she does?" said Penny. "I would very much like to read it."

"I sure will," replied Mike. "I do have two final questions. What year did the government sign the Indian Removal Act?"

"1830," replied Arthur. "It was a devastating piece of legislature signed by President Andrew Jackson. He used it to relocate several of the Native American tribes who lived east of the Mississippi. The bill forced them to settle out here in the western states. Some went peacefully, but others resisted. Many died on the long walking journey to their new homes."

So, Two Ponies lived all the way back in 1830, thought Mike. *Yes, that would account for the isolation of his village.*

"And your second question?" asked Arthur, breaking into his thoughts.

"In your family's history, does it say who Moon Flower married? I'm just curious."

"Well, let's have a look," said Penny. Rising, she led Mike into the small living room. Retrieving a large black, leather-bound book off the fireplace mantel, she held it up for him to see.

"This is our Diyin God Bizaad, our family Bible," she said. "My maternal great-grandmother, Braids Sweetgrass, insisted we have one. Before she died, she recorded our family's history. Since then, I've kept it up to date."

While Penny flipped through the pages, Mike took one last glance at his painting of the blue-eyed Indian. His face immediately broke into a wide grin. He knew this face!

"Hello, Gray Wolf," he whispered. "Safe journey, my old friend." After this weekend, the origin of the painting was no longer a mystery. Where was the sacred mountain where the young Two Ponies envisioned it? Even the painting of the deer turning into an Indian warrior, now came to life for him. As with the image of the blue-eyed Indian, would he also recognize the face depicted in that painting? Would the man wear a crooked grin?

"Here it is," said Penny, drawing his attention. "It says here that Moon Flower married a man named Three Feathers in the spring of 1831."

So, it was Three Feathers she chose, thought Mike, looking down at the page. He was glad. Three Feathers was a brave man who would protect her with his life. He smiled at the small twinge of jealousy that suddenly swept over him. Silly.

"I was just curious," he said, softly.

"Now we must get you on the road," said Penny, closing the Bible. "You have a long drive ahead of you."

"I do," said Mike. "I'll just go and gather my things."

Standing outside his Jeep, Mike reached down and shook Arthur's hand.

"Thank you, Arthur, for inviting me into your home," he said. "I had a very … interesting time."

"You are welcome, Miguel," said Arthur. "Please come back and visit us soon. We have much to discuss, you and me. When you return, we'll build a fire under the stars and smoke a pipe of friendship."

"I'd like that," said Mike. "And I *will* be back, Arthur. I'm suddenly up for another adventure."

"The Spirit will provide," said Arthur. "Here, I have something for you, Miguel. Hold out your hand."

When Mike looked down at the small object Arthur placed in his palm, he smiled. It was a small bear carved out of white stone.

"Keep this with you, always," said Arthur. "To the native people, the bear represents spiritual protection and courage. Whenever you are faced with a difficult task, just hold this amulet in your hand, and your path will soon become clear."

"Thank you, Arthur," said Mike, slipping the small amulet into his pocket. "I'll keep it close."

Turning to face Penny, he looked into her eyes. For a fleeting moment, he could have sworn they turned a deep blue! Was he seeing things? Glancing at Arthur, the old man just smiled and nodded. When he turned back to Penny, however, he once more gazed into alluring hazel eyes flecked with gold.

"Thank you, Penny," he said. "I've enjoyed your company and your lamb chops. Take care of Arthur, will you? His wisdom reaches far beyond this world, I'm sure."

"I'll watch out for him," she promised, giving him her dazzling smile. "Here are the directions to the Little Painted Desert. And, Mike, be safe in your travels. Someday our paths may cross again. When they do, our spirits will greet each other as old friends."

Suddenly he understood his mother's words. 'We all live many lives,' she'd told him. Did certain souls *follow* each other on the path to enlightenment? They had to. How else would Penny now repeat the exact words Moon Flower said to Two Ponies 186 years ago? Could it be just a coincidence?

"I'll definitely be back, I promise," said Mike, slipping Penny's directions into the front pocket of his jeans. "My soul is drawn to this hot, arid land. And now I know why. Goodbye, my friends."

"Safe travels, my son," said Arthur. "May the magic of the journey go with you."

"Oh, it will, Arthur," said Mike. "I may even start believing in the Easter Bunny again."

Climbing into his Jeep, Mike started the engine and slipped on his sunglasses. *What a strange morning*, he thought, as details of his dream again tumbled through his mind. Shape-shifting wolves from outer space? The she-snake from Alpha Draconis? And what about the star helpers from Arcturus? Really? It would all make a great Sci-fi movie. But if he honestly thought about it, most of the things in the dream could have stemmed from the stories Arthur had told him. The strange black rock falling from the sky, was only one of his stories. It was no different than the time his mom took him to the circus, and that night he dreamed he had a pet elephant. Having resolved it all in his mind, he pulled his Jeep out onto the long driveway leading to the main road.

Entering the little town of Dilcon, Mike pulled out Penny's directions. They were simple as always. He stopped at a four-way intersection and looked around for the sign leading him onto Indian Route 15. Locating it, he pulled out onto the paved, two-lane highway and headed west. When he lit up his cell phone, he was not surprised to see it still refused to connect to the mother ship. Once again, he had no choice but to rely on dinosaur technology.

Out here, low, baren hills stretched out as far as the eye could see. Occupying the bottom of their little valleys were isolated homesteads where a lone tree struggled to provide shade and sand covered the yard instead of grass. He passed several dirt roads leading off into no-man's-land and he wished he could spare the time to discover where they would lead him. From one of these roads, a black beat-up 1968 Ford pickup truck pulled out in front of him, and he allowed it to set the pace. In its bed, a huge white tank of water sloshed in rhythm with the dips in the road. A sense of déjà vu hit him, and he thought of Julius George and his water delivery to Arthur's goats. Had their chance meeting only happened twenty-four hours ago? It felt like a week had passed since Julius found him at the border of the reservation.

When the pickup truck turned off, Mike trained his eyes on the far horizon ahead. To him, the long stretch of empty highway seemed extremely lonely. After a couple of miles, he glanced down at his speedometer. He was shocked to see he was doing nearly eighty! He quickly slowed down, remembering Julius's warning about the suicidal cows that grazed fence-free along the highways.

When he approached the junction of Indian Route 15 and AZ-87 S., he came to a stop. The sign ahead instructed him to turn left for the Little Painted Desert County Park. A right turn, he noted, would take him to the Hopi reservation up on Second Mesa. His mind immediately recalled the old shaman, Black Fox, and his two faithful companions. How could he forget the young Spotted Dog, who fiercely protected the Hopi's ancient knowledge? Or the peaceful Painted Hair, who put aside his aversion to fighting so he could be a part of saving his world.

He turned left and headed south. Glancing down at his phone he moaned. Still zero bars. *This really is dinosaur country,* he thought. Without his iPhone he was lost. But, at least the roads were well marked. This road held much of the same. Low hills and the occasional homestead. As he drove, he thought of the other players in his dream. What of Winter Bird and his trusty long knife, or the tall Standing Deer who gave his life to save a young girl named Little Doe. When the face of Sky Feather appeared in his thoughts, he smiled at the memory of the man who had taken in the little orphaned Two Ponies and raised him after the tragic death of his parents. What of the father-son bond *they* shared? Mike suddenly found himself mourning people who didn't exist. It was like missing the fictional characters in a good novel. Of course, he couldn't pass it *all* off as a dream. Wasn't the marriage of Three Feathers and Moon Flower recorded in Arthur's family history? *Here's where believing in magic comes in*, he thought.

When the sign for the Little Painted Desert County Park loomed ahead, Mike slowed down and turned right onto Painted Desert Rim Dr. From here he could see the far rim of the deep valley beyond, and he was glad he'd taken the time to see this wonderful sight. Pulling into the parking lot, he was relieved to find it empty. Spotting two massive stone pavilions, he parked in the shade of the closest one and got out. Someone had personalized a small cement utility shed by spray-painting the word "DINE'" on its exterior wall in huge black letters. This he now knew was the true name for the Navajo nation.

When he stepped up to the edge of the little valley, he knew why Arthur had suggested he visit it before leaving the area. The view was magnificent! From his vantage point on a small stone outcropping, the valley opened before him like a massive gray-and-pink wound in the earth. Patches of sage and tumbleweed dotted the valley floor like tufts of dried hair. Despite the early hour, the distant rim was already being swallowed up by the slowly building haze. Off to his right, he spotted the sandstone cliffs that gave the valley its name. The geological strata did indeed look as if the hand of God had painted it with a giant cosmic brush. The layers of sandstone ranged in colors from dark gray to light peach. Glancing up at the sun, he decided he could spare a few minutes, so he sat cross-legged on his small cliff. *Now this is Zen*, he thought. Placing his hands on his knees, he breathed deep as his soul drank in the timeless beauty.

He was watching the flight of a hawk as it circled above him, when something floated downward toward him. Without thinking, he extended his left hand and caught it. It was a white feather! The moment he closed his hand, he caught movement on a small gray outcropping of rock to his left. What he saw made his heart skip a beat.

Closing his eyes, he willed his heart to slow down. *I'm going to open my eyes, and what I saw will be gone*, he thought. *It is not real!* When he slowly turned his head, however, there was no denying what he was looking at. Twenty feet away, four Indians, stood smiling at him. Were these the same four Indians the psychic said were following him around? At that time, Mike thought of them as some unknown macabre haunting. Now, he looked on each in eerie recognition.

The first to step forward was Winter Bird, who grinned broadly at him as he patted the trusty long knife hanging on his belt. *Here's a man of many stories,* thought Mike. Next to him stood the Hopi called Painted Hair, with his three-fingers-wide streak of white hair running down through his long black mane. Always the peaceful warrior, Painted Hair soberly placed his right hand over his heart and nodded in Mike's direction. Third in line was Standing Deer. When he stepped out, his mouth curved upward into a huge grin as he pointed to the single black eagle's feather tied to his long ebony hair. This, Mike knew, was his trophy for having cheated death. *Bioregeneration*, thought Mike, and gave Standing Deer an enthusiastic thumbs-up.

The last to step forward was Red Otter. For Mike, time seemed to tumble backward, as his soul felt again the special childhood bond they'd shared as two young warriors. Restored to health, Red Otter, too, wore a single black eagle's feather in his long black hair. When his face broke into his signature crooked grin, Mike couldn't help but smile back. Then Red Otter's face took on a more serious expression as he laid his closed fist against his chest. Without hesitation, Mike did the same.

"I, too, am *your* brother," he said, softly.

What strange magic transformed the psychic's four Indians, into the band of brothers standing before him? He knew one thing for sure: he would never again fear them, nor would he question the origin of the images he painted onto his canvases. When all four men raised their hands in farewell, Mike did the same. Then, one by one, they faded away.

Remembering the white feather trapped in his left hand, Mike opened his fingers. Before he could examine it closer, a sudden gust of wind snatched it from his hand. He sat watching it as it floated high into the sky, until it disappeared from sight. When he at last lowered his gaze, the lone figure of Sky Feather stood watching him from the same small gray outcropping.

Seeing him again, brought Mike to his feet, and his sudden rush of unconditional love quickly erased the 186 years. Sky Feather's appearance was all the otherworldly proof he needed, that his dream of the night before, was somehow a strange reality.

"Hello, Sky Feather," he said, his voice breaking with emotion. Before he could say more, the image changed and he found himself looking into the face of Bob, the father he'd lost in 2002. No longer ravaged by the cancer, he again wore the muscular physique of his youth. Suddenly the significance of the moment hit Mike, and he smiled through his tears. Sky Feather and Bob Aul were the same soul! Somehow, across time and through two lifetimes, they had both loved him as their son. Now, as he stood looking at his dad, Mike knew he was being handed a rare and precious gift—the chance to fulfill a wish he'd carried around in his heart for fourteen long years.

"Goodbye, Dad," he said aloud, his emotions tightening his throat. Raising his arm in farewell, he spoke from his heart. "I miss you, and I love you so much!"

His dad smiled broadly, laid his hand over his heart, and faded away.

Although he could no longer see his dad physically, Mike could now sense his spirit lingering beside him. Recalling the last words that Sky Feather had told dying Two Ponies, he at last made the connection. 'Death for us is only a temporary separation, as we are destined to share the father-son bond' he'd said. If they *were* destined to cross time together, then he would indeed see his dad again someday. His only wish now was to live the kind of life that would make both men equally proud of him.

CHAPTER 25

M ike climbed back into his Jeep and started the engine. The day was already heating up, so he switched on the A/C. When he reached for his sunglasses on the dash, something dangling from the rear-view mirror caught his eye. He carefully slipped it off. *One more miracle to add to this most incredible weekend*, he thought. In his hand lay the Q-link Jin gave him at the river. Or did he give it to Two Ponies? It no longer mattered. To him, they would forever be one and the same. After his "dream" in the sweat lodge, he had no doubt the heart of a courageous young warrior called Two Ponies still beat within him. Then he heard the voice of Jin, the Arcturian from the stars, play in his mind.

Greetings, my earthly friend, he said. *Remember you promised to wear this and never take it off?*

Mike's face broke into a huge grin.

"I will never take it off, Jin," he said, aloud. "I promise."

Dropping the Q-link over his head, he slipped on his sunglasses. Making his way back to the highway, he turned right onto AZ-87 and headed south.

Suddenly, the open road ahead no longer seemed paved with lonely miles. After his experience at the Little Painted Valley, he only needed to turn around to find four loyal friends who were willing to follow him on this journey called life. To find his dad, he only needed to look into his heart. Saying goodbye to him, face-to-face, meant everything, and he felt closure for the first time since his dad's death. He was suddenly anxious to return home to Michigan and tell his incredible story to his friend Jenna. Being Native American herself, she would see it for what it was—a true miracle of time. By following his heart and painting the blue-eyed Indian, he'd unknowingly set in motion a stranger-than-life adventure that had forever changed him.

Twenty minutes later, the sign for I-40 West loomed ahead and Mike swung his Jeep up the ramp and merged into traffic. The interstate traffic was light, so he cracked his window and reached for his first cigarette since arriving in Dilcon, the previous morning. Pulling out his lighter, he realized he hadn't even thought about his cigarettes in all that time. Even now, it felt foreign in his fingers and he slipped it back into the pack. Perhaps Mordecai Ruby had given him more than just the insight into four friends.

When his phone chirped, he was thrilled to find he now had full internet service. It felt good to be back in touch with the world. Bringing up his GPS, he settled in for the three-hour drive ahead of him. As was his custom, his mind began to lay out the rest of his day. By midafternoon, Jake would be back from his encounter with the *Galactic Warriors III* and Chloe, and he looked forward to trading alien stories with him.

When his phone rang, he quickly answered it.

"Hello, Momma," he said.

"Hi, Mike," she chirped. "Did you go to the Navajo reservation this weekend?"

"I did," he replied. "I'm driving back to Phoenix now."

"Did you by chance find me a story about UFOs and aliens?" she asked, hopefully.

"Sort of," he replied. "Are you sitting down?"

"I just made me a fresh cup of coffee," she replied.

"I must warn you—it's a pretty strange tale," he said.

"I'm a writer, Mike," his mom reminded him. "Nothing is too strange."

Putting his Jeep on cruise control, Mike decided to start at the beginning.

"Well, Mom, it all started in a goat yard."

ABOUT THE AUTHOR

Kathleen has lived with the dream of becoming an author since the age of twelve. Realizing that dream took fifty years. Today, that dream is finally a reality. An avid book reader, she lives in Ohio with her husband.